THE GIRL WHO CROSSED MOUNTAINS

LELITA BALDOCK

Storm
PUBLISHING

This is a work of fiction. Names, characters, business, events and incidents are the products of the author's imagination. Any resemblance to actual persons, living or dead, or actual events is purely coincidental.

Ebook ISBN: 978-1-80508-547-8
Paperback ISBN: 978-1-80508-548-5

Cover design: Eileen Carey
Cover images: Arcangel, Shutterstock

Published by Storm Publishing.
For further information, visit:
www.stormpublishing.co

ALSO BY LELITA BALDOCK

The Baker's Secret

PART 1

1936–1938 – CIVIL WAR

ONE

1981 Donostia – San Sebastian

"Abuela, Grandma! He's here, come, come!"

I look up from my morning paper, squinting into the bright morning light. A soft breeze, salt-heavy and warm, drifts up off the bay, collecting the bright pink ruffles of my granddaughter's dress. Little legs pump hard as she runs up the hill from the river below.

"You are sure it is him?" I call back. There is a fluttering in my heart already, a squeeze of my chest. I breathe in deeply, intentionally.

"You said to look for a grey suit, and he was looking all over the place." She has made it to my front porch. Panting slightly, hands placed firmly on her hips, she concludes, "Definitely lost."

So small, so feisty. A smile teases at the corners of my mouth, but it wouldn't do to show my amusement. I love my granddaughter's internal fire. It comes from her abuelo, I think.

"Then, let's not keep him waiting," I say.

I stand, stiff, creaky, perhaps before my time. A life of manual work takes its toll.

She watches, a small frown forming between her eyes. "Madre says you do too much, Abuela."

"Your madre should remember who her madre is," I quip.

My daughter fusses. She takes after me, I think.

Collecting my cardigan and handbag, I make my way down to the cobbled road where she waits, body already half turned back to the train station below, face excited.

She takes my hand. The small bones of her fingers slip into place alongside mine. Natural, seamless. I glance down at the brown curls that spring from her head, bobbing in the breeze. Alive, everything about her is alive.

We were right to return.

Laia is proof.

Hand in hand, we make our way down the hillside to the train station near the Puente de Maria Cristina. To our right, the tamed natural Urumea river cuts a path to the sea, neat boulevards and ornate bridges line her waters.

The bay opens out before us, the warm sandy beach, the fishing port, the rambling old town. Rising above it all, mammoth, imposing, the fortified hillside, lined now by a scenic walkway and sightseeing locations. My town, my Donostia. I can call her by her Basque name once again. After years of Francoist rule, San Sebastian is learning to celebrate its traditions once more.

We cross the bridge and come to the station. The resting train hisses as it cools. Tourists spew out of its carriages to take in all that San Sebastian has to offer: sandy beaches, warm sun, fresh seafood, local crafts. These outsiders burst from the trains daily now. The summer season floods the streets with new faces, new languages, new eyes. It is not unusual; there have long been visitors in San Sebastian after all. But somehow, this feels... different.

Things are changing, they always do. It is the only thing in life I know to be truly true. That and the love I bear for my family. I am learning to trust change. In the new democracy of my country, change is a good thing. At least I hope it is. I have to believe. I cannot remain in the past.

Most of the arrivals have already disbursed, carried forth in rusty old cabs, or on excited legs, from this edge of the river and into the heart of San Sebastian. I hope they brought heavy wallets.

He is standing by an old wrought iron streetlamp, its black paint pocked with rust and exposed grey metal. Hat in hand, fingers tented over his eyes to block the bright morning sun, grey suit. Definitely lost.

Laia and I approach slowly and his eyes turn, landing on us. He squints, subconsciously leaning forward as he works to assess my face. Then, recognition, confidence and a flashing, broad smile. His grin has lost none of its brilliance. I stop, taken aback by the flood of memories, the pulsing of my heart ratcheting up, my blood throbbing in my veins.

And the question that has haunted me since I opened the letter, asking if he could visit: will I tell him the truth? That I lied, all those years ago, that he should have returned to France when the war was done.

That there was a reason for him to come back.

"Abuela?" Laia enquires, looking up at me. I squeeze her hand. I can't move my eyes from him.

He steps forward, closing the gap between us.

Suddenly awkward, he pauses. His hands flutter, his eyes scanning me, then Laia. A smile forms on his lips as he gazes at my grandchild. I understand this. She is a delight.

His eyes return to my face and I see the kindness that always swam in those deep blue pools. A gush of air escapes my lungs and I find my own smile.

"Bonjour Gilles. Welcome back."

"Bonjour, señorita..."

"Señora," I interrupt. "Señora Garcia."

"Of course." He nods. "It has been a while."

"Thirty years. I thought you'd come sooner."

He shifts nervously. Eyes tracking off to the waters beyond the port.

"I am sorry," I say, "that wasn't how I meant it. We only returned ourselves six years ago. When Franco died." I pause. "I understand why you waited. But I am glad you have come."

He nods, grateful, and turns his attention to Laia. "And who is this lovely young lady?" he asks. "Does she speak French?" He holds out a hand, formal, polite.

Laia glances up at me, and I nod. She grips his palm and shakes firmly. "Oui."

A huff of surprise and he looks back at me. "Laia," I say, "this is my dear old friend, Monsieur Fortin. Monsieur, this is my granddaughter, Laia."

"Call me Gilles."

It is a kindness, a step towards breaking the formality between us. But I am not ready for that yet. That wall of propriety is all that is holding me together.

Gilles is smiling. A small tear forms in his eye. "She looks like you."

"She does."

I lose time for a moment, staring at him. His fair hair is now peppered with grey, but his shoulders are still wide, and firm, his step sure. Time has rested gently on him. I am glad for it.

"You must be tired after your journey. Come to the house. My daughter has prepared refreshments."

"You are most kind," Gilles says, falling into step beside me.

"It is the least I can do after you have come all this way."

As we start up the hill to my home, Gilles gazes out over the Bay of Biscay. The waters are shining a perfect blue today. No clouds are gathering on the horizon, and the sun is bright. It is a good day. "It has been too long," he whispers.

"You are here now," I say.

He smiles.

At the house, we settle in the dining room. A pitcher of lemon water already waits on the table. The sound of my daughter fussing in the kitchen echoes through the open space. "Go see if your madre needs help," I say to Laia and she skips off on command.

Gilles's eyes watch her as she slips from the room. "She is a good child," he says, "and her French is exceptional."

I pour two glasses of cool lemon water, and hand one across the table to him. "Her mother spoke French first, in Bayonne. But we had returned before Laia was born. She has taken to both tongues very naturally."

Gilles sips his drink. A long blink shows his pleasure at the taste. My Adelina has always been fabulous in the kitchen.

"You have a lovely home," he says, taking in my beautiful pastel-painted walls, the carefully decorated shelves filled with ornaments and family photos.

"Juan has been a good husband," I reply.

"Will I get to meet Señor Garcia?"

"Perhaps, he is out to sea. His return depends on the tides."

It is a truth and a lie. I doubt that he will return before Gilles's train departs this evening.

"So..." Adelina bursts from the kitchen in a flurry, bringing with her the comforting scent of grilled fish and herbs. Apron firmly tied around her ample waist, she leans over the table, placing a heavily ladened tray of pintxos before us. It is only mid-morning, not usually the time for snacks, but we have a guest.

"I wasn't sure what you liked," she says, eyes focused on the food, not looking at Gilles. "So I have made an assortment. Omelette with potato, Idiazabal sheep cheese, Tolosa beans, bread, and some peppers in oil, from my garden." Her glance flicks up to Gilles at that. She is proud of her garden. "Eat up, enjoy." She turns to me, loosening the apron tie as she leans down to peck me on the cheek. "I must get back, lots to do before the oldest gets out from school, and Alain will have had enough of the baby by now. I will send Laia to collect you later, si?"

"Thank you, my dear." I smile up at my beautiful daughter. Her dark eyes are tired, her hair a mess of curls forced rather unsuccessfully into a bun at her nape. She is a good girl. "I will see you later." She squeezes my shoulder, offers Gilles a single, slightly challenging glance, and then exits back into the kitchen.

"Don't mind her," I say. "She is just a little..."

"Protective." He smiles. "You have a beautiful family, señora. Thank you for welcoming me into your home after so very long. My letter must have come as a shock."

"I don't know how you found me." I know it wasn't Camille.

Gilles leans back in his chair. "The Canadian War Records Office loves a story of escape. And honours all those who helped those soldiers to survive. You saved my life."

My throat tightens, hard, knotted. Tears spring to my eyes, and I feel the skin around them constrict as I work not to cry. I didn't save him. Not really.

She did.

She saved me too.

I feel a warmth on my hand. Gilles has leaned across the table, taking my hand in his. Beside us Adelina's food offering steams in the cool room, filling the space with the rich scent of food.

Neither of us notice.

Our eyes meet and he smiles.

It is time to remember.

TWO

ABENE

1936 Donostia – San Sebastian

Abene Ortiz stepped out of the cool of the small grocery store where she worked, securing the large wooden door behind her. It was closing time. Señora Morritz was long retired for the day. The store, perched on the edge of the old town, had been in her family for generations, or so her boss liked to proudly announce, legs braced wide, bright floral-patterned dress hugging her well-padded hips. Señora Morritz had birthed eight boys from those hips. She'd earned them. One day, the oldest would take over the store, the others dispersing across the city, perhaps even into the countryside to find their own paths, as was the way in the Basque region. But for now, Abene worked in the store with the ageing lady. Long, tiring days; only Sundays free. It was a good job though, and the money was important for Abene's family. So, she would never complain.

Plus, she was good at it. She'd been too old to benefit from the new Democratic government's education push, building schools, training teachers, but it had not held her back.

Numbers came easily to Abene, learned in her younger days as she helped her father to record his catch. She'd also picked up some French from her great-grandmother as they knelt together, tilling the soil for vegetables in the small family plot on the outskirts of town that belonged to Abene's parents.

Sometimes the señora would buy their produce. It had once been a thriving farm, but times changed. Small now, without enough crops to sustain a family, it drove her grandfather to the bay to fish, the work her father now toiled in.

She looped the padlock through the metal hook attached to the door, clicking it shut and securing the store for the evening. Pausing on the doorstep, Abene wiped the sheen of sweat from her brow then stretched out her lower back, arching, hands pressing into the muscles that tightened there after a long day on her feet. Cramp relieved, she breathed in fully. The early evening air was warm and salty, moisture-laden from the bay just beyond. Above her, the sky still shone blue, its hue not yet deepening towards dusk. She loved this time of year, how the light lasted long into the night. It meant earlier mornings, overheated siestas in the storeroom, but also hours left to enjoy when the day's work was done.

A secret smile curved her lips as she made her way along the cobbled paths of the old town, heading for the port. About her the other shop owners were closing up, the rattle of their keys ringing down the lanes, their shouted evening farewells a chiming echo in the balmy air. Abene waved to the old lady who made traditional pots, spun on a wheel, her gnarled hands moulding the clay. Then she turned downhill, following the natural fall of the land to the water below. Out across the bay, the Isle de Santa Clara reared up from the waters, calm now, the tide on an ebb. Along the sweep of land before her ran a golden stretch of beach, dotted with holidaymakers from across Spain, drawn by the warm waters and fresh sea air. And directly below her, the Puerto.

From this vantage, she could already make out the fishing boats that had returned from a day on the sea, nestled hull to hull in the port, her father's vessel among them. She picked up her pace, drawn as always to the salt of the waters below. Abene dreamed of sailing on their white-crested waves, of the heat of the sun turning her skin to tan and the taste of salt on her lips. Her soul craved the freedom of the water – a release from the tight streets of the old town, from the reality of the life of hard work and manual labour that she'd been born into.

The port sang the song of the ocean, freeing her spirit, as the various boats bobbed against their moorings, the wind whistling between the lines of their sails. The heavier fishing vessels rocked more slowly. The metal clang of their hulls meeting the grey stone windbreaks that held the storms at bay sounding dimly against the slap of the waves below.

At the far end of the dock, a figure came into view. Bow-legged and stooped, moving in rhythm with the currents below, her father strode towards her, mouth wide in a grin. Abene smiled. Arms open, he pulled her into a sweaty, smelly embrace. She didn't resist, breathing in the familiar brine and fish of his flesh.

Pulling apart he looped an arm around her shoulders, turning her to walk back along the jetty towards the beach beyond.

"Good catch?" she asked. The bounce in his stride had already answered her question, but it was right to ask, give him the moment to share his good fortune.

"Full haul." He patted her shoulder, his hand heavy against her thin cotton dress.

"Excellent news."

"The waves were kind today."

"You'll celebrate then? At the cervecería, the tavern?"

"I will. The men deserve to blow off some steam. It's been a long off-season."

Abene nodded her understanding. Fishing life was tough. What the currents gave, they also took away, until the season was right. Thankfully, they had turned early this year.

"I'll tell Madre. We can eat late."

"No, no," her father smiled, "eat when you are hungry. Never wait on me."

Abene smiled back. He always protested. Her mother always waited.

Coming to the port edge they paused, the unspoken understanding of familiarity between them. "Drink happy," Abene said and watched as her father rolled away, waving goodbye high above his head.

Turning back, she paced along the docks to her father's boat. The fish were long gone, delivered to the packing docks on the next cove over, ready for processing. But the boat needed cleaning. And that was always the job of the newest crew member.

"Juan!" she called. Her friend's dark head popped up, followed quickly by the gushing spurt of water thrown from a bucket. Shrieking with fake horror, Abene skipped to the side, narrowly avoiding a blast of lukewarm water.

Laughing, Juan Garcia turned back to his job, scrubbing down the decks, and clearing away the salt spray, sweat and fish bits. *A clean vessel takes care of you*, her father always said.

Task complete, Juan emptied the last dregs from his bucket into the bay and called, "Bittor going to the inn?"

"He is, all the crew are invited."

Juan nodded, placing the bucket and sponge in a box and checking the lock on the engine room.

"That means you too, Juan."

He was the son of her mother's oldest and most beloved friend, Udane. Lourdes had struggled to have Abene, her body refusing to conceive until she passed her fortieth year. By the time Abene first stirred within her mother's womb, she and Bittor had all but given up on having a child. Juan's mother suffered a different challenge. She had conceived throughout her childbearing years, but none had lived to birth, until Juan. Their mothers had shared the challenges and fears of pregnancy together, and the joyful arrival of a child of their own after so many years of hope and loss had bound the women more tightly than blood. And when their babies had been born a girl and a boy, both women had set to hoping for a more formal bond between their families. Unfortunately for this hope, Juan and Abene had been raised so closely together there could be no other way to view each other than as siblings.

And Juan could be an annoying older brother, if only by a month.

Finished with the boat, Juan leapt neatly over the railing and onto the docks. Looping a grease-slicked arm over her shoulders in much the same gesture as her father had just done, the two friends strolled back towards the beach.

The sands were emptying now, tourists, red and hot from a long day sunbathing, gathered up their towels and chairs and headed back to the hotels that dotted the shoreline. The winds had shifted, pouring inland off the bay, cooler and heavier. In the distance, deep grey clouds were gathering, a summer storm building beyond the edge of the bay. Common for San Sebastian, the warm rain was nothing to fear on land. But holidaymakers preferred to stay dry.

"Ah, there she stands." Abene felt the deep sigh of longing as it rumbled through Juan's chest and grinned knowingly to herself. Looking up, she spied exactly the person she'd known would be standing on the concrete rise above the beach. Tall and slim, arms resting lightly on the worn green railing that protected the unsuspecting from plummeting from the roadside down onto the sands, she stood, eyes forward staring out to sea.

"Every day," Abene said.

"Every day," Juan said. "In summer at least."

"Perhaps she likes the view."

"The salt."

"The shirtless holidaymakers..."

"Hey, don't tease!" Juan gave her a playful shove. "That's my future wife you are disrespecting."

Abene snorted a laugh. "Only in your dreams, Juan. She's from the 'other side'."

"A man can dream."

"A man can, sure. Which man are you talking about? I can't see him." She dodged her head on either side of Juan, pretending to search for a third person.

"Very funny," Juan drawled, but amusement played at the corners of his mouth.

They fell into step again, Juan's arm back in place around her shoulders. "She is beautiful though," he said, voice reverent, soft.

Abene looked across at the woman. The soft material of her bright summer dress lilted in the gathering breeze, and her hair, a perfect set of curls set about her chin, barely moved. Abene flicked one of her own tight, unruly curls from her eyes and frowned. It was true, the woman in yellow was beautiful. Older than her and Juan's twenty years, but not by much, just enough to add sophistication, elegance.

Abene still remembered the first day she and Juan had laid eyes on the woman, then just a girl, dressed in white lace-trimmed skirts as she trailed her father through the Saturday fish markets. And Abene still remembered what she'd done to her.

"I bet her hands are as soft as silk," Juan continued, distracting Abene from her reverie. Shoving the memory aside she joked, "Wouldn't you like to know!"

They fell into peals of laughter, turning to take the path

away from the beachfront, out towards their homes on the edge of the city.

"You'll join father at the inn?"

Juan made a study of his feet. Abene let him have the moment. It was hard, she knew. Xavier, Juan's father, had passed away only two years before. The family had fallen on hard times. Juan left town for several months, seeking work in the neighbouring provinces of Spain. But he soon returned. He missed his mother and the salt waters of Donostia. Bittor had offered him work on his fishing vessel. Juan had seen it as a favour to a family friend and did not believe he had earned the work. He felt that Bittor looked down on him. But he took the job. His mother would have been destitute if he hadn't.

That belief sat heavily between the two men Abene loved most in the world. Gone was the easy companionship between them, replaced with awkward silence. Both were too stubborn to give the misunderstanding a voice and clear the air.

"Maybe," he said at last.

It was a start.

Lourdes's ttoro stew bubbled softly on the hob, filling the small family home with the comforting scent of monkfish and cod. It wasn't much, a small stone-walled cottage of two bedrooms and a living space with a kitchen in the corner. Red tiles on the roof, vegetable patches outside.

Abene shifted on her chair. Across the table her mother rose, hands twisting nervously as she paced to the pot to check the stew. She'd done the exact same check only moments ago. It was clear that Lourdes was worried.

Abene glanced out the window, framed by flimsy flower-patterned curtains. The night sky had begun to show, but it was still light out.

Bittor never stayed this late at the inn.

A grumble in her stomach made up her mind. Abene stood.

"I'll go collect him. No doubt Luis or Alvaro are talking his ears off about fishing tips, expecting him to share his good fortune. You know how the men get jealous."

Lourdes placed the wooden spoon down on the edge of the pot. Wiping her hands down her apron, she turned to her daughter.

"Straight there and straight back, yes?"

"Si, madre, of course."

"All right. But be careful."

It was darker outside than she'd thought. The air was heavy with the coming storm, pulsing with an energy that promised it would be a big one. Despite that, the night was warm, and Abene could imagine how her father might have lost track of the time. Rain storms were so common in San Sebastian that no one really worried about the deepening clouds above. Though, it was preferable to be indoors when they broke, dumping their burden down over the tiled roofs of the city in a blast of power.

Pulling her coat tight, Abene hurried down the hillside from their little plot of land on the edge of the city, to collect her father.

The inn was tucked into a small corner of the old town. The warmth of its lights spilled from the windows onto the darkening streets beyond. Usually, it was a quiet place where the men gathered to restore themselves after a long day on the water, but today was different. Abene could hear the tension before she'd even cracked the door. Angry voices shouted over each other, a bustle of fear and aggression.

Taking a deep breath, she stepped inside.

The inn was in chaos. The fishermen, one hand clutching a beer, the other gesticulating widely as they threw heated words across the space. Behind the bar the innkeeper watched on, eyes equally ablaze with passion.

"They are coming for our freedom," Luis cried, thumping

his glass onto a wooden tabletop and sloshing the contents over the rim to spill on his hand.

"They will overrun the country. Return us to the oppression of the king!"

"The rebels don't want the king. They want the nation."

"But we are a democracy now. We vote."

"If you believe that is assured, then you are more foolish than I realised."

"Enough!"

On the far side of the room, Bittor stepped up onto a table. Legs spread wide, he eyed the men jostling below him. Somehow his presence commanded them and slowly the din fell silent.

"I know you are afraid," he began. "Our freedom is so new. We all know the feel of the king's boot on our necks. But we are Basque! This is our land. No one is going to take it from us."

"And if the rumours are true? That an army is building in the south, coming to conquer..." Luis challenged.

"Then we fight," her father said simply. "We have won our land back, wrestled independence from the crown. We will not give that up. Never again. If they come for us, we fight."

A roar of agreement erupted from the men, glasses of beer thrust into the air in unison, a call to arms, a promise to battle.

A warm hand landed on her shoulder. Abene jumped, spinning. Juan smiled. Leaning close, he whispered, "It will be a long night. I'll walk you home."

"No, no," Abene protested. "I came for Father."

They both looked over to where Bittor stood, the crowded inn of fishermen all in his thrall.

"He will be a while yet."

Abene turned to her friend. "Is it true? What they are saying? Is fighting coming to Spain?"

Juan shook his head, a wry grin curving his lips. "The king

left without a fight. We have had two democratic elections since then. Spain is free. We have a voice now."

"Then what do they fear?" Abene gestured to the jeering fishermen, the scent of salt and beer, fresh and stale pulsing through the air.

"They are old men. They know what it was to be Basque before democracy. They fear the return of that life. But we are one nation now. And here in Basque Spain, we have our own government, our own leaders. They won't give in to some political rebels in the south."

"So you think my father is right?"

"I know he is. The time for revolution is past. But we are new to peace, and scared. All will be well, Abene. You'll see."

Abene glanced back at her father, now down from the table, surrounded by his friends, talking with intensity. A fresh beer in his grasp.

"I will tell Madre, Father will be a while."

"I will see you home."

"No need, you stay. This is where you are needed tonight."

"Are you sure?"

"A storm is about to break, the streets are empty. I will be fine."

"All right, see you tomorrow?"

"See you tomorrow."

Abene made her way out of the inn, but her mind was uneasy. She wanted to believe her father's words, Juan's assurances. But there was something behind their eyes, a wariness, a concern. They didn't believe their own promises, at least not fully. Why else would her father have agreed they would fight? If he didn't believe it could come to that, he would have discarded the notion as wasting time in fretting over the future.

Everyone knew Bittor was a man of the moment. He didn't plan his sea routes to fish, he waited until the last moment to sign with a cannery each year. He didn't even know he was going to propose to Lourdes until he found himself on bended knee.

So why would he agree they would fight if it came to it?

Why acknowledge that possibility?

Troubled, she decided to take a stroll before turning for home, aiming to skirt along the edge of the bay, past the port, following the road that braced the beach, holding its waves back from the city beyond. As she walked the first fat drops of the storm that had been brewing all day smacked into the dust that coated the streets. She didn't mind. The weather was simply the weather. Buttoning her coat over her light cotton dress she strolled on.

As the curve of the beach came into view, she paused, blinking in surprise. The rain was coming in heavily now, the clash of the cool water and warmed street cobbles causing a thick mist of humidity to rise up, obscuring the way ahead. But still, Abene could see her.

Standing with her arms resting on the rusty railing, eyes towards the bay, just as she had been hours before, was the woman in yellow. Gone was her elegant poise, her perfectly curated image. Replaced by how any woman standing in torrential rain would look. Wet, bedraggled.

What on earth was she doing?

Abene's mind reeled back, a memory of childhood guilt uncoiling with it. She had been wrist-deep in fish guts and scales when the wealthy man stopped by their stall, a little girl by his side. The man and Abene's father had begun the talk of trade, stepping aside to view the various varieties of fish on offer that day. The girl, wide-eyed with curiosity, had moved shyly towards Abene.

"It looks like hard work," she'd said, hands clasped before her, expression open.

Abene had looked up at this girl, with her perfect hair, her shining shoes, her heart-shaped face. She had everything, *was* everything Abene would never be.

She still didn't know if she'd intended it, whether it was meant in fun or malice. But Abene had flicked her wrists, sending a spray of fish blood and salty brine flinging across the space between them. The girl had jumped back, but too slow, the pure white of her skirts now splattered with fish gore.

Shock dropped Abene's jaw, at the mess of blood that now marred such a beautiful dress, at what she had done.

That shock curdled to fear at the rough voice of the wealthy man, the clap of his polished shoes on the wooden dock as he stomped towards them.

"What have you done?" he screeched at his daughter. "I told you to be careful. Useless child. Your mother will know what to do with you."

He gripped the girl's upper arm fiercely, turning her away from the stall and hauling her off.

Abene could have stepped forward, could have confessed her fault.

She didn't.

And the girl did not tell on her either. She just looked back at Abene with large baleful eyes. Mouth closed. Silent.

Abene had felt the heat of her father's stare. Looking up at him she'd shrugged innocently, but Bittor had not been fooled. Kneeling down before her he'd brought his face close to hers, voice soft, but firm.

"Jealousy is a nasty thing, Abene," he'd said. "Not all is as it seems on the surface."

At the time she'd not understood those words.

Over the years she'd spied the beautiful girl, then teenager, now woman as she went about her life in San Sebastian. Always dressed in the latest fashion, always perfect and pale in the glowing sunshine. And always alone.

One time, as Abene and Juan had chased each other across

the harbour, pails of water sloshing against their bare legs as they raced to splash the dirt from her father's boat, Abene had looked up. There across the docks the girl stood, watching. Their eyes had met and in the instant before the girl had looked hurriedly away, Abene had seen it. Her sadness. Her longing.

And Abene had known, in her madre and papá, in Juan laughing at her side, she had more in this life than she realised.

Now, seeing the woman standing alone in the rain, concern wrinkled Abene's brow. A part of her wanted to turn away, to head up the hillside to the warm and dry of her mother's hearth. But the other part, the larger part, knew she had to check on the woman.

Abene picked up her pace, feet stepping lightly over the now slippery cobbles, rivulets of water gushing between the tracks in the stone,

"Excuse me, señorita?" She stopped a few steps back, not wanting to alarm the woman.

Nevertheless, the woman flinched, her head snapping around at the sound of Abene's voice.

"Sorry, sorry," Abene said, holding her hands, palm out before her, in a calming gesture. "I could not help but notice you here in the storm. I wondered if you needed help home?"

The woman regarded Abene with wide, beautiful eyes that curved delightfully at the corners. How could she still be so beautiful? Abene wondered, even wet as a rat!

The woman blinked once, slowly, before a spark of recognition lit in her eyes. Then, with what appeared to be extreme effort, she shook her head and spread her plump lips into a smile.

"Thank you, señorita, but I am quite well. You may safely leave me be."

Abene watched as she turned away, eyes focusing out to sea once more. Abene huffed in exasperation. She had done what she could, she'd checked on the woman. She could return home...

No, she decided, not good enough.

"Come along then, señorita," Abene said, stepping forward and grasping the woman's arm. "The hour is late, safer to walk as a pair. Where is home?"

Startled again, the woman turned, surprise writ across her face. "I live? Oh, well, I..."

Subconsciously, she glanced away from the bay, towards the line of expensive tourist hotels that lined the Urumea River.

Of course. She was the daughter of a hotelier. That explained the expensive clothes.

"The hotel street? What a lovely place to live. Come along then, it's on my way. Let's get you home."

"Oh really, there is no need..."

Abene ignored her protests, removing her coat and wrapping it around the woman's slender shoulders. It was as if the warmth of the coat reminded the woman that she was cold, and her body broke out in a prolonged, deep shiver.

"Yes, all right then, thank you," she said, stepping forward to follow Abene's lead.

It wasn't long before the woman stopped on the path before a grand entranceway lined with marble. "This is me," she said lightly. She mounted the first stair to the doorway then turned, as if remembering. "Oh!" she exclaimed. "Where are my manners? My name is Miren," she said, thrusting her hand out before her.

An amused smile spreading across her face, Abene gripped Miren's soft flesh and shook. "Abene."

Miren nodded. "Well, Abene. Thank you. It was most kind of you to see me home. I hope our paths cross again soon."

She nodded once then spun on her heel, racing up the stairs and into the luxurious-looking building.

Abene stood on the street, alone and wet, watching as she went.

Miren hadn't returned her coat.

Laughing softly to herself, Abene turned away. It was time to get back; her mother was waiting.

Rich people, she thought, are so impractical.

She bent her head back, allowing the cooling rain to wash over her face, embracing the wet.

She'd always loved a storm, and what harm was a little water anyway?

THREE
MIREN

Ringing blasted from the telephone. Miren jumped, the sound a high-pitched assault on her nerves. Hand fluttering at her throat, she reached down and seized the receiver.

"Good morning, Señor Torres' office." She was proud that her voice remained steady, despite her shattered nerves and her rapidly beating heart.

She never did well when he was out of town. Especially with all the talk of political upheaval. And her father's angry threats...

A pause at the end of the line, then the wobbly strains of Señora Barta's familiar voice. A complaint then. Not news. The wealthy of the city loved to criticise.

Miren took a deep breath, as quietly as possible lest she alert the señora to her impatience, and settled her voice to calm. It was a skill she had recently mastered. Working for the local government demanded it.

At length, the señora finished.

"Thank you for bringing this to my attention. I will be sure to pass on the information to Señor Torres when he returns to the office."

"And when are you expecting his return? San Sebastian is his responsibility, he should be here, watching over his people."

"He has been called to Barcelona for important meetings but will return shortly. Be assured, our community remains his top priority."

Signing off the call, Miren rested her forehead in her palms. The headache that traced along her brow had been pulsing for hours, threatening to bloom into a proper migraine.

"Pull yourself together," she whispered to herself, forcing her body to sit straight in her chair. "You are a grown woman!"

Yet without him...

She was always like this when Anders Torres was away. Distracted, emotional, unseated. She'd even kept that dear girl's coat the night before. Hadn't realised until this morning when she saw it hanging in her closet. It was a rough coat, torn and patched in multiple places. A poor person's coat. She remembered Abene, the wild girl she'd watched as a child as she ran across the sand beside the boy with fire in his eyes.

How Miren had longed to join them. To discard her shoes and play in the soft grains of white that lined the shore.

But Miren didn't play. And she certainly didn't run around the city, feet bare, hair streaming free behind her.

Her father would not have allowed it.

An old grief swelled in her chest. The heavy loneliness of a childhood spent separated from her peers. The reproachful eye of her father always watching.

She shook her head, casting the thoughts aside. This folly was not becoming of the secretary of the esteemed Señor Torres, and certainly not of his future wife. Miren could do better, must do better. Abene's strong face floated in her mind, her wide features, the determined line of her mouth.

How Miren wished she was as brave as the fisherman's daughter...

The commotion in the hallway beyond her office door

alerted her, and she knew he had returned even before the telltale four-click knock that was their code.

She rose from her chair as swift as a winter wind, but he still made it into her office and around her desk before she'd taken a step.

Gathered into his arms, his lips on hers, everything melted away.

Anders was home.

He held her to his chest, his hands rubbing soothing circles across her back. "I am sorry," he breathed into her neck. "The talks took longer than I expected."

"It is no problem. I know how important your work is."

He pulled back, holding Miren before him as he studied her face.

And she fell. Into his deep brown eyes, his full lips, his very being, just as she had the first moment she'd beheld him. Tall, with broad shoulders, and a steady gaze. She'd noted the manicured nails that tipped his elegant, soft hand as he took her own and asked her to dance. He'd led her through the gathered crowd of local politicians, to the circular dance floor in the centre of her father's hotel ballroom, and swept her off her feet.

At his suggestion that she apply to work in his offices, Miren's knees had wobbled; the thought of working close to him, day in, day out. Of what might grow between them...

Her father had believed it a marvellous idea; he was nothing if not ambitious. And Anders was a growing power in Basque political circles. If her father had known the scandal that would follow, he would never have agreed. Just last night her father had threatened to rip it all away from her...

And he could, Miren knew. He could take it all.

"And *I* know how you worry," Anders voice broke through the fog of her anxiety, the grip of fear that held her hostage whenever he was away from her side. "With what is happening in Madrid, you have good reason."

"Is it bad?"

Anders heaved a sigh, releasing her and moving to take a seat on one of her visitors' chairs. The secretary to the minister often had visitors.

As he settled his long body into a chair, she saw it. His shoulders slumped, his face fell into lines of strain. She perched on the edge of her desk, her dress pulling tight around her thighs, and waited patiently.

Rubbing a hand across the stubble that shadowed the sharp line of his jaw, Anders faced her.

"There has been an assassination in Madrid. The socialist Lieutenant José Castillo Seria is dead. Monarchist leader José Calvo Sotelo has been killed in revenge," Anders said.

Miren's breath caught in her throat, as a wash of shock flashed through her body.

"We have had political violence before, but this is different," he continued. "General Francisco Franco and others of the military elite have continued stoking division. I believe a coup is coming. The others refuse to see the risk. They won't arm the people. A group is travelling to Madrid today, still believing talks will save us."

"And they won't? We are a democracy!" Miren exclaimed.

"And what is a vote before the power of an army?" Anders' eyes searched her face, intense, hopeless. "It is hard to believe Franco will stop before the people's will. He has the church on his side and the army generals. Neither was happy when the king left. They lost power. No man accepts that lightly."

"But they are just a rebellion. How can they succeed against a nation?"

"Are we a nation?" He paused, shaking his head, before sighing heavily. "When the king accepted his fate and went into exile, the people believed change was coming, finally. A new, elected government would stand up for the poor, the workers.

Would lead us to equality. It was a beautiful idea. A perfect dream."

He stood, pacing to the window, eyes lowering to watch the bustling streets of central San Sebastian. "You know it hasn't delivered."

"But things have improved. Everyone has a say now. The new social programs..."

"Are not enough. The poor are still poor. Desperately so. And the men in Madrid are too focused on holding majority government to actually make real change. They are squeezed. Caught between the ire of the Church and the cries of the peasants. And we are no better here. Autonomous Basque government; it sounds good. But are our people any better fed than under King Alfonso XIII?"

"Things are shifting, it will be better. I believe it will."

"Perhaps it might have. But I fear we have ignored these machinations for too long, and now it is too late."

Miren gasped.

He turned back to her. "I do not wish to scare you," he said, coming to her side. "But I cannot deny the very real danger we are facing. Franco will come for us. The mines and metal manufacturing are here in the north. He will need our lands to fight his war."

All the moisture dried from her mouth in an instant as he spoke that one terrifying word: war.

"War? Against his own people?" She shook her head in disbelief.

"Men will do anything for power."

She swallowed, her mind racing. "What do we do?"

Anders' eyes softened and he placed his hands on her shoulders. "I need you to be strong."

Her face fell as realisation dawned. "You are leaving again? Now?"

"I must go to the government in Bilbao. After events in

Madrid, we cannot stick our heads in the sand like the Catalans. We must arm our people. We have to be ready to fight."

"And me?"

"I need someone here that I can trust fully. I need to you stay and hold the fort in San Sebastian until I can return."

"But you said the army is coming. How can you leave me alone when that threat is on our doorstep?"

"Peace, my love." He cupped her chin with his hand. "I would never leave you in harm's way. I will be gone for only a few days. A week at most. When I know what our plan is, the Basque plan, I will return for you."

Supressing a sob, Miren pressed her forehead into his chest. "I hate being apart."

He soothed her hair, fingers tangling gently in her neatly cultivated waves. "It will be the last time, I promise."

"I wish we were already wed."

She felt his amusement in the twitch of his arms and looked up at him. Met with his wry smile, the twinkle of humour in his eyes, she frowned, pulling back. "You find that funny?"

He stifled a laugh. "No, my love," he said, tucking a loose strand of her hair behind her ear. "It is a day I also dream of. My divorce from Lucia will be finalised soon, and then I will race you to the altar. But, married or not, I would still need you here. In truth, your father's home is safer than mine right now."

"I only feel safe with you."

"A hotelier is not a target. A politician is. I would have you far from the risk of harm."

"But you will put yourself in its path? How is that fair?"

"I will be fine, Miren. It is not just the protection of our region that drives me to Bilbao. It is for my own safety. We must arm our people, for all our sakes."

Miren nodded. She understood. She hated that he was right, but she knew he was.

"I will stay. But you must ring me, daily. Twice a day. You must keep me informed as to what is happening."

"I will." He pulled her into a crushing embrace. She pressed herself into him, breathing deeply the musty scent of his body, savouring the warmth of his arms. "I will be home soon."

"I will hold you to that," she whispered. "Or I will never forgive you."

After work, Miren took a detour on her way home, stopping at the home of Anders' sister, Carla who lived in a small first-floor apartment off the Plaza de Gipuzkoa. The two women had been instant friends, Carla's welcoming warmth a balm to Miren's natural nerves. Isolated from her peers as a child by her father's insistence on private tutors, to Miren this bond with Carla was something new and wonderful. When the rumours of an affair between Señor Torres and his secretary began to circulate through the upper echelons of San Sebastian society, Carla had stood by Miren. When Anders announced his intention to divorce, Carla cast Lucia aside and chose Miren, without hesitation.

To Miren, unused to the bonds of friendship, it had been a miraculous choice. Divorce might be newly legal in democratic Spain, but in the lives of everyday people the Catholic church still reigned supreme.

Carla didn't care.

Ushering Miren inside with a beaming smile, Carla fussed in the kitchen making coffee, while her young son Daniel entertained Miren with the story of his day. Climbing into her lap, he snuggled close before leaning back so he could wave his arms as he chatted away.

"And then Mamá took me to the park, and I played with the other children."

"Did you?" Miren exclaimed. "And what did you play?"

"Chasy, I won."

"Good boy."

"Now, now, Daniel, give your Izeba Miren some space. She has had a busy day. Here, a nice fresh coffee."

"Thank you, Carla," Miren said, ruffling Daniel's hair as he jumped down from her knee. He wandered over to his mother for a kiss on the cheek before heading to the lounge and the wooden train set his father had bought him last Christmas.

"He is a darling," Miren said, and meant it. Daniel was a delight, and Miren longed for the day she would have a child of her own. A child with Anders.

Carla smiled, looking at her son as he played on the floor. A small frown creased her forehead as she returned her attention to Miren. "So, what does Anders say? Are the rumours true? That the military is gathering."

Miren sipped her coffee, buying time to consider her response. She'd known Carla would ask. It would have been easier to simply return home to the hotel, but she'd needed the strength of her friendship with Carla, she needed someone to talk to, someone who would understand.

"The government is gathering in Bilbao, Anders is going with them."

"When do you leave?"

"No," Miren shook her head, eyes fixed on her cup. "Not me. Anders needs me here."

She heard Carla's exhale of irritation. "My brother really can be a fool sometimes."

Miren looked up, an expression of acceptance on her face. "He says he will only be gone a few days. He wants to convince the leaders to arm the men."

"So he believes a fight is coming."

"He says it is prudent to prepare for the worst. But..."

"But?" Carla prompted.

"But I fear he will be gone longer. And that is difficult for me."

Carla narrowed her eyes at Abene, mouth pursed. "He has threatened it again, hasn't he?"

Miren waved a dismissive hand, wishing fervently that she hadn't spoken. Carla reached forward, capturing Miren's hand and holding it tight. "Anders will fight for you. Do not fear your father's words. He cannot stop the love between you, even if he tries."

Miren nodded, a wobbly smile on her lips, grateful for the reassurance, even if she didn't believe it. Jose Perez could be formidable. He wanted the best for his daughter, partly for Miren's sake, mostly for his own. A high-powered marriage for Miren had long been his goal, as he brought suitor after suitor to her door. But Miren had eyes for one man alone. The only reason her father had given his blessing to Miren and Anders planned engagement was Anders' political power in the region. But with that at risk...

Carla released her hand, and added sugar to her coffee, stirring slowly. "I have some news." She leaned forward, eyes bright. Her palm came to rest on her belly, and Miren knew.

A squeal of joy erupted from her lips and she bounced to her feet, rounding the table to embrace her friend, her own worries forgotten. The two women broke apart, and Carla gave a small laugh. "So, have you told Daniel he is to be a big brother?"

"Not yet. I am a little worried about how he will take it. But Diego is sure Daniel will be proud and excited."

"He will be a wonderful big brother."

Carla looked at Miren, fear and hope warring in her eyes. "Not the best timing, with the trouble brewing."

Miren squeezed her shoulders. "It will be all right," she offered. "The fight is not with us. It is political. We just have to stay small."

"Yes," Carla agreed. "Thank you."

Miren settled herself back into her chair. "This is good news, Carla, a new life, that is always a beautiful thing."

"I know, you are right. I just worry."

Miren understood that. She was worried too. In fact, the whole of Spain was worried. It was that uncertainty that had led her here to Carla's kitchen, seeking the reassurance of her friend. But now she realised it was up to her to give the confidence. She straightened in her chair, squaring her shoulders.

"Whatever happens, we will rise above it. We always do," she said, though the skin around her mouth remained taut.

Carla met her stare, nodding firmly. "And we will greet it together, as a family."

The huff of joy escaped her lips before she could stop it, her heart fluttering at Carla's words. Oh, how she longed to truly be a sister to this woman.

"As a family," she agreed.

Daniel burst from the lounge, arms spread wide as he ran across the room. "Daniel, what are you doing?" Carla cried.

"I'm a bird," Daniel shouted, voice high and piping. "And I am flying!"

Miren stood, catching the boy up in her arms and swinging him in a small circle. "And just like a bird, you will always be free," Miren said, eyes flicking to meet Carla's across the room.

Daniel giggled in delight and clasped his hands to the sides of her face.

"I love you, Izeba Miren."

"I love you too."

FOUR

MIREN

Anders was right and wrong. Franco was coming, but they didn't have a week. Days after the assassinations in Madrid, the military coup began. Seville was taken and Madrid was besieged as military districts across the country rose up against the government. General Francisco Franco crossed to the mainland from Morocco, soldiers at his back. Though the coup did not conquer the country, a revolutionary army charged through the centre of Spain, cutting a swathe through the heart of the nation. The poor of the countryside – the workers and farmers, overlooked for centuries and seeing no change under government rule – put up little resistance, even joined willingly.

Neighbouring Navarre was captured, sending women and children fleeing from Spain across the Pyrenees. The threat became immediate. San Sebastian would be next.

"You must get the children out," Anders' voice was tense, pitched high, crackling down the phone line. "I have convinced the government to send guns. At last, they see sense. Every man in San Sebastian will be armed. But the fight is coming to our city. Miren, you have the lists of families with children under ten. They must be the priority. Work with Manuel. Secure any boat you can. Fill them to the brim. Get the children out of the city."

"It is in motion," Miren breathed into the receiver. "We have already requisitioned all the fishing vessels. The fishermen did not argue. The first will leave before sundown."

"Be on one of those boats, my love."

"What about Carla and my family?"

Anders sighed heavily down the line. "The order is children and caregivers... Carla won't leave Diego and won't be parted from Daniel, she won't leave. You could bring your mother. But your father will be expected to fight."

Miren pressed her eyes closed. Her father would fight. She could try and convince him to run but...

"I can talk to Carla, and try to get her to see sense."

"You can, but please, my love, put yourself first. Whatever happens, you have to get yourself on a boat."

"I will be on a boat tomorrow."

She heard him sigh in relief. "I am in talks with France. We are working to ensure the safety of our people who have fled there. It is temporary. But it is essential. I need you here. Safe. You have heard the tales from Pamplona, of what Franco's men have done to the women..."

Miren swallowed, her throat tight with horror, as the imagined images of screaming women flashed through her mind. She still did not fully believe the reports that had landed on Anders' desk. Rape. Hangings in the streets. Execution-style killings on the roadside. Against your own people? How could it be true?

She shook herself, forcing her mind to focus on the task before her.

"And is Bilbao safe?"

The silence stretched, pregnant with the unspoken truth. A voice sounded, hushed and distant on the other end of the line. She heard the scrape of Anders' chin against the phone as he turned, his voice muffled as he spoke to someone behind him, then clear again as he returned to her. "I have to go. Be on a boat, tomorrow, Miren. I will meet you at Puerto de Bilbao."

"I will be there, my love. Be safe."

"You too."

Carla refused to leave. Miren had begged her, but she would not be moved.

"I cannot abandon Diego."

"What about Daniel, what about your unborn baby?"

"We are family, we will stay together."

She'd given Miren no choice. Now, as she stood on the docks, Miren listened to the knocking as the waters of the Puerto bobbed gently against the boat hulls. At her side only her mother, Maria, stood, her eyes wet with tears. Miren tented her hand over her eyes and looked out over the glistening waters.

The port side was awash with action, men climbing over boats, readying the vessels for sea, and children, lined up all the way back to the beachside, each with a single small suitcase, their mothers fussing beside them, pressing down stray locks of hair, wiping away errant tears. Near her and Maria stood a fair-haired boy, his darting eyes misty with tears, but his head was held high, firm. He was afraid, alone, but he refused to show it.

Brave lad.

Miren took her mother's hand. "It will be all right, Madre, you will see. A short trip over the waters and we will be safely in Bilbao with Anders."

Her mother released a loud sob, pulling her hand free to blow her running nose heartily. Miren suppressed a sigh. She was sad too, and scared. But they were the adults here, they had to remain in control of their emotions, and set an example for the children milling around them. "Mamá, please, calm yourself. The children are scared, we must be brave, for them."

Maria glanced around her, and slowed her breathing, wiping her eyes dry with the edge of her sleeve. Good, Miren thought to herself, that seemed to have worked.

Behind them, the city streets were buzzing with action. The last of the men of San Sebastian who had not already made the journey to fight the advancing forces were gathering at preset locations, ready to be collected for the front. Army trucks drove up and down the narrow streets, their hulls filled with guns and weapons, handing them out to any man too old to be taken to fight. Readying them for the invasion of their very homes.

Her father was among them. She'd tried to convince him to leave, begged, cried. This was a political conflict after all, and her father had always courted those in power. His associations may damn him. Maria had too, accusing him of putting the city before his love for her, for Miren. But even that astonishingly brutal attempt at manipulation had failed. "To flee is to admit a fault. We have done nothing wrong. I will not be driven from my home," he'd declared.

They'd left him sitting in the reception hall of his hotel, a rifle across his knees. Miren prayed it would not be the last memory she would have of her father.

The line ahead moved forward, forcing him from her thoughts. A hand pressed to her mother's elbow, she gathered up her suitcase and moved them on.

An old, gruff-looking sailor stood at the helm of his boat, one suntanned arm raised to usher them forward. Several children were already aboard, their small, frightened faces turned up, watching the man. He turned, beaming a welcoming smile down upon them all, the creases of his cheeks squishing up to bury his eyes. "You are aboard the *Safe Seas*," he said, voice strong and firm despite his obvious age. "She'll see you safely on. And safely home when this business is done. Now settle down, bums on the deck. That's the way."

The children obeyed wordlessly, all sitting as ordered.

Miren felt a flash of gratitude and smiled at the man. He stepped forward, holding out a grease-slicked hand to help her across. She took it, the callouses of his workman's palm scraping over her skin. She stepped from the dock, crossing the invisible barrier between the land of her city and this vessel of deportation.

Her heels clicked on the metal of the deck.

"Safely aboard," the fisherman said, before turning to offer his hand to Maria.

Miren looked up, waiting. Maria moved forward then paused, her hand mid-air towards the waiting sailor. Her eyes looked down, gazing into the waters below. The sailor spoke again, "No need for fear, señora, the waters are gentle today. I'll have you in Bilbao before the sunset. Come on now."

He smiled again. Maria looked up and met his eyes. Then stepped back. The waiting line of children flowed forward around her, sucking her back from the fishing boat.

"Wait! Madre!" Miren called, hands gripping the vessel's railing so she could lean over towards Maria. "Mamá, what are you doing?"

Maria's eyes were wide and wild, her head shaking back and forth. "Get on this boat!" Miren ordered. Beside her, two more children had crossed onto the vessel, their parents stepping back to wave goodbye, just as Maria had done. The boat would soon be full.

Miren stepped up to the sailor, placing herself in the way of the next to board.

"Madre, I have a passage for you. On this boat, now, with me. Come here, now!"

But her mother would not move. Slowly she raised her head, her smile watery and unstable as she met her daughter's eyes.

"I will stay here. I will stay with my husband."

Panic shot through Miren. "Mamá, this is silly. Papá wants

you to come with me. He needs to know that we are safe – that both of us are safe."

"I will be safe. With Jose, I am always safe. You must decide where you are most safe."

Miren stared at her mother. She loved her father with all her heart, but San Sebastian would fall, and if the invaders chose brutality, there would be nothing her father could do about it.

She opened her mouth to protest, but the sailor beside her spoke. His voice was soft, pitched just for her. "She has made her choice. It is only you who must now decide."

Miren turned to him. His deep brown eyes shone from a face etched with lines, the grey stubble on his chin catching the sunlight. "We must leave, now. You must choose. To go with your mother, or stay bound for Bilbao. It is up to you."

Miren watched his face, expecting judgement, a hint of expectation over what she should do. She found only patience.

She turned back to Maria, her own eyes now filling with tears as she stepped up to the boat's edge. To step off and stay with her family, or leave and trust Anders. Where was she the most safe?

Her body hovered on the edge of the boat, halfway between both decisions, both worlds: her childhood and her adulthood.

She lifted her foot and stepped back down onto the boat deck.

As the vessel pulled away from the docks, Miren scanned the faces still waiting along the jetties, hoping for their own place in a vessel to freedom. Her mother was already gone.

A weight, sudden and pressing, smothered her, pulling her down as if through the deck. In a daze she made her way to the opposite side of the boat, hands gripping the railing, seeking comfort, something solid to cling to. Feeling a presence at her side, she glanced down.

The small boy with fair hair she'd noticed before stood at

her knee, large round eyes gazing up at her. Fear laced his features, but his cheeks were dry. She knew she should smile, should offer this child the comfort and reassurance of an adult. But her body would not obey.

The boy raised his hand, holding his plump fingers up to her.

"You can hold my hand if you like," he said, voice high with youth and trembling with sorrow.

Miren's heart cracked. Prying her hand from the railing she had gripped with all her might, she reached down and took his offered palm.

"We can travel together," he said, fingers wrapping about hers. "We can be brave together."

Miren watched as he puffed out his chest in a gesture she was sure he mimicked from a beloved father. How hard it must have been for his parents to send him away, how desperate. Her mother had done the same, she realised with no small amount of irony. Maria had sent her daughter to safety, had stayed behind to defend her home.

Acceptance. There was nothing else to do.

Miren squeezed the boy's hand. "My name is Miren," she said. "Thank you for your comfort."

"I am Eduardo," he said, eyes smiling now. "And you are welcome."

FIVE

ABENE

A hand, heavy and warm, smothered her mouth. Abene's eyes flew open, her body rearing up from her bed in terror, hands flying out to hit her attacker. It was a hot night. She'd left her window open in hopes of a cooling breeze. A mistake when the invaders were so close to their city borders. They'd come. They'd come for her Donostia.

Arms flailing, hands formed into fists she hit out, striking her attacker hard against his firm chest.

"Sssh, Abene, ssh, it's me, it's me!"

As her eyes adjusted to the dim light of the moon, a set of familiar features materialised before her.

Juan.

"Oh!" she gasped, throwing herself forward and wrapping her arms around her friend, pulling him tight.

It had been almost two months since Juan and her father sailed for Bilbao, the *Safe Seas* packed to the brim with children from their city and its surrounds. They hadn't returned. Bittor had sent word that they had joined the fight on the borders of Viscaya, but since then, nothing.

Relief flooded her, as she embraced her friend. But Juan

flinched, pulling back slightly. Abene frowned, releasing him. Her arm came away slick and sticky.

"You're hurt!" she exclaimed, realising he was bleeding heavily from one side.

"Quiet, don't be loud. It's nothing."

"Let me get soap and water..."

"Abene, stop." Juan's voice was tight, forced.

Abene stilled, watching her friend in the moonlight.

His mouth worked, lips trembling. "Abene, you must wake your mother. You have to pack. Light, and quick. Solid shoes, no heels. We are leaving."

"Leaving? Juan, what has happened?"

"I promised your father..."

"Papá? Where is Papá? Is he with you..." She moved to rise from the bed, but Juan grabbed her hand.

"Abene, listen. We don't have time. The line broke. The Nationalists will be here within hours. I have run all night to beat them, but we don't have long. We must go and fast."

Shock and fear sluiced through her, her head felt light, disconnected. The Nationalists were coming. Here, for her home. Where was her papá?

"Abene? Did you hear me? The port is overrun, we must travel on foot. We have to go."

"Go where?"

"To France. The people of Navarre fled to the border and were welcomed warmly. We have to get out of Spain."

"And Papá?"

"Come on," Juan rose, pulling her to her feet. "Wake your mother, be ready within the hour. I must go and collect my mother. We have to move."

He turned, aiming for the door.

"Juan!" Abene cried, making him pause. "Papá, he will meet us there, si? He will meet us in France?"

"Pack your bags, Abene. This is no longer your home."

Without another word he turned, disappearing into the dark hallway beyond her room, leaving Abene alone with the unbearable weight of her unanswered question.

She knew the answer without him saying it. She knew.

Sorrow, gut-wrenching and sharp, stabbed into her belly. "Papá," she whispered, tears springing to her eyes, a hole opening in her heart. She wondered how it had happened, and when? If it had been quick, or if he had suffered? Questions and fears tumbled through her as a numb resolve stiffened her limbs. She would pray for him, in the quiet moments, when she was alone.

For she would not tell her mother. Not yet. Without Bittor, she could not trust that Lourdes would fight on, as she knew they must. They were leaving their home, leaving everything they knew and trusted. Lourdes would need to believe that she would be reunited with Bittor if she were to get through all that was coming. Abene had to keep the hope alive to keep her mother going. She could lie for that.

They waited on the dirt road outside, the first rays of the new dawn just peeking over the horizon, illuminating the ripples of the Bay of Biscay in the soft pink promise of the dawning day. Lourdes and Udane embraced, both women fighting back tears at the reality before them.

"We will be all right," Udane assured her friend, wiping tears from Lourdes' eyes.

"We will make it together," Lourdes agreed.

Blinking furiously and swallowing hard, fighting to control her pain, Abene stepped forward to Juan. "It is a long way. I packed bread and cheese."

"A wise move. We will likely need to beg along the path. I think it will take us several days of walking, and the mountains..."

They both looked at their mothers. Beloved, healthy for their age, but softened, rounded by time. Lourdes stood taller, straighter, her oval face full, where Udane's was newly hollowed. The years since her husband's death had slimmed Udane's limbs and greyed her hair. "Food feeds the body, love feeds the soul," Lourdes had once said. Watching the two friends as they gathered themselves to depart, Abene felt the full force of those words. Concern knitted her brow even as she gifted a firm smile to her mother. Would she shrink in Bittor's absence as her friend had done after her husband's death?

She pushed the thought aside. That was a worry for later. First, they had to hike across the mountainous terrain of North Spain. Could their mothers withstand the trek to come?

"We will make it," Abene affirmed, voice firm. She would accept no alternative.

"We will," Juan agreed.

They set off up the hillside, striking away from the coast. "We must travel a little inland," Juan explained. "Avoid the major ports. We will be passing through land occupied by the Nationalists. Quiet and fast, we don't want to draw the attention of soldiers."

No one argued, they simply fell in step, in silence.

As the sun rose over the farmland of Gipuzkoa, casting the fields in bright yellow daylight, it became clear they were not the only people seeking escape over land. Groups of women, a few older men who had not travelled for the front, children who'd missed a place on a boat to Bilbao, all clustered in bundles along the roadside, all with the same destination in mind: France. Abene scanned their fellow travellers, eyes downturned, expressions tight with fear. She didn't see Señora Morritz, or her sons. She hoped her employer was somewhere safe.

Udane developed a blister on her heel before lunch on the first day, spending the afternoon trek with an arm slung about her son's shoulders, limping forward. Lourdes huffed and puffed, her cheeks rosy with effort, but her face set in grim determination.

Neither woman voiced even a murmur of complaint.

They camped that night by the roadside, and another family group settled a short distance beyond them. Juan ventured over to talk with the older man who led them; they swapped bread for dried fish and shared water. As the dark of night descended over them, a cool breeze blew over the drying husks of the corn fields, the air scented green and dusty, but warm. Abene was grateful for that warmth. It was stifling on a still night indoors, but out here, under the open sky of Spain, the heat of the early autumn night was welcome. This journey in winter would be fraught.

In the face of fleeing their home, and the uncertain fate of her father, it wasn't much to cling to, but as her feet pulsed with the pain of a long day on the road and the sound of her mother's laboured breathing filled her ears, Abene would take what she could get.

Small mercies.

Two nights later having crossed rivers and deep, craggy ravines, they stood on the edge of the town of Irun, nestled at the base of the Pyrenees, the snow-tipped mountain peaks shining in the evening light. The line of refugees had thinned as they travelled, leaving them alone on the edge of Spain. Before them the hard, brutal cliffs seemed to radiate cold and challenge. A natural border that lined the division between Spain and France. All that was left between them and the safety of a foreign land. Franco's men controlled the town, the bridge across the river patrolled by soldiers day and night. But Juan had a plan to bypass their watch.

"We will rest tonight," Juan said. "It will be a big day tomorrow."

"How will we get past the soldiers?"

"Downstream, a little swim. It will be all right."

"How long do you think it will take us to cross the mountains?" Abene asked.

Juan's eyes strayed to his mother. Udane was already sitting, shoes off with her foot resting on her bag. The blister had burst the day before, leaving a ruin of blood and fluid to leach into her stockings. Her heel was a mess. It needed proper treatment and rest before infection set in. Things that were not available until they reached their destination.

"It will take as long as it takes."

"But, Juan, how can we do this, really? We don't know the paths, it is not an easy climb."

"I know the way," he said, eyes tracking away from her.

"What? How?"

Juan eyed her in the dark, face serious. "You remember when I left Donostia after Papá died?"

Abene nodded, brow creasing in a frown.

"Work was hard to come by, but I found some. It was not strictly... legal."

A gasp sounded from Abene. "Juan, are you telling me you worked as a *Gaulan*? A nightworker, smuggling across the border?"

Juan shrugged. "It paid well."

"What if you had been caught? Juan, you know what shame that would have brought to your mother."

"And now, it is that shame that will see us to safety," Juan snapped. Abene fell silent, he was right, after all.

Aside from Udane's heel, they had been lucky so far. The trek had passed without incident, no run-ins with stalking soldiers and plenty of fellow travellers to trade supplies with. She just had to believe a little longer.

"I am sorry, Juan," Abene offered. "It has been a long day."

"Get some rest, tomorrow the real journey begins."

Mercifully, Juan's plan to wade through the river was

helped by the slower currents of summer's end. They crossed without incident, climbing up the opposite bank drenched, but unseen. She had to admit, he did know the way. And right now, that was what mattered.

As they began their ascent of the mountains of the Pyrenees their luck ran out.

A wicked storm had been gathering to the west, the first winds of true autumn ready to blast away the last of the lingering summer warmth, ushering in the season of transition.

Abene smelt it on the wind the moment she woke. Looking at Juan in the pre-dawn glow; she knew he smelt it too. They should have waited. Stayed another night at the base of the mountain range, and rode out the storm. They were Basque, born and bred, they knew the power of the winds and rain. But they were tired, desperate, dirty and hungry, with the threat of rebel soldiers at their backs. So they ignored their instincts and forged on.

The storm hit at midday, the winds high and wild, slapping rain, fat and cold, down on them, transforming the rocks of the Pyrenees into a treacherous, slippery passage. As the wind rose, and the skies above darkened under the roiling black of thunderclouds, they knew they could not go on.

Abene, Lourdes and Udane hunkered down against a large round stone, while Juan scouted ahead, looking for anything that could pass as shelter. Time stretched and dilated, rainwater soaking through Abene's coat to her skin, the winds freezing her to the bone, rendering her a shivering puddle of fear.

Juan returned as the sun's rays slipped beyond the mountain, taking with it what little light the storm had not blotted from the sky. He gestured, and they followed, slow, stiff and wobbly, struggling with each step to find purchase on the rain-slicked rock.

Miraculously, he'd found a hut. Old and weathered, but whole, likely a shepherd's shelter for the men who ran their goats across these unforgiving valleys. Empty but for a single worn chair in the corner, the hut was basic but dry. They all stripped off their wet clothes, wrapping themselves in blankets from their packs that had remained somewhat dry. There was nothing with which to start a fire, no extra warmth to be had. Instead, they gathered together, bodies pressed close.

Abene relaxed her muscles into the warmth of her mother's ample body, listening to the pounding winds and claps of thunder that pummelled the outside world. Somewhere between the slash of rain against the wooden roof and the hum of her mother's chest, Abene's eyes grew heavy and carried her to rest.

SIX

ABENE

Southern France

They exited the Pyrenees two days later, dirty, exhausted and starving. At the border crossing into France, they were met by soldiers in military uniform. Their names were taken and they were loaded onto the back of a truck. They travelled for an hour, the coastline of the Pyrénées-Atlantiques, the land of the French Basque, a glimpse of blue in the distance, before arriving at a purpose-built set of buildings near the port of Bayonne,

They were sent to a medical tent, examined, and jabbed with various vaccines. Shown to showers and given basic but clean clothes, then sent on to reception centres throughout Bayonne.

Funded by the French Government, these reception centres had opened up across the country in community halls, manor houses, schools and churches. Abene, Lourdes and Udane were placed in a hall run by the small Catholic community of The Church of Saint Maria, the nuns were welcoming and warm. Juan, being male, was sent further out to a centre on a farm that bordered the city. Udane watched as Juan was loaded onto a separate truck, the sagging lines of her cheeks deepening with sorrow at another separation from her son.

As Abene sat on her small cot in the long, narrow hall of the church, her mother and Udane snoring softly beside her, the stress and worry of the week before crashed down upon her.

Sobs, uncontrollable and strong, wretched from her very soul. Her mother stirred, sitting up to pull her daughter close. Soon her own tears began, the salt of mother and daughter mingling on wet cheeks.

"We are safe now, my daughter," Lourdes whispered softly. "We are safe."

Abene nodded, unable to form words through the heavy press of sorrow that had her chest in a vice. Eventually, her tears subsided into dreams. She did not wake until the warming rays of a new day shone through the windows of their new home.

The next morning Abene took a walk to see the boats arriving from her home. She longed for the sea, to feel the open freedom of the water beyond, to know the call of the waves still sounded, despite all that she had been through. But the port of Bayonne rested on an inland curve of the river. The briny scent of the tidal waters would have to do. Around her the city glistened, its white walls and brightly painted shutters and flower boxes catching the autumn sun. She followed along the Adour River that cut down the middle of the city, fishing boats bobbing peacefully along its banks. Reaching the dockside, she sat on the dry grass of a small hillock. At the port, a new boat had just docked, and a stream of children and a few adults stepped from her decks. Abene watched as French soldiers ushered the new arrivals along the jetty to the waiting medical tent, then led them up to waiting trucks to be transported to their temporary homes. People fleeing her homeland.

A flash of movement in her periphery caught her attention.

Abene looked over to see Juan making his way along the river to join her. She watched him approach, his rolling gait comfortingly familiar, and nodded as he settled on the grass at her side.

"Mother said I would find you here."

They sat in silence, watching as the last of the passengers stepped from the vessel onto French land.

"They look so small from here," Abene said.

"They are small," Juan replied. "They are children."

"So many..."

"Bilbao will fall," Juan said, eyes set on the horizon. The city around them was peaceful, strafed in the golden beams of the morning sun. A world away from what they knew was unfolding in the north of Spain.

Abene sucked in a deep breath. "You are sure?"

Juan nodded, a muscle beneath his stubble-covered cheek twitching as he fought his own inner battle. He scratched at a patch of dirt that crusted his worn calloused hands; fisherman's hands. "I met a group of others from the front," he said, eyes lowered. "They arrived yesterday, evacuated from the fighting in Gipuzkoa. They said the politicians were sending men to the east. Decamping to Barcelona. Now that San Sebastian is taken, Bilbao will be the focus. It is only a matter of time... Soon, Catalonia will be the last remaining freehold of Spain. The last stand."

Abene eyed him, an odd, tingling sensation starting along her arms. "A last stand? But what chance can Catalonia have against the rest of the country?"

"We have to fight. We cannot give up."

"We?"

Finally, Juan turned, fixing her with his eyes. "There is a convoy, trucks arranged by what remains of the Basque government. It will drive the evacuated soldiers to the East Coast, and down to Barcelona. There they will fortify the city. They will hold them out.

"I am going with them."

Abene stared at him, her face contorting in pain. She opened her mouth to argue. He'd already fought, he'd been wounded, he'd done enough. But the understanding of a lifetime together held her tongue.

Juan knew his mind. As children, hungry and bored, they'd hatched a plan to climb onto the roof of their local church, hoping to steal eggs from the pigeon nests that lined the eves. Abene lost her nerve. Juan didn't. As he'd shimmied up the rough stone wall, Abene had begged him to stop, to come down, but Juan would not listen. Hands full of eggs, he'd overbalanced and fallen, landing in a mess of egg yolk and dirt, his arm twisted beneath his body. His father scolded him, his mother lamented the sacrilege of the church, and Juan promised he would not try anything so reckless again. Months later, when the break was healed, he'd climbed the roof again.

If Juan had decided, no one could change his mind.

"Have you told Udane?"

Juan looked away, eyes returning to the horizon. "Not yet. But I will, once I have packed."

They fell silent, each watching the gentle sparkle of the sun on the currents before them.

"Our home is gone," she whispered.

"Yet we remain," Juan said, hand gesturing down to the evacuees' boat, now bobbing empty in the port.

Abene leaned over, resting her head on Juan's shoulder, he bent his own to hers, the strong curls of his hair twinning with her own.

"You will come back," she said. It was not a question. But Juan nodded anyway, his head moving against her temple.

She sat back up, turning to him. "Papá," she began. "Tell me, what happened?"

Juan eyed her, his thick brows creasing above his eyes. "You know."

"I do," she agreed. "I know he is gone." Her eyes flashed to the sky, a silent prayer to God on her lips. "But I want to know how. I deserve that. Mamá deserves that."

"She knows?"

"She hasn't asked, which is the same thing." Abene had seen it, the quiet emptiness in her mother's stare, the downturn of her lips.

Juan blew out a heavy breath, shoulders slumping.

"When I found my father's body, Madre was my first thought too." He paused, picking at a loose fingernail. "We were manning a barricade. The nationalists fired a munitions round. It threw us back, lifted us from the earth, to crash back down. I caught shrapnel in my side." He placed an absent hand over the injury, better now, but still not fully healed.

"There was dirt everywhere, over everything, over me. More mortars were exploding around us. I could see the earth flying into the sky, smell the smoke and fumes. But my ears... they just rang and rang.

"I managed to get up. But everything felt slow, like I was wading through mud. I looked around, but I could not see Bittor. I called out for him, but I couldn't hear my own voice."

He paused, hands now clasped together, shaking. Abene swallowed, tears forming in her eyes, her chest a gaping hole of pain.

Lips trembling, Juan continued. "I found him behind a tree. He must have crawled there. I don't know how, his injuries..." he heaved a breath, voice cracking as he remembered. "Blood was everywhere. He'd been hit directly. His legs..." he trailed off.

The tears spilled down Abene's face at the unspoken suggestion. Her father had been blown apart.

"His eyes were wide open, he was still breathing. I made it to him, I took his hand.

"You and your mother were his final thought, Abene. He

made me promise to get you out. He made me swear." His voice broke and a soft keening wheezed from his throat as his head dropped into his hands. Shoulders quaking, Juan cried. Abene wrapped herself around her friend. The image of her father, bloodied and dying, covered in muck and dirt. She would never find peace with it. She could not.

"Thank you," she managed, voice thick with sorrow.

"For what?" Juan cried. "Bittor didn't make it. I didn't save him..." He collapsed into a fresh round of tears, chest heaving in her arms.

"But you were with him. He didn't die alone. You were there, you were there..."

As the words formed, she realised they were true. It was something to hold on to, a small mercy for her beautiful papá. It would be the part she would tell her mother. It was the only part that mattered.

Eventually, they came apart, Juan's face a wreck of tears and snot. Abene's was little better. Drying their tears they stood. "Is it time?" she asked.

"Yes."

Hand in hand they made their way down the small rise to the river's edge.

"I will be here when you return," Abene said. "We all will be."

"I know," Juan said. "And I will come to you."

He gestured to the port, to the row of children still making their way into trucks. "They will need mothers until they can return home."

"They will. But we are Basque. We will all take care of them."

"They are who we fight for... who I fight for."

"I know. I understand."

Arriving at Abene's church accommodation, they embraced once again. "Return soon," Abene said and turned sharply away. She didn't want to see Juan's face as he answered, didn't want to read the doubt she knew swam in his eyes.

She had to believe.

Hope was all she had left to cling to.

Rallying her resolve, she made her way back to the hall she now called home. Juan was right, the children of her region needed mothers. The government had done well, sending teachers, nurses and nuns to watch over them. But more hands would always be welcome. It was time for Abene to take action.

It was time to do her part for her people.

Across the evening, two new groups of evacuees arrived at the church hall. Abene rolled up her sleeves, helping the patient nuns assign cots, while Lourdes and Udane worked in the kitchen to cook stew to feed more hungry, scared mouths.

The next morning when the small group of government-assigned nurses arrived to check on the new arrivals, Abene was ready. She made her way to the little desk and the fair-haired, round-faced nurse who always came to their church. Smiling at the first waiting child, she gently pushed past. The nurse looked up, her eyebrows high on her forehead.

"Qui? Vous aidez?"

A local then. Abene paused, sifting through her brain to find the basic French she knew from childhood. "Bonjour," she said, "I would like to help."

The woman stared at her. Clearly, Abene's French was not enough. She tried again, tapping her chest. "J'aide. I help," she pointed back along the line of waiting children.

Understanding lit the woman's moon-shaped face. "Tres bien, very good," she announced, coming to her feet. Taking an apron from a hook by the door she looped the garment around Abene's neck. "Come."

Abene followed the woman behind the makeshift curtain that allowed some privacy as the new arrivals were inspected for disease and had their wounds treated.

"You speak some French," the woman said. "And fluent Spanish. I speak some Spanish and fluent French. Between us, we can translate, yes?"

Abene nodded her understanding.

"Bien," the woman said. "Merci for your help. I am Camille Cambourd." She tapped her chest.

"Abene Ortiz."

"Pleased to meet you."

A boy and an old woman appeared at the curtain's edge, steps hesitant, eyes nervous.

Abene plastered her warmest smile across her lips. "Come in, come in," she said.

Her work had begun.

SEVEN
MIREN

1937 Bilbao

Miren was overwhelmed. On her desk, piled higher than her head, lay page, after page, after page of applications. The bulk of the Nationalist army was approaching at speed, leaving a trail of destruction in its wake. An Iron Wall of fortifications and defences had been erected around the city of Bilbao, but few believed it would hold Franco's forces at bay. Since he'd been declared the head of state the October before, nothing seemed able to stop his advance. They were living under siege, bombardments reducing whole quarters of the city to rubble, the threat of capture a heavy, constant shadow at their backs.

Her own city of San Sebastian had fallen, fast. It had been months since she'd chosen, months since she watched her city disappear from the deck of a boat. She'd still not been able to get word to her mother, to find out how her parents were, whether they had survived. Perhaps these mountains of applications were a gift; they kept her mind distracted from her worst fears, at least.

All the parents of the Basque region were now desperate to

send their children away. But there was nowhere safe left in Spain.

Anders was working tirelessly overseeing the evacuation effort in Bilbao. Having secured safe harbour for Basque citizens to France, Belgium, The Netherlands, England and even as far away as Russia, there was a lot of paperwork to ensure every child was properly tracked. The hope remained that they would return. Every one of them. Soon.

But as was the nature of all plans, there were cracks, and in this case, ruptures big enough to flood a city. Specifically, more children than places on vessels. They had set up an application system; parents had to make their case for sending their children away. With Anders busy in government talks all day and most of the night as the politicians worked not only to evacuate their citizens but to keep them safe abroad, the processing of those applications, the responsibility of choosing who could escape and who had to stay, fell on Miren.

It was a lot.

It was too much.

How had it come to this? How could it be that putting your child on a boat with strangers, and sending them to a foreign land, was the best option?

The reports from San Sebastian flashed in her mind. Photos of streets strewn with the bullet-ridden bodies of soldiers, the feet of hanging victims swaying in the breezes off the bay. The mayor had been executed without trial. She closed her eyes. She'd send her child away too.

Each day she toiled, assessing, deciding. She'd made sure the small boy from her escape from San Sebastian was safe, little Eduardo, listed for France. It was a small thing. It was something to hold on to.

She longed to go home, back to the one-bedroom apartment she had been assigned here in Bilbao. Emergency accommodation near the buildings of parliament, mercifully near to

Anders' hotel. She wanted to crawl under her blankets and bury her head in the soft pillows, wrap her arms around herself and pretend that Anders held her. That they were together somewhere, anywhere, but here.

It wouldn't work though. The soft, welcoming bed could only keep her from her thoughts momentarily. Soon the worries, the fears for her parents, for her people, reared up in her mind. It didn't matter where she went, or what she did, her brain and her thoughts were still with her.

She should have stepped off the boat.

A soft knock on her door.

"Come," she said, lifting her head, forcing her features to calm.

A young man entered, hair neatly greased back, two small pimples gracing his forehead.

"The British ship has docked," he said. "Señor Torres is making his way to the docks, he asked me to see if you were free to join him?"

"Yes, thank you, Manuel."

It was an altogether different scene at El Puerto de Bilbao than what she had experienced the day she left San Sebastian. The ship, a hulking naval vessel, loomed up from the waters, shiny and grey, the proud blue, red and white flag of the United Kingdom flying from her decks. Along the dock stood the children, each with a single suitcase dangling from their hands, barely clearing the wood below. A neat row, punctuated by the occasional adult, a teacher or a nurse, the carers who had been assigned to go with them. Their parents had already been separated, standing outside the port area, watching, wide-eyed, cheeks shining with tears in the early spring sun.

Anders stood beside a man in a white naval uniform, golden metals pinned to his chest. Miren approached cautiously, not wishing to interrupt. Spying her, a wide smile spread instantly across Anders' face and he held out a hand, welcoming her forward.

"Señorita Perez, I am pleased to introduce you to Rear Admiral Redford. He will be seeing our children to the safety of British shores. Admiral, this is the incredible young woman who has been processing our myriad applications. Your country cannot know the gift you are giving to our people."

The admiral turned his gaze to Miren, his eyes shrouded by white fluffy brows. "Your people will owe you a large debt, señorita," he said.

The blast of emotion surprised her. Her lips trembled and her heart hammered as she took the admiral's hand to shake. It was one thing to process the applications for this evacuation, it was quite another to be acknowledged for it.

"In times of war we must make difficult decisions," he continued. "I can only imagine the challenges behind your choices. But know this, you have saved lives this day."

"Thank you," she breathed, as he released her hand.

As the admiral made his way back to his vessel, she felt Anders' eyes on her. Stepping to her side he took her elbow, leading them from the docks back towards the city. "I thought you should see what you have done," he said. "I know how this task has weighed on you. But look," he paused, gesturing at the line of children. It shuffled forward slowly as a sailor at the boarding plank checked each child's paperwork. "You have saved them."

Tears, hot and plump, sprang into her eyes and a mix of pride and guilt churned within her. "But the others..."

His fingers dug into her flesh. "Not here," he whispered.

She nodded, dashing the betraying tears from her cheeks, lifting her head in a gesture of confidence she did not feel inside.

"Well done," Anders' whispered, continuing them on their

way. "You are to take the remainder of the day off. I think you need it."

She nodded her agreement, not trusting her voice to speak.

"Let us share lunch. It has been too long since we had a moment together in the midst of this chaos."

Surprised, she turned to him. "But your work, the advance of the Nationalists. The only way to save the rest of them is to stop Franco."

"A break to eat will not make the difference," he replied, eyes set forward now, pace increasing. She caught the flex of the muscle that lined his jaw, saw the bob of his throat and knew there was more to this sudden moment of normality together.

She opened her mouth to ask, to press him to reveal what was behind his focused eyes. But as they walked to his waiting official car, the words dried up.

She didn't want to know. She simply wanted to exist in this rare moment, just her and Anders and the promise of time together. Knowing what was behind his change of routine would only spoil it. If she remained silent she could ignore the gnawing doubt that clawed at her belly, the heavy shame that she had chosen him over her family, leaving them behind in San Sebastian; the guilt she bore for each child she'd failed to get out of Spain, and just be with him, for one perfect afternoon.

She would take every moment she could get.

He dismissed his driver and they walked the blasted streets of Bilbao arm in arm, the buds of spring impossibly green along the tree branches. At her apartment, she made paella with chickpeas. Meat of any kind was too difficult to source in the siege. They ate on her balcony. Miren savoured the view of the lush green mountains that surrounded the city, ignoring the knowledge of who waited in those hills.

After lunch Anders took her to bed, slow and tender, unrushed. His hands flowed over her body as if to memorise every curve, every rise and hollow. As he finished his eyes gleamed wet with tears. She didn't ask why, she'd made her choice. Reaching up she drew him to her breast, running soothing fingers through his thick dark hair.

"I love you," she whispered. His arms tightened about her waist, gripping her to him.

"Everything I do, you are the reason. Everything."

She nodded, silent, banishing the creeping fear that continued to writhe its way along her bones.

She didn't want to know, she just wanted this.

As it happened, she didn't have to wait long to find out anyway.

EIGHT

MIREN

Manuel burst into her office, slamming the door shut behind him. Miren looked up in shock. "Manuel?" she said, coming to her feet.

"He is sorry, señorita. He is truly sorry."

Miren frowned, cocking her head to the side. "Manuel...?"

She was exhausted. Five days before the government of Bilbao had ordered the evacuation of the civilians of the city. Miren had worked night and day on the logistics and transport, working to get as many people out as possible. The sound of exploding bridges, destroyed in an attempt to slow the advance of the Nationalists, an accompaniment to her sleepless nights.

"There was no choice, he wants you to know this. There was no other way."

"No other way, Manuel, what are you saying?"

She rounded her desk, stepping towards her young assistant.

"I am here though. He asked me to watch over you, and I will. It will be all right. You haven't done anything. You are just a secretary. No one can blame you for protecting children."

"Blame me? Manuel, what are you talking about?"

"They are here."

Miren froze mid-step, her flesh turning to ice. She didn't need to know who "they" referred to; only one force could drain the colour so thoroughly from Manuel's tanned face.

Terror, bone deep and primal, stole the strength from her limbs and she felt her body begin to shake.

"Where is Anders?"

And suddenly she understood. Manuel's flustered ramblings clicked into place and Miren slumped back against her desk, hand fluttering to her chest.

Anders was gone. Anders had left her.

Worse, he had planned it all along. She'd known it. As he smoothed the hair from her forehead and said goodbye, she'd known.

Manuel stepped forward. "The Basque Government left for Barcelona last night. It was the best way."

She held up a hand, stopping his progress. She needed a moment to herself, she needed time to process. There was no time.

"Where are the Nationalists?"

Manuel blinked, pupils dilated with fear. "They have entered the city. They will be here within the hour."

An hour. Her gut plummeted, her heart pounded in her chest. She swallowed. There was no time for her own pain just now. She had to act.

"Send everyone home, and bring me the multi-cut scissors, we must destroy the documents."

An hour later, as the heavy footfall of highly polished military shoes echoed up the stairs to her office, Miren sat alone, cross-legged on the floor, piles of shredded paperwork surrounding her. She had sent everyone else away, including Manuel.

It was the first time she saw him, but it would not be the last. Not tall, but imposing, barrel-chested, he stood erect, head high, turning his eyes down to her along the length of his proud nose. A man who expected obedience.

"Stand," he commanded.

Blurry-eyed, wrung out and abandoned, Miren pushed herself from the floor. She was too overwhelmed to be afraid.

"Name and role."

"Miren Perez, secretary to Minister Anders Torres."

A small tick of a heavy eyebrow was the only indication of his displeasure before he launched at her. Pulling back his arm, he swung, the back of his hand connecting with Miren's cheek with a loud crack. She didn't preempt it, didn't see it coming. As the full force of his bodyweight concentrated through the bones of her face Miren saw a flash of light and collapsed to the floor.

He stood over her, panting slightly, then straightened his jacket.

"Stand," he repeated.

Dazed and shocked, Miren tried to push herself up, but her arms gave out beneath her, her head spinning.

"I do not expect to repeat myself," he said. "Stand."

She tried and failed again.

The edge of his boot connected with her ribcage, forcing the air from her lungs. She fell flat to the carpet, her chest cramping as her muscles spasmed against the explosion of pain.

"Stand," his voice now a whisper.

She couldn't. She knew she couldn't.

And yet somehow she did.

On her feet, hunched over her chest, struggling to breathe, Miren focused on the red patterned carpet, trying to stop the whirring in her mind, trying to think.

"Good girl," he said. "You understand my displeasure surely?" His voice crooned as he moved closer, circling her like prey. "Señor Torres is no minister. He, and the rest of the fake government of the Basque, are no more than upstart troublemakers."

He stopped behind her, his breath hot and menacing on the

back of her neck. She closed her eyes and willed herself not to faint. "But it is all right now," he continued. "We have arrived to set you and your people free. I would have expected more gratitude... Yet..."

He gestured at the piles of shredded paper at their feet. Miren swallowed, still working to simply draw breath.

He stepped before her, then lifted his arms out in a gesture of unexpected warmth. "Do not worry, I am in a good mood today," he said. "I grant you forgiveness. This time."

He lifted a hand, clicked his fingers and two soldiers, rifles strapped to their backs, entered the room.

"Escort Señorita Perez home," he ordered. Hands, rough and harsh, gripped the bare flesh of her upper arms, hauling her from the room.

"Oh and, señorita?"

Her progress halted, the soldiers were at the man's beck and call.

"My name is General Sergio Hernandez. You would do well to remember me."

She blinked rapidly, her mind still unable to catch up with everything that was happening around her.

Sergio flicked a wrist, turning to her desk, and the soldiers moved, drawing her from the room, down the stairs and out into a Bilbao forever changed.

The army truck bounced over the dirt roads that surrounded San Sebastian. Miren grimaced, trying to brace her ribs against the shunt of the vehicle. The bruises on her upper arms pulled with the movement. Breathing against the shooting pain from her core, Miren rested her head back against the truck. Beside her sat others from her office. Her *former* office. Men and women loyal to Anders, now unemployed, being returned home to San Sebastian.

Part of Miren felt overwhelming, shameful relief that they were all alive, and mostly unharmed. After the stories of the fall of San Sebastian and the executions on the streets, she had feared the worst. But part of her was just too tired to even care.

The Nationalists had kept her under house arrest for a week, delivering minimal food, and necessities, even a priest to hear her confession. During that week General Hernandez had visited daily, each time with a new set of questions and the unspoken threat of his fists.

Miren hadn't held out. She had no real secrets to keep.

So she talked. About the agreements with foreign countries to evacuate the Basque children, and later as many civilians as possible. Of the fear the people felt, fear for their lives.

He'd "tsked" at that.

"But, my dear woman," he said, "what have you to fear from your fellow countrymen?"

She'd wanted to scream at him. To stand and beat her fists against his proud chest. To smash his face as he had hers. He and his soldiers had decimated her country, murdered her people, and threatened the life of the man she loved. What did she fear?

Everything.

Now, having served whatever use the general required, she was being returned home.

The truck stopped before her father's hotel with a jerk and Miren was hurried out onto the pavement. The Maria Crista rose above her, regal and elegant as always, yet along her walls new holes marred the once perfect sandstone where the blast of gunfire had torn the stone away. A pockmarked canvas of war. It took the breath from her lungs. All the reports she'd read of events in San Sebastian, all the photos of bodies and prisoners, had not prepared her for this confronting moment. Suddenly, it was real.

The fighting had come right to her parents' door. Had they

remained safe within? Or, in her absence, had the unthinkable befallen them?

She mounted the stair on unsteady legs, swallowing hard as she made for the door. Terrified of what she may find, lips forming a silent prayer, she stepped inside.

Her mother stood at the reception desk, her perfectly fitted dress immaculate, a stark contrast to the ruin of the walls outside. Mother and daughter faced each other across the room.

"Jose!" her mother cried. "Jose, Miren is home."

Her father appeared in the office doorway, standing straight, the bob of his throat the only emotion he allowed himself to display.

Maria rushed forward with uncharacteristic haste. Spreading her arms wide she enveloped Miren into the comfort of her embrace. At the softness of her mother's skin, the familiar scent of fresh soap off her flesh, Miren broke down. All the fear, the stress, the sorrow, the grief, all the pain of shattered hope flooded from her soul. Relief that her parents were alive, were safe, warred with the guilt of her choice to leave them. The realisation of what she had come so close to losing. Sobs tore from her throat as her knees gave way.

"My daughter, my daughter," her mother whispered, holding her up with the strength of pure will alone. "Madre is here, Mother is here."

Slowly the sobs subsided, the pain of her bruised ribs forcing her to calm. Her mother led her to the kitchen, placed the kettle on the hob and returned to take her hands.

"I prayed for you every day. I prayed you would be returned to us."

Miren looked at her madre, her face a wreck of shame. "I am so, so sorry, Madre."

Maria smiled softly at her daughter.

"Where is Anders?"

Miren closed her eyes as a fresh wave of grief threatened to overwhelm her. "He left me," she whispered. Maria took her daughter's hand and squeezed it tightly. "Oh, Madre, I am such a fool!"

Maria cocked her head in silence, giving her daughter the space to find her words.

"I left for him. I left you." Miren's voice cracked, fresh tears spilling down her face. "He asked me to follow him. I did, without question. And then... and then he just left! Fled with the rest of the Basque government and left me behind. Why would he do that?"

She broke down, placing her head on their entwined hands, shoulders heaving.

"Peace, my daughter, peace," Maria said, smoothing her daughter's rich brown hair. "Look at me."

Breathing in ragged gasps, Miren lifted her head to face her mother.

Maria held her daughter's eyes, waiting for her grief to settle.

"You made a choice. Anders made a choice."

Miren stilled, watching her mother's face, waiting for her to continue. "Life is a choice. We cannot question those of others, their choices are theirs. As ours are ours."

The kettle sang out, whistling the boiling was done. Maria stood, padding over to the hob. She poured the scalding water into a teapot, then broke fresh herbs from her windowsill plot to flavour the liquid. Returning to the table she set the pot to steep, steam rising from the spout between them.

The robust scent of rosemary filled the room, warm and comforting. Maria poured the herbal tea into delicate porcelain cups, painted blue birds flitting across their white rims. "Drink up, my child," she said. "And then to bed. It is time for you to rest."

"Gracias, Madre," Miren whispered and sipped her tea.

Her father had not followed them in, he stood at the kitchen door, watching, Looking up, Miren met his eyes across the room and instinctively shrank from what she saw glimmering there. Shaking his head he turned away.

Miren felt her lips tremble as the weight of his disappointment settled over her shoulders. And she knew: she'd gambled and she'd lost. She'd chosen a man mired in scandal, had left her family for him. Aligned herself with the democratic cause.

And Anders had left her. The Nationalists had won.

What came next? Miren didn't know. But it wasn't over. Not for her, or for her family.

She'd brought this to her parents' home. This uncertain future they now faced. Would they ever forgive her?

Would she forgive herself?

NINE

MIREN

San Sebastian

Miren woke to a city she could hardly recognise. It started in her home when she woke to the still silence of an empty hotel. The Maria Crista was one of the oldest and most successful hotels in the region, even in winter they would welcome a steady stream of guests, holidaymakers and businessmen. In a normal year. But this was not a normal year.

The halls echoed, and the kitchen sat dark and unused. Her father had sent the maids home, leaving only a skeleton staff to keep the rooms orderly. As Miren crossed the polished floor of reception her heels clacked loud and telling, ringing through the bare hallways, an auditory reverberation of change.

On the streets of the old town, a sea mist drifted thick and cloying, covering the stone-walled stores in a damp promise of the coming storm. Clutching her coat tight around her neck, Miren made her way through the centre. It was quieter than normal. The usual bustling energy of San Sebastian replaced with a sombre silence. People went about their business, heads lowered, eyes furtive. The only men standing tall were the

Nationalist soldiers. Patrolling in pairs, seemingly at every street corner, eyes peeled, watching.

She saw her before the San Vicente Church, walking quickly, one hand manoeuvring a pram, the other clutching her son. Carla. A smile of pure joy spread across Miren's face, the first in months. Holding her arms out wide she called to her friend across the square, "Carla, Daniel!"

Carla's head snapped up, surprise and fear etched across her face. She stopped, stepping back. But Daniel surged forward. His little arms held high, a smile beaming on his lips as he cried "Izeba Miren! Aunty!"

It all happened so fast.

A nearby soldier whipped around, face stern. Carla reached forward, grabbing Daniel's arm and wrenching him back to her. Turning him to face her she slapped his little face, open-handed and hard.

Miren stopped dead, shock rattling through her as her friend hissed at her son. "No!"

Tears of confusion filled the little boy's eyes. Carla straightened, and glanced at Miren. She saw the terror in Carla's expression. The soldier was advancing. Then Diego materialised, addressing the soldier politely, his body language small and submissive. It was so unlike him that Miren gaped.

"Please, the boy is young. He simply forgot himself..."

The soldier stared at Diego, then down at the sobbing Daniel. He gave a grudging nod, then turned away.

Diego rounded on Miren. He stepped forward, coming towards her, but stopping some distance apart. "Stay away from us."

Miren stared at him, and over his shoulder at Carla. Her long-time friend kept her eyes down, not meeting her eye. Then Diego turned. Scooping a sobbing Daniel into his arms, he led his wife and children away.

"There you are!" An urgent whisper at her side brought

Miren from her shock. Her father stood at her elbow. His fingers clamped around her arm. "Come."

"Papá, what are you doing here?"

But Jose wasn't looking at Miren. Across the square people were spilling out of the San Vicente Church, fast, faces harried.

"Quickly now."

"But, Father, wait. What is happening?" Miren pointed at the church. She felt her father's fingers tighten on her arm. He pulled.

Just then, two soldiers appeared at the church entrance, an old priest held between them. They dragged the ageing preacher down the stairs and out onto the street, before throwing him bodily to the hard stone cobbles. The priest sprawled across the path, hands rising to protect his head. A soldier stood over him, shouting. Then he unslung the gun from his back and, holding it high above his head, brought the butt down against the priest's head. Blood spurted, bright and red from where the gun had connected.

Miren stepped forward, mouth wide in horror. What was happening?

"No," Jose hissed. "Come away."

"But, Father, he is an old man. And a priest!"

"And it is none of our business."

More shouts rose as another pair of soldiers appeared from the church, grasping an orderly between them. He was thrown to the street beside the priest, the two men clutching onto each other. The orderly held up a hand in pacification. A soldier slapped it away, forcing the barrel of his gun into the man's face. The orderly then brought his hands together and began to pray.

Two hands gripped her shoulders and her father forcibly turned her away from the now-empty square.

Dazed by shock, Miren did not resist. Shouts from the soldiers rang across the square behind her. As Jose pressed her around the corner of a building a single gunshot rang out across the sky.

Jose did not slow their pace, urging Miren forward on trembling legs along the Urumea until they were back in the hotel. He steered Miren to the family living space. There Maria stood, wringing her hands before her. The couple exchanged a look and Maria hurried from the room as Jose settled Miren on a large couch. She sat, shaking, hands clutching the armrests. Maria returned with a cup of coffee.

"Here, daughter, drink."

Miren took the cup in unsteady hands, and brought the warm liquid to her lips: sweet, milky. For the shock. As she sipped the sweet coffee, its warm tendrils slipping through her body, the trembling of her limbs began to subside. But not the fear and confusion.

Looking to her parents, she asked, "Father, what just happened? Diego told me to stay away, Carla slapped Daniel, and the priest..."

It was too much, the tremors started again. Maria took the wobbling cup from her hands and took a seat beside her on the couch. "Darling, much has changed here in San Sebastian. Surely you know this?"

"I read the reports, paesos, arrests. But that man... he was a priest!"

"A Basque priest," Jose said, pacing to the small fireplace that lay cold and empty against the wall. "Father Arimeni praised the Basque culture, our ways of life. He was a leader of our community."

"And a man of God!" Miren could not understand it. "Papá, Spain is a Catholic nation."

"Spain is Franco's nation, now."

Miren fell silent, mind whirling. "And Carla? She slapped Daniel. I have never seen her do such a thing."

"The boy spoke Basque. It is forbidden. As is calling our

city by her Basque name, Donostia. We live in San Sebastian only now. There have been arrests for smaller transgressions..."

"But Carla is a new mother, and Daniel is just a child."

"Even pregnant women have been executed."

Horror sluiced through Miren, her hand coming to her mouth in shock. "Pregnant women..."

"The soldiers have been indiscriminate. Daughter, this is not the city you knew. And it is not the country I love," he paused, eyes going unfocused as he looked away across the room. Then he turned back to Miren. "These are dangerous times, my daughter. Fear walks the streets. They've rounded up teachers, academics, politicians and imprisoned them, or worse, just for who they are. The soldiers look for any hint of disobedience or subversion. We stood against them, and we lost. Now we must be small and quiet. Unseen."

Realisation dawned over Miren. "Diego, he told me to stay away from them..."

Jose closed his eyes, sorrow filtering over his features. "You worked for Señor Torres. You were in the very offices of the Basque government in the Plaza de la Constitución that Franco has overthrown. You are dangerous. Worse, you are *in* danger. It is why I came to find you today. You can't be out on the streets. You are lucky, so, so lucky that you are here and alive. When we heard Bilbao had fallen..." Jose looked up at Maria, raw emotion, missing yesterday when she'd returned home, now carved lines through his face. "We prayed."

Miren swallowed, understanding. She'd read the reports that came into Anders' office in Bilbao. Of arrests and summary executions. Of show trials. But they had been targeted at soldiers who fought against the Nationalists. This, this was against the civilians. Against men of God. Their crime? Being Basque. It was too much, incomprehensibly awful. It shook her to her very core. The foundations of her life had been ripped away. But there was nothing she could do, only heed her father's words, stay out of sight, and pray.

"I understand what you are saying, Father, Mother. And I will listen. I will be careful."

Jose nodded sadly, eyeing his child. "The hotel is a good place. We can keep ourselves separate. Weather this storm. We will do so together, as a family, si?"

"Yes, Father," Miren said. "Together."

And Miren kept her word, passing her days within the walls of the Maria Crista hotel, listening to the radio and reading the newspapers, learning of the horrors inflicted on her people beyond those bullet-ridden walls.

A prison, roughly constructed of brick and mortar, was set up on the beach. Exposed to the elements, the beating sun and the freezing winds, those sent within its walls were not expected to survive.

As the months passed the true hardship for the everyday people of the city began to show itself to Miren. As her father explained, the Basque language was banned; to speak it meant instant arrest. Whole families were taken prisoner because of a slip of the tongue from a child at school. The normal flow of activity on the streets dwindled, with people securing themselves at home to keep distant and hopefully safe from the seeking eyes of passing Nationalist guards.

Food became more and more scarce. Fruit and vegetables were older, and supplies of flour for bread and cereals ran low. The fish caught in the waters off the coast didn't make it back into the communities the fishermen came from. What her father would normally source for the hotel was impossible to purchase. But without the holidaymakers from Madrid, or the visiting politicians from Barcelona in residence, perhaps it didn't matter. For Miren and her parents, it meant hollow bellies and food boredom. For the poorer of San Sebastian, it signalled starvation.

As the full heat of summer began to burn down on the city, the usual holiday visitors from out of town did not arrive. Children did not play on the beach, adults did not fill the squares and bars chatting away the balmy hours of evening.

War had ravaged the nation of Spain, and it still held Barcelona in its grip.

And Miren had heard nothing from Anders. She knew he and the Basque government of Bilbao had fled to Barcelona, the surrounds of the city were now the centre point of the war. Now that Franco's Nationalists held the north, they controlled the mines and manufacturing. How long could the fighters in Barcelona hold out without access to fresh weapons and supplies?

And why hadn't Anders sent word? Even just a letter to tell her he was alive and safe?

Perhaps that was an impossibility. In this nation at war, how could a politician from the losing side really do anything?

Yet she heard the stories of the refugees in southern France. She knew how much work the Basque government had done to secure safe passage for the children of the region, the work they still managed in secret. If they could coordinate and facilitate the supply of food and medicines for people outside of Spain, surely something could be sent to her to ease her fear and grief?

The adjustment of returning to work at her father's hotel was a tough one. She'd left to be Anders' secretary more than a year before, a young woman full of hopes and dreams. Now she was firmly back where she'd started, yet everything had changed. She'd lost her career, her fiancé and her country. The sorrow lay heavy and large on her heart, an ache that she could not lift. Her parents must have seen the desolation in her eyes, yet neither spoke a word to her about all that had befallen her in the months in Bilbao. The burden of their own experience was too great to overcome.

As the seasons drifted towards the chill of winter the streets were deserted. Children, waif-like and hollow-eyed, appeared on street corners, begging for food, only to be moved on, roughly, by Nationalist patrols. A pall of fear and hunger gripped the city in its clutches, and Miren could not see a path through.

It didn't stop her from checking the hotel mail daily, hoping against hope to find a letter addressed to her in Anders' tight handwriting. He had left her, she knew. Had fled to Barcelona, leaving her to her fate. But she could not bring herself to give up on him, on them. If the Nationalist threat had not come to their city, he would still be with her. He loved her, she was sure of it. And she loved him.

So she waited, and prayed that he would send word, let her know where he was, how he was, when he would return for her.

No letter came.

There was nothing to be done except endure. Day, after day, after day.

TEN
ABENE

Bayonne

"Another boat is arriving. I need your help."

Abene looked up from her knitting. She was in the church courtyard, passing a cool October afternoon with Sister Agnes. The old nun had been a champion for Abene and her fellow Basque refugees. After the fall of Bilbao and as the siege of Barcelona had extended, the sister had held nightly prayers for the people of Spain and promised that no matter how drastically the French government cut their funding, there would be a place here in Bayonne for them to seek refuge.

And cut funding they had. After the influx of refugees that landed when Bilbao was claimed by the Nationalists, fear of this new population becoming permanent had swept France. Political tensions murmured across the border with Germany and Italy also, causing French citizens to begin to look inward. The long shadow of the Great War had never really faded.

Reception centres across France began to reduce their services. Many Basques ran fundraiser days – cultural performances, soup kitchens and fêtes – in an attempt to find the money to continue their time in France.

Talk of return was growing.

With all that at her back, Abene met Camille's face, expression urgent. "Another boat? But the boats were stopped?"

"It is an emergency evacuation. Children only. They will be spread across the centres in the city, but I was hoping we could house a group here?" Her eyes sought Sister Agnes.

The ageing nun stood slowly, joints tight and stiff. "There will always be room here for the innocent."

Camille nodded. "I will ring through that we can take a group. Can you start to set up the cots, and medical supplies?"

"Of course," Abene agreed, following Sister Agnes into the main hall.

Abene enlisted her mother and Udane, as well as several other women from the centre. Together they ported extra cots, mattresses, sheets and blankets into the hall, squeezing those already in place closer together so as to fit in more for the coming children.

Next, she set up a small privacy curtain, table and chair, ready to help Camille examine the children as they arrived. She was laying out the medical tools, stethoscope, reflex-hammer and thermometer when she heard the bustle of their arrival.

Coming around the curtain she watched as a line of small children filed into the hall. They were of various ages, some as young as four, some on the cusp of teenagers. They walked in pairs, hands gripped tightly together, eyes wide as they scanned the room, step unsure.

Abene beamed out her best smile of welcome and helped to usher them into the hall, assigning them beds. At the back of the line, a small boy caught her attention. He walked hand in hand with an older girl but was clearly dragging his feet. Abene moved to his side and knelt down, bringing herself into his line of sight. "Hello there, child. What is your name?"

He regarded her with bright brown eyes, a fair curl bobbing in the centre of his forehead. "Eduardo," he whispered.

"Welcome to Bayonne, Eduardo. I am Abene, it is wonderful to have you stay."

The boy shuffled his feet, eyes cast down nervously. Abene smiled up at the girl. "You go on in," she said. The girl nodded, dropping Eduardo's hand and moving through. Abene returned her attention to the small boy. Cocking her head at him she said quietly, "I can see you are a good helper." She paused as his eyes flicked up in cautious curiosity. "I wonder if you would like to help me finish in the medical area? It would be good for me to have an extra pair of hands."

A small smile tickled at the edges of Eduardo's mouth. "I am a good helper," he said, standing taller and puffing out his little chest. "And I am very brave."

"Well then, you are just the one I need," Abene said. "Come." She stood up, offering her hand. Eduardo clutched it in his own, his grip solid, and they made their way to finish setting up for Camille's check of the children and their health.

The first winter at the reception centre had been tough, the close quarters in the church hall and food rations creating the perfect environment for illness to spread.

This second winter, with the sleeping space filled with children of all ages, things were worse. Sickness had ripped through the hall, a series of colds and fevers. And such illness targets the young. The children of Spain who had arrived healthy and hale began to cough and sniffle and were sent to bed, one after the other. Sick children need their mothers. The teachers and caregivers were run off their feet, trying to offer comfort to their small charges.

Abene joined them, adding her time and hands to the service of the children of northern Spain. She'd needed time to process, to recover after losing everything she had ever known, and the pain of the death of her father. But as time stretched on, Abene knew she needed more. Juan had known too, prompting her to act even before he left to fight. Working with Camille, translating for the newly arrived refugees, had been one thing, but caring for sick children was soul-filling.

Abene was grateful. Mopping the brow of a feverish child and spooning broth into their mouths brought comfort and calm she hadn't realised she needed.

Wind rattled the wooden slats of the hall roof. Outside a night storm was building off the coast, the air thick with moisture and ready to burst. Lamplight flickered soft and glowing, illuminating the row of cots that lined the wall. They kept the sick children separate, hoping to limit the spread of the fever that confined them to bed. Abene strolled along the row of sleeping children, pausing at each to check their temperature, placing cooling wet clothes on their foreheads and soothing their brows. Most children slept, fitful and tossing, but at rest. Only one set of eyes remained bright in the lamplight.

"Mi cariño, Eduardo," Abene said, settling herself on the edge of the child's bed. "You are not sleeping?"

She smoothed his hair back from his face, his blonde locks damp with sweat. The child lifted his hands and took hers, squeezing her fingers gently, his skin clammy and hot. "Will you sing to me?"

A smile curved Abene's lips. "Of course, dear one. What shall I sing?"

"Something you like."

Abene nodded, thinking. The song came unbidden, an old folk tune of the sea and the waves, of storms and danger and love. Of hope. She sang in a whisper, her voice a soft sound floating gently to Eduardo, for his ears only.

As she sang his eyes drooped, the lids lowering fraction by fraction. His breathing slowed, the rattle in his chest settling to a wheeze, his hands relaxing their grip on hers. Soon his head rolled to the side, the peace of deep sleep smoothing his features. But Abene didn't move, choosing instead to stay sitting by his side, her fingers still tangled with his, watching the gentle rise and fall of his chest beneath the sheet. "Mi cariño," she whispered, "be well soon."

ELEVEN

ABENE

1938

As the dusting of frost that covered the cobbled streets of Bayonne melted with the warming winds that promised spring, Abene continued her work caring for the evacuees of San Sebastian and Bilbao. Though tolerance in France waned, some funds still made it from the government in exile in Barcelona, keeping centres such as The Church of Saint Maria's Catholic Hall open. It was a mercy and a blessing for the people who could not or would not return.

With the fall of Bilbao the June before and the establishment of Franco's Nationalist rule in the region, fear of retribution had intensified. Everyone thanked God for their safe harbour here in the Pyrénées-Atlantiques. Now Franco turned his attention to Barcelona, the last remaining stronghold of the Republic of Spain. What would happen if Catalonia fell?

It was a fate too terrifying to face. So few did, instead turning inward and focusing on making their lives in France as comfortable as possible.

"Now, Eduardo," Abene said, eyeing the small boy sitting before her, legs swinging off the edge of the cot. "Courage."

Eduardo nodded, squeezing his eyes tightly shut as Abene pressed the alcohol-soaked pad to his scuffed knee. As the sting of disinfectant fired through his nerves Eduardo sucked in a hiss of breath through clenched teeth.

"Bravo, brave boy," Abene said, tossing the bloody pad into a waiting pan and gathering up a spool of gauze. Carefully, she wound a length of fabric around the boy's knee, protecting the open wound from the elements while it healed.

"And you are all fixed up," she said, smiling at Eduardo. "Now, remember, what did I say? You can play, but you must always...?"

"Go slow around the corners," he replied, a sheepish curve to his lips.

"Exactly. Good boy. Now, off you go."

He dropped down from the cot, feet already running as they hit the floor, tearing off for the door. In his haste, he almost collided with Camille. "Perdon!" he cried, brushing past her and out the door.

Camille let out a low laugh. "That boy will be back in here within the week," she chuckled, a fond smile spreading over her face.

Grinning her agreement Abene came to her feet, wandering to join Camille in her inventory of their supplies.

"We have come through the toughest months well prepared," Camille said. "It is good. We are still well stocked."

"Let us hope that continues," Abene said, picking up a box of miscellaneous wound wrappings. "The bumps and scrapes are easy to mend..." she trailed off.

Camille eyed her, frowning. "You are thinking of your friend? Juan? You still have had no word?"

Face flat, Abene shook her head.

"But the news from Catalan is good, no? The Nationalists are still held out?"

"They have not taken the region. But they hold the rest of Spain."

"Calm, my friend," Camille placed a gentle hand on Abene's shoulder. "Your fear, I do not know myself, but my country does. It was only twenty years ago we too were occupied. But it did not last. We are France once more. And always were, in here."

She tapped her chest proudly. Abene sighed, turning away. She was grateful for Camille's gentle presence and friendship. The women had formed a profound connection over their months working together. As Abene's halting French had smoothed and improved, they had shared more and more of their lives, their countries. But Camille still thought only as a Frenchwoman. She did not see the difference between a war with a foreign enemy, and one that called itself your countryman.

She felt Camille's sharp eyes on her back and knew her friend could read her disagreement.

"Growing up on a farm," Camille began, "I learned the rules of the crops, the seasons, the planting weeks, everything outlined in a neat little book of dates and seedlings. And then I learned to follow the pattern of the skies, not the date on a calendar, and trust my body, my nose and the feel of the season on my skin. As my father did.

"'There is a time for every planting', he would say to me, 'it isn't told by a rule, but by the ways of nature.'

"Life is like that too, I think," she paused, walking to Abene's side, turning her friend to face her. "The time for your return to your home will come," she continued. "When the season is right."

Abene nodded. She didn't believe it, not in her heart. But Camille's words were soothing nonetheless.

"You are full of courage."

"In the end, courage is all we really have," Camille said. "When my mother died, I didn't think I could go on. Father was lost without her. But life gives. A neighbour, Madame Marguerite, took me in and cared for me as my father came to terms with his loss. She makes the most extraordinary sponge cake." A peaceful smile drifted over Camille's face. "We endure. There are those who care," she said. "You are not alone."

The two friends stared at each other in silence and Abene smiled, shoulders relaxing. "Merci, my friend," she said.

Camille gave her shoulder a squeeze before turning back to her inventory of supplies. Abene untied her apron, hanging it on the hook by the doorway.

"You are in Bayonne again tomorrow?" she asked, one hand on the doorknob.

"Oui," Camille replied.

"Then I will meet you at the station and we can walk the Adour together before we start."

"A lovely idea," Camille agreed. "Until the morning."

"Au revoir."

Abene made her way through the hall, heading for the kitchen building where she knew her mother and Udane would be found. As expected the two friends were hovering over the set of large stoves, sweat plastering their hair back, beading on their foreheads, sleeves rolled up to their elbows. The scent of chicken stew and thyme was thick in the close air, humid and cloying from the cooking steam. Abene paused a moment, savouring the homely, familiar sight. Her mother stood over the pot, wisps of her greying hair escaping her bun to frame her round face. Lourdes had weathered the loss of her husband far better than Abene had expected. Where Udane had withered in her grief, her mother had solidified, mouth set permanently in an expression of defiance that softened only when she smiled at her daughter.

For Abene it had been a challenging two years living in this foreign land. Learning the ways of the French Basque, processing the deep, soul-loss of her beloved papá. Lourdes had shouldered that grief for herself and Abene; she had carried them both into this new uncertain future.

Looking up Lourdes spied Abene hovering in the doorway.

"Ah, daughter, just in time. The carrots need peeling."

Gathering a different apron, stained with the juices of food, Abene set to work on the carrots, falling into the rhythm of the kitchen as naturally as breathing.

"Another family left today," Udane began, pensively, her movements small and cautious. "Returning to San Sebastian, hoping..."

"Bah!" Lourdes interrupted, voice shrill. "Foolish chance. How can they risk their children so?"

"Surely no one would harm a child!" Abene looked up, spying Helena, one of the teachers who had made the journey here in a parental role for the evacuated children.

"Why do you think they sent their children here then?" Lourdes challenged.

"Well, because... because of the fighting. The risk of accidental harm."

Lourdes snorted in derision. Udane's eyes narrowed on the young teacher. But neither woman spoke, their silence an accusation in the humid air.

Abene cleared her throat, lifting a handful of chopped carrots and dropping them into the soup pot. "Will you be returning then Helena?' she asked, voice light.

"I... yes. I have fulfilled my duty to the children here. I want to go home." She paused, hands fluttering before her.

"And you, Abene?" she asked.

Abene didn't look up, remaining focused on the rolling carrots before her.

"San Sebastian is no longer my home," she replied.

TWELVE

ABENE

The breeze off the waters was fresh and salt-tinged, the briny river currents flowing quickly. Strange how different to San Sebastian it felt here. The Adour River opened to the same body of water as her childhood home, the Bay of Biscay, but here, everything was different: the tides, the scents, the colours that glinted off the water. So close yet so far from home. Camille walked beside her in silence, not pushing, allowing her friend time to find her words.

Abene spoke, "We can't return. But increasingly, I see that we cannot stay."

She fell silent, listening to the crunch of her feet in the sand, and the caws of seagulls overhead. "France wants us out."

Camille nodded silently. "There are changes happening in my land, threats building to the east. We are uneasy after the Great War."

"It is more than that," Abene said. "My government is failing. The funds have slowed. More and more it falls to us to raise our own money. You know this."

"Yes."

"More people return today. I feel... I feel I have failed them..."

"Failed them?"

"Since we arrived, after the experience of the Pyrenees... I promised myself I would never allow anyone, man, woman or child, to face what I faced. Never again. But..."

"But it is not in your control. War is never in anyone's control."

Abene nodded, stopping her walk to gaze out over the gently rolling river. The waters twinkled pale in the early morning light.

"They will live, I believe that. Franco's men are not inviting them back for slaughter. But the San Sebastian they return to is not the same. They will not grow up Basque. Not really."

"There are many ways to hold on to culture," Camille said. She paused. "Do not forget what you have done for Eduardo. You have made a difference there."

They continued walking, falling silent once more. Soon they came to the centre of Bayonne, the tall buildings of the town rising gracefully around them. Abene loved this walk, the way the scent of the salty sea gave way to the murky mud of the river. It had become her sanctuary. She did not want to leave, but she knew a decision had to be made. And soon.

"Things are coming to an end. I am called back to Saint-Jean-de-Luz. No more funding for my work here," Camille said. "Do you want to stay in France?"

Abene sighed, shrugging her shoulders. "I believe we must. We are tied to the fighters. We escaped with a soldier. My father fought..." her throat tightened. She squeezed her eyes shut to hold back the tears that still sprung to her eyes when she thought of Bittor. She doubted that ache would ever leave her. "But I don't know how to stay... if Barcelona falls..."

"Come to the farm."

Abene's face shot up, eyes locking with her friend's. "The farm?"

Camille reached out, taking Abene's hands in hers. "It is a small square of land, more a fermette, but my father is ageing, the upkeep taking its toll. Strong hands, Basque hands, would be welcome."

"But my mother... Udane."

"Are solid women too."

Abene watched her friend's face, and read the honesty of her words in her eyes. "You would offer this to me, to us?"

"If the alternative is losing you, I will insist!"

Abene puffed a breath through her nose, the sound part joy, part a deep well of emotions she could not yet fully understand. A swirl of feelings – relief, hope, gratitude – too many to sort through in this moment.

"How?"

"We will employ you, to work on the fermette. I am needed to help the local doctor. I cannot help my father work the land," she paused. "But even more than that, as my friend, I would have you stay. I would have you here, safe."

The flood of emotions threatened to overwhelm her, and Abene threw herself forward, clutching her friend in a tight embrace. "This, I can never repay."

Winding her own arms about Abene, Camille smiled against her friend's neck. "The debt is already paid."

"But what of Eduardo? What will happen to him?"

Against her better judgement, reason or thought, and yet from the purity of humanity, Abene had formed an attachment to the small blonde child. Barely seven years old, but brave and calm, he had needed her comfort in his sickness and had continued to seek her out since. A natural transition of affection and love.

Camille's face turned grim. "Helena thought you should know, privately," she said.

Abene's stomach dropped as though a stone plummeted through her bowels.

"He is to return home? But it's not safe!"

Camille paused, heaving a sigh of bitter sorrow. "Eduardo has not been called home. And he may never be."

Abene frowned, mouth opening in an unspoken question. She looked at Camille and read the sadness in her friend's face. "Oh!" a hand flew to her mouth, covering her horror. "His parents?"

Camille shook her head sadly. "Executed in San Sebastian, just days after the fall of the city."

"But that means..."

"Yes, they passed almost two years ago. Deemed traitors..."

A sound of disgust ripped from deep within Abene's throat. "A show trial, nothing more. What crime had they committed but to fight for their home?"

"The news has only just made it through the channels. Eduardo is orphaned."

Abene closed her eyes, pain slicing through her heart.

"What will become of him?"

"He will not be returned. The government of France has decided to keep the orphans, for now at least. Specific centres are being set up around the country to house them, there will be a large one inland at Saint-Jean-de-Pied-de-Port, but also others. Eduardo will be sent to one. He will be cared for. He will be safe."

Relief flooded through Abene. But was quickly doused by realisation.

"But he will be motherless."

"Citizens can adopt, and some have. Perhaps the boy will be lucky."

Abene swallowed, chest tight with sorrow. "Does he know?"

Camille shook her head in silence.

"Let's not burden him yet. It is enough he must leave

another home. The truth of his parents can wait." She paused, thinking. "I will tell him about Saint-Jean-de-Pied-de-Port. It should come from me."

Camille squeezed her shoulders in a gesture of comfort. "Would you like me to come with you?"

"No, I think he will need that moment alone with me."

"I understand."

The two friends fell silent, parting without a word as they each turned for their destinations. Abene followed the peaceful tidal river of Bayonne, the waters glistening gently in the soft sun. A beautiful counterpoint to the turmoil unfolding within her.

Such a contrast of fortunes: an answer to the safety of herself and her family, but also a wrenching separation.

Eduardo.

Could she really let him go? Cut these newly formed bonds of love that had grown from her heart to his, and trust the world to keep him safe?

Yet what was the alternative? She was an outsider, here only on the sympathy of the French Government and people. She had no rights to claim an orphaned boy, had no security to offer his future.

Camille was right, she knew. Eduardo's continued safety was in the hands of France and the newly drawn up orphan program. He would be protected, fed and cared for. He would be safe.

For that she had to let him go.

Coming to the pale stone walls of the church Abene slowed her step. Shouts of joyful play echoed from the small courtyard at the back of their residence hall, the high-pitched tone of Eduardo piercing her heart with love and sorrow. How well she knew his voice, its timbre, the meaning in the tone. Right now, he was full of life, of soaring joy.

The corners of her mouth tickled as she imagined his smile,

wide and pure as he raced after his companions in play. She longed to make her way to the courtyard, to greet his grinning delight with her own exuberance and allow herself to be swept up in his happiness. Instead she turned away, pacing for her cot, tread heavy. He would see it on her face, she knew. One glance and his joy would turn to ash. And she would have to face the truth. Would have to tell him.

She wasn't ready. It was too fresh, too raw.

She needed time to process it for herself before she explained it to Eduardo.

For now, it was her burden to carry, alone.

Abene left it to the last day to tell Eduardo. The knowledge, a lode stone in her heart tethering her to sorrow and the anticipation of loss. As the other children began packing on the morning they were to depart, she took the boy aside. "Mi cariño," she said, smoothing his hair with her palm. "You know that I love you, don't you?"

The child beamed, throwing his arms about her neck and squeezing tight.

Hot tears flooded Abene's eyes as her soul cracked open. She wanted to wrap him up in her arms and run, far, far away, where they could be together and safe, always.

Gathering her strength, she gently disentangled his arms. Holding his hands, she took a deep breath and explained.

"The government has set up a wonderful new centre, just for children! It will have games and songs and fun. All the food you can eat, and wonderful teachers to ensure you have the best education. It will be perfect."

Eduardo regarded her, eyes scanning her face. Concern creased his brow. "For children?" he asked. "Are you coming too?"

Abene forced herself to smile, blinking back the tears that

threatened to spill down her cheeks. "The centres are for children," she said. "You will be so very happy there."

"No," Eduardo said. "I want to stay with you."

Pain cleaved Abene's heart, as she worked to brace herself against her own sorrow. "Mi cariño, you cannot stay with me. The centre for children is the best place for you."

"No!" Eduardo stamped a foot then threw himself back into her arms, clutching onto her with all his might. His little arms shook with the effort of hanging on.

The tears coursed from Abene's eyes and she held him to her, rocking him gently, a moment of shared pain at the thought of separation.

"It will be all right," she crooned. "You will see. It will be all right."

"But I want to stay with you..."

Camille appeared in the doorway, face full of pity. Abene nodded to her friend in silence. Dashing away her tears she pulled away from Eduardo. "It is time to go, mi cariño. Be strong my brave, brave boy. All will be well. Trust in God."

Eduardo stood before her, shaking as desperate sobs wracked his little body.

It was too much. Abene couldn't do this. She looked up to Camille, a desperate plea in her eyes. Please let me keep him, her heart begged. Please tell me there is a way.

Eyes sad, Camille moved forward. Hands on Eduardo's shaking shoulders, she manoeuvred him away. As he rounded the door he looked back one last time, his face a portrait of pain. Then he was gone.

Abene slumped to the floor and gave in to her sadness. How many loved ones must she lose to Franco's evil ambition? How much more could her heart take?

She stayed on the floor, knees gathered to her chest, tears streaming from her eyes until the last sounds of the children's high-pitched chatter faded into silence.

Soon the silence was replaced by the gentle click of heels. Camille crossed to her and came to sit by her side. Without a word her friend embraced her, holding Abene to her chest as if she were the child. They sat together in the strange new silence of the church hall as the sun faded from the world outside. No words passed between them, just the warmth of love and friendship, and the gift of understanding.

When Lourdes' voice rang through the hall, calling her for dinner, the two friends stood as one.

"You did the right thing," Camille said.

"I didn't have a choice," Abene replied.

"I know. But heed your own advice, my darling. 'Trust in God'."

Abene smiled at her friend and squeezed her hand. Together they made their way to the communal dining table.

And Abene wondered if she had any hope left for the word of her Lord above.

THIRTEEN

1981

"It's all so much," Gilles says, shifting in his chair.

"It is what it is."

Suddenly the room feels too small, too close. I stand, pacing to the window. I consider opening it, but I know the heat of the day outside is too strong right now. I must be patient. Patience is one skill I have developed well. The most important things are worth the wait. My love of Juan, the arrival of my daughter. I would wait a thousand lifetimes for them both to return to me.

I pray I never have to.

Gilles is shaking his head, hands fidgeting on the table, "I don't know what was worse – staying in Spain, or being forced to flee."

I snort softly. "I am not sure there was much difference, in the end. Francoist Spain was a place of fear and control. France was invaded by Hitler." I shrug, "At least Hitler lost..."

"It is not something you learn about, in Canada. What happened here during the Spanish Civil War. The memories must be sharp. Why did you return?"

I tip my head to the side, pondering. Was it me that wanted to come back? Or was it my husband? My mother and father were gone by then, his too. What was it that drew us to this little house on the hillside?

"I was born here, grew up here. I am Basque, but I am Spanish too. So many people fought for this land to find freedom again. So many sacrificed so much. It just seemed the natural thing to do."

"Has there been justice? For the people wrongly killed? An investigation?"

I wave a hand, coming to sit once more. "There are murmurs. But 1936 was a long time ago, and the rule of Franco was thorough in the years between. Many were killed without record, and dumped in shallow graves on the roadside. I am glad I never saw it..."

"What of the men who ruled? The generals, officials? They still hunt Nazis across the globe."

"I suppose some investigate and search. But it isn't something I choose to think of. I have a house and a family now. A future. I don't wish to go back to the past."

I think of my family: my daughter, her husband, their children. All of my heart. Complete. Everything.

Sadness filters over Gilles' face. "Thank you for seeing me, regardless."

Pity washes over me and I smile softly. "Gilles, you are always welcome here."

"I did wonder... when I took so long."

"The shadow of war is cold and dark. You came when you could. Will you visit other parts of Spain?" I ask, redirecting his thoughts from the darkness I see swimming in his eyes.

He blinks rapidly. "Bilbao next, then Madrid. I want to know this country, your country. Finally, Barcelona, my flight leaves from there."

I breathe deeply through my nose. "I have never been to Barcelona," I say.

"Really? But it was the centre of your resistance."

"And the end of it all. The civil war was bad, Gilles. But the worst came next."

PART 2

1938-1942 - A NEW WAR

FOURTEEN

ABENE

1938 Saint-Jean-de-Luz

The fermette was picture-perfect. A sizeable two-level farmhouse sat neat and settled on the crest of a gentle grassy mound. Spread across the front of the property were rows of vegetables. Abene spied leek, spinach, courgette, aubergine and more. To the rear, obscured by the high-pitched roof, apple trees, their leaves glossy and green in the afternoon sun, swaying in the gentle breezes that rose through the valley.

As Abene walked up the hill beside Camille – Lourdes and Udane striding confidently behind them – a tentative sense of peace settled over her chest, bringing hope to her tired mind.

Camille's father Pierre met them at the door. Broad and strong and greying from age, his smile was wide and warm. As Abene watched him embrace his daughter, the light of genuine love shining in his eyes, she felt the loss of her father anew, a cold ebbing pain that she doubted would ever fully heal. As the old farmer turned from Camille, his arm stayed slung around her shoulders.

"Welcome to your new home. It's yours as long as you need it."

They were ushered inside, and given a brief tour: kitchen and living space downstairs, bedrooms upstairs. Lourdes and Udane were to share, as were Camille and Abene. Tight but comfortable. Bodily maintenance took place in an outhouse a short walk from the back door.

After depositing their possessions and freshening up, the travellers gathered in the large country kitchen. Pierre served a supper of ratatouille and eggs, all provided by the garden around them. The food was hot and delicious, filling Abene's belly with warmth and comfort.

Beside her, Udane spoke up. "A wonderful meal, we thank you for your generosity, and for giving us a safe place to stay."

The words were honest but tinged with doubt. None of them believed they would be allowed to stay here. It was too kind, too generous, too noble.

Abene swallowed a mouthful of stew, glancing up at Pierre.

He bit off a chunk of oven-warm bread and chewed slowly, eyes settling on Udane. "You are confused," he said. "You don't understand why I have allowed my daughter to bring you here."

Udane shrugged. "We have been well cared for in France. The Sisters at Saint Maria in Bayonne gave all they could."

"But they are holy women, bound to God. And I am just a farmer."

"I meant no disrespect..." Udane stammered.

"Peace," Pierre said, holding up a hand in a calming gesture. "I jest." He paused, heaving a deep and tired sigh. Looking out of the nearby window that overlooked the apple orchard behind the house, the trees now cast in softening shadow, he continued. "You look at my lands and you see safety and calm, yes?"

They nodded collectively.

"It was not always so. France has known war. All of Europe has, and recently. I fought." He paused again, eyes turning down to look at his hands, palms up on the table, as if in prayer to God above. "I was a medic at the Somme. It was a... difficult time. I have seen the horror that war brings. I have stood in its filth and smelt death as it rose up to try and claim me. Somehow, I got out alive." He turned to Camille, reaching over and taking her hand in his. "I got home to my family. Not all were so lucky."

Father and daughter stared at each other a moment, eyes bright with the tears of memory and fear. Abene's body washed with sorrow. Such bitter joy to see their love and connection, a gut-wrenching mirror of her own loss: her papá, her Eduardo. Shaking his head, Pierre returned his attention to the table at large. "You have been lucky. You made it out. But you need a safe harbour. I promised myself a long time ago, that if someone needed help, and there was any way that I could give it, I would. Others have done so for me. I will return the favour, however I can."

His voice had grown tighter, filled with unexpressed thoughts as he spoke. Now he looked away, subtly wiping a tear from his stubbly cheek, before fixing Abene with a stare. "You have been a friend and support to my daughter. That is reason enough to grant you a place to lay your head."

Abene felt her stomach flip at the intensity of his gaze. "It was hard for me when she decided to pursue medicine." He glanced again at Camille, pride shining in his eyes. "But I should have known she would. Always my little nurse. When she said she wanted to help the Basque from Spain, I could not have stopped her. I felt only truest pride."

"Oh, Papá!" Camille beamed, clearly moved by his affection and love.

A smile now firmly in place, he raised his hands to the sides. "So, you are welcome here. But don't forget," a twinkle now lit his eye, "this is a farm. And I need workers!"

"And we know how to work," Lourdes said confidently.

"Good, good," Pierre slapped the table. "Now, enough of that, we have supper to finish."

As they were clearing away the dishes and preparing to clean up, a knock sounded on the farmhouse door. Camille answered, bringing in a woman and young girl, hair in two neat blonde plaits.

"Papá, look who has come to visit!"

"Ah, Marguerite!" Pierre embraced his new guests.

"When you told me your daughter would be returning I knew I had to bake," Marguerite said, producing a tea towel-wrapped parcel from the basket at her elbow.

"Ooooh!" Camille exclaimed, taking the parcel from her. "It is, isn't it?"

"Your favourite, but of course."

Abene watched as Camille placed the parcel on the table and unwrapped the cloth, revealing a decadent sponge cake layered with cream and jam. "Thank you, oh how I have missed you."

"I have missed you too."

"Let me introduce you all," Camille said. "This is Marguerite, our neighbour from Starling Farm just down the road. And this is her beautiful daughter, Giselle."

Giselle beamed up at Camille, hands gripping her skirts as she turned side to side in her excitement.

"Papá, put on the kettle, we have dessert to enjoy," Camille said. "Will you all join me? Marguerite is the greatest baker in the region."

"Oh, you compliment me too much, Camille."

"Nonsense. Now, Giselle, will you do me the honour of accepting the first slice?"

That night Abene lay on her new bed, restless and wide-eyed. The warmth of the day still held the stone walls in its grip. She kicked a leg out, seeking the cool breeze from the open window. Around the house, a gentle quiet had fallen with the setting sun. A few birds still tweeted their goodnights across the fermette, but otherwise, silence. On the bed beside her, Camille was breathing the deep, soft breath of sleep. But Abene remained awake. The events of the last few weeks were turning over in her mind. Seeing the love between Pierre and Camille was beautiful, but it split her heart. The loss of her own father, killed on the battle fields of Vizcaya, was still raw, even after two years of grieving. She would have to check on her mother; no doubt the same pain, but even sharper, still sliced her soul.

And young Giselle. The girl was of an age with Eduardo, but taller and altogether a different child. But just seeing her, happy and smiling at her mother's side, had brought the sorrow Abene felt at leaving the boy behind flooding back.

She'd bonded so deeply and honestly with the child; she wanted him to have everything he deserved in life. Had hope bloomed in her heart when she learned that he was orphaned, a thought that she could fill that void? What a selfish and cruel dream. Yet he was alone, motherless and at the mercy of the protection of institutions. Abene would have him know a life with family, surrounded by love. She would give that willingly. But she could not. Displaced herself and living on the kindness of strangers, she had no power here in France, no rights as a citizen. She too lived at the mercy of the state.

So they had parted and remained alone.

She wiggled in her bed, seeking comfort and oblivion in the light sheets that cocooned her.

"What are you thinking about?"

Abene turned her head to the side. "Did I wake you? I am sorry."

"It's all right. I don't think I had fully drifted off. Are you all right?"

Abene rolled on her side to face her friend across the room.

Camille's pale eyes shone in the moonlight that peeked through the curtains. "I do not wish to sound ungrateful..."

"But you are filled with sorrow."

"This is a beautiful home, and we are all so lucky to be here."

"But it is not Spain."

"No, it is not... and little Giselle, she made me think of Eduardo and Father and Juan and, well, everything. I am sorry, I do not wish to be so negative. You have done so much for me, for us all."

"Not at all," Camille said, reaching out a hand between their beds. Abene gripped Camille's palm. "You have had to make so many choices and give up so much. Grief is only natural. But I hope, in time, you can find your way back to happiness. Here, with Papá and me."

Abene smiled softly in the darkness. Camille's words helped settle her mind, it was good to have a friend so true and dear. "I think life here can be beautiful," Abene said, though the words rang false in her ears. "I will find my way."

"I know you will," Camille replied. "And I will be there beside you, always."

Her friend squeezed her hand and then released her grip, rolling onto her back. "The rooster will crow with the dawn, he is loud! Try and get some sleep before then."

Abene nestled back down into her covers, closing her eyes, and choosing hope. For Udane and her mother, for Juan at war still on the outskirts of Barcelona. For Eduardo to find a family. For her country to find freedom and peace, and for herself to find a place to call "home" once more.

The months that followed were slow and calm, the soft warmth of late summer giving way to the cooling turn of the leaves of autumn. Abene, Lourdes and Udane learned the patterns of farm life: the early rise with the rooster's call, the feeding of chickens and collection of eggs, the hearty breakfast before a long morning in the fields of vegetable or orchards of fruit, the satisfying lunches of stew and bread before more toil and then finally the rest of evening by a fire, sharing stories or knitting, singing or reading. On Saturday there was the trip to the market in Saint-Jean-de-Luz, a day of community, friendship and hard bargaining. Pierre came alive on the streets of the market, chatting with old friends, swapping seeds and goods. Lourdes and Udane took over the planning of weekly food on the farm, learning some of Pierre's preferred dishes, and introducing him to some of the peppery flavours of the Spanish Basque. Camille was still a nurse in town, an aid to the overworked local doctor. Her days were not spent in toil on the land, but crossing between the many farmhouses that bordered the coast, meeting with families with sick relatives, or new babies. As the work of the farm slowed for winter, the shortened hours of daylight and dwindling crops drawing all inside, Camille's work intensified as the cold winds brought sickness and fever.

Abene could have helped. She knew Camille would have welcomed her support with her tasks, but she could not. Despite the peace and security, the routine and warmth of the fermette, Abene felt adrift and heavy. Her limbs were like wooden branches weighing her down, her thoughts slow and difficult to comprehend.

All this peace and safety was simply too at odds with her soul for Abene to settle. She'd lost too much, hurt too deeply. Her father, her home, her Eduardo. And Juan, her lifelong friend, still out there, somewhere, his fate unknown. How could her heart accept this sanctuary, this good fortune and comfort, when her loved ones faced the unknown, alone, afraid?

Why was she gifted this privilege of protection, while others suffered? She did not deserve this, not when they went without it.

If she could have traded places with Juan, with Eduardo, with her father, Abene would have.

But such a choice was beyond her ability. And it sat heavily on her soul, drawing her down, down, down into sorrow and despair.

She could pretend, forcing a smile or a laugh, but she knew the light never shone in her eyes. Her hair grew lank and dull, her skin ashen, despite her healthy hygiene routine. As the darkness of winter solstice approached, she welcomed the blacked-out sky, using the longer nights as an excuse to stay abed, longer and longer.

At first, no one pressed. The past years and months had been hard on them all. But soon Abene saw the disapproval in their glances.

They were done with her indulgence, they wanted her to lift.

Part of her wanted that too.

But a bigger part, the greatest chunk of her soul, simply wished for it all to end.

FIFTEEN

ABENE

"The refugees of Basque Spain have started cultural gatherings in town. I thought of you."

Camille bustled into the farmhouse, bringing the wintry winds of December with her in a flurry of cold. Her nose and cheeks were flushed red from braving the elements, her eyes wide with passion.

Abene looked up from the stew she was cooking on the stovetop in the large kitchen. Root vegetables and dried herbs. The steam from her cooking had filled the room, warm and hazy. The windows dripped with condensation where the warmth met the cold glass that held the outside chill at bay.

Abene frowned. "'Gatherings', what do you mean?"

"There is a large French Basque community in this region, as you know. Well, as the reception centres have been closing, groups of refugees from Spain have settled here. Some orphans too. The local Basque church of Saint John the Baptist is running language and culture classes, on Sundays, after Mass and mid-week for the children. A way to keep the Basque traditions alive and welcome the newcomers. You could contribute."

Abene turned back to her stew, face solemn. Orphans. Eduardo. No.

"I am not a teacher."

"But you speak the Basque language, and Spanish and French. And you know the folk songs, I have heard you sing them—"

"I need to be here, working, earning my keep."

"You should try it, my daughter." Lourdes stood in the doorway, knees still muddy from the fields.

Abene met her mother's eyes, and saw the sorrow embedded there, and the worry – worry over Abene.

Abene sighed heavily, running a hand over her brow.

"Look," she said, regarding the two women before her, two women who loved her dearly. "I know what you are trying to do. I know I have been... distant. It has been hard adjusting, that's all. But I will do better. I swear."

"No one blames you, daughter," Lourdes said, coming into the kitchen and placing a hand on Abene's shoulder. "We understand. I understand. Some time in a Basque community, helping others, helping children, may help."

Abene met her mother's stare. "But, Mamá, they will remind me of him..." Tears broke free from her eyes, the memory of Eduardo's pleading face, desperate to stay with her flooding her mind. Lourdes wrapped her in a tight embrace, rocking her gently.

"We must go on," she whispered gently into Abene's ear. "We must go on."

Abene allowed herself to be held and comforted until the pain in her heart tempered once again to a dull ache in her chest. Extracting herself from the embrace, she dried her cheeks on her apron and faced Camille. Strength and love shone from her friend. Abene's eyes flicked around the room, taking in the solid, safe walls of this home that held her and her family safe. She had lost so much, too much, and uncertainty still hovered above her. But here, in this kitchen, with these women – Camille, Lourdes, Udane – was her life now.

Fate had seen her here, had kept her safe. She owed it to her father to live when he could not. She had to go on.

"All right," she said. "I will try."

Camille accompanied her into the town, a place of white-painted walls and bright red shutters, interspersed with old stone churches and official buildings. They crossed the Nivelle River that ran through the centre, fishing boats bobbing on the gentle currents. Abene paused, watching the rise and fall of the hulls, her mind drifting away to another time, another town, a familiar boat.

"Come, we are nearly there," Camille prompted gently.

The church of Saint John the Baptist was on the other side of town, a cream stone building, its steeple modest in comparison with the grand Buen Pastor Cathedral in San Sebastian. Inside the adjacent church hall, a kindly woman, her dark hair losing the battle with grey, greeted them warmly.

"You must be Abene?"

She made tea and they talked. As Denise described the classes they held for the children and adults of Basque Spain, something within Abene's chest began to thaw. By the end of their meeting, the whisper of a smile touched her lips.

"So, will I see you on Sunday for folksong?" Denise asked.

"I would like that," Abene agreed.

That Sunday as the rooster crowed to the dawn that shone softly on the fermette, Abene snuggled lower in her blankets. What had seemed a nice idea earlier in the week, in the warmth of the church hall kitchen under the dulcet tones of Denise's soft Basque, now weighed heavy and impossible on her soul.

How could she sing folksongs with lost children of her homeland? It would conjure up her father and her Eduardo.

No, it was a foolish idea. Her mother needed her at the fermette, and here she would stay.

Camille had other ideas. Her friend bounced from her bed across the room and threw the covers off of Abene.

"Hey!" Abene cried, covering her eyes with her arms to block out the morning light. "What are you doing?"

"I am making sure you keep your word."

"It wasn't a promise."

"It was to me."

Abene lowered her arms and looked up at Camille. The concern on her friend's face forced her into action.

"Fine," she grumbled, climbing from the bed.

At the hall Denise greeted her personally, showing her to a seat in the back row of the gathering. Men and women turned to watch her enter, nodding. Before them children sat on the floor, little legs crossed, outnumbering the adults three to one. Orphans of Franco's war.

Abene's heart squeezed. Gripping her skirts, she sat down. At the front, Denise and another woman led the group into a new song, a folksong for farmers. Abene's lips curved in a smile as the familiar melody filled her ears. Her father had sung it on his way to the boat, an old song from his farming days.

An hour later the singing came to a close and everyone stood, forming into groups to chat amiably while the children rushed around playing.

That was when she heard him.

A high-pitched exclamation of surprise her heart knew intimately. Abene whirled around just as two arms and two legs, longer and stronger, leapt into her embrace.

Eduardo.

"Mi cariño!" she cried, cradling the boy to her chest. "What are you doing here?"

Denise came forward through the crowd. "You know our Eduardo?" she asked, a beaming smile on her face.

"Si, si, he was at the church in Bayonne with me and Camille. But I thought he and the other children were sent inland?"

"Many were," Denise confirmed. "But more arrived, and there were simply too many in Saint-Jean-de-Pied-de-Port. So, some came here to Saint-Jean-de-Luz."

A huff of laughter mixed with joy escaped Abene as she squeezed Eduardo tight, her heart filling with love, so full that she felt it would burst. How could this be? It was too beautiful, too wonderful. Tears wet her cheeks as her arms trembled, the solid warmth of this child she loved filling the emptiness within her, the cold space in her chest flooding with the sun of love.

He pulled back, taking her face between his hands, his palms sticky with childhood games. "I missed you," he said.

"I missed you too."

"Denise and I have devised a plan. If you are willing."

Abene and Camille were making their way along the Nivelle River, heading home after a Sunday at the church. Abene was a regular at the cultural activities now; in the weeks since that first folk day, she'd not missed a single Sunday Mass or Basque gathering and was in talks with Denise to run her own session in a week or two. Denise was keen to expand their offerings. The return to worship and the company of her fellow Spanish Basque was more comfort than she'd expected. And of course, there was also Eduardo.

"A plan? To do what?"

Camille eyed her conspiratorially, her eyes shining. "A plan to find Eduardo a home."

Panic shot through Abene. Her connection with the small boy had returned instantly. Every Sunday when she arrived at the church hall, he was there, waiting to run into her arms. They passed the morning activities together, hand in hand.

When the time came for him to return to the house for boys with the young teacher who watched over the orphans, it was always hard. He would hug her tightly, unwilling to let go, though he knew he must. In his eyes, she saw the fear that they would once again be parted. And she could say nothing to ease that fear. She could not promise him anything. His life and those of his fellow orphans, was at the behest of the French government. The only path to stability was adoption.

Abene looked away, subtly wiping a tear from her eye. It was selfish to feel this way. Eduardo deserved a loving family. And if Camille and Denise had found a willing couple, she should be happy.

Yet the thought of parting from him once again skewered her soul.

Swallowing her sorrow, she nodded. "How wonderful for Eduardo. How did you find a family? They will love him, he is impossible not to love—"

Camille's sharp laugh broke into her sentence. "Not another family!" she cried, eyes bright. "Do you think I would suggest separating the two of you again? I see the way you are together. Your souls have bonded, as truly as any mother and child. I would not send him away."

Abene frowned, turning to her friend. "Then what are you suggesting to find him a home?"

"I will adopt the boy."

Abene blinked. "What? You want to adopt?"

Camille laughed again. "No, no I don't. But I am a French citizen, and I can adopt him, for you."

"For me?" Abene stared at Camille open-mouthed as understanding dawned. "You would take on this responsibility, for me?

A smile spread across Camille's face. "I will sign the paperwork. But we will know the truth, the boy is yours."

"A ruse?"

"A truth in your heart... and a subterfuge that will keep him here, under your guardianship."

"Merci," Abene breathed. "Thank you for this, for everything. I can't believe it!"

She stopped. "I will have to tell him then... the truth, about his parents."

Camille looked down at her feet. "He needs to know."

Abene nodded. "Yes, he does. And he deserves the choice. To stay with the other boys, or to come with us, with me."

"You can't think he would choose to stay?"

"His life has had few choices. I will allow him this one."

Silence fell between them, the heavy knowledge of all Eduardo must learn, the truth of his parents' fate, weighing down this moment of joy.

Camille said nothing, only took her friend's hand once more and squeezed.

"I will go now, to the boys' home. Speak to him."

"I will wait for you at home, with hope in my heart."

Abene found Eduardo playing in the yard at the back of the house, trouser bottoms rolled up, feet bare. He squatted with two other boys, their hands in the dirt, eyes focused on the ground.

"Eduardo?"

The boy looked up instantly, a smile already growing on his lips.

"Tante Abene! Come, come," he gestured enthusiastically.

Abene's heart sheered in love and sorrow, this beautiful, happy boy, whose joy she would shatter. Pushing down her hurt, she chose to give him this last moment of innocence, a final time when the truest horror of life was still to reveal itself. Forcing calm to her movements she joined the boys crouching in the dirt. There was a small mound of dirt, piled up around a hole, at its centre teamed the black backs of ants, scurrying to and fro.

"They built it," Eduardo explained.

Abene tousled his hair affectionately. "They did, it means rains are coming."

All three boys sat back on their haunches, looking up at her, faces open, curious. Abene leaned forward, finger pointing at the ants. "If you look closely you can see sand on their backs. One tiny grain each, look."

Dutifully the boys followed the line of her finger, watching the busy ants. "I see!" one child exclaimed. Beside her Eduardo gripped her arm in excitement, "Me too!"

"Good," Abene continued. "They carry the sand, grain by grain and build a ring around the entrance to their home beneath."

"Why?"

"Well, the pile protects the hole from the rain." Abene looked up and pointed at the sky. Grey clouds gathered above. "The ants know the rain is coming, so they build up the pile to protect their home."

"How do they know?" the other child asked.

"I don't know," Abene answered honestly, "but they are never wrong."

Eduardo leaned forward, watching the ants again, wonder on his face. Abene steeled herself. "Eduardo, will you come with me?"

He followed her happily, taking her hand and swinging their arms lightly between them.

She led him to his bunk, sat him beside her in the dim room. She held tight his hand as she spoke, telling him of his mother, and his father, that they had gone to heaven.

He cried, but not overmuch. The tears seemed more of confusion than a true understanding of the loss she conveyed. When he climbed into her lap, she let him, holding him close to her heart as his tiny body shuddered.

"I won't see Mamá again? Nor Papá?"

"Not on this earth, but after, when your life is done, you will see them next to God."

He sobbed and leaned back to watch her face. "How do you know?"

Abene smiled and soothed his cheek with her palm. "I don't know, I just do."

"Like the ants?" he sniffed, rubbing his eyes with the back of his hand.

"Like the ants," Abene agreed. Then, pressing her forehead to his she said, "Until then, you can stay with me, if you like."

Eduardo looked at her closely, then, in a trembling wail threw himself back into her arms. "Promise?"

Arms wrapped tight around his tiny frame, Abene fought back her own tears and worked to steady her voice, contouring her tones into what she hoped was firm and assured. "I promise," she said.

SIXTEEN

ABENE

1939

Her feet were sore, her back ached, but she wore a peaceful expression. It had been a nice day helping Pierre with the barn repairs. Heavy rainfall had found cracks in the roof that could not be left until summer. After that, the walk into town to collect Eduardo from school, the highlight of her day, every day, had calmed her soul. Sodden grass squelched beneath her feet as the boy strolled beside her, his hand holding hers, skipping lightly as he chatted about his day. The adoption process had been swift, the government was more than happy to release children from their responsibility. So, Eduardo had come to the fermette. He'd settled in quickly, instantly gravitating to Pierre, always keen to help with any suitable farm work.

About them, pines reached for the pale blue sky, their evergreen needles pimpled with drying raindrops. Backlit by the soft yellow of day's end, the stone house they now called home came into view. From its chimney, smoke curled into the still air, an offer of warmth and comfort. Surrounded by the grasses of winter, rows of onions, scallions and broccoli grew green and hardy against the chilly season, a group of chickens scratching at the muddy earth, searching for worms. In a few months, this land would be a hive of activity as workers brought in for the season bent their backs to the soil to plant spinach, beets, broad beans, courgette and pumpkin.

But for now, the pace of the farm slowed, slumbering in wait for the coming sun. The food barn remained full, buckets of potatoes harvested in November, still fresh and waiting. Stored corn and jars of pickles, bags of flour for bread. Abene's diet had shifted, but it was no less satisfying.

It was a joy to return here.

Coming to the step that led to the front door, Abene crouched down to pat a pecking chicken, enjoying the soft, silky feathers that lined her back. A smile, faint and weary, but no less honest, ghosted on her lips.

Opening the door, she removed her jacket, stomping her boots on the landing to clear the mud and water, before stepping into the warm embrace of the fire-heated cottage. Inside was silent, still, only the scent of wood smoke in the air. Her brow creased in thought, she'd expected her mother and Udane to be cooking by now...

"Upstairs," she said to Eduardo. "Dry clothes, then you can have some bread."

The boy trotted off happily, leaving Abene to investigate.

Making her way to the large kitchen that opened out across the back of the cottage, she rolled up her sleeves, already too warm in the closed space of the stone walls. She found her mother there, and Udane, Camille and Pierre. They sat at the table, collected together as if in Sunday prayer, heads bowed forward, hands clasped.

Her heart reacted before her mind, strumming up a rapid beat that pounded against her ribs.

"Madre? Camille? What has happened?" she asked, stepping into the spacious room.

Lourdes looked up, cheeks wet with tears.

"My child," she said, holding out a hand. Abene took it, coming to her mother's side. Her eyes tracked straight to Udane, her worst fear on the tip of her tongue. The woman was crying, but still, oddly calm.

Knowledge, weighted by inevitability, settled over her body, her shoulders slumped, her eyes closing in resignation.

Lourdes spoke. "It is over, our home is lost. Barcelona has fallen."

"When?" Abene asked.

"Yesterday. The final blow was an all-out assault on the city. Bombing raids, ground troops. The Republic had no chance," Camille said, voice soft.

"And the government?"

"We don't know. Reports say some got out."

"Soldiers? Juan?"

Udane clasped her hands together, lips moving in a fervent prayer.

"Refugees are making for the French border in the east."

"Juan is amongst them," Abene said, face set in determination. She would believe nothing else, she simply couldn't. It would break them beyond repair.

Udane began to cry, a soft sniffling sound. Lourdes wound an arm about Abene's waist, pulling her daughter close. Abene understood the gesture, a mother's need to know her child was safe in the face of the loss of another.

"Juan is coming," Abene said again, firmer, louder. "He made it out once before, he will do so again."

"But how will he find us?" Udane sobbed, turning to Abene, eyes bloodshot from crying.

Abene looked up to Camille, who answered, "We left this

address with Sister Agnes, if he comes to Bayonne, she will direct him here."

"What is being done in the east?" Abene asked. "Is there a camp there for the refugees? Did our government plan ahead?"

Camille shook her head slowly. "I do not know, but I think we can safely expect the refugees will be looked after. As you were here."

Abene kissed to the top of her mother's head, blinking rapidly to halt her own tears of sorrow.

The war in Spain was over. The Nationalists had won.

Her nation would never be the same,

Taking a seat beside Lourdes, Abene realised she didn't care. Spain had been lost to her for more than two years, and after the war took her father, in her heart, she'd never believed the Republic could win.

No, Franco's forces were too powerful, too well-trained, too brutal. It may have taken time, but this had been inevitable.

Now, sitting in the warmth and safety of Camille's family farm, Abene could accept this truth, and acknowledge it.

It was all right, she realised. She was willing to give up her country, to turn away and make a new life. It was a sacrifice she accepted. On one condition.

That Juan made it back to them, alive.

The soft scuff of a heel on wood drew her head up. Eduardo stood in the doorway, eyes wide. A fleeting burn of shame flooded through her body. In her own sorrow and grief, she'd not thought of the child.

Forcing herself to display a calm she did not feel, Abene came to her feet. Crossing the floor she opened her arms to Eduardo. "My darling," she said, kneeling as he ran the short distance between them, burying his head in her neck. "Shh, shh, calm," she crooned rocking him in her arms.

Eduardo shook against her chest, his fingers pitching into her flesh. Gathering him up into her arms she carried him from the room to the small cot they shared. There she sat with him in her lap, holding him until his sobs subsided.

Then, gently, she turned his face to hers. "Dear one, talk to me. Why do you cry?"

Eduardo huffed, and sniffled. "Because you are leaving."

Abene blinked in surprise. "Leaving? I am doing no such thing. Why ever would you say that?"

"Because 'home is lost', your mamá said so... I don't want to be lost from you!"

Sobbing claimed him once again and he threw himself back against her, arms wrapping like a vice about her neck. "I don't want you to go!"

"Eduardo, mi cariño, peace, peace," she soothed, rubbing his arms, trying to disentangle herself from his grip. "No one is going anywhere, not me, not my mamá, not you... we are staying here, on the farm. Together."

"But Lourdes said, 'Home is lost'."

Abene sighed, wiping a tear from Eduardo's eye. "Si, mi cariño, yes. Our home in Spain is no longer ours. And we cannot return. But here in France is a new home, and here we can stay."

Eduardo eyed her, sobs slowing, face guarded. "Then why does Udane wail? Why does Lourdes cry?"

"Because they are afraid for people they miss. Like you, they don't want to be apart."

"Are the people in heaven? Like Mamá and Papá?"

Abene blinked rapidly, willing herself to calm. "I don't know. Udane hopes not."

"But heaven is wonderful," Eduardo said. It was the statement of a child repeating what they had been taught.

Abene answered carefully. "Heaven is wonderful. And we should be happy for our loved ones who are there. But we still miss them, while we wait to see them again."

"Like I miss Mamá?"

"Exactly like that."

The boy fell silent, fingers clenching and unclenching against her shoulder as he thought. "I wish Mamá was still here," he said.

Abene smiled, feathering her fingers over his cheek. "I know."

SEVENTEEN

ABENE

Dusk was her favourite time. Before her the small farm lay still and calm, the last rays of the spring sun painting the darkening sky in dabs of pink and purple. A gentle breeze stirred in the valley, brushing past the hair that curled at her chin, tickling her skin.

"Abene, come, help!" Eduardo called.

Gratitude swelled in her chest as she looked across the grass to where the boy ran, arms wide and flapping as he attempted to herd the chickens towards their pen for the evening. The lengthening days meant warmer evenings, and the birds had little desire to turn in for the night. But foxes prowled the farm, seeking any opportunity for an easy chicken dinner.

"Ha!" Eduardo straightened from a bend, arms full of fluffy chicken. "I have caught Elise," he announced proudly.

Laughing, Abene walked toward the boy. "Well done. Careful with her wings. Good boy. Take her to the cage. I will join you to round up the others."

It was a new chore, freshly added to Eduardo's growing responsibilities. At almost eight years old it was time for him to begin to learn more about farm life. They would be staying.

Pain, at once cold and hot, gripped her heart and Abene's smile faltered.

Four months. It had been four months since the fall of Barcelona. The final stand of her people against Franco's invaders. With that victory, Franco had sealed her country from her grasp. She could never return. France, this farm, this new family, this was her life now.

And it was a good life. She had found happiness here, working the farm, helping Camille on her nursing rounds, attending Basque cultural events, caring for Eduardo.

But a black cloud hung about her shoulders, ever-present and pressing. Juan. What had become of her childhood friend? Did he share her father's fate? Fallen on the field of battle outside the city of Barcelona. Had he been captured? Taken prisoner for his fight against the Nationalists? Suffering now, alone in a beach-side prison, at the mercy of the elements?

Or, impossibly, had he escaped?

At first, they'd prayed for news. Hoped beyond hope that he would appear. Their welcome to France in 1936 had been warm and open. But the political climate had changed. Murmurs of war rippled across the continent from Germany's charismatic leader. And Franco held Spain. Feeling pinched between two unpredictable powers, France didn't want to antagonise their southern neighbour. So they set up detainment camps and imprisoned the soldiers who fled the civil war.

Even if Juan had made it out of Spain, would he have got through the French soldiers at the border?

Abene shook her head, refocusing on the task at hand.

Eduardo had secured Elise in the chicken coop. Now, face flushed with exertion, he jogged to her side, eyes gleaming with joy. She wrapped an arm around his shoulders. He'd grown taller since she took him into her care, some of the softness of childhood had sluiced from his features over the cold winter that now faded at their backs. But he was still a boy.

Smiling down on him she said, "Come, you go left, I will go right and we can pin them in."

He nodded and moved to follow her plan.

Later, after a simple supper of root vegetables and soup, Abene and Camille sat on the small bench at the front of the farmhouse, sharing the deepening evening, listening to the final chords of birdsong as the blackbirds and swallows settled for the night.

That was when she saw him.

Silhouetted in black by the final rays of the sun, hobbling, crouched, shuffling.

Yet she knew him instantly.

"Udane!" she cried, leaping to her feet. Turning to Camille she said, "Fetch Udane. He is home!"

Spinning from Camille's startled face, Abene hitched her skirts above her knees and ran as fast as her legs could carry her, down the grassy hill towards the road that lined the farm.

She met him at the gate. His hand rested on a fence post, head down. She paused, watched as his body trembled, and heard the ragged edge of his breath.

Then the head turned up. Two eyes gleamed from a haggard face, bright against a thick bushy beard. No longer familiar, but unmistakably him.

She swallowed, tears springing to her eyes.

"I found you," he said, before pitching forward, stumbling bodily against the fence post.

"Juan!" she exclaimed, pushing open the gate to gather her friend in her arms. He was impossibly thin, light against her embrace. The stench of sweat and dirt and blood assaulted her nose. Despite his withered body, he was heavy, the dead weight of his collapsed strength pressing her down.

"Help!" she called over her shoulder. Pierre appeared at her side, carefully taking Juan from her grip to shoulder his body with his own. Abene stepped back, wobbly from exertion and shock. Her heart pounded mercilessly in her chest.

Udane stood a few paces back, one hand clasped over her mouth, eyes wide. At her side, Lourdes, young Eduardo nestled under her protective arm.

"Come, young man," Pierre said to Juan. "Let's get you inside."

"I found you," Juan repeated, eyes opening briefly, their whites flashing in the last of the sunlight before he collapsed once more. Camille and Abene moved to help Pierre and between the three of them, they manoeuvred his limp body into the farmhouse.

Eduardo and Abene gave up their bed for Juan. Carefully, they lay him on the mattress, his limbs twisting awkwardly within their grip. As Abene eased the rotten shoes from his feet, Juan groaned, arms flailing a moment before exhaustion claimed him once again.

"Come, Eduardo, it is your bedtime," Lourdes said softly. "You can sleep in my room tonight." Abene was dimly aware as the child hugged her tight, whispering "good night," before allowing himself to be drawn from the room. She remained, eyes trained on Juan as his breathing stuttered painfully from his chest.

"He has a fever," Udane said. They lit a fire, despite the mild night, and piled blankets over his body, but still he shivered.

"I'll make broth," Camille announced, and padded silently from the room, taking her father with her.

And so the vigil began. Mother and would-be-sister sat, hand in hand on the bed's edge, eyes trained on the man before them.

"What has happened to him?" Udane croaked, tears spilling down her cheeks. "What has been done to him?"

Blinking back her own pain, Abene squeezed the old woman's hands tight. "He is safe now," she said. Their eyes met in the dim firelight. Abene watched Udane take a determined breath before turning back to her son. They had to believe. Once again they began to pray.

Juan awoke in the early dawn. Udane had fallen asleep at his side, her body curled around her trembling son. Abene remained away, watching from the small chair that sat at the fireside. Seeing his eyes open she stood, pacing softly to his side. She took his hand, held it to her lips and pressed a kiss to his dirt-crusted fingers.

She watched the tears fill his eyes, glistening in the pale morning light. His mouth moved but she silenced him with a gentle finger to his lips.

"Shh," she whispered. "It is all right. You are with us now. You are safe. We won't leave your side, not even for a moment."

His hand gripped hers tightly. "I promise," she said softly.

Slowly his eyelids began to droop, his features slackening with sleep. Abene smoothed his greasy hair back from his forehead and heaved a wobbly sigh. It would be a long road to recovery, she knew. But she would walk it with him. Every single step.

EIGHTEEN

ABENE

It was two days before Juan was strong enough to wash. In the meantime, Udane sponged what she could from his face and hands. But, at noon on the third day, Pierre boiled water and filled the tub in the outhouse to the brim. Abene helped Juan to the tub, his impossibly thin legs too wasted for him to stand without support. As Udane loosened his trousers, Abene stood firm, eyes focused on the wall. She felt Juan's puff of embarrassment as the last of the rags were removed from his body. But she didn't care. It was just a body, after all. And he was her brother.

Udane paced away with the flimsy remains of his clothes and Abene braced his arms as he stepped into the tub.

A hiss escaped Juan's lips as his worn flesh met the steaming bathwater, and he paused. Abene waited patiently as he eased himself beneath the water. He leaned back against the edge of the tub and Abene stepped back, eyes averted, "I will leave you to wash. Take your time."

"No, wait!" Juan's arm shot up from the water, gripping her skirt. "Please don't leave me."

Abene met his eyes. Gone was the mirth that had always swam there, the wry humour waiting to dance free from his mouth. She nodded. Pulling up a rickety chair she took a seat. Seeing her settled, Juan relaxed back into the water. After a moment he took up the rough cake of soap and began to work the suds across his chest. Abene waited in silence as the water sloshed and the scent of oil and flowers filled the room.

Juan rested his head back against the tub's edge, a long sigh sounding from deep within his chest. "I forgot how nice a bath is. Can't believe I ever argued with Mamá about taking one."

An unexpected smile twisted Abene's mouth. "Do you remember the time you hid in Father's fish shed, when we were playing hide and seek? Udane had to practically chase you through the streets to get you to wash off the stench of fish."

Juan glanced at her, a grin cracking his lips. "I got away from her, but my stomach betrayed me. I had to return home for supper. And she wouldn't feed me until I was clean."

"I can understand that! You smelt like the cannery."

"Hey, what's a little fish between family?"

Abene laughed. "I've smelt worse."

It was the wrong thing to say. Juan's face fell as his eyes turned back to the water that lapped around him, now whirling black and oily.

"I didn't mean..."

"It's all right."

"... I teach Basque children in town. The amount of wee..."

"It's all right!" Juan's voice had risen, high and tight.

Abene fell silent, guilt twisting in her stomach. They sat in silence, the only sound the soft crackle of the unseasonable fire and the occasional drip of water from the long beard that lined Juan's chin.

"Tell me," Abene whispered.

Juan stared at the wall, eyes going distant, lips parting. "It wasn't like when we crossed. January, winter in the mountains, is a different beast. I travelled alone. Around me, people fell, knees first into the snow. Exhausted, wounded, starving. Old men and women, children. I didn't stop, I could have..." he trailed off, pausing, alone with his memories. Eventually, he continued. "I made it to the border, many didn't." He stopped and swallowed. "The French guards separated the men from the women. They locked me up in a cell. No light, no water, a bucket for our business. Five of us. We could not all lie down at once, there wasn't enough floor space. We took it in turns to sleep. I... I thought I would never see the sun again."

Silent tears spilled down Abene's face and she clenched her jaw tight to hold in the sobs. It was one thing to know about the detainment camps, it was another to hear about the experience of them.

She did not want to hear Juan's story; it tore her soul to see him brought so low. But she knew he had to speak. She would listen, so Udane could be spared.

"It was their idea to run. The others in my cell. They planned, but I didn't listen, I didn't believe. When they left, they still took me with them." His eyes tracked up from the tub, settling on the ceiling, seeing something far beyond the walls of the farmhouse.

"Only two of us made it. Me and another man, he was well-spoken, probably rich. I don't know his name. I never asked. We travelled together for a time. But he wanted to go south, back to Spain. He asked me to join him, to continue to fight..." Juan slumped forward. Drawing his knees up he hugged them to his sunken chest. "I didn't say no. That night, while he slept, I snuck away. I couldn't... I couldn't admit it to him."

Abene frowned. "Admit what?" she asked gently.

Juan turned two large, sorrowful eyes to hers. "That I am a coward."

"Juan..." Abene began. But her friend turned away, exposing his back to her, lined with the angry red of healing scars. The signs of torture. Abene sucked in a ragged breath of shock, falling silent.

"I don't know how long I walked," Juan continued. "But I didn't stop until I found the church in Bayonne. They wanted to take me in, to feed me, but I knew I could not rest. If I did... They gave me directions to the farm and I continued. One foot, then the next, until I saw you."

He turned, where pain and guilt had twisted his features into a wreck of sorrow, now his forehead lay smoothed, relaxed. "There you were, running down the hillside. And I knew I was home."

Abene collapsed onto her knees, hands grasping his across the rim of the tub. "Yes," she said, voice breaking.

"If they find me, they will lock me up again."

Abene took a steadying breath. She knew it was true. They would have to keep Juan's true identity secret.

"Juan, this is your home now. Pierre will keep you safe. I will keep you safe. You are home."

He nodded sadly. "I know. Donostia is gone. We can't return but, Abene, I won't leave you or Mamá, ever again."

As the days of spring lengthened into summer, Juan's body slowly healed. At first, his ribs pressed painfully through his skin, his legs so emaciated from starvation, as a soldier and a prisoner, that Abene could not fathom how he had made it across the hundreds of miles to the fermette. But soon the healthy and abundant produce of the land – roast chicken, root vegetable soups and pies, Camille's baked cheesecake and cream – began to fill his features once more.

Pierre fashioned him a cane from a sturdy tree branch and Juan took to hobbling about the grassy lawn of the farm, helping Eduardo to herd the chickens to their nightly rest. The exertion was good for him, and Abene watched as his balance and strength slowly returned, a small smile gracing his lips as Eduardo leapt and bounced about the garden in search of wayward fowls. The boy was good for him, Abene could see it. Touched himself by unspeakable pain, somehow Eduardo had never lost the innocence of youth, the ability to live in moments joyfully and wholly. He was a blessing to them all.

Though the days showed continued progress in Juan's condition, the nights were a different matter. Udane and Abene took turns sleeping beside him in the small bed that Abene had once shared with Eduardo. Juan could not handle the dark. His dreams, filled with horrors, woke him from his sleep, thrashing and screaming. In the midst of the grip of his memories, nothing could calm him, except for the firm embrace of strong and loving arms. But slowly, as the shadows of autumn gathered, even those nightly hours of trauma began to slowly fade.

Until Germany invaded Poland.

Dark whispers of gathering conflict had been swirling through the streets of Saint-Jean-de-Luz for months, as Adolf Hitler, the ruler of Germany, called for the return of his once great country, his words setting Europe on tenterhooks. But no one saw the invasion coming.

Immediately, France and Britain declared war on Germany, with the whole country mobilising for war.

That night, Juan woke, his screams piercing the night. His writhing body was so slick with sweat that at first Abene did not notice the warm spread of acrid urine. Wrapping herself about him, she soothed his tremors, his quaking limbs and spasming muscles. Only then did the warm seep of urine register in her mind. Without a word she disentangled herself from her friend, helping him to rise from the wet sheets. She sat him on the wooden chair, gathered up the sheets and whisked them from the room. In the outhouse, she filled a bucket to soak them, collected a towel and fresh blankets and returned. Covering the wet patch on the mattress with the towel she offered clean trousers to Juan, turning from the shame that laced his face, and led him back beneath the blankets.

Despite events in Poland, nothing much changed in the Pyrénées-Atlantiques, and winter's chill passed without advance of the conflict. Life on the farm plodded on and maybe Abene allowed herself to believe that nothing further would come to knock upon their door.

Then, on 10th May 1940, Germany invaded France.

They learned the news over the radio. Gathered in the common room, hands clasped together in horror, they listened as the disembodied voice of a presenter spoke of the Invasion of Belgium, France and the Netherlands, a mass assault pushing into sovereign lands.

Peace was finished.

Abene allowed Eduardo to climb into her lap. His limbs had grown long these past months, but she gathered him as close as she could.

"It will be all right," Pierre declared, eyes alight with passion. "The Maginot Line will hold."

Abene hoped it was true.

She slept beside her mother, Eduardo's arms wrapped around her neck. Despite the muggy heat of the night, she snugged him close. When Juan's screams began from the next room, Abene met her mother's eyes in the moonlight and knew neither of them had been asleep. Lourdes' lips began moving in silent prayer. Soon Abene's did too.

There was nothing else to do but pray.

NINETEEN

ABENE

1940

Within days, the streets of Saint-Jean-de-Luz were flooded, young men leaving in droves to travel to Paris and fight. Shouts of confidence and passion rang through the streets, the people of southern France were determined that they would fight back and win.

But despite the country's fervour, the Maginot Line didn't hold and the German army swept towards Paris. Abene was at the church hall, showing the children how to craft the neat geometric patterns of Basque knitwear when Denise appeared at the door, fidgeting nervously.

"Home time, everyone," she announced, walking in, steps clicking loudly on the floor.

Abene froze, her hands going still in mid-air as she demonstrated a particularly challenging loop.

"It's not yet time, is it?" she said, frowning in confusion.

"The carers are here. We are closing early."

Reading the barely contained panic on her friend's face, Abene turned to the children and smiled.

"All right, mes enfants, leave your work in the box on my desk and I will see you all next week."

The children filed out dutifully, Eduardo coming to stand at her side.

"Tante Abene, why are we finishing early?"

Abene flashed a smile, brimming with as much reassurance as she could muster as she guided the class from the hall. At the entrance, their carers milled in wait. After the last child had lined up to return home, Abene turned to Denise.

Her face was ashen with fear, her eyes wild. "Paris has fallen," she said simply.

Shock shot through Abene and she stared at Denise. "But the fortifications—"

"They didn't hold."

"What is happening?" Eduardo asked.

"Nothing, young man, all is well..." Denise stammered.

But Abene swiftly interrupted. Eduardo had lived through war before, he deserved the truth. "Mi cariño," Abene said, taking the boy by his shoulders and turning him to face her directly. "You know that the German Army has invaded France?"

Eduardo nodded.

Swallowing, Abene continued. "They took Paris today."

"What does that mean?"

Abene flicked her eyes up to Denise. "Even in the Great War, Paris held..."

She turned back to Eduardo. "I don't know, not really. But we have survived war before, you and I. And we will do so again."

"I don't want to leave the fermette!" Eduardo said suddenly, arms crossed in defiance.

"Peace, my brave boy. I have said no such thing. It is far too soon to decide anything. For now, we go home."

Pausing to collect a shaking Denise into an embrace, Abene whispered, "It will be all right. We will endure."

Releasing Denise, whose tears now followed freely down her cheeks, she wrapped an arm around Eduardo's shoulders and headed back to the fermette.

A rapid knock on her bedroom door brought her from her sleep. Sitting up, her eyes adjusted to the dim light of early dawn, revealing Juan pacing to her bedside, step steady now without his walking stick.

"Stay inside, do not make a sound."

"What has happened?" Abene hissed, fear choking her throat.

"Soldiers, in the trees. I have been watching... They are passing through the fermette, heading towards town."

"Germans?"

"I don't know. But I am going to find out."

"Juan," Abene gripped his arm, "wait, don't go out there." As her fingers curled into his jacket, she realised he was already dressed or perhaps had never made it to bed that night at all.

The mood at supper had been sombre, fearful. Paris was still a long way from the fermette, tucked as it was on the border with Spain. But it had been conquered and Paris had never been conquered. A pall of fear had fallen over the whole of France and her citizens held a collective breath, and prayed.

Juan took her hand in his, squeezing tightly. "I have to see who it is. If they are Germans..."

He left the rest unsaid, for if they were in fact an invading battalion, what could they do, really?

Abene read the determination in his eyes and saw there was no arguing with him. The moment Germany had crossed into France a change had come over him. A fire, a resolve, an anger.

The soldier within him, the man shaped by battle on the outskirts of Barcelona, had flared back to life.

Releasing a breath, Abene nodded. "I will lock the door behind you and keep the others inside. Be careful, please, please be careful."

Mouth set in a line of grim determination, Juan squeezed her hand once more, then strode from the room.

Abene stood to follow.

"Tante?"

Looking over at Eduardo's newly installed cot, she saw the boy sitting up, eyes shining wide and bright in the gathering dawn. Camille was also awake.

"Stay here."

Quickly she followed Juan downstairs. Pierre stood in the hallway, shovel in hand.

"You saw them too?"

Juan nodded.

"We go, now, together. Here." He handed an axe to Juan.

With barely a glance back at Abene the two men exited the house. She took the key and locked them out, the click of the mechanism too loud in the silent morning. She paced swiftly back up to her room in the pale blue light of the waking sun. There she found Eduardo crouched on the floor with Camille, both peeking between the curtains.

"Come away," she whispered urgently.

"I see a soldier," Eduardo said, eyes not leaving the window.

Abene rushed to his side, kneeling down to see for herself.

The boy was right. There, secreted behind an apple tree, was the unmistakable figure of a man in uniform, a gun slung over his shoulder. The soft light of morning cast him in grey, making it impossible to tell if he were French or German. Abene closed her eyes, lips moving in a silent prayer to God.

"I see Juan."

Abene's eyes flew open as panic seized her limbs. Eduardo

was right. There, on the edge of the orchard, Juan crouched, body rigid, still. He'd seen the same soldier they had. He was stalking him.

"Oh God," Abene breathed, hand coming to her mouth.

Juan paced forward, stepping carefully.

Abene's heart pounded in her chest as she watched. She longed to look away but could not tear her eyes from the scene unfolding before her. Juan continued, closing the gap between him and the soldier, axe before him. So far, the soldier hadn't noticed him, he was facing the other way, planning his next move.

Then another soldier appeared in the distance, coming toward Juan and the man he stalked.

"No," Abene breathed.

The second soldier was moving through the trees, fast and low. It didn't yet seem that he had seen Juan, but with each step, he drew closer. He soon would, even in the half-light of dawn. Abene's throat closed over. She wanted to scream out, to warn her friend. But she knew she could not. It would alert them all, and with Juan in the middle of two unknown soldiers, place him at even greater risk.

She could only watch on, and pray and pray and pray.

The second soldier continued forward and then stopped dead. Abene sucked in a breath. Juan paused, cocking his head as if listening. Then suddenly, without warning, the second soldier charged. Juan spun on his heel, turning to face the soldier, axe up. The first soldier, now at Juan's back, also turned, arms flailing in surprise before he too began to run. Juan glanced over his shoulder, realising he was pincered between the two advancing enemies. Time seemed to pause, the scene unfolding in slow motion. Then Juan pivoted, turning back to face the original soldier, and sprinted forward, a cry escaping from his lungs. Everything snapped back into real time as Juan advanced on the soldier. The man paused, perhaps in shock at Juan's charge. Then he turned, running away. But Juan did not stop. Like a man possessed he rushed in pursuit, axe raised above his head. Behind him the second soldier stopped, unslinging his gun and aiming it directly at Juan's back.

A cry of horror escaped Abene's lips.

Then, like a miracle, Pierre appeared out of nowhere, shovel swinging through the air. It connected with the second soldier's head and he collapsed, gun with him.

At the same time, Juan threw his axe aside and launched himself in a dive, straight into the back of the fleeing soldier. They crashed to the ground in a tangle of limbs and shouts.

And all went silent.

Abene was on her feet in an instant. She flew down the stairs. The commotion outside had woken the household and Lourdes and Udane met her in the hall. Abene pressed a finger to her lips and brushed past them, Camille following. The friends paused a moment together before rushing outside. Camille headed straight to her father and the fallen soldier at his feet. Abene raced to Juan. He was sitting up on the soft, dewy grass. Beside him, the soldier he had tackled was dusting himself off. Abene slowed her pace as she approached.

"Not German," Juan said quickly, holding up a hand.

The soldier looked up sharply at his words. Seeing Abene he raised his hands to show he was no threat.

"Out. Beach. Out," he stammered in broken French

Abene looked at Juan and he shrugged. "I don't speak his language, but from his name, I think he's a Pole. Sounds like an evacuation on the coast."

Behind them, Pierre and Camille were helping the other man to his feet. Juan stood and offered a hand to help his soldier to stand. They made their way over to Pierre and Camille, the second soldier now hanging between them, unsteady on his feet.

"I think they were making their way to the beach, an evacuation," Juan explained.

Pierre nodded thoughtfully. "This fellow's not walking anywhere for a while yet." He paused and turned to Camille. "Go fetch the truck from the barn. We'll drive them into town."

Camille nodded. Transferring the weight of the soldier to Abene, she rushed off.

The soldier was heavy, his breath sour, the smell of his sweat and unclean body puckered Abene's nose.

"They've come a long way," Pierre said, face drawn. "Let's help them get to safety."

At the truck, Abene helped the soldier inside before climbing in herself. Juan looked at her sharply, eyebrows raised.

"I'm coming too," she said simply, preparing to argue.

But Juan only nodded, squeezing in beside her. Pierre fired the engine and they set off: Pierre, Juan and Abene in the front, the two Polish soldiers in the back.

The beach and fishing pier of Saint-Jean-de-Luz were brimming with soldiers. They streamed from the town, down onto the sands, forming into groups. On the horizon large ships sat in wait, anchored beyond the break in the deep of the Bay.

Pierre pulled up and they helped the soldiers down to the sands. A group of fishermen were making their way to the docks that lined the Nivelle River, and Juan broke off to join them. At the beach they were met by other soldiers, jogging up the beach to take the injured man from them. Nods of thanks and smiles and they turned to rejoin the men milling on the sands.

Juan reappeared. "They are ferrying the men to the big ships. Using the fishing boats. It's a huge evacuation. These soldiers fought in the Battle of France, but have been driven back by the advancing German army. After the Maginot Line broke they were told to rendezvous here for evacuation."

Abene looked up at the skies, grey and cloudy. "At least the heavens are helping. The Luftwaffe won't be able to fly in that." She pointed to the clouds. Since France had been invaded the shadows of fighter planes had periodically darkened the skies above Saint-Jean-de-Luz, on route somewhere, or simply scanning the coast, Abene didn't know. But the planes looked evil, menacing.

"Let's hope it holds," Pierre agreed.

"I'm going to help," Juan said.

Abene looked at him sharply. "What do you mean?"

"They need fishermen to drive the boats to get them to safety. So many have gone to fight. But I am here. And I can drive a boat."

"But, Juan, those boats will be a target."

"You said it yourself, the sky is shrouded. I'll be safe. The sooner we get these men to safety, the better."

"I don't think—"

"I'll be all right," he interrupted, gifting her an overconfident grin.

"We'll wait here for you," Pierre said. "Drive you back when you're done."

"Thank you," Juan said, then turned and ran across the beach to the fishing dock.

Abene wrapped her arms around herself, seeking warmth against the chilly morning breeze that blew in from the bay, and against the fear that snaked up her body.

"He knows boats?" Pierre asked.

"He does."

"Then he is the man for the job."

As the sunlight strengthened around them Abene kept her eyes trained on the skies, praying that the gathering warmth did not dispel the cloud cover. It was all that stood between Juan and a Luftwaffe machine gun. As the fishing boats chugged out against the rough currents, the smoke of their engines filling the air, she thought of San Sebastian and the effort to get the children out. Her father and Juan had ferried children then, out and away from war.

Eduardo had been on one of those boats. What had he seen? What had he felt? Alone and adrift on a strange boat, heading to a city he didn't know, his parents waving goodbye from the dock.

She sucked in a deep breath through her nose, working to still her nerves. This evacuation had to succeed. It had to.

The day passed slowly, the steady shuttle of fishing vessels out and back, the lines of waiting soldiers dwindling. Abene watched as the smaller fishing vessels, buffeted by the increasing strength of the waves in the bay, struggled to dock against the large passenger ships that lay in wait, and prayed none would capsize. Overhead, the clouds held. As the first breezes of the early evening brought the smell of salt and seaweed blowing across Saint-Jean-de-Luz, Juan returned to the truck, step heavy, shoulders slumped. Exhausted.

"Come on then, let's get you back," Pierre said.

Back at the fermette, Lourdes plated out oven-warm quiche and bread. Juan fell on his food, stuffing his face with abandon, before slumping back in his chair.

"They were so scared," he said.

The table fell silent, looking at him as one.

"The men. I could see it, in their eyes. Fear. I know that look."

Abene pressed her lips together, swallowing her words. For she knew it too. She'd seen it in Juan's eyes when he returned from Barcelona.

Juan pushed back from the table, walking out into the night.

Udane went to move but Abene stilled her with a gentle hand. "I'll go," she said.

Outside Juan stood by the chicken coop, the red tip of his

cigarette bright in the deepening dark. Abene joined him in silence. They stood together, watching the sky blacken, listening to the rustle and chirp of the nesting birds. It was calm and peaceful.

It was a lie.

France was at war. And not just in the north. Soldiers all the way from Poland had come here, to their town, seeking rescue. Despite their distance from Paris, the events of today proved the fear in everyone's hearts. Nowhere was safe from Nazi reach.

Placing a hand on her friend's back, she stood with him in silence, offering her presence. It was all she could give.

TWENTY

ABENE

The Armistice signed by Marshal Petain on 22 June 1940 created a north-south divide through France, with a French government ruling the south from the coastal town of Vichy. It didn't take long for this "rule" to be exposed for what it truly was: a subordinate government to the German rule in the north. Money, gold, food and supplies were gathered from the south and sent north, funding the German war effort and feeding their troops. But goods were not the only thing being collected for transport, as Abene would soon witness first-hand.

She was in the church hall leading a group of young Basque refugees through a folk song when two local policemen entered. Abene continued singing, keeping her face a mask of calm, as Denise approached the unexpected visitors. Abene watched as her friend spoke with the officers, then turned to lead them to where Abene was teaching. The frown of concern was clear on Denise's forehead.

Abene brought the song to an end, waiting calmly for the children to settle. One officer stepped forward, coming to stand beside Abene.

"We just have some questions for the children," he said softly, smiling at the watching group.

"Questions?" Abene asked, glancing across to where Denise stood rigid on the edge of the space. "These are young children, sir. Not one is more than twelve. I am not sure they can help with your inquiries..."

"I assure you, they are just right," he said, turning from her to address the children sitting cross-legged before them.

Smiling down, he began. "Hello, mes enfants, I am Officer Laurent. You might have seen me and my men around town. I won't keep you long. I just have a few questions for you all. Is that all right?"

The children nodded, a chorus of, "Oui, monsieur," issuing politely from their sing-song mouths.

Abene took a deep breath and waited.

"A show of hands, how many of you live with your parents?"

Around half of the children raised their hands. "Good, good, and how many stay at the orphanage?"

The other half put up their hands. Abene gripped her skirts. Why was that information relevant?

"Who here remembers life in Spain, before you came to France?"

Some shuffling this time, whispers of uncertainty. It had been years since most had made their way here. Some hands went up but with less confidence than before.

"I see," Officer Laurent continued. "Now, a very important one. Who here goes to church on Sundays?"

Abene blinked, looking up sharply at the officer. Most children raised a hand, straight and tall. The officer nodded, a small smile on his lips. "And those of you with parents, raise your hand if you go with mum and dad... now raise your hand if you go with only one parent."

Abene exchanged a look with Denise, confusion bubbling up within her.

"Some children have only one parent," Abene interrupted, unsure what information the officer was fishing for.

"Ah, of course," he said. "Thank you." Then turning back to the class. "Who goes to church but a parent, or someone else who lives with you, stays home?"

A few hands went up. "I will need their names," the officer said aside to Denise.

"Whatever for?" Abene asked.

"Just their names." He returned his interest to the class, raising his hands in a gesture of warmth. "Well, I won't keep you any longer. Thank you for your time."

Nodding to Abene he moved to Denise, following her into her office.

Blinking rapidly, Abene forced herself to smile and organised another activity with the children. She waited until the officers had left, and the children were calmly playing together before crossing to speak with Denise.

Her friend looked up from her desk. "Close the door."

Abene complied, before coming to stand by Denise. She looked up at Abene, "They wanted their names. The children who don't go to church, or who know someone who does not."

"But why?" Abene said, mind unable to draw a connection.

"Jews."

"What?"

Denise released a heavy breath. "You have read the news, yes? Seen the talk of Jewish corruption? Well, what are you, if you don't go to church on a Sunday?"

"Lazy."

Denise snorted, and shrugged, "Or you aren't Christian, which means you are..."

"Jewish. Oh God. But what does it matter? Why do they want to know?"

"I don't know," Denise said. "But they asked the children. Small ones, who don't know to lie."

The two friends stared at each other, fear uncoiling between them.

"We must warn the families."

"Yes, but of what?"

"Whatever is coming."

It came a week later. Policemen streaked through Saint-Jeans-de-Luz, ordering Jewish families to pack a suitcase and loading them onto trucks. They were gathered at the station and herded onto a specially chartered train and transported out of the city.

The radio announced the strength of the Vichy government in ridding the region of the Jewish Scourge. Abene felt deep concern. She had experienced the conflict of citizen against citizen before, a divide based on race and belief. She did not know what fate the Jewish citizens of the Pyrénées-Atlantiques were rolling towards, but she feared for them, deeply.

The police arrived at the door to the fermette one week later. It was late evening, the household had already eaten and tidied the dishes. Abene and Eduardo were sitting in the lounge, working through his letters and numbers. Lourdes and Udane knitting and chatting in the corner, when the loud knock reverberated through the wooden walls. Pierre stood, eyes instantly alert. Juan appeared from the kitchen where he'd been mending boots. Pierre waved him back and marched to the door.

Wrapping a protective arm around Eduardo, Abene craned her neck to watch, ears pricked to listen.

"Good evening, Pierre, nice night."

"What are you doing here, Henri? It's late. No good cause to be out disrupting people's evening rest."

The policeman gave a too-casual smile. "I won't keep you.

I'm here following up a report about a new farmhand you are keeping on the property."

Abene's breath caught in her throat. *Juan.* Her eyes skipped across the room, meeting her friends. He stepped back into the darkness of the hallway.

Pierre was shaking his head. "I have no new help," he said. "Just the women from Bayonne. But they've been here for years, I consider them family."

"I am not talking about the women, and you know it. I mean the man. You were seen driving back from the coast with him in your truck."

A tense silence fell across the room, but Pierre stood firm. "A traveller, he needed a lift. He is not in residence."

"Pierre," Henri leaned forward, "don't be a fool. You were seen with a man. Are you hiding someone here? A Republican from Spain? A rebel soldier who escaped the camps? Or is it worse? A Jew?"

The air went out of Abene's lungs. This hunt for citizens based on race and religion had become a plague on the country. A dread, deep and intrinsic, the like of which she'd faced as Franco's men bore down on her beautiful Donostia, had returned to plunge her new home into shadow. This time, she had nowhere to flee.

"There is no one here but myself and the women and little Eduardo, who is just a child. Your information is mistaken."

The policeman leaned forward, lowering his voice. Abene strained to hear. "Be careful, old friend. War makes enemies of friends. Choose carefully what you are willing to sacrifice. And who."

Pierre straightened, knuckles going white where they gripped the door. "Good night, Henri."

He started closing the door and the policeman stepped back. The door closed, and Abene watched as Pierre stood, pausing a moment before the entrance before turning within.

They all sat in silence, the full import of what had just occurred slowly sinking in.

"I will leave," Juan said, stepping from the hall into the common room.

"Don't be a fool, son, I'm not going to turn you out."

Juan eyed Pierre. "It is time that I signed up and joined the fight. This just proves I have waited too long."

Abene sucked in a deep breath. "But, Juan, you aren't even supposed to be in the country. You are a soldier from Spain. How can you join the army? They'll send you to a camp."

"No, they won't care, they need the men."

"France is already lost." She regretted the words the moment they left her mouth. Her eyes flicked up to Pierre. He shook his head, looking away.

"Perhaps," Juan answered. "But we have to try. We can't just give in."

"Juan, you already did try. In Spain. You nearly died."

"But I didn't," Juan replied. "Don't you see? This is our home now. This land, here in the south of France. This farm is where we have been welcomed.

"Spain is gone. But here, hope remains. I can help. I know how to fight."

"There is talk of a regiment. Americans, outside Bordeaux. Some of the men were discussing it at the tavern. They plan to try and join. I could speak to them, and ask if you could join," Pierre said. "You have to go quietly. Vichy, France, can raise no armies against Germany."

"Thank you," Juan said. "This is a good plan."

"But, Juan!" Abene felt Udane's hand in her own and turned to see the older woman's face, resignation in her eyes.

"I can do this, Abene," Juan said. "I can help. And maybe, if we try, we can win. We can't give in so easily. Then we have already lost."

She turned and stared at him, her heart breaking, because as much as she wished to refute his words, she could not. She saw his point and felt it keenly. Udane's iron grip in hers, a silent symbol of defeat.

All she wanted, from the moment she'd arrived at the fermette, was to hide away here. Safe from prejudice and danger, safe from war. Even after the fall of Paris, she'd told herself it would be okay. Germany hadn't come this far into France, and the agreement with the Vichy government would keep the Pyrénées-Atlantiques safe.

But war had come to them today. Walked up and knocked on the door, dressed as a local.

She could no longer pretend they were safe here.

She could no longer believe it would all go away.

She stood and closed the gap between herself and Juan, drawing him into a firm embrace.

"Promise you will return."

"I will," he said. "Promise you will be here."

"I will be," she swore.

TWENTY-ONE

MIREN

1941 San Sebastian

Spring was easily Miren's favourite season. The gathering warmth brought life to the streets and smiles to people's faces. Things in her city had settled over the years since the end of the war, the flow of food and goods recommenced, and the tension of occupation had thawed.

It had also brought acceptance to Miren's heart. It had been four years since Anders fled Bilbao, abandoning her to her own fate. With the space that time afforded, Miren had come to understand their relationship in a different light. She saw how Anders had loved her and kept her close only when it suited his needs. The invite to be his secretary as he faced an unhappy marriage, the apartment in Bilbao as he fought his political battles. Their engagement, the promises of forever, were nothing but dust in the face of the full horror of war. With the fall of Barcelona over two years before, and the declaration of General Franco as Caudillo, Military Leader of all of Spain, Miren had finally found a path to surrender. Anders was gone.

Somehow, her life continued.

The end of the war had been met with silent resignation and fear in San Sebastian. The economy of Spain was on its knees. War spending, rationing and death had created hardship at every level of society. The country had been run into the ground, and the cessation of gunfire was not enough to allow the people to bounce back.

Grief and sorrow at the loss of husbands, sons and brothers darkened every corner of the nation. Then, on the heels of the end of their own conflict, news of the German army's activities just over the border with France brought further disquiet. The invasion of France, the murmured fear that the Wehrmacht may stream down towards the Spanish border. The expectation that Spain choose a side.

The newspapers spoke of Franco's cleverness, his diplomacy and tactics in courting both sides of the conflict abroad. He'd not declared for either side, keeping Spain neutral.

In truth, after their own civil war, they had nothing left to give to anyone, and there was little appetite within the nation for further bloodshed.

But it was easy to see that Hitler was not happy with this arrangement. The men shared a common philosophy of control and order. So Hitler had sent bombers to raid Bilbao and Barcelona in support of Franco's mission. Repayment for that support would be expected. And with the growing presence of German tanks deeper and deeper into the south of France, border regions along the Pyrenees grew wary. So Franco played a game. Spain was neutral; her people were prevented from joining the war abroad.

And Nazis were invited to visit.

A film crew had arrived only months ago, here to document the ways of the Basque. A pure race, they called Miren's people. The disconnect astonished her. Her people had been subjugated by Franco and his Nationalist regime, forced to abandon their customs and their language. Yet now he invited Hitler's men to celebrate the uniqueness of the Basque.

Soldiers arrived in droves, their open laughter and full wallets a sharp contrast to the people of Miren's nation. But their lavish spending and expensive tastes brought an unexpected boost to the struggling economy. Her father's hotel was once again booked out, the halls ringing with the clipped and unfamiliar tones of the German language.

Here, the invaders of Europe were guests, invited, welcome. On the other side of the Pyrenees, they were tyrants. The stories of German cruelty were known in San Sebastian, the round-up of Jewish citizens, the forced labour camps. Yet the people of Biscay smiled and greeted them warmly, adding their own comments about the 'scourge of the Jews' as they pocketed coin to pay for food.

Miren would never understand politics.

Running a hotel with her ageing parents was far, far simpler.

As she made her way back from the local market, arms full of fresh, seasonal flowers, ready to adorn the reception desk and dining room of the hotel, Miren breathed in the salty air of her city, light and fresh today, the thick sea mists driven from the streets by the warming sun, and chose to smile. The only way to survive this life, she'd come to realise, was to keep going.

Mounting the stairs to the hotel with a skip in her step, she pushed through the door into reception, words already on her lips. "Madre, I found the most beautiful blooms at the stall today. I think they will be perfect for the dining room. See?"

She turned to the desk, arms raised high to display the bright blooms and froze. Even from behind, she knew him. The breadth of his back, the roundness of his shoulders.

Tremors started along her limbs, her breath catching in her throat as her mind whirled back, back, back, to a cold office room, shredded paper on the floor, and the heavy stomp of advancing soldiers, the hot pain of a slap, the rough carpeted floor.

General Hernandez turned slowly, his proud face, dominated by a hooked nose, confirming what Miren had known in her body. She lowered her arms, bringing the flowers before her like a shield.

"Miren, darling," her mother said, rounding the reception desk. "We have a very special guest to welcome today, This is General Hernandez. He is highly ranked in our Caudillo, General Franco's army, very decorated," she preened.

"You are too kind, señora," Hernandez said, voice gravelly and low. He pierced Miren with a stare. "But I do believe your beautiful daughter and I have met before."

Maria looked up at her daughter in surprise and Miren swallowed, before bobbing a courtesy. "Welcome to the Hotel Maria Crista," she managed to squeak.

Hernandez's lips twisted in a slow half smile. "It is good to see you so well," he said. "Political life was clearly not for you."

Miren gave a wobbly smile, still frozen to the spot, unable to decide what she should do.

Thankfully her mother stepped in. "General Hernandez will be staying with us for a few weeks, while his residence is set up. He is to support the police in keeping order throughout San Sebastian. General," she turned her attention to Hernandez, "you honour us."

"The honour is mine," he answered, eyes never leaving Miren.

Finally, her limbs decided to cooperate and Miren started for the door to the kitchen. "We will do all we can to make your stay as comfortable as possible," she said. "Now, I must get these flowers into water, if you will excuse me."

"Of course, señorita," Hernandez said. "We will have plenty of time to speak later."

His words rang with an intent that Miren did not understand. Nodding to him she made her way swiftly to the door to the back rooms of the hotel. In the kitchen, she dumped the flowers in the sink, their beauty forgotten. Hands now free, she clutched the edge of the bench as if her life depended on it.

The air whooshed out of her and she sagged over the flowers, her body giving in to the terror of her memory. Slowly she lowered herself to the cool tiles that covered the floor, white, edged in blue trim. Hugging herself she closed her eyes, breathing deeply in an attempt to calm her rattled nerves.

General Sergio Hernandez. The man who had led the invasion of Bilbao's government offices, the general who had ordered for her to be locked in her apartment, questioned, brutalised then returned to San Sebastian. The man who knew of her connection to Anders, to the Basque ideals.

He remembered her, he'd made that clear. Would he expose her politics? Use her as an example that even now, years after the war was done, Franco's rule would find you, expose you and punish you?

Miren hadn't done anything against the Nationalists, not really. But she'd worked for the enemy, slept with him, loved him. Would that be enough to damn her?

Bracing herself, Miren wiped the tears of fear from her cheeks and pulled herself back to her feet. He'd let her go in Bilbao, sent her home. And he'd come here by chance, not in search of her.

1937 was years ago. Spain was different now. And Miren had done nothing but toe the line since her return to the hotel. All would be well, she promised herself, she just had to keep living as she had been. One day, and then the next.

All would be well.

The quaking of her hands refused to be still.

. . .

That Friday evening her father held reception drinks in the hotel's fancy ballroom. A lavish, wood-panelled space, dominated by a shining chandelier and marble-framed fireplace. The presence of Señor Hernandez was an honour, and Jose would acknowledge it.

Resident guests, dressed in their finery, made their way into the room from 6 pm for drinks and refreshments. The women glittered in jewels and silks, the men stood, crisp and starched. The laundry service had been run off its feet in preparation. Miren wore a pale green gown that clinched at her waist, around her neck a string of her mother's pearls, and matching earrings dangling tastefully from her earlobes.

The room looked spectacular; her father really had outdone himself with the decorations. Pots of fresh flowers overflowed on tables covered in pale linen tablecloths, the glass of the chandelier twinkling above.

Hernandez stood in the centre of the room, surrounded by a press of men in suits, cigar smoke puffing up in a cloud over their heads. She kept to the edges of the room, hoping to avoid notice. At first, she believed her tactic was working. It didn't last, however. Within the first thirty minutes of the evening she felt his presence come up behind her, the stench of cigar smoke on his breath as he leaned in close to whisper into her ear. She repressed a shudder, turning towards him and stepping back, hoping to create space between them.

"You didn't think I had forgotten you, did you?" Hernandez breathed.

Miren forced a smile to her lips. "Not at all, General, you are in high demand this evening."

"Indeed." He cocked his head, regarding her unashamedly. "So beautiful," he crooned, "and yet unmarried. Why would that be?"

Miren willed her body to calm its raging pulse, but his proximity filled her with terror. "All happens in God's time," she said.

Hernandez snorted, mouth twisting in amusement.

It was an evasive answer, and he had seen straight through it, she could tell. At almost thirty years of age, Miren was well passed marrying age. She should have children of her own by now. Yet she still remained beneath her parents' roof. It was a situation her father lamented, his beautiful girl still in waiting. In her mother's eyes, she saw glimpses of understanding, of what Miren had found in Anders and then lost to war. But she knew their patience was coming to an end.

"It is remarkable," Hernandez said. "How beautiful you remain. Even more so, in fact, than that first day when I met you in Bilbao."

Miren's throat went dry, her eyes widening with fear.

She saw the light of amusement sparkling in his eyes. "Come, come," he said jovially. "You must not be angry with me for those days."

His words floored her. Where was he going with this line of conversation? It was not what she'd expected. "It was war," he continued. "I had to be sure you knew nothing. I should not have pressed you so hard. You were just a young woman after all. But war is war." He shrugged, taking a sip of the wine in his hand. "You understand, si?"

Unable to trust her own voice, Miren nodded.

"It has been a wonderful moment of fate that brought us back together here, in a liberated Spain."

Miren felt the hairs on the back of her neck rise. Spain had not been "liberated", not by this man and his Nationalist soldiers.

"I am looking forward to coming to know your city," he continued. "I was hoping you might agree to accompany me on a tour of the highlights, perhaps tomorrow?"

There was nothing Miren wished to do less, yet as she opened her mouth to refuse she caught her father's face staring at her over Hernandez's shoulder and knew instantly that she could not refuse.

"I would be honoured," she said, voice soft, heart resigned.

"Bah!" Hernandez spat. "'Honoured'. No, no, I'd prefer 'delighted'." He eyed her, face expectant.

Miren blinked in realisation and repeated his instruction. "I would be... 'delighted'," she said.

"Wonderful!" he raised his now empty glass in a mock toast. "Now, I will keep you to myself no longer. Until tomorrow."

As Miren watched him stride back into the centre of the room she felt the walls of the ballroom pressing in on her. She wasn't sure what was happening, or why this new enforcer of their city wanted her time and attention. But whatever the reason, she knew it could not be good.

"San Sebastian is a beautiful city."

They were standing before the Buen Pastor Cathedral, the most grand cathedral in the city. Miren looked over at Hernandez, he appeared genuinely happy as he gazed up at the spiral towers that reached above. Despite her fears and misgivings, the morning tour of the city had passed amiably. Hernandez took her lead and listened as she spoke of the history of the old fishing port and her people's ingenuity on the water, the ebb and flow of the hotel trade and the press of the sea on the seasons.

"Madrid is a far larger place," he continued. "But now that I have spent time on the coasts of Spain, I realise how drawn I am to the sea."

Despite herself, Miren smiled. As a child of a beachside city, she could not imagine living inland.

"I think I will enjoy making this my home."

Miren looked at him. A sense of wistful distance had come

over him, as if his mind was floating away into the past, seeking something else, something different. "This is not what you expected?"

Hernandez shrugged. "I always thought I would return to Madrid. I was born and raised there after all. With the Germans advancing on the border, this is where I need to be. To keep the peace for our people. The peace I fought for. But it will be nice to have some time for me, as a man, not just a general."

His eyes scanned over her, slowly, with unabashed intensity.

Miren felt her skin crawl. "It must be hard. Your duties," she said, hoping to redirect his thoughts.

"Not at all," Hernandez said, the determined set of his jaw firming back into place. "Franco and I, we share a vision for this nation. It is the greatest achievement of my life. And I will do anything to protect it."

Miren's stomach churned at his words. For a brief moment there, she'd thought she'd seen behind the armour, a glimpse of humanity within the General's façade. But the moment it peeked from behind his walls, it vanished on the breath of his ideology.

"You must be getting hungry," she said, changing the subject. "Lunch approaches. Let us return to the hotel, and out of the heat of the day."

"Lead on my beautiful guide," Hernandez said.

And Miren did; there was no other choice.

TWENTY-TWO

MIREN

The month of General Hernandez's stay at the hotel passed like molasses for Miren. Every meal service and evening he was there at her side, wanting her time and attention, his eyes roving, his hands too familiar. Fortunately, she'd been able to avoid any further trips about town with him; the work of overseeing the local law enforcement had kept him occupied most days, but every moment he was in residence at the hotel, he expected her to attend to his needs.

It wasn't difficult work, bringing him wine for dinner, suggesting which meal to try from the menu and accompanying him to the parlour for a casual chat before they retired for the evening, but Miren despised every moment of it. This man, with his dark hair and proud features, was arrogant to his very core. He believed in his right to victory over the freedom of Spain so completely that Miren realised nothing could ever help her to warm to him.

He was a brute. She knew that well enough from personal experience. He loved power and enjoyed lauding it over those who worked beneath him. The glimmer of humanity she'd seen as they stood before the Buen Pastor Cathedral had not shown itself again. After four weeks of bending herself to his every whim, Miren knew it never would.

When the sleek black government car pulled up at the entrance to the hotel, ready to transport Hernandez to his official residence, newly renovated and elaborate, Miren had breathed a sigh of relief. He was an unpleasant man, trapped in his beliefs and all too sure of his importance and power.

On his stale breath, the trauma of Bilbao drifted, recalling Miren to the worst day of her life.

As the car pulled away from the hotel, she sent a prayer to God that she never had to endure the presence of General Sergio Hernandez again.

She should have known better. When had God ever listened to her?

The extent of her folly was revealed to her a week later when her father called her into his office. Miren walked in, taking a seat before his large oak desk. Her shoulders were tight, her head lowered. She knew what this would be about. Suitors. No doubt some new man had come forward expressing interest in courting the successful hotelier's daughter. How her parents worked to marry her off! But she would oblige, go on a few excursions with whichever young man, and then feign surprise when the dalliance came to nothing. Miren was beautiful, she knew it was true, Anders had always said so. But with his disappearance, and no word of his fate, the light within her had gone out. She didn't know how to open her heart to another man. More, she didn't want to.

She would play her role though, ever the dutiful daughter.

What she didn't know was that her time had already run out.

"Daughter," Jose began, and instantly Miren knew something was different. She looked up, meeting her father's joyful face. He was positively beaming. A frown creased her usually smooth forehead. "I have the most wonderful news."

He paused, watching her expectantly. Miren blinked, realising he wanted her to play along, to fuel his excitement. "What news, Father?" she asked.

Jose rose from his seat, clapping his hands before him. "A proposal of the most excellent kind!"

Again, he paused, milking the moment. Miren suppressed her building impatience and confusion. Her father came before her, kneeling to bring their faces in line, and he took her hands.

Now Miren began to worry. Why was her father being so jubilant? Since the war, he'd been reserved, pensive. During Basque rule he'd loved to entertain and network, but under the Nationalists he'd kept himself small, cautious. And Miren and her mother had followed suit. What had changed now? And what did this proposal have to do with her? She hadn't been seeing any suitors lately. Her responsibilities tending to General Hernandez's needs had taken her time...

A terrible thought popped into her mind. Hernandez. No surely not...

Before her, Jose continued to grin like a cat that got the cream. "I see the light of realisation in your eyes, daughter," he said. "And then the shadow of self-doubt." He stood, leaning back against the table behind him. "I know it has been hard for you," he said, eyebrows lowering in a parody of sympathy. "The war disrupted the prime of your youth. Suitors have been scarce in the wake of our country's trials. But! A most excellent proposal of marriage has been made. General Hernandez visited me this morning."

Miren clutched the arms of her chair, her knuckles going white with the force of her grip. Her breathing shortened, a cold sweat breaking out across her body.

"He has asked for your hand in marriage." Her father clapped again, delight in his voice. "You are to be a wife! And soon. I must say the man was rather impatient to make things official." He paused, chuckling to himself. "I guess I was the same with your mother... But I have insisted on at least a year of engagement, it is only proper."

He prattled on, something about her mother's joy at the news, the cathedral he preferred, the date of the engagement announcement, but Miren wasn't listening.

She felt as though her head had been stuffed with wool, the world was spinning, the light fading, the walls pressing in on her once again.

"No!" The word was louder, sharper than she'd intended. But it had the desired effect. Jose stopped mid-sentence, turning to face Miren, the joy fading from his face.

"No? What do you mean 'no'?" His eyes had darkened, and tension pinched his lips together.

Miren swallowed. "I cannot marry General Hernandez, Father. It is not a good match."

Jose frowned, staring at his daughter. "Why not? He is the most eligible man in San Sebastian. A powerful general in Franco's regime, here to oversee our city. He has a direct line to our illustrious leader. Darling? Do you think yourself unworthy?"

He could not have been more mistaken. Miren shook her head. "Father, please. General Hernandez is a Nationalist, he stands for everything that our people fought against. How can I marry him?"

"Shh!" Jose hissed at her. "Are you a fool? That is dangerous talk. Basque governance is long gone. Spain is united under the new rule. Whatever we may have hoped for... that is the past. We do not speak of it!"

Miren curled in on herself against the onslaught of his words, the power of his anger. "You should be grateful that General Hernandez is willing to overlook your past... associations."

"Anders was not an 'association'. I loved him!"

"Enough!" Jose roared. "I will not hear that man's name, not under my roof.

"You are talking like a fool, and I will not allow it. With this marriage, you place yourself above suspicion. Your choices in the civil war are absolved. And you will have a life of luxury and privilege. Miren, you will marry General Hernandez. I order it."

"Then you are damning me to a life of sadness," Miren cried, coming to her feet.

Jose's eyes bored into her, his face a mask of rage. "You forget yourself, girl." He ground from deep within his chest. "You forget the danger you brought to this home, to this family. Fraternising with that politician. You ran away and aligned yourself with the Basque. Do you realise how your mother and I fretted? How I have continued to worry, never knowing if the sharp edge of consequence will come knocking on your door?

"You have seen the executions. The people who were dragged from their homes to face their choices."

"You believed it too," Miren whispered.

"But unlike you, I see what is before me now. Enough indulgence, I have tolerated it long enough. I have already given the general my blessing. You will marry General Hernandez and secure your future and your safety. Don't you see? As his wife, you will be untouchable."

Tears slipped down her cheeks as a sob ratcheted up from her very soul. "You have killed me," she cried, turning and racing from the room.

"No, daughter," Jose shouted at her retreating back. "I have saved your life."

There were more words, shouted from his desk into the dimly lit private quarters of the hotel, but Miren didn't hear them. She fled up the stairs into her chambers, securing the door behind her before throwing herself onto her bed and giving in to the sobs of sorrow that refused to be contained.

As the night drew its cloak over the streets of San Sebastian, Miren paced hot and frustrated, to her window, throwing it open to the sea breezes that blew in from the bay beyond. Salt thick and warm, the air brushed over her skin, bringing the scent of the waves, the promise of freedom just out of her reach. She slumped against the windowsill, savouring the cooling air, the smell of dust rising from the overheated streets below. There would be no reasoning with her father. There was no one who would come and save her.

She was trapped. There was no choice. Despite her hatred and fear of General Hernandez, Miren was going to be his wife.

TWENTY-THREE

MIREN

The ballroom was warm and stuffy, despite its size. Her father had lit a wood fire in the grand fireplace, the marble frame shining in the flickering flames. The fire was more for show than practicality, but her father always insisted on the flames, especially for Christmas. It had been Jose's idea to combine these events.

Around her, people milled, dressed in gaudy finery. Painted lips open wide in tittering laughter, heads haloed in cigar smoke. Waiters carried trays of bubbling champan, the Spanish version of champagne from Catalonia, in crystal flutes, appearing and disappearing from the kitchen beyond, a constant circle of refreshment.

Miren ran her hands down her own glossy gown. Pale pink satin, figure-hugging, slippery. Fiddling with the string of pearls at her neck she stepped forward into the room. Immediately her father appeared from the crowd, hands out in welcome, eyes shining.

"My princess," he crooned. "You are a picture."

"Gracias, Papá.' Miren allowed him to kiss her on both

cheeks. A small frown formed between his eyes. "Chin up, daughter, this is your engagement, the start of your wedding celebrations. General Hernandez will be overcome when he sees you. You are a vision."

Miren swallowed, eyes tracking across the room in search of her fiancé. She found him easily. His broad, squat frame and straight back commanded attention. Around him the men of the city gathered, each making important conversation, hoping to gain favour with Franco's favourite general. She suppressed a shiver, glancing away.

"Come, daughter, nerves are natural," her father continued. "Hernandez is a powerful man, but he chose you, remember..."

"Husband." Maria appeared at her father's elbow. "The waiters are asking which wine to open next."

"Ah, yes yes. Thank you, my dear."

Her father turned, striding for the kitchens. Miren took a bracing breath. How her father had sourced so much wine for this night baffled her. With the industry still struggling to recover from Franco's conquest, and trade with France halted by war, wine had become a luxury. Despite that Jose had found a way to impress his future son-in-law. Maria came to Miren's side, hooking their arms together. "Don't forget to smile," she reminded Miren and walked her across the room to Hernandez.

He turned to her, dark eyes gleaming, lips twisting in a dangerous smile. His hand flashed out, gripping the soft flesh of her bare upper arm, fingers digging painfully into her skin. She would bruise, she was sure.

"Gentlemen," he said grandly. "My fiancée, Miren Perez."

Ridiculously, the men encircling Hernandez clapped, one even gave a cheer.

Hernandez eyed her and puffed on his cigar. "Your father has done a stellar job with this party," he said. "Señora Perez, you have a beautiful business here.'

"Thank you," Maria said, bobbing a curtsy. "I know my husband wanted this to be just right for Miren... and you."

"Of course." Hernandez turned back to the assembled crowd of fawning gentlemen, dismissing Maria with the turn of his back. His fingers remained clamped around Miren's flesh, holding her close, preventing escape.

The evening passed in this fashion. Hernandez regaled the men who surrounded him with stories of the war and his great victories, while Miren stood beside him, a beautiful silent statue.

Sometime after tapas the small band started a more upbeat song and couples began to make their way to the small dance floor space. Miren's stomach flipped. Would Hernandez expect her to dance with him? The thought of his body, pressed close to hers, swaying to music, made her feel physically sick.

Feeling light-headed from the wine, Miren excused herself for the bathroom.

"We will dance," Hernandez announced. "When you return."

Miren nodded, knees feeling weak, and made her exit. As she made her way across the ballroom, she could feel his stare, like an arrow between her shoulder blades.

At the sink she splashed cool water over her face, careful not to ruin her meticulously placed make-up. Staring at herself in the mirror, she worked to slow her breathing, to return some sense of calm to her body. It was no use. The heat of the ballroom, the cloying scent of cigar smoke, the cruel sparkle in Hernandez's eyes, how had she got herself into this mess?

She'd dallied too long, she knew. Bracing herself she headed back for the ballroom.

And walked into a ghost.

The band finished a song with a flourish, the music giving way to applause and cheers from the happy dancers. And Miren's eyes locked with his across the room.

Anders.

He stood in the middle of the space, a secret smile on his plump lips. His face was thinner, his eyebrows unkempt, fine lines around his eyes. But it was him.

Her heart flew into a pounding race. Wary, unsure of her step, Miren advanced towards him. He stepped up to her, taking her hand as if nothing had happened between them.

"May I have this dance?"

Her voice wouldn't work, her lips couldn't move. Joy flushed her senses even as rage pulsed on her blood. It had been four years since he'd abandoned her in Bilbao. Four years without a single letter, phone call, anything. Four years not knowing what had become of the man she loved. If he had been killed in the battle of Barcelona, if he had been taken captive. If he ever thought of her...

How was Anders here?

Mind frozen from shock, Miren nodded and allowed Anders to guide her to the dance floor. Hernandez would likely be furious that she danced with another man. But in that moment, Miren had no choice. Following Anders was all she could do.

The band struck up a new beat, not slow, not fast. Anders pulled her into his embrace, effortlessly moving her through the steps. Somehow her body complied and she moved to the music smoothly.

"How?" she managed to croak. "I..."

Anders twirled her gently, then brought her close, his lips to her ear.

"I have missed you every day."

Miren jerked back, body stopping still, completely losing the rhythm of the song.

Anders stared into her eyes, not looking away. "I longed to reach out to you—"

"No." The word came out louder than she intended, flat

and hollow. Then her hands began to shake, a terrible trembling rattling along her limbs. The room seemed to press in, the heat of the fire crackled and snapped, the air too thick to breathe. She had to get out.

"No," she repeated, spinning on her heel and making for the door once again.

Guests glanced at her in surprise as she passed, but Miren didn't care. As the door slammed shut behind her she broke into a run, shoes slipping dangerously on the polished tiles of the reception hall. She did not slow at the front door, did not stop to collect her coat, just strode out into the icy December night. Her feet sloshed in a puddle on the road, the air around her hazy with misting rain. The chill shocked her chest, causing her to take a sharp intake of breath, the cold of winter coating her lungs. She crossed the street, pace clipping, not stopping until she reached the rusty barrier that lined the Urumea River. There she gripped the railing, leaning out over the edge and opened her mouth and screamed. Her cry was caught on the wind, swallowed up and whisked away out towards the bay beyond. Met with the echoing silence of the night Miren stood, chest heaving desperately as she watched the waves crash powerfully against the rocky outcrop where the river met the sea. A glint of light caught her eye. She looked down at her left hand and the sparkling diamond that encircled her ring finger. Fury, sudden and intense shot through her. She gripped the diamond ring, wrenching it from her finger. Raising it above her head she braced to fling it over the railing to the currents below.

"I wouldn't recommend that."

His voice was soft, steady.

Miren twisted around, hands coming in front of her in a gesture of self-protection.

Anders stood in the soft moonlit street, a dark umbrella shrouding him from the rain.

He stepped forward.

"Stop!" Miren cried, hand shooting out to hold him at bay.

"I only wish to offer you the umbrella. This rain will ruin your hair."

Miren's heartbeat pulsed, a drip of water running down from her forehead to cup her chin. Too late to save her appearance, but Anders stepped forward anyway, and she let him. Stopping a pace before her, he offered the umbrella. She took it, her eyes never leaving his face.

He didn't step back. Neither did she.

The silence stretched, Miren staring into a face at once so familiar, so beloved. And now, so confusing.

Her red-painted lips parted. "I don't understand," she managed.

Anders blinked slowly and sighed. "I am sorry," he began. "These past years have not been easy. I should have approached you differently. This..." he gestured back towards the hotel. "This was too much."

Miren stared at him, mouth working, mind rejecting his words.

"You are hurt, I understand," he continued. "Miren, if it could have been any other way, I would never have left you. You have to believe me."

"I don't *have* to do anything!" Miren squeaked. "You left me alone in Bilbao. You should have taken me with you."

"Barcelona was not safe—"

"You never wrote! I heard nothing, nothing. The city fell and you were gone. I thought you were—" She broke off, the sorrow and confusion breaking through her resolve. Sobs heaved from her heart as she turned away, unable to face him any longer.

She stood there as the rain of a winter storm fell in a circle around her, tears streaking down her face, silent. Alone.

A small scuff of footfall, warm hands on her bare upper arms. A soft, gentle voice. "I am sorry."

Miren stiffened, pulling away from his touch and turning back to face him.

"Why are you here? This is the celebration of my engagement."

Anders eyed her, she saw his mouth twist in disbelief at her words. She had just been about to throw away her ring after all. But he didn't say anything about that.

"I am working with France."

"What do you mean, 'working' with France?"

"Information gathering mostly, against the German invasion.

"I fled there, after Barcelona. But they were not happy to see us. There were some... bad years. But then the war in Europe started and things changed. I had something to offer the French, intel mostly. And I was able to get back to my beloved Spain. But not back to you." As he spoke he raised his hands, reaching for her.

"Please," Miren said. "Don't."

Anders nodded sadly, returning his arms to his side. "I know this is bad timing. I didn't plan to approach you, at least not tonight. But when you walked into the room, nothing else mattered."

"Why are you here? You know this is my father's hotel. You must have realised I would be here."

"I was to meet a contact ."

"A contact? You mean for France?"

"And for Spain."

Miren stared at him in shock. To think there was a resistance network, more, that some part of it was operating from her very home.

"The people I work with in France need a way to get messages to the British Embassy. My contact works for the

British Consul in Bilbao. He is staying at your father's hotel. You are perfectly placed to pass messages—"

"Stop, stop!" Miren held up a hand, realisation seizing her guts. She knew the guests well, and Anders had just given away his inside man. A small, brisk fellow, with a genuine smile. Mr Chalmers was the Attaché for the British Consul. "You say too much and forget I know this hotel. Why are you involving someone else in your schemes?"

"It is dangerous for me here. I am known. The Basque politician. Anti-Nationalist. It was a grave risk to come here tonight. To come to you."

Miren shook her head, "That may be true. But it doesn't excuse you. I thought you were dead."

She hadn't meant to give him hope, but obviously, something in her reply buoyed him and he stepped forward, suddenly eager. "Please, Miren, give me a chance to explain. If we could just sit together..."

Reaching up she wiped the rain from her cheek. Cringing at the smudge of mascara she was sure to have cast across her face, she brought her eyes up to meet his.

"How?" She knew she looked a mess, unhinged, distressed. Yet despite herself, Miren was curious. She wanted to know.

"There is a coffee shop, in town. I am there every Friday morning. Routine is good in my work... You could meet me there."

"I can't just visit coffee shops as I please."

"You are soon to be married," Anders said, voice soft. "You have reason to be out shopping..."

His words felt like a slap and Miren felt herself pull back from him. "That is why you are here then?" she said. "To scuttle my chance at happiness? You didn't care before. For four years I didn't matter. But now that I am engaged—"

"Miren—"

"No, no, I understand. It has always been the way hasn't it,

Anders? When you need me, I am there. When you don't, you disappear."

"Miren, please. I longed to contact you. These years apart, they have been torture."

A laugh, bitter and harsh, scraped from her throat. "Really?" she said, voice dripping with derision. "Tell me, Anders, how long have you been back in Spain?"

Anders glanced away, "That's not relevant– "

"No? Strange, I think it is very relevant. See, I want to know how long you have been working with the French and British across San Sebastian. And why you came here, tonight of all nights?"

"I told you, my contact."

"It seems a very big coincidence."

"It isn't like that." His voice was small, hurt. Some part of Miren mellowed then, as she looked at this man who had owned her whole heart. Who she'd believed dead and cried for.

"What is in these messages? What work are you doing?" she asked.

Anders looked up. "Transport. I can't say any more. I won't risk you further than I must. But, Miren, the French are key to the freedom of Spain."

"What? They are at war."

"They are, for now. But if we help them in their war, then maybe, maybe they will help us in turn."

"Anders," Miren sighed, "our war is over. We lost. Spain belongs to Franco. That dream... that dream has passed."

"Perhaps, but what I am doing? It is still the right thing. And I need you, Miren. I need your help."

Miren stared at him in the darkness and saw the hope and belief on his face. And the love she'd held for this man came flooding back, she could not help it.

Taking a deep breath she said, "I will think about it."

Anders' eyes snapped to hers. "Meet me at Cafe Més Que, 11 am on Friday. I will be there, I promise."

She nodded, handed him back his umbrella and moved away. Her legs felt shaky and unsure as she made her way to her father's hotel. She did not look back at Anders, not once. At the hotel door, she paused, slipping her ring on her finger before pressing her weight against the bulky door and returning to the familiar embrace of her home.

The party continued to rage beyond the entrance to the ballroom, but Miren made her way upstairs to her chambers.

She had a lot to think about.

Anders, the man she loved more than herself, the man she'd left her family for. She'd feared him dead. But without confirmation, she'd been left in limbo. She'd prayed for news. Fought an inner battle for acceptance. Yet he lived. And he wanted to see her.

It was dangerous, what he was doing. Messages between allies. Spain was neutral in this European war, but Miren was no fool. She'd seen the Nazi officers strolling the beach on their leave from the war and had heard Franco's messages of support for Hitler in the press. Spain would turn on Anders and his rebels in a heartbeat. Anything to gain favour with the power of Germany.

It was a risk to meet with a man who worked against Franco, who actively worked for the resistance. And to pass on messages? It might sound trivial, but it could land her in jail, or worse. And why should she take such a chance? For whom? Her lover who had abandoned her? So he could find closure, and ease his guilt?

It was foolish to get involved. It was not her war or her problem. And Anders was no longer her responsibility.

Yet, as she slipped between the cool sheets of her bed Miren already knew. She would be in that cafe on Friday.

Because, despite it all, despite the years of questions, of

thwarted grief, the sense of abandonment, a flame of love still burned for Anders, a dream of a life together tucked tight within her heart. And he believed in her, needed her. As he fought for the freedom of Spain and her people, he still needed Miren. She had stepped up once before, worked to save the children of her region from Franco's army. She would do it again.

And maybe, just maybe, this time it would set her free.

TWENTY-FOUR

MIREN

Cafe Més Que was loud, the scrape of the wooden chairs echoing through the space. The waiter placed a cup of coffee before her with a nod and a smile. Miren stared at the cup. Her chest was tight, her breathing ragged. Realising she was picking at her fingers, she clamped her hands together in her lap, closing her eyes and willing herself to still. Opening them again she glanced at the clock on the wall. She was early.

Trying to distract herself she picked up her coffee, hands shaking so violently that she sloshed the dark liquid over the rim of the cup. She put the cup back down with a clank and gripped the table, fighting for calm.

The door opened. The water-laden air off the coast rushed in to mingle with the heat of the cafe, the scent of salt and coffee assailing her nose together.

He strode into the cafe, black suit, newspaper tucked beneath his arm. After a brief exchange with the waiter, he came to sit behind her, back to the wall. Miren sat ridged.

"You came." His words were soft, warm and soothing. Miren nodded. Cleared her throat and moved to turn to him.

"Don't."

She froze. Of course, this was a secret meeting.

She folded her hands in her lap and listened to the rustle of his newspaper as he unfolded it to read. Silence stretched; the scent of his skin, his musky cologne, drifted across her senses.

"I have a letter for you to pass to Mr Chalmers." His voice drifted gently to her ears. "And also a letter for you. From me. I will bend down now and place them in your handbag. I hope you will read it, and understand my feelings for you."

"I might," she whispered over her shoulder, before reaching out and clutching her coffee cup. Shakily she brought the cup to her lips and sipped. The liquid had cooled, but it was still good to have something to do with her fidgety hands.

She heard him move and felt his breath on the back of her calf. Glancing down she watched him slip a large manilla envelope into her bag, a small one with it. Then a touch. So fleeting she could not be sure she didn't imagine it. Warm fingers wrapped briefly around her stockinged ankle. The touch was gone as fast as it came, the skin of her ankle suddenly cool. Then the scrape of his chair, the bustle of his movement.

"I hope I see you next week."

He strode across the cafe and back out onto the street. Miren sat unmoving, mind reeling, heart pounding. She stared at her cooling coffee and listened to the chorus of chatter that enveloped the cafe, the tick of the clock, the hiss of the coffee machine steam. Then she stood, gathered her bag and left.

Back at the hotel, Miren slipped behind the reception desk and quickly scanned the guest register. She made her way up the stairs towards the guest rooms. Stepping lightly, she crossed the carpeted hall tiptoeing to door thirty-three. Mr Chalmers' rooms. Her chest tightened. Her breath panting as she glanced back down the hall, checking for prying eyes. The hall remained empty. Bracing her muscles against her trembling nerves she bent down and slipped the large envelope under the door. Knocking three times she pivoted on her heel and headed for her own rooms as fast as she could while retaining her dignity. Inside she pressed her door closed, turning the key in the lock with a loud click. A swoosh of air escaped her lungs and relief flooded her limbs as she leaned back against her door, taking a moment to steady herself. Then, kicking off her heels she padded across the soft, comforting carpet and took a seat at her bureau. Carefully she pried the envelope of Anders' letter open. Reading his words her soul lifted, and she knew her heart had forgiven Anders the moment she'd seen him, alive and well in her father's ballroom.

The next Friday came swiftly and Miren could not wait to make her way to the coffee shop and the man she loved waiting inside. A fresh pile of envelopes sat fatly on the reception desk, as Miren descended from her room. On the top, white and gleaming in the light from above, was a letter stamped with the British Embassy seal. Mr Chalmers' response to Anders. Miren swallowed, moved to the desk and gathered up the mail.

"I'll just drop these to the post office," she said, voice breathless with anxiety. The trip to the post office a ruse to separate the secret correspondence.

Maria looked up in surprise. "Daughter? What has gotten into you?"

Miren halted. Did her mother suspect something? What had given her away?

She raised an eyebrow in question, unable to trust her voice as her throat closed over.

"It's only 7 am child," Maria chided, laughter in her voice. "The post office doesn't open until nine. Come have some breakfast, you are skin and bone these days..."

Relief and embarrassment washed over Miren and she allowed herself to be led to the kitchen for toast and eggs. She'd been so caught up in her plan to visit the cafe, her head so filled with the thought of Anders, that she'd completely forgotten the practicalities of the day.

Crunching her toast, Miren watched the clock as its hands ticked slowly towards opening time.

At the cafe, Miren managed to sip her coffee without spilling it. When Anders appeared at the door, her heart leapt, but her body remained still.

"He wrote back," she whispered, his presence behind her radiating energy into her very flesh. "It is in my bag." When he bent behind her to fish the envelope from her bag, his breath ran along her leg. Another touch, this time to her elbow, a gentle squeeze, a memory of more, so long ago.

As he left Miren released a long, heavy sigh, a small smile curving her lips in anticipation of the next week, and the next, and the next.

TWENTY-FIVE

MIREN

The winter days passed swiftly, dark, cold weeks punctuated by the promise of Anders and their secret meetings. But with the spring came a pause. Mr Chalmers returned to Bilbao, removing the need for Miren's role as courier. And Anders stopped appearing at the cafe. For weeks on end he was absent. Miren kept up her routine, hoping for a stolen moment with him, however small, but with each Friday that passed, her heart sank a little lower.

Had he moved on once again? Set off for a distant city, or country, driven by his own needs and goals? Left her once more without saying goodbye?

By the time the blossom of April arrived, Miren was distraught. Not only had all contact with Anders ceased, but the day of her nuptials was approaching fast. So distracted had she been by her little dalliance with the resistance, she'd ignored the pressing matter of her wedding. She needed to arrange a dress fitting, decide on her jewellery, approve the cake... Her mother pressed her daily, asking for details and offering to help. But Miren had shimmied and twisted and avoided. It was a reality she didn't wish to face, an inevitable event she could not avoid. A choice she had to make.

And Anders was nowhere to be seen.

Had some part of her believed he would rescue her? That at the last moment, he would gather her up and whisk her away from San Sebastian and Hernandez and this union she feared so deeply? Had she believed Anders would be her husband, as she'd dreamed so many years ago?

Foolish girl, she should know better.

Yet the dream was there. In her quiet moments, working at the reception desk or helping her mother with the management of the hotel, her mind would drift. Her perfect white wedding dress, the beautiful cathedral and standing at the altar in a tailored black suit, Anders, his smile open and warm and all for her. It was a deception she knew, but the daydream gave her comfort and strength. And pain.

On the first truly warm morning of the season, Miren awoke in a slick of sweat. Visions of Anders and Hernandez had haunted her sleep, the two men blending into one awful amalgamation of their worse traits. Rough and cruel Hernandez, absent and selfish Anders.

And Miren decided. Despite it all, the doubt, the hurt, the fear, she wanted something for herself. She would not allow Anders to be done with her, not this time.

She dressed carefully, applying her make-up with extra care. Gathering up the day's mail she made her way to the cafe. It was not a Friday; she was actioning the emergency protocol Anders had promised would work. She saw the momentary look of surprise on the waiter's face and knew her ruse had worked. Within the hour Anders appeared, eyes scanning worriedly, the obligatory newspaper pressed beneath his arm.

So, he hadn't left the city after all.

His step was faster, the snap of his newspaper more

pronounced. The tables had turned, and now he was the anxious one.

"What has happened?" he whispered, voice tight.

"Nothing," Miren replied, a small smile of revenge curling her lips. She was surprised by how good this felt.

"Then why are you here?"

"It has been four weeks—"

"Miren, I have been busy with other details. You shouldn't be here."

She didn't reply, allowing the silence to stretch between them.

She heard the rustle of his newspaper, and the exhale of exasperation as he shifted in his seat.

She waited a moment longer, then whispered, "Midnight tonight, at the maid's entrance to the hotel. Be there, Anders. Or you will never see me again."

Miren stood, collected up her handbag and made for the door.

She did not look back.

He met her under a silver moon, pale and narrow in the warm spring night. Miren stepped from the maid's door and gripped the lapels of his jacket, pulling him towards her bodily and pressing her lips to his. He resisted, but only for a moment before his muscles melted against her, their bodies aligning, at once familiar but also foreign and exciting. Breaking the kiss Miren eyed him in the moonlight. His face had darkened, his gaze intense. Turning, she drew him behind her leading him up the stairs to her room. They moved swiftly, steps light on the plush hallway carpet. In her chambers she shut the door behind them, locking it. It would not do to be disturbed. She moved to the bed, her silk robe slipping from her shoulders as she walked. Sitting on the bed's edge she pulled the last clip from her hair, allowing her curls to fall in a cascade over her now naked shoulders and breasts.

Anders crossed the room to her. He stood between her legs, eyes dark with desire, lips slightly parted, a question on his face.

She answered with her body. Hands gripping his shoulders she pulled him down to her, shimmying back on the mattress until they lay entwined.

"I never forgot your touch," she breathed into his neck, the stubble of his cheek rough against her softer flesh.

"I've dreamed of the taste of you each day."

"Not tonight," she whispered and buried her face in his chest before laying back and giving herself to him fully.

Soft light filtered through the pastel of her curtains. Miren lay, limbs heavy with satisfaction, legs twisted with the sheets. Moving languidly, she rolled onto her side and watched the speckled light that danced across Anders' bare chest. Reaching over she wound a finger through the dark curling hair that spread thick and dense across his torso. Smiling down at her Anders caught her hand, bringing it to his mouth to kiss.

"I should go," he said.

She shuffled closer, resting her head on his shoulder and linking a leg around his. He was right, but she was not quite ready, not yet.

Warm in his embrace she breathed in the musky scent of him, eyes drifting closed.

"I will end my engagement," she said softly. "I will do it today, as soon as I can."

Beneath her Anders shifted, drawing her from him, to stare at her face.

"You cannot do that, Miren. Your connection to Hernandez is useful."

"But the wedding is only weeks away. I can't marry him. I want to be with you."

Anders' lips twisted in amusement. "You think I care if you marry? It makes no difference to me."

Irritation shot through Miren. She sat up stiffly, pulling the sheet up to cover her nakedness.

"You want me to marry him?" The words croaked from her.

"It is best if you do."

"You want me to vow my life to him, before God? For what?" She turned sharply, piercing him with her stare.

"I don't care what God thinks either," Anders said smoothly, sitting up beside her. He ran a warm hand over her bare skin, but the touch was no longer welcome. Miren shrugged him off, anger and hurt building within her.

She heard him sigh, deep and heavy. "Miren, you know my divorce from Lucia was never finalised. Even if it had been, by Franco's new laws, I could not remarry. There is no path for us in this Spain. That is why I must keep fighting, to make a Spain where we can live together and be free.

"Your engagement, and marriage to Hernandez, it keeps you safe. If you break off the engagement now there will be a scandal, you will be vulnerable. Your past associations will be called into question. He would harm you, Miren. You know he would. There will be a time for us..."

He fell silent. But his words rang in Miren's ears, an echo of her father's as he forced her to accept Hernandez's proposal. How could her life have come to this? To a place with no choice, or self-determination? Miren dashed hot tears from her eyes.

"I wish things were different," she whispered.

"I know, I do too. We were so close... But, we have won democracy before, we can do it again. What I am doing, it is bigger than you and me. It is for Spain. It will make a difference—"

"What is it that you are doing?" Miren said suddenly, cutting him off. "What are you 'transporting' that is so important? More important than me?"

"Miren, it is best if you remain ignorant—"

"Tell me!" she demanded, shifting away on the bed so she could fix him with her eyes.

They stared at each other across the bed, eyes locked, the soft light of day strengthening around them. And Anders relented. "Allies. Soldiers from England, Canada and America. Men who have been shot down over France. We are a network, a trail of supporters from the south of Belgium down across the Pyrenees. The men are snuck here, then it is my job to get them safely out of Spain."

The breath left Miren's body, she felt her jaw drop open in shock. "You are rescuing soldiers? How? What?" Terror, hot and raw surged through her body, causing her to begin to shake. "Anders, if you were caught—"

"I won't get caught." He moved across the bed, drawing her into his embrace. "Franco is playing both sides. Spain is neutral, but if the soldiers are discovered they are turned over to the Nazis. We know what fate would await them. I have to help."

Miren swallowed, body going limp as she allowed herself to be held.

As Anders smoothed her hair down her back he continued. "Messages come to me when a new group has successfully made it to San Sebastian. Then I work with the British Consul in Bilbao or Madrid to arrange transport out of Spain, to Gibraltar. Either by sea, or land.

"It is safer than other work I have done for France..."

Miren shook her head slowly. Trembling from shock and fear she pulled back from Anders' arms.

"It is not our war..."

"It is injustice, and it is a way to fight for what is right. Then our time will come."

"Anders, we lost. Spain belongs to Franco—"

"For now, yes. But we cannot stand by while other countries face the same fate, or worse. Hitler says that he won't invade Spain. But can we be sure that is true? His ambition seems far greater. If we help the Allies, we help the fight for freedom across Europe. And the fight for freedom here in Spain too."

Miren watched his face, saw the fervour that lit in his eyes. "How long?"

Anders blinked, surprised. "How long?"

"How long must I be wife to that man? How long until you rescue me?"

His eyes softened and he took her hands in his. "I do not know, my love. But Hitler is overstretched. The allies are strong. We must help the soldiers until the end."

"And then?"

"And then I will come for you."

Miren watched him in the dawning light and felt the weight of disappointment bearing down on her heart.

She did not want to wait. Did not want to be a part of this global fight for justice. She wanted safety and security. She wanted Anders.

Once again she faced a choice. To follow the word of the man she loved, to choose him, against everything else.

And once again, she did.

"I will marry Hernandez. I will play my role. But, Anders?"

"Yes, my love?"

"Do not abandon me again. Whatever happens, this time, you tell me. You take me with you."

"I will," he promised.

And Miren believed him.

TWENTY-SIX

MIREN

Miren dragged herself through the breakfast service. Each guest seemed more aggressive, and more demanding than usual.

"My coffee is cold."

"This omelette is flat."

Plastering an accommodating smile on her face she went through the motions, trying to keep her mind distracted from Anders and his revelation.

Rescuing soldiers. Technically they weren't enemy soldiers, true, but the risk was still great. Anders had mentioned Franco's desire to play both sides in this European conflict, and Miren had seen enough newspaper reports to know it was true.

Just last week there had been a report of two British men being captured in the foothills of the Pyrenees and turned over to German-occupied France. And now that Hitler was making noises about moving further into French territory, Spain would only be more keen to court the alliance.

If Anders was caught...

Miren shook her head quickly, forcing the thought away.

For years she had believed him dead. The only man she had ever loved. When she'd seen him standing before her in her father's ballroom she'd nearly fainted. She'd hated him, at first. Knowing he had been alive, and in Spain, but hadn't contacted her.

But the love was always there, just below the surface. And it wasn't long before that won her back.

Last night in his arms Miren had surrendered the last of her anger and fully embraced a future with Anders. She hadn't expected him to ask her to still marry Hernandez. In the heat of their lovemaking, the promise of their future had been offered and sealed.

Anders had explained, but it still broke her heart.

She would have to trust him. Her heart could do no less.

Collecting the final plates from the breakfast room, smears of greasy fat and sauce congealing on the white porcelain, Miren made her way to the kitchen and wondered if she could sneak up to her rooms for a nap before lunch. Her midnight activities had left little time for sleep. Fatigue only made her nerves feel more frayed. No doubt a nap would set her anxious heart to rest.

Leaving the plates to the kitchen staff she washed her hands before making her way to reception to check if her mother needed her for anything before slipping away.

But the moment she rounded the doorway her heart seized in her chest.

Hernandez stood at the desk chatting amiably with her mother, his wide frame imposing on the space around him, sucking away the very air in the room. Or so it seemed to Miren.

Instinctively she froze, hands fluttering to her chest.

What was he doing here?

Did he know about Anders and her meeting the night before?

Or worse, did he know about the transport?

Maria looked up and saw her hovering in the doorway.

"Miren, dear! Look who has come by to see you." Her voice was high and gay, not a hint of concern.

Hernandez turned slowly, his dark eyes rolling over her body. Miren swallowed, running her hands swiftly down her sides to dry the clammy sweat that now collected on her palms.

She smiled but knew the gesture did not reach her eyes.

"My darling," Hernandez said, spreading his arms wide and crossing the room towards her. Miren stood still, unable to move, mind racing, heart pounding in fear.

He came to her and took hold of her shoulders, pressing a kiss to each cheek.

"It is good to see you."

"What are you doing here?"

Hernandez frowned theatrically, heavy brows creasing in confusion. "Does a man need a reason to call on his beautiful fiancée?"

"But it is a work day..."

"Ah, I see. It is as I feared." He turned back towards Maria and in a loud stage whisper confessed, "I was right."

Maria positively beamed at the man, hands fussing with some documents as she grinned.

Hernandez turned back to Miren. "You must accept my sincere apologies, my beautiful Miren," he said. "Clearly I have neglected you. I've been so busy with the affairs of Spain that I have not made time for my most precious jewel. So, today I have taken the morning off. And you and I will be going for a little treat."

Trepidation dried her throat. Miren glanced up at her mother. "But Mother needs me here."

"Nonsense," Maria chided gently. "I can manage just fine for one day. Go and enjoy some time with your fiancé. It is not long until the wedding, you two will have plans to finalise."

"See?" Hernandez said. "Come, let's get your coat."

He led her out into a brisk spring morning, the haze off the bay light and sweet with moisture. Miren focused on the cobbled paths before her, working to keep her breathing under control, the click of her heels so loud it jangled her nerves still further.

"Where are we going?"

"A cafe," Hernandez answered, eyeing her slyly. "I think you will like it."

Her guts turned to water.

A cafe.

He knew. About Anders and their meetings, about the messages.

Oh God.

As they approached the square where the Cafe Més Que was nestled, Miren's knees began to wobble, the sweat of fear beading on her brow despite the temperate morning air.

She should run. Turn tail and flee.

But where?

She didn't know where Anders was staying and had no way to contact him other than the cafe.

As the little shop front came into view she slowed her pace. Perhaps the cafe owner would realise, would send for help...

Perhaps Anders would come.

She began to turn for the cafe and Hernandez stopped before her.

"Where are you going?" he asked.

Miren turned, subtly wiping a drip of perspiration from her temple. "The cafe," she gestured feebly.

"No, my darling. Do you think I would take you to such a lowly establishment?" A sickly smile on his face, he took her arm at the elbow. "I have a far grander location in mind. Come, it is not much further."

He led her on, but Miren felt no relief. Her mind continued to churn with questions, concerns and possibilities.

They passed the town hall and the old offices she'd once

worked at with Anders. They trailed along the boulevard of political offices, the government buildings opulent and imposing with their sandstone arches and shining brass door knobs. Eventually, they came to the Plaza de Gipuzkoa and a small cafe situated between the grand buildings of the square. A series of neat, white-painted iron chairs sat on the cobblestones. Men in black suits read oversized newspapers while women with neat curls chatted over cups of coffee.

Hernandez led her to a spare table and pulled out the chair for her.

"It is a nice morning to be outside, I think." He said, before taking a seat himself.

Miren settled herself in the chair, eyes flicking around the elegant space. It was a beautiful location, the hotel at her back rose large and shining, while the streetscape offered a view of the beautiful central architecture of San Sebastian.

A small man in white serving attire appeared.

"Two coffees, black. And some of that sponge I enjoyed yesterday, but only for me. My fiancée isn't eating treats this close to our big day," Hernandez said, not even asking Miren what she might enjoy.

Miren watched as he arranged his bulk on the small chair, and wondered if the spindly legs would snap beneath his weight. They were stronger than they looked, she guessed.

"So," Hernandez began, leaning forward, fixing her with his stare. "How has the planning been going? With only a few weeks to go, I expect all is in order?"

Miren worked to find some moisture in a mouth parched by fear, gave up and simply nodded.

"Come, my darling, tell me. Do not mistake my commitment to my work for disinterest. I want to know all you have arranged for our vows at the Buen Pastor Cathedral."

Buen Pastor Cathedral. Stunning, crisp sandstone walls,

complete with gothic spirals, traditional. As a girl, she'd dreamed of marrying beneath those sacred vaulted domes. As a woman, she only wished to run. She blinked rapidly, fighting for composure.

Fortunately, the waiter returned, a tray of coffee and sponge floating before him.

"Thank you," Miren whispered, clutching her cup in a white-knuckle grip and taking a sip of the scorching hot liquid. Its bracing bitterness fortified her. Replacing her cup on the table she straightened. What could she say? In truth, she'd arranged only the bare minimum. Some part of her hoping and praying that God would intervene and stop this whole event from happening.

"Most details are in hand," she lied, fighting to urge to cross herself in apology to God. "But I am afraid that my work at the hotel has meant a rush of finalisations."

"Come now," Hernandez said, scooping a large, cream-laden portion of sponge from his plate. "You have been out and about all over town for months. You can't expect me to believe you have not got the whole day planned to perfection." He eyed her over the spoon and then sucked the creamy cake into his mouth.

Miren's hand began to shake.

Out all over town.

Had he been watching her? Or was this simply a throwaway comment?

She offered a wobbly smile and took another sip of her coffee. "Well, yes, I suppose I have done rather more than I have said. But Mother has warned me there is much still to do. I simply do not wish to be complacent."

Hernandez chewed slowly, then scooped more sponge into his mouth. "Perhaps fewer visits to that poor little cafe then?" he said.

Heat flushed her cheeks, and she gripped her hands together, clammy and hot.

"Oh, it is just an easy little place," she said, breathless.

"Indeed. But, I wouldn't want you to forget your real mission."

Mission? Miren's chest clamped tight around her lungs. He had been watching her... But what did he know? Surely if he knew the truth about Anders he would have had her arrested? What was this little game he was playing?

"I—"

"I am merely teasing you, my darling," Hernandez interrupted. "I am sure you and Maria have everything in hand. Though as your husband-to-be I would prefer you keep to the most reputable establishments in future. Can we agree to that?"

"Of course," Miren croaked, smiling weakly.

"Excellent, now finish up your coffee. The day is rushing away and I must let you get back to your planning."

They passed the walk back to the hotel in silence, the cry of the fat seagulls and the rumble of passing cars the only sounds.

At the entrance to the hotel, Hernandez gripped her shoulders, pressing two kisses to her dewy cheeks once more.

"It will not be so long before I see you again," he said. "I promise."

Miren nodded; words were truly beyond her.

"And soon, I will see you every day. I cannot wait. Good day."

Miren watched as he strolled away, his gait solid and confident, head high and arrogant.

He didn't know about Anders, of that she was sure.

But this had not been the casual meeting of a husband and wife-to-be.

Hernandez was having her watched, that much was clear. He hadn't found anything to accuse her of, but he was letting her know that if there was anything, he would find out.

Stomach churning from the strong coffee and a healthy dose of fear, Miren pushed through the doorway into the hotel and sent a prayer to God for his protection.

TWENTY-SEVEN

MIREN

The crowd cheered. Miren stood on the steps of the cathedral, her veil now turned back over her head, flowing down her hair and back to spread expansively over the stone stair. At her side Hernandez beamed, the medals of his military uniform glinting in the harsh afternoon sun as he waved to the assembled guests and curious onlookers, drawn by the loud ring of the cathedral bells that chimed joyously overhead. Their music filled the streets of San Sebastian, proclaiming that it was done. Miren was married.

Taking her arm, Hernandez led her down the steps, a rain of rice falling from the air to sprinkle over them as their gathered guests threw the small white grains in celebration, wasteful when so many starved from food shortages across Spain. Miren's pointed shoe crunched on the slippery grains. Instinctively, she gripped Hernandez to prevent herself from falling.

"Do not worry, my darling. I won't let you fall."

She smiled weakly at the man, meeting his eyes. They shone with the same ravenous intensity as they had the first day she saw him, all those years ago in Bilbao. The glow of conquest.

At the bottom of the stairs, a sleek black car waited to transport them back to her father's hotel and the lavish reception that had been arranged. It would be the final hours of her safety, cocooned in the warmth and familiarity of her family hotel, before she would make her way to Hernandez's grand house on the hill. She pushed the thought of the night to come aside, breathing deeply the burning humid air of her summer city, and slipped into the waiting car.

The ballroom was more elaborately decorated than it had been for their Christmas engagement celebration. Bouquets of flowers, white lilies and bright pink roses spilt lush and plump from tall crystal vases. Trails of green ivy wound around the ceiling-high windows, small candles flickered about the space. Waiters in serving white hovered on the edges of the room, trays laden with wine poised to serve.

Behind them, their guests surged into the room, a wall of joyous chatter and happy laughter flowing before them. Miren was swept forward by the celebrating crowd. A cool glass of wine was pressed into her hand. Music struck up from the corner and the room came alive with the sound of a party. Hernandez split off, gathering with him the ever-present group of sycophantic young admirers from the Nationalist Party. Miren made her way to the edge of the room. Standing alone she surveyed the celebrating guests. Gathered for her special day, yet she stood separate and alone. She sipped her wine. The cold liquid seemed to curdle in her empty stomach, sour and acidic at once. She closed her eyes and pictured that wonderful day, so many months ago now, when Anders appeared, suddenly, unexpectedly and magically in this very room.

She scanned the room, part of her hoping to see him somehow materialise from the crowd. Part of her horrified at what that would mean and how it would make her feel.

As the rays of hot summer sun dimmed, casting the ballroom in the soft oranges of dusk, Hernandez appeared at her side once more. His eyes were glazed from drink, his breath sour from wine and brandy.

"It is time, I think," he said. Without further discussion he led her from the ballroom, the crowd behind them jeering a different note now, more lecherous, suggestive.

Her father appeared in the entranceway, her suitcases in his hands. Her mother pressed a single kiss to her cheek, her eyes bright with unshed tears.

The journey to Hernandez's home was short but winding. They trailed out of the city centre, into the gentle hills that lined the back of San Sebastian. Her husband sat beside her, cigar burning in his lips, the smoke thick and acrid building up in the airless space of the vehicle. The day was still hot, the warmth of a summer evening weighing on the car. Miren felt beads of sweat run down her spine, the close lace of her dress too tight to be comfortably breathable. She longed to wind down a window, to flush the stench of cigars and sweat and heat from the car. But she dared not move.

Soon the grand house came into view. A sweeping drive lined by trees led to a sprawling two-storey abode. Hernandez helped her from the car and walked her to the impossibly large double doorway. Behind them, the driver couriered her suitcases.

Inside was cavernous. The click of her heels echoed through the dimly lit space. The high ceiling and hallways that ran from every side seemed to go on forever. The air was cool, despite the warm evening outside. Miren hugged herself, feeling a deep chill run over her skin.

"Welcome home," Hernandez said. "I have given my maid Juileta the day off, but she will be back tomorrow. She'll talk you through the mechanics of the house and the logistics of running my life then." He paused and gave a dismissive smile. "I thought you should enjoy your first night of marriage without such burdens." His eyes grew dark and he moved toward her. "Come."

He led her up the stairs to a carpeted landing and a room on the left. Inside opened into an expansive bedroom. The furniture was old but elegant, with carved wood and plush cushions.

No ornaments sat on any surface, no photos or paintings.

"You will need to decorate, of course."

The driver placed her bags on the floor. Hernandez spoke a few words to the man and then he departed, leaving Miren and her new husband alone.

Miren stood motionless, her heart pounding as Hernandez came up behind her. Two heavy hands landed on her waist, squeezing tight. His breath was hot and pungent on her neck.

"I'll leave you to settle in and freshen up. I will return later."

The hands left her waist and he moved for the door.

"Wait up for me." The door closed softly.

Miren exhaled, sinking to the floor in relief, however momentary. She was here and it was done. There was no turning back now. Slowly she lay herself down on the soft carpeted floor, a hand on her chest as she focused on her breathing, seeking calm.

He would be back, her night was not yet done. But at least she had this moment to gather her strength and prepare. Rising stiffly she shuffled into the small bathroom that sat to the side of the room and ran a cool bath. It's as all she could think to do to ready herself for the night to come.

It was long past midnight when her door creaked open again. Miren lay in bed, book in hand, reading fitfully by the light of a single lamp. She looked up and blinked to steady herself.

Hernandez crossed the room, unbuckling his belt.

Then he was on her. His hands, rough and insistent as he hitched up her silken nightdress and shoved her panties aside.

Hard and forceful he entered her, no soft and easing touch. Miren gritted her teeth and focused on the ceiling above. He thrust fast, his stale breath blowing hot over her skin. Then a guttural groan and he rolled away.

Miren lay still, her groin aching and raw, the smell of his sweat still on her skin.

Beside her Hernandez reached down for his trousers and produced yet another cigar, lit it and puffed, a halo of smoke forming above his head.

"At your age, I knew you wouldn't be a virgin," he said. "Still, it is a disappointment. If you pray enough, God will forgive you."

He drew in more smoke, breathed it out slowly, then rose, pulling up his trousers and re-buckling his belt.

"I will leave you to get your beauty sleep. It is your one asset after all. Juileta will be ready for you at 8 am sharp to explain the house. I will see you for dinner."

With that, he strode from the room.

Miren lay still, listening to the rasp of her breath as she processed what she had just experienced. Tears welled in her eyes and she dashed them quickly away.

"Stop it!" she ordered herself. "You knew this would be hard. Be strong."

Gingerly she unfolded herself from the bed and padded back to the bathroom. There she ran a tap and flushed her vagina fully with water, hoping to cleanse all of his seed from her body. A baby with Hernandez could not happen. She would never allow it.

Running a second bath she sank into the warm liquid and closed her eyes. The worst was over. One day at a time, she would learn this new routine and life, and wait, wait, wait until the day Anders came to rescue her.

TWENTY-EIGHT

1981

Juan's heavy tread draws us from our conversation. I know my husband's gait. And it's past midday, he will be ready for food. I wasn't sure he would come today. Fishermen don't always adhere to the traditional lunch and siesta rhythm of our people. And today, Juan has an extra reason to be away. Yet he has come.

Of course he has. He is here for me.

Gilles sits up, straightening his shirt as Juan enters the small dining space.

His dark eyes land on Gilles immediately. Gilles stands, offering a hand. Juan pauses, one moment, two, then offers his own in return. The shake is firm, two men facing off. It is like watching teenagers. Stupid, after all these years. I clear my throat loudly and stand.

"Husband, come, help me to plate."

"I can be of assistance," Gilles says. "It is the least I can do to thank you for your hospitality."

I glare at Juan pointedly.

"Nonsense," Juan says, under sufferance. He's been out on his boat all morning, I can see the fatigue beneath his eyes. We both slept poorly last night, knowing what today might bring. But that's no excuse for being an ill-mannered host. "You are our guest," he continues. "Can I interest you in a cider? I made it myself, the traditional way. It will go nicely with my wife's food."

He emphasises the word "wife", and despite myself, I feel a surge of pride. Even after all these years, my husband wants to claim me.

"Thank you, a cider would be nice," Gilles agrees, returning to his seat.

"We won't be a moment," I say, leading Juan into the kitchen.

He makes straight for the drinks fridge, while I gather bread and cheese. A pot of marmitako bubbles softly on the stove, the scent of tuna strong in the air. It's been cooking down all morning. It will be perfect. That's the trick with marmitako stew: slowly, slowly.

As I begin to ladle soup into bowls I feel Juan's arms come around my waist. I put down the ladle and lean into his embrace. His arms are strong, and firm. His stubble grazes my cheek, rough and familiar. His skin smells of salt and sea air, the bay is a part of him, wedded to his soul. He smells like home.

I breathe him in, savouring this moment together.

"Have you told him?"

I shake my head against his cheek.

"Will you?"

"I don't know."

"Still?"

"Still."

He nods, accepting this without argument. We've talked it through, Juan, Adelina and me. Weighed the options, the pros and cons. We could not agree on what was best. We did agree that ultimately, the choice would be mine.

And still I have not decided.

It is a large responsibility. A burden. But I can bear it.

We take up the soup and return to Gilles. He accepts a cool cider from Juan and the two men drink, the unspoken tension between them slowly fading. It is a lot, this history between us all.

After we've scraped the last of the stew from our bowls, Juan stands to collect the plates. Making his way out he presses a kiss to my head and shakes Gilles' hand.

"It is good you came," he says, voice sincere.

"I think so too," Gilles replies.

No siesta for Juan today. I knew he wouldn't, it has been a lot for him, meeting Gilles. Two men, so linked, but never in the same room before. As my husband makes his way back to the bay, his boat and his sea currents, a smile touches my lips. He is a fisherman to his very bones. Donostia has always been in his blood. I guess it is in mine too.

PART 3

1942-1944 - RESISTANCE

TWENTY-NINE

ABENE

1942

As the first chilly winds flowed through the region, German tanks rolled into Saint-Jean-de-Luz, breaking the agreement with the Vichy government and bringing the Pyrénées-Atlantiques under occupation. It was a clear tactical move; Hitler wanted the whole French coastline, a barrier to Allied invasion. He also wanted to edge closer to Spain.

Abene and Camille stood in the front garden of the fermette, hand in hand, as the tanks lumbered past.

"Now, things change," Camille said.

Abene remained silent.

That evening Marguerite arrived at the door, face tight with worry. "I don't want Giselle walking into school alone, not now."

"Come in, come in," Camille ushered her inside.

Over cake they made a plan. Abene and Marguerite would alternate days to walk the children into town and safely behind the school doors, then return in the afternoon to collect them.

That night as Eduardo slept peacefully and unaware in his cot by the fireplace, Camille and Abene whispered. "We need to stay closer to the house," her friend said. "Fewer trips into town."

"I will go to the hall tomorrow, and speak with Denise. She will understand I cannot come in as often, even for the children."

Camille eyed her in the dark. "Don't stay longer than you need."

The walk into town the next morning was crisp and cool, the happy chatter of Eduardo and Giselle a strange counterpoint to the dread building within Abene as the city's edge came into view.

The streets were oddly quiet and still. Smoke curled from chimneys into the bitter air, blending with the grey clouds above. Then she saw them. Two soldiers in the field-grey of German military uniform, strolling casually along the road. Abene moved herself between the children and the patrol, angling the children away. As they advanced into the town centre and the small building that made up the school they passed more patrols. They were concentrated around the central train station; in the town hall square, a row of tanks sat, large, metal and intimidating.

At the school Mademoiselle Lulen met them at the gate, guiding the children within the safety of the schoolhouse swiftly and efficiently. "I will be back to collect them at the day's end."

"As will most parents," the teacher said, eyes furtive, nervous.

Leaving the school, Abene took a circuitous route to the church hall, seeking Denise and any news.

The older woman drew her inside, locking the door behind them.

She led Abene to the back office, putting a kettle on the hob in the small kitchen before coming to sit at the table, hands clutched tight before her.

Abene reached forward, taking Denise's hands in her own, a gesture of solidarity and strength.

"They arrived in the early hours and drove right into the square," Denise said, eyes darting side to side. "We all stayed away, we knew not to be out. Not with them on the streets." She swallowed, visibly unsettled. "In the afternoon they came here, walked into the church itself, didn't even dust off their boots... The officer was so polite, so friendly. He wanted to ask about the Basque activities we held and said how he respects such an ancient culture.

"He'd seen a film, he said. The Nazis made a film about our people!"

Denise fell silent. Abene sat still and stunned, unable to properly process what her friend had just shared.

"We must be careful," she said finally, though the sentiment rang hollow. "I don't think we should hold Basque activities anymore."

Denise agreed. "I doubt people would come now anyway. We must stay home and go unnoticed."

Abene nodded. What else was there to do?

As Saint-Jean-de-Luz adjusted to the presence of the German occupiers, things changed. A line of armaments was set up along the coast, the Atlantic Wall, as it came to be known. A defence system intended to keep the Allied forces at bay. In the north the defence looked skyward, watching for bombing raids aimed at military targets, that blew up civilians as collateral. In the south, the focus was the sea, a line of guns pointing out into the Bay of Biscay holding back boats and deterring a land invasion.

To Abene it was a blight on the beauty of her new home. A shiny grey metallic threat that kept them all in fear.

Every day that she walked Eduardo and Giselle to school she passed patrolling soldiers, guns over their backs, cigarettes dangling from their lips, puffing grey into the cold air. Food supplies dwindled, with the soldiers taking supplies for their own use and distribution.

It wasn't long before they arrived at the fermette, truck engine blaring as they raced up the small hill to the farmhouse, churning up the muddy grass.

Pierre had no choice but to hand over his chickens and stored potatoes.

As the truck bumped its way back into town, they all gathered in the front room, watching as their winter rations drove away.

"It will be all right," Pierre said stoically. "We will make do."

No one agreed.

THIRTY

ABENE

It was a cool, wet December morning when Abene first laid eyes on her.

Abene was returning home through the streets of Saint-Jean-de-Luz after dropping Eduardo and Giselle to school, when her tall, slender frame wrapped in a deep blue coat, hair neatly pinned into a bun at her nape, flashed into view. The woman moved with the elegance of a Parisian, her perfectly painted lips startling. She gripped the elbow of an older man, his hair tucked under a hat, small dark curls escaping from the rim. He was bent over at the waist, so thin his clothes hung off him. Abene wasn't sure why the couple caught her eye. But, as her heels clicked along the path outside the train station she saw them and could not look away.

Slowing her step, she watched as the woman paused by the kerb, eyes darting left and right, furtive, tense. Abene watched on, her heart beating faster. She didn't know this woman, or her purpose in Saint-Jean-de-Luz, and yet somehow she intuitively knew: she was in trouble.

Two German soldiers, grey uniforms perfectly pressed, rounded the corner. The woman visibly flinched as they strolled into view, turning the man away from their prying eyes. Unfortunately, the movement drew the soldiers' attention. Steps ringing purposefully off the cobbles the Germans advanced. Abene stood frozen on the opposite side of the street, galvanised. Something was happening before her very eyes, this woman and the man who followed her clearly wished to avoid the soldiers. There was nothing strange in that, yet they seemed desperate. And the soldiers were interested.

So Abene decided to act.

Without a second thought, she stepped into the street, raising a hand, a false smile across her lips. "Tante Clare! Bonjour!" she cried, voice aimed at the retreating woman's back. The woman glanced over her shoulder, eyes wide. Smile anchored in place, Abene hastened to cross the gap between them. Coming to the woman's side she hooked their arms together. "Sorry I am late to meet you," she announced, too loudly, ensuring the following soldiers could hear her. "Let's get you home!"

Abene lowered her voice to a hiss, "Trust me," she whispered, praying that the woman would follow her lead. The woman regarded her with suspicion but offered no resistance as Abene pulled her forward, coaxing them into a swift walk. As they rounded the station corner Abene risked a peek back towards the soldiers. They had slowed their advance but were still in pursuit.

As the station wall covered their passage Abene forced the couple into a run, aiming for a small side street. The woman picked up her pace, the man lagging behind. As the soldiers appeared at the station corner, Abene and her charges slipped into the shadows of the lane. But they could not rest yet, Abene could not be sure that they had not been seen. She urged them on. "I know a place," she panted, herding the couple down the lane, heading for the Church of Saint John the Baptist.

A few streets later they arrived. Abene shoved the door

open, ushering the man and woman inside. At her desk, Denise looked up in surprise. "Abene?" she said. "It has been a while." She eyed the couple, her expression melting into realisation. "Come," she gestured to the office space at the back of the building, closing the door behind them. "Sit," she ordered.

Abene guided the couple to the small oval table that sat in the centre of the room. The man collapsed onto a chair, his breath coming in wheezing puffs, his face pale and drawn.

"I'll make tea," Denise announced, bustling from the room.

"Thank you," Abene called to her back. Denise gave a gesture of dismissal before disappearing into the adjacent kitchen.

Abene turned back to the couple. The woman rounded on her. "Who are you? Why did you interfere?" her eyes blazed in fury, her mouth set in a determined line.

Abene blinked in shock. "I think the phrase you are looking for is thank you," she chided, pulling out a chair to seat herself. The woman glared down at her, and Abene looked away, feigning disregard. Inside, her stomach roiled, her chest squeezed in fear. She didn't know this woman she had saved from the soldiers. She had risked her own safety to get them hidden. She hoped she had gambled rightly.

The woman released a long sigh. "We would have been all right. I have done this before," she said.

Abene narrowed her eyes at the woman, "They had noticed you. And he..." she pointed directly at the older man, "is clearly a Jew."

The man's head shot up, the colour he had regained while sitting drained from his face.

The woman stared at Abene, mouth twitching. Finally, she drew a chair and took a seat. Offering a hand across the table to shake, she said, "I'm Sophie. This is Felix."

Abene accepted her hand, and shook firmly. "Abene."

"You are not French?"

"Basque, from Spain."

Sophie nodded slowly. "Then you understand."

Abene closed her eyes briefly at that statement. The plight of people fleeing their own country because of invaders? Oh yes, that she most definitely understood.

She pinned Sophie with her eyes. "What are you doing in Saint-Jean-de-Luz? We are occupied. This is not the free France of the south."

Sophie glanced away, eyes tracking about the small office, clearly contemplating how much to share.

"Have you heard of the Comet Line?"

"No."

Sophie paused. "We are a group working to get people out of France: downed airmen, Jews."

"Out of France? To where?"

She held up a hand. "No more details. It is not safe." She looked over at Felix, expression tight. "Felix cannot stay in France. We are to meet contacts here, at a farmhouse on the edge of town. But I am unsure of the way..."

"Tell me where; I can show you."

Sophie took a deep breath, obviously conflicted. "Can I trust you?"

Abene gave Sophie a withering stare. "I risked myself for you when those soldiers were advancing. I could have turned away..."

"But you did not."

"But I did not."

Sophie paused, then nodded firmly. "It is known as Starling Farm."

Abene swallowed hard as cold fear washed over her body. Her friends. The house Eduardo often visited. What were Jeans and Marguerite involved in? How often had they put Eduardo, the boy who was now her child, at risk?

"I know it."

Beside them Felix began to cough, his painfully thin chest spasming beneath his heavy cloak.

"Is it far?"

"Around an hour's walk. Let's rest a while first, so Felix can recover."

"All right," Sophie agreed.

Denise appeared with a tray of tea made from rosemary; tea leaves were scarce now the Germans had come. She placed the tray and some biscuits on the table before them. "I took the liberty of a peek outside, no soldiers in the lane. I don't think you were followed."

"Thank you, Denise," Abene said, taking her friend's hand in hers. "I am sorry to put you in this position. I didn't know where else to go."

"Nonsense!" Denise said, eyes scanning over the couple. "You always come here, when you need."

"Thank you."

As the streets slowed for lunch hour, Abene led Sophie and Felix from the church. They took the small laneways and paths, avoiding the town centre and the open space of the riverside. Once they reached the outskirts of town, Abene increased their speed, eager to get them to their destination and be done with whatever folly this was.

At Starling Farm, Marguerite opened the door. Seeing Abene, her face split into a wide smile of greeting. It quickly melted as Abene gestured behind her to her companions.

She watched Marguerite's throat bob, her hands gripping the door nervously.

"You'd better come in." She swung the door wide.

Abene didn't move. Fixing her friend with a cold stare, she said, "You will collect Giselle today, I am taking Eduardo home early."

"Abene—" Marguerite began, but Abene was already

turning away. Head high, shoulders set firm she strode from the farmhouse back towards town.

That night as she lay in her bed listening to Eduardo's soft breathing float through the air, Abene's mind could find no rest.

When Sophie had said Starling Farm, purest panic had gripped Abene's heart. The thought of the young boy, sleeping peacefully just across the wooden floor being in danger, tore her soul in two. She would not allow it. Not ever, ever again.

Yet part of her understood Marguerite's choice. This war, like the one she had escaped, was a terrible, brutal thing. The innocent died, and the powerful conquered. The men of the Basque region had rallied, Juan with them. Joining the French army to fight for freedom.

It was a hope Abene could not believe in. Not after San Sebastian and the nights in the cold of the Pyrenees, not after learning the truth of her father's death. The Nazis were here in Saint-Jean-de-Luz and they would not be routed. Abene had chosen to be small, to keep her head down and survive.

Juan had not.

Despite all he had seen on the borders of Barcelona, despite the memories that haunted his eyes and had stolen his smile, despite the end of hope for Spain, he had not given up.

She rolled onto her side, watching the dust motes that danced in the silver strip of moonlight that poured across her sheets. It didn't matter how she rearranged the facts; she could not believe in a French victory. The country was lost, Europe too, perhaps. The might of Germany seemed to eclipse even the power of Franco and his Nationalists. What chance did anyone have against that?

But the innocent were fighting, and dying. Giving their lives for freedom, for hope.

They did not deserve their fate.

Juan was out there, fighting for their new home; this place in the south of France that had opened its arms to her and her family, given them refuge and a future. She glanced across the room, eyes falling on Eduardo, and watched the gentle rise and fall of his chest.

Fortune had also brought him into her life, this beautiful boy that had stolen her heart and made her a mother. He slept in peace, safe beside her, and she would do anything to keep it that way. Eduardo had faced too much loss in his short life, had been driven from his home, from his mother's arms once before. Abene could not let him face that fate again.

She'd felt powerless. Hiding on the farm had seemed the only option. But the bravery of Sophie and Marguerite had opened her eyes. Like Juan, and her father, it was time for Abene to join the fight for what was theirs. For Eduardo and for herself.

Perhaps there was something Abene could do after all.

The next morning after seeing Eduardo safely to school, cutting a wide birth around the train station, Abene returned to Starling Farm.

Marguerite opened the door. "Come in," she whispered softly, face wary.

Abene followed her to the expansive kitchen. Gathered at the table were Sophie and Felix; Jeans was probably out working the fields.

"I'll make tea," Marguerite said.

"You will sit," Abene said.

Silently her friend obeyed.

Abene ran her eyes over the three of them, but only Sophie met her stare, expression defiant.

Marguerite sat forward, placing her hands on the table, palms up in supplication. "I am sorry, mon amie, we just want to help the victims. A group of Basque priests are working for the line, when they came to us for help—"

Abene interrupted, hand in the air, "I want no details."

Marguerite paused. "We never meant to endanger Eduardo. I would never—"

"Eduardo never sets foot here again, understood?"

Sorrow flooded Marguerite's face, she nodded silently.

"...And when you have 'guests'," Abene eyed Sophie, "Giselle stays at the fermette with me. It is not right to involve the children."

Marguerite stared at Abene, her mouth going slack. Glancing between Abene and Sophie, she said, "You don't think the children would be blamed? They are innocents."

Abene snorted in indignation. Turning to Sophie, she asked, "Do you believe that?"

Eyes hard Sophie paused. Abene could see she knew it was a test. She shook her head. "No. I believe the Nazis will punish anyone."

"Good, then we can proceed."

The three others looked at Abene, waiting. Slowly Abene drew out a chair, sitting herself down, arranging her hands in a prayer position before her.

"No more trains," she said.

"We have already realised this," Sophie interjected, her voice was brisk, annoyed. Abene ignored her.

"We thought Saint-Jean-de-Luz would be small enough to use the station and not be noticed," Marguerite explained.

"You thought wrong. The men will have to walk. Where is the safe house before here?"

"Just north of Acotz," Sophie said.

"Then I will meet them there, guide them to this farm. You cannot be seen near here, not after yesterday."

Marguerite stared at her friend. "You want to help?"

Abene eyed Sophie. "You are taking them to Spain, yes? Across the Pyrenees?"

Sophie's mouth hardened into a line.

"So the next safe house, it is in Hendaye ? At the border?"

Sophie nodded. "After they have recovered here, I will guide them to Hendaye. But no further."

"Do you want to know what happens when they arrive in Spain?"

"I want nothing but the meeting points for transfer."

"Why are you offering this?" Sophie asked.

Abene paused, the sound of artillery fire filling her ears, the hollow pools of Juan's eyes breaking her heart. "I know what it is to run."

She met Sophie's stare, a moment of understanding passing between the two women.

"Welcome to the team," Sophie said.

THIRTY-ONE

ABENE

1943

Abene approached the old oak tree slowly. It stood tall and silent in the barren field on the edge of Acotz. The night around her was dark, yet mild, the earth still radiating the warmth of the mid-autumn day. But the leaves of the oak were browning, signalling the turn of the season. Soon the days would grow shorter, colder and these transports would grow more treacherous. But not yet. As she drew closer two figures stepped into view. They must be the soldiers she would be transporting.

She raised a hand in a casual wave, indicating she saw them, and that she was no threat.

She'd been working with Sophie and her network of smugglers for months now. On a designated night she would creep from the comfort of her bed and trek two hours to this overgrown field to meet Sophie and whomever they were working to rescue that day. Abene's job was to get the men to Starling Farm before dawn. There they would rest and recuperate, eat a hot and hearty meal, and wait out any inclement weather before

Abene led them to Hendaye at the base of the Pyrenees to meet the guides who would help them cross into Spain.

This would be her third transport.

Her task was relatively safe, obscured from view by the veil of night and the isolation of the countryside. The guides who braved the crossing at the river in Irun faced a far greater danger. The guards on the Spanish side of the border suspected something, she knew. And had increased their patrols of the river crossing. So far they had been lucky, but Abene wondered how long that luck would hold out.

Coming to the men, she unslung her pack and pulled out bread and cheese, offering the food to be eaten. They accepted gratefully, munching quickly on the simple fare.

Abene scanned around, looking for Sophie. She materialised from the darkness behind the oak, and Abene blinked in surprise. Sophie was not alone.

Standing beside her was a child. A girl, small, maybe six years old, though the sunken cheeks of malnourishment made it hard to determine; she could be years older. She wore a coat several sizes too large for her and clutched a suitcase to her chest. Sophie's hand rested on the girl's shoulder.

Abene crept forward. The girl tensed, stepping back behind Sophie. Abene's heart stuttered. So small, so scared. Her arms ached to wrap around the girl, to soothe her fear. What had befallen this child to bring her to this moment?

Coming to Sophie's side, Abene whispered, "A child? Is she for the crossing?"

Sophie glanced down at the wary child. "Yes."

Abene blew out a breath. "Can she make it?"

"I've waited until I had two men, strong and fit. They are willing to carry her, if they must."

"It is a grave risk. Why transport a child?"

Sophie eyed her in the darkness. "She's a Jew."

The words hung heavy and tense in the balmy night air. "Her parents?" Abene asked.

"They didn't make it. They were hiding in a neighbour's attic in Lyon, but their quarter was bombed by the Allies. Exposed, they had to run. Only Ana and her father made it to Bayonne. They hid for a while before making contact. By then her father was sick. Perhaps if he had come to me sooner..." Sophie trailed off.

Abene's heart cleaved in sorrow for the small pixie child hiding in the night. "All right now," Sophie whispered to the girl. "Go with Abene." She stepped back, gently pushing the child forward, but the girl resisted, eyes wide with alarm.

"She doesn't trust adults," Sophie explained.

Abene could understand. What horrors had this child seen?

She addressed the girl. "Hello, ma cariña," she began. "My name is Abene. I am a friend of Sophie's. I am here to take you and these men to safety."

The child remained rooted to the spot, her small hands gripping her suitcase before her protectively.

Abene felt her face fall into lines of pity as she regarded this waif-like reflection of her Eduardo, orphaned and alone. Abene understood; she was so young, too young, to face this challenge. But they needed to move. It was a long walk to the safety of Starling Farm and the dawn would not wait for them. She could not force Ana though, her time with Eduardo had taught her that much. Taking a deep breath, she knelt down, bringing her eyes in line with Ana's, and spoke into the fogged terror she met there.

"My son was scared too, when he first arrived in a new place. But he decided to be brave. He took my hand and now he sleeps warm and safe in a beautiful farmhouse."

Curiosity lit the girl's eyes. Encouraged, Abene continued. "He has a best friend, a little girl named Giselle. She lives in the house I am taking you to. Her parents are lovely. You will be safe there. And then I will come and guide you to the next stop. And these men, they will be there with you, every step of the way. They will get you to your own farmhouse, and a warm, safe bed. Does that sound nice?"

The child nodded. Abene felt the approach of one of the soldiers. He knelt next to her. "Hi, little one, my name's Benjamin. I have a younger sister, just like you, back home," he said. "I will make sure you get to Spain safely." He reached a hand out between them.

Abene glanced at the man in the dark and smiled. She doubted he would have a sister so much younger than him, but it was a good story. And it worked.

Ana stepped forward and took his hand.

Above them, Sophie released a breath of relief.

Abene stood and the two women embraced.

"Be safe," Sophie said.

"You too," Abene replied.

She collected up her backpack and started across the field. The two men and little Ana falling into step behind.

A week later Abene trudged through a damp, sticky night, Ana's small hand in hers. Storms had set in the morning after they arrived at Starling Farm, delaying the next stage of the journey. It had been a tense week. German patrols rarely came out as far as the farms, but it was still preferable to move people on quickly. Less chance of discovery. The rains had broken that morning, so, despite the thick and slippery mud, Abene had gathered the soldiers and child and set off for Hendaye.

They were approaching the town when she heard the truck. It was well after midnight, the moonless, cloud-covered sky the perfect cover for their intent. But headlights cut through the dark.

The engine rumbled in the distance. Pivoting on her heel she gathered Ana into her arms and sprinted from the road side, hoping the two soldiers behind her followed her lead. She could not shout out to warn them, it would give them away. She crashed through the overgrown roadside as the headlights came into view over the small hill in the distance. She glanced back and her mouth went dry. Germans. What were they doing out of town in the middle of the night?

She ducked behind a tree, Ana pressed to her chest, her small hands gripping onto the lapels of Abene's coat. The soldiers appeared beside her, hunkering down below the grass line to obscure themselves from the road. They were all dressed in dark colours. Abene hoped it would be enough to shroud them. The truck lumbered nearer, its engine loud in the still and silent night. Abene closed her eyes and said a prayer. The vehicle passed by, the bright headlights slipping over them and leaving them in the dark.

Then it stopped.

Abene held her breath. Why had they stopped in the middle of the road? Had they seen something? The white of an eye, the flash of reflection off a coat button?

She hugged Ana closer, pressing her lips firmly together to hold in her scream of fear. A soldier, black knee-high boots gleaming, dropped down from the truck and walked to the road-side. He turned his head left and right scanning the trees.

Tucked low, a bare five paces from his position, Abene and her group held their breath and prayed.

The man paused, eyes focused just beyond them. He was so close Abene could see the twist of his mouth, the squint of his eyes as he stared into the darkness.

He raised a hand.

Then turned back to the truck, calling out something in German before swinging his door wide and climbing into his seat.

The three adults exhaled a collective sigh of relief as they watched the truck continue on down the road and out of sight. Once the last beam of the headlights faded from the road they slowly stood, brushing the sticky mud from their knees.

Ana was still tucked against Abene's chest, her frail body quaking with terror.

"It is all right," Abene soothed, smoothing the child's hair from her face. "We are all right."

She placed the girl on the ground and took her hand once more. Waving the men forward she led them back to the road and on to the safe house. Too close, she thought to herself. That was too close.

And what was a patrol doing out so far, so late?

Worry creased her brow, but she strode on. The sooner they reached the safe house, the sooner these travellers would be on their way to Spain.

It was all she could do for them. She had to remain strong.

As the first rays of dawn peeked over the horizon Abene stood at the door to the safe house. The guide, Mateo, had returned to her after ushering the soldiers and Ana within.

"Anything to report?" he asked.

"A patrol truck, around 1 am. I've not seen them out so far, so late."

Mateo nodded thoughtfully. "We have noticed increased activity recently. Something is up."

"Do you think they suspect our work?"

He shrugged. "Hard to say. Tensions run high across the region. The locals aren't happy at being occupied. We Basque have never taken well to foreign rule."

Abene snorted a laugh. True words.

"Likely it is just a show of force. To keep us repressed." He looked over his shoulder at the men and child now sitting inside. "She's a small one."

"Jewish, there is no choice."

Mateo nodded solemnly. "I'll get her across."

Abene squeezed his shoulder in gratitude. "I must get moving. I'll just say goodbye."

A smirk twisted Mateo's lips as he moved to allow her inside.

Abene crouched before Ana and took her into a tight hug. "Be good," she said. "Do exactly as Mateo says. He will see you to safety."

The girl wrapped her arms around Abene's neck, her fingers small and warm on Abene's skin.

"Au revoir."

She pulled from Ana's embrace, her little face full of sorrow.

How many goodbyes had her short life already endured?

It wasn't right, all this pain and loss. War had ripped Abene's land apart, and now it enveloped her new home in darkness. She couldn't let the armies win, not again. She felt the fire of her purpose flare within her gut anew. She would go on, for her mother and Udane, Camille and Pierre. For Eduardo. For children like Ana.

Abene stood and turned to the men she'd helped. "Good luck," she said to the soldiers.

"Thank you," Benjamin said, rising to shake her hand. "You have risked so much for us."

She accepted his handshake, nodding once. "Mateo knows the way. You will be in Spain before you know it."

"We could not have made it this far without you."

"Don't get blown from the sky again," Abene said. The man released a laugh and Abene smiled.

Ruffling Ana's hair a last time she made her way into the misty light of dawn. She would keep to the woodlands for an hour or two, then make camp in the forest and wait for the night to fall. As she made her way from the small house on the edge of Hendaye, Ana filled her thoughts.

May she make it across. May she find a new place to call home.

She prayed for the girl with all her heart.

THIRTY-TWO
MIREN

Hans' laughter rang through the dining room. Miren stood by the doorway, her tight silk dress clinging to her body. She fussed with the shoulder of her gown. The back was cut low; it was hard to keep the clear line of her too-thin ribs covered sufficiently.

She doubted Hans would notice anyway, but Hernandez wouldn't like it if he saw them. Her overly thin frame irritated him. But Miren simply could not keep the flesh on her bones.

Juileta appeared at her side. Tutting she reached up and smoothed a hair back into place behind Miren's ear. "Better," she said. The gesture was so natural, so maternal, that Miren felt her throat close over with emotion.

Swallowing, she smiled softly at the maid. Grateful for her gentle touch, for this moment of companionship.

These past months of marriage had not been easy for Miren. Her duties in the house were simple enough, but they left her with large tracks of time alone and dithering. Never one to have many friends, in the years since Franco's defeat of Spain, Miren had found herself cut out, isolated from the circles she'd thought of as hers. Carla, that loss still bled her soul.

Now, as the wife of General Sergio Hernandez, even her parents kept a distance.

Her husband was a general to his bones: a man used to the strict obedience of soldiers, he would tolerate no less from his wife. It did not matter how hard she tried to do everything right, to be a good and dutiful wife, he always found fault. The only authority Hernandez recognised as higher than his own was God.

Prayer, supplication, penance; Miren had to atone for every slight, real or imagined. The first time he'd drawn his rosary beads, from the pocket of his trousers she'd begged forgiveness. But Hernandez was passionate. He believed in a vengeful God. And Miren was a sinner for forgetting the butter in the shopping order, for spilling his evening wine, for wearing the wrong colour to a gathering, for being Miren. Angered, he would force her to her knees in prayer, the click of his rosary in his hands as he fingered the shining beads. As he hovered above her, a menacing evangelical angel, Miren prayed and prayed and prayed, until he deemed her cleansed.

She feared the day her prayers would not be enough to satisfy his disappointment.

Without the quiet presence of Juileta in the house, Miren may well have lost her mind and the last of her hope. Nodding to the kindly maid, Miren arranged her features into a careful expression of neutrality and moved to join the small group of men gathered by the fireplace.

Fortunately, for the most part, Hernandez ignored her, but when he was entertaining, she was expected to play the beautiful, dutiful wife.

"Ah, my darling," Hernandez said as she approached. "I was getting impatient for your arrival. But now I see your perfection I realise it was worth the wait."

He drew her to him and pressed a kiss to her temple, hand gripping her waist in a gesture of ownership.

"I am grateful for your patience, my husband," Miren replied, eyeing the assembly of guests.

She only knew Hans, the Nazi officer who had been staying in San Sebastian during a recovery from his duties on the front.

"Gentlemen, may I present my wife, Miren. Miren, you know Hans. And this is Pieter Weber and Karl Lind. All are on leave from duty, and have been gracious enough to visit our beautiful city."

"Welcome to San Sebastian," Miren parroted as she took in the three Germans before her. Sharply dressed in Nazi grey, hair and nails perfectly trimmed. Commanders for certain, not foot soldiers. These men clearly came from privilege.

Hernandez ran his hand up her spine, his fingers probing her tender flesh. She stifled her wince of revulsion at his touch.

"There is no more beautiful city in the world," Hans said gayly, swigging from his glass of deep red wine. "Except of course for Rothenburg ob der Tauber in the Fatherland. You must visit one day, General. When this silly war is over and Germany is returned to her rightful place of power."

"I would be delighted to visit your beautiful country, Hans. Wouldn't that be a wonder, Miren? I don't believe you have ever left Spain?"

"No, I've not," Miren answered simply.

"A proper Nationalist," Hernandez beamed. "I look forward to showing you off around the world, once proper order is restored."

Miren smiled meekly and lowered her eyes. She knew her role, pretty and quiet. A showpiece for her husband's ego.

The evening wore on. Dinner was served, chicken, fish and potatoes, then they retired to the smoking room for more drinks. The smoke of cigars swirled around her head, even now after all the evenings she'd endured with Hernandez the scent still sickened her stomach.

A soft knock on the door and Juileta appeared at Miren's side. "A phone call for you, señora."

Miren looked up in surprise. "Is it my mother?"

"A friend, I believe."

Miren's mind raced. She had no friend who would call her, no acquaintance, especially this late in the evening. She didn't miss Juileta's evasive answer. Forcing calm to her voice she rose saying, "Apologies, gentlemen, can you excuse me briefly?"

"Return quickly," Hernandez eyed her suspiciously.

"Of course."

Miren followed Juileta into the hall.

"Hello?" she held the receiver to her ear, concern snaking through her body.

The phone line buzzed and crackled. Miren's breath caught. "Hello?" she repeated. "This is Miren speaking."

"Can you talk?"

The voice was soft and deep and an arrow for her heart. Anders.

Why was he ringing her at night? This was risky, even for him.

Miren glanced around the hall. Juileta had returned to the kitchen to collect further refreshments for the men and she was quite alone. Still, she must be cautious. Hernandez could be unexpected.

She lowered her voice. "I can, what has happened?"

A deep breath, and sigh. "Meet me at the gate at the back of your garden in thirty minutes."

The phone hung up. Miren held the receiver before her, looking up at the large clock that hung above the mantel. 10:30 pm. She replaced the receiver and rejoined the men in the smoking room.

As the clock struck 11 pm Miren stood, one hand pressed to her head.

"Forgive me, gentlemen," she said. "But I have developed

the most dreadful headache. Please excuse me, I must retire for the night."

"Of course, of course," Hans cried affably. "Women are not made for the long hours like we men. We thank you for your company until so late."

The three German officers stood and bowed to her in farewell. Miren nodded her thanks and turned for the door. She didn't miss the glare of disapproval that burned in Hernandez's eyes. She knew he would be up for hours yet, entertaining. The men liked to drink well into the night. But when they finished he would come for her, to make his displeasure at her early departure known. She had to be back, secured beneath her blankets, before he came to punish her.

Outside she rushed across the cool grass of the manicured yard, heading for the far end of the garden and the gate that led to the lane that bordered Hernandez's impressive home.

The gate swung open easily and she stepped through into the quiet of the lane. The silence of the tree-lined suburb enveloped her.

He waited in the dark, smoke from a cigarette curling into the night sky. Miren fell into his arms, smothering his face with fervent kisses, clutching him to her in desperation.

He held her, but his body barely responded to her touch. Miren pulled back. "My love? What is wrong? Something has happened, hasn't it? Tell me!"

Anders scanned her face, as if memorising every feature, then gently smoothed a curl that had escaped its clip from her forehead, back behind her ear.

"I am sorry to have called you, but it is urgent. The maid—"

"—was discreet. I believe she will not say anything about who she heard on the phone," Miren said, and realised she knew it was true. Juileta would not go to Hernandez.

Anders nodded, mouth turned down, grim.

"I have news from France. It is not good."

Miren blinked; focusing on his expression she saw deep lines of fatigue that cut down his cheeks, a new darkness beneath his eyes that even the night could not hide. She waited.

Anders ran a hand through his hair, stepping back from her. He took a long drag of his cigarette. Exhaled.

"I've had a warning. A group of escapees were caught at the bridge crossing in Irun."

Miren gasped in horror, her hand flying to cover her mouth.

"The Spanish guards handed them over to the Germans in France, for questioning."

The last words fell from his lips, heavy and defeated. She stared at him in the dark, seeing the hopelessness that weighed down his shoulders.

Swallowing, she placed a hand on his arm, gently. "Are you revealed?"

He eyed her in the dark. "I do not know. Have you heard anything?" he gestured back towards the mansion.

Miren shook her head. "No. He is entertaining tonight, three Germans. But there has been no talk of the Comet Line, or of rebel discoveries."

Anders nodded. "Good, that is good."

"Anders," Miren pressed, "I think... I think this is a sign. You have risked so much, but this, this changes everything. It is time to stop."

He looked at her, expression sad. "Almost." The word was barely a whisper.

"What do you mean?"

He licked his lips, feet shuffling, clearly uncomfortable. "We have three in hiding now. Two airmen and a little girl. They have waited some time. I have arranged a passage from the port tomorrow night. We leave at midnight."

Hope blazed through her. "We?"

"They..." he gestured vaguely. "It will be my last transport. I must get them out. I can't leave the child in danger. Then, I agree. You are right, my love, I must stop."

Miren blinked away her disappointment. "And we will run?"

"I can't think on that now," Anders said, voice sharp, irritated.

Miren flinched, hurt.

His gaze softened. "I am sorry, my darling. I am tired and stressed. The discovery of my contacts was unexpected. I am afraid for the lives in my care. For my own life. I just need to get them out."

Miren drew him into her arms. "I understand," she whispered. Though his reaction still stung. The hope of their escape from Spain, the dream of her future with Anders was all that kept her going in the long days and nights as Hernandez's wife.

Just a little longer.

Anders held her before him. "You will listen tomorrow. Keep vigil? And if you overhear anything from your husband, anything at all, no matter how small or insignificant it sounds, you will call me?"

Miren nodded, her nerves rattling in her chest. "Of course."

He drew her close, his lips finding hers. The kiss was soft at first and then it built. A sudden urgency gripped his body and he lifted Miren from the ground to straddle his hips. Pressing her against the stone wall of the fence, one hand cupped her buttock while the other worked to free his trousers. Miren responded. An arm about his neck, the other hitching her dress over her waist. He thrust hard, his breath coming in pants. Soon her own breathing quickened as the pleasure of his touch swept through her body. She threw her head back in ecstasy, biting her lip to keep from crying out as she found release. They stayed tight against the wall, limbs entwined, sweat blending on their skin as their passion calmed. Then Anders set her back down.

"Call me if you hear anything," he said then pressed a kiss to her forehead. "And Miren?"

She looked up from arranging her skirts. "Yes?"

"Never forget that I love you. I truly do."

With that, he spun away disappearing into the night before she had a chance to reply.

"I love you too," she whispered to the salty breezes that rose from the bay far below. She hovered in the laneway, watching the space where Anders had stood moments before. Nausea rose to burn the back of her throat as anxiety permeated her senses. This was the danger of Anders' choices. She'd known it, felt it haunt her in the quiet of night, and now it had arrived. She had to trust to his network, his plan. All she could do was pray.

Hernandez visited her that night. She'd known he would. He expected her to stay and entertain until he granted her permission to retire. It did not matter that Hans had believed her deception. Her husband would be angry. And his anger must be satisfied.

She sat up in bed at the sound of her door, bracing herself against the bedhead.

"You embarrassed me." His voice was husky, slurred with drink.

"I felt unwell."

"You were too focused on yourself to do your duty. As my wife, you entertain my guests. It is your role in this house."

He had not raised his voice, he didn't need to. The threat was enough.

"Stand up."

Miren slipped from the bed. There was no point resisting. Compliance made it go quicker.

"Undress."

She slipped her silk gown from her shoulders, allowing it to fall to the floor, pooling at her feet. She heard the rasp of his rosary beads as he drew them from his pocket, his approach slow and deliberate.

"You have to learn," he said, step heavy on the floor as he closed the space between them.

Miren said nothing; there was nothing to say.

"Kneel and pray," he said, and Miren's body obeyed, muscles flinching as he placed the beads across her shoulder, cool and slick.

It was always this way. He never touched her, just stood close, his physical presence a threat, the possibility of violence hovering on the edges of the moment.

She gripped the beads and, taking a deep breath, began her penance.

She felt she'd prayed for hours, her voice hoarse from repetition, her knees and thighs aching from kneeling rigid by the bed. When at last he slipped the beads from her neck, Miren blinked in gratitude, but she dared not move. Not until she was alone.

At the door he paused. "We should try for a baby," he said, then shut the door firmly behind him. Miren's posture collapsed, her head coming down to rest on the softness of her mattress. Her muscles spasmed as a sob, deep and raw, croaked from her throat and her eyes filled with tears. The tension and fear of kneeling beneath Hernandez's ire rushed from her body in a shuddering jerk of limbs and soul.

If Anders knew the truth of this, the veiled threats, the constant control, would he take her away? She wondered, her body trembling in the cool night air. Perhaps she should have told him, perhaps it would have changed his choices. But something stopped her. Shame? Some deep fear that Hernandez was right – that she was a terrible wife, a sinful woman?

The worry it would make her seem weak to a man who was so strong? The belief it would turn Anders from her?

She didn't know.

But she had endured. She was still here, still alive.

And it would not be long. Not now.

Anders had one last job to do, and then his resistance would come to an end. And he would come to her, free her from this life. From this marriage, from Hernandez, from her broken country.

Carefully she slid up to lay across the bed. She should bathe, she knew. In case he returned, in case he wished to take her body. She would. Later. Now she was too tired. Too overwhelmed.

Her eyes drifted closed, her mind floating away to the familiar dream of the future. Her only future with Anders.

THIRTY-THREE

MIREN

Juileta's soft touch woke her early the next morning. The kindly older lady placed a tray of coffee and toast by her bedside. "General Hernandez has already left for the day," she explained. "You can take your time."

Miren nodded, grateful for the maid's thoughtfulness. She'd said nothing about the male voice on the phone last night and asked Miren nothing now. Though she never said anything against her employer, she seemed to understand Miren's fear of her husband. And with small gestures like this morning's breakfast, showed Miren she was not alone in this looming, empty house.

Miren dressed in a loose-fitting cream blouse, clipping pearls to her earlobes and applying soft make-up. Her housewife outfit and a uniform to survive the day.

She passed the morning at her bureau, going through correspondence and listing what wines and cheeses needed replacement after hosting the night before. When Hernandez returned home that evening she found reasons to hover near his home office, listening for the phone, watching for any sign of urgency, any indication he knew about Anders and the escapees.

They dined together in silence. Juileta had made red meat. The bloody steak repelled Miren and she could barely stomach it. When the dinner dishes were cleared away, she sat tense, waiting to be excused. Leaning casually in his seat at the opposite end of the table, Hernandez swirled his freshened glass of red wine, a sleepy expression on his face. He was tired, Miren noted. The long nights of entertaining, the heavy drinking and his advancing age were catching up with him.

His fatigue was also a good sign for Anders' plans. Hernandez was relaxed. He didn't know what would be happening at the Puerto in a few hours' time.

When her husband nodded his approval for her to retire, she fussed in the library, pretending an interest in finding something to read, while keeping an eye on Hernandez, and an ear out for any visitors. At 11 pm she trailed her husband up to their chambers, bidding him a polite goodnight before disappearing into her own room. There she undressed slowly before sliding beneath her sheets. She lay on her stomach, exhausted and spent, but her eyes would not close. Mind still whirling she watched the clock on her bedside tick, counting the seconds to midnight, ears pricked for any movement on the landing to indicate Hernandez being called to action.

As the clock arm ticked over 12 a smile of relief parted Miren's lips. The boat would have left by now. Anders' plan had worked. The last of his transports was done.

Soon he would come for her. Her eyes closed and she gave in to the heavy lethargy that weighed on her body and soul.

It would not be long now.

She slept late, her frayed nerves needing the time to heal. Juileta didn't raise her, and Miren was glad of it. She felt fresher for the extra rest. She dressed in pale blue, checked her face and set her hair in a small bun at her nape. She really needed to wash it tonight.

Hernandez sat at the breakfast table, newspaper spread before him, coffee cup empty. Juileta shuffled in with a plate of eggs and toast for Miren, and a fresh pot of coffee for Hernandez. Miren took a seat in silence. The newspaper flicked down. "You are late."

"S-sorry. I overslept..."

"It is all right. I've had a busy morning as it turns out, so I barely missed you. Eat up. There is much to do."

"Of course."

He stood and strode from the room, leaving Miren to push her eggs around her plate despondently. She simply could not face the grease, but knowing she needed something in her stomach, she forced some dry toast down her throat.

The day passed calmly. Miren asked their driver to take her to the bayside and, wrapped in a cloak, took a walk through the biting cold winds that blew up the coastal path. Standing at the railing she gripped the rusting metal, felt the flaking paint beneath her skin. Breathing in the misty droplets that formed over the water, Miren watched the currents rippling out over the sea, and the grey clouds that rolled through the skies. It was good to know the airmen had escaped. Anders had done so much for the Allied forces. She was proud of his determination and strength, even if it meant she had to wait.

But no longer. His job was done. Now it was time for her.

Returning home Juileta handed her a stack of mail. "Thank you," Miren said, as she made her way to her bureau to sort the correspondence. She leafed through the envelopes casually, most were bills addressed to Hernandez.

"Señora?" Miren turned, Juileta stood in her doorway.

"Yes, Juileta?"

"Another letter came, hand delivered. For you alone."

Miren's eyebrows knitted as Juileta lifted her hand, a small envelope – crisp, white and thin – secured between her fingers.

Scanning Juileta's face, Miren took the letter. Her mouth opened, a question forming on her lips. But Juileta curtseyed quickly and retreated from the room. Miren watched her go, alarm rising within her. Juileta had brought her a secret note. Followed her to the privacy of her office to deliver it. Why?

Setting her confusion aside, Miren took her seat at her desk and slid the letter opener under the seal.

Dearest Miren...

She dropped the letter. Instantly tears sprang into her eyes. "No," she whispered. "No."

Hand shaking, she retrieved the letter from her desk, forcing herself to read, and then reread. Her mind fought against every word.

I love you. Please believe my words. It is only the truth. But I cannot stay in San Sebastian. It is too dangerous for me there. I have left with the airmen, bound for the safety of Gibraltar. There I can find a way to continue my work for the freedom of Europe.

I know this is not what you wanted. But it is not the right time for us. Not yet.

I will come for you, later, when the war is done.

Until then, be strong, my love, and hold me in your heart.

Sincerely,

Anders

Hands shaking violently Miren rose from the desk and began pacing around the room. A scream broke from her lips, ripping from her throat in a raw howl, her fingers twining in her hair, pulling at the roots as she collapsed to the floor.

How could he do this? How could he leave her again?

He'd promised.

And then the memory, his words the last night she saw him, "We are leaving." She'd challenged him but he'd dismissed her concern. And then he'd made love to her. Hard and fast and urgent against the stone wall. He'd known. He came to ask her to listen out for him, and to say a goodbye.

He'd known he was leaving.

He'd lied to her face.

Anger pure and hot shot through her. She sprang to her feet and took up the letter. Gripping it between her two hands she ripped it apart, tear, tear, tear until it was a mess of scraps littered across her floor. Then she picked up the letter opener and flung it across the room. It crashed against the window, shattering the glass.

Miren stared at the broken pane, breath heaving in her chest.

A soft knock on the door. Juileta's questioning face. The woman took in the scene: torn paper, shattered glass.

"I will call the repair man. No need to trouble General Hernandez."

Miren stared at her in shock. The letter... Anders must have hand delivered it to Juileta, knowing Miren trusted her. All his planning, just to run away, to leave her, again. Miren saw the understanding in Juileta's face. She knew she must look a mess: eyes red-rimmed, hair awry, snot on her lip.

But Juileta ignored it all and simply bent to collect the torn paper from the floor.

Miren lowered herself to her knees to help. In silence the

two women worked, carefully plucking the shards of glass from the carpet.

When they were done Juileta rose and nodded. "Supper will be ready at six. I suggest a bath for my señora before then."

Their eyes met, and Miren knew she could trust Juileta with this secret. The ageing maid would not go to Hernandez about the private letter, or Miren's extreme reaction. A bond had formed between the two women who lived beneath Hernandez's roof. Juileta would keep her confidence. "Thank you," Miren whispered, and she meant it.

Juileta nodded once, then exited the room, leaving Miren alone, hands clutching the torn pieces of Anders' farewell to her chest, her heart as shredded as the pages.

Hernandez was already at the dinner table when Miren arrived. He sat hunched forward, red wine at his elbow. As she entered, he studied her; eyes gleaming in the soft light of the room, like a lion hunting his prey.

"Good evening, husband," Miren said, taking her seat.

"Good evening," he replied, taking up his glass and downing a large gulp. Juileta appeared with a tray of soups.

"Not yet, Juileta," Hernandez said. "We will eat later. First, I want some time to celebrate with my wife."

Juileta bobbed a curtsy and left the room swiftly.

Miren angled her head at Hernandez, mind racing. Celebrate? Had she forgotten an important date? It wasn't their anniversary, or his birthday...

"Will you join me in a glass of wine?"

"I—"

"Of course you will, this is a momentous day!"

Miren swallowed, nodded, then bracing herself, said, "Husband, please accept my apologies. I seem to have forgotten something very important. Forgive me—"

"No, no, my darling," Hernandez cooed. "How you fret. You have forgotten nothing. I have news!"

He paced to her side, glass and bottle in hand, and poured her a healthy serving. Miren watched the rich red wine slosh into her glass. It reminded her of blood.

Hernandez put down the bottle, collected his own glass and strolled to the mantel, resting his elbow on the wooden top. "Join me," he said, holding out a hand.

Miren rose stiffly, nervous, and went to stand with him.

"Cheers," he clinked their glasses together then took another huge gulp of his own. Miren sipped at hers. The wine was fruity and heavy. It felt like acid in her throat.

She watched as Hernandez savoured his own wine, a smug smile of self-satisfaction on his face.

"You will be proud of me, wife," he began. "Today I have done a great thing for Franco, for Spain."

He paused, clearly waiting for her to engage with his tale.

Miren rallied her acting skills, perfected now after almost eighteen months of marriage. "How exciting," she said. "Don't hesitate, tell me all."

"Oh, my darling, I will," he leered at her, expression dark and deep with malice.

"It pertains to a mutual friend, in fact," he said. "Can you guess who?"

Miren frowned. Mutual friend? She had no friends. Hernandez had seen to that. "I am not sure I—"

"I tease, I tease," Hernandez interrupted. He was clearly enjoying the moment and her discomfort. "It is likely you would not even remember the man. It was an awfully long time ago. Though I do believe you two were... close."

Miren raised her head, face tightening, lips parting. Hernandez stared at her, mouth twisted in a cruel smile. "I had a report this morning," he continued. "An unexplained fishing boat off the western coast. It seemed a small matter, but you know me, I like to ensure order in my region."

Miren's mouth went dry. *Oh God, no.*

"You would never guess what we found inside?"

Another pause. He expected an answer.

"I've no idea," she managed, the terrible knowledge that she *did* know sinking through her gut.

He crossed the room to refill his wine. "More?" He held the bottle up in offer. Miren shook her head. "The boat was not out fishing. It was smuggling! A little girl, two British soldiers and a man from San Sebastian. Our mutual friend."

Miren felt the blood drain from her face; suddenly light-headed, she swayed on her feet.

"And I think you know to whom I am referring..." He skewered her with a hard stare. "Your former boss. Anders Torres."

"Oh!" she breathed, unable to form words, her eyes now wide with fear.

Hernandez smirked. "Do not be afraid, my darling, you are quite safe from that man."

"What do you mean?"

"He is already dead."

The room spiralled away suddenly airless and cold. She reached out a hand to clasp the mantel in an attempt to steady herself.

"How?"

"I had him executed, of course. The man was a traitor to our nation. And he was working with Britain, against the interests of Spain. Thankfully one of the airmen talked. And we have handed over the information to Germany..."

His voice continued to wash over her, as he explained his orders. Anders, shot dead on discovery, right there on the boat. The airmen handed over to the German Army in France, the little girl...

It was too much. Her hand slacked, dropping her wine

glass, the liquid splashing across the polished wooden floor. Her knees gave and she fell to the boards with a bang. She felt his eyes on her back, boring into her soul, her secrets. But at that moment it didn't matter. The truth had stripped her of her ability to pretend.

Anders was dead.

She couldn't comprehend it.

Booted feet at her side, Hernandez towered above her. Miren flinched instinctively. A hand twisted through her hair. "You will honour me for my success," he said, wrenching her to her feet. Miren staggered up, pulled by the roots of her hair. Hernandez shoved her bodily across the room, his first act of physical violence towards her since the day they'd met in Bilbao so long ago. It had been coming, Miren had known.

At the table he swept an arm over the surface, clearing the cutlery in a crash of metal. Then he forced her face to the table with one hand, his other unbuckling his belt. Miren went limp. She didn't fight back. Not as he pushed her skirt up and dragged her panties down. Not as he spread her legs with his hips. She just stared, silent and lost across the shining surface of the table. What he did to her didn't matter, not anymore.

Anders abandoned her.

Anders was dead.

There was no escape, no rescue coming.

Miren was dust.

She watched as she floated away. Specks of hope materialised before her eyes, dancing in the firelight before the air sucked them up the chimney, up, up, up.

There was nothing left.

Miren was no more.

THIRTY-FOUR
ABENE

The cold earth crunched beneath her shoes, her breath a cloud of white before her face. Abene stomped her feet, trying to force some feeling back into her numbed toes. Around her, the November night was still, silent. Abene knew Sophie didn't like to run a transport so late in the year. The cold of the mountains was dangerous, the rivers on the Spanish side were deeper. But in war, sometimes, waiting was not a choice.

Above, the dark sky twinkled with a perfect vista of stars. It was beautiful, but Abene barely glanced up, her eyes and her focus trained on the old oak tree that stood in the middle of the field. It was the perfect landmark for the handover.

But Sophie was late, and that was unusual.

Abene paced back toward the tree, circling it once again, checking that she hadn't missed a group of hidden Allied soldiers leaning against its trunk. Silly. There were meant to be four in total. Three men to evacuate, and Sophie. She hadn't missed them in the dark. They simply weren't here.

At first, it hadn't bothered her. The walk from Bayonne was long, so Abene simply assumed they were running behind schedule. But as the hours slipped by concern furrowed her brow. It would not be long now before the dawn light spread across the grasses of the Pyrénées-Atlantiques. Soon farmers would be stirring. Even if Sophie arrived now, it would be too risky to transport the men to Starling Farm. They would have to wait. She dallied a moment longer, torn between her wish to see Sophie, to know that her friend and their charges were safe, and her own safety. She had to get back to the fermette before sunrise. If she ran into a German patrol on her return...

Puffing a breath of cloud before her, Abene made her decision. She would go home, wait for the next night and return. She paced back to the oak and unslung her sack of supplies from her back. It wasn't much, some water, hard cheese and bread. Intended as a refuelling snack before the trek to Starling Farm and the waiting hot meal Marguerite always provided. But it would have to do.

She knew Sophie would understand; eat the food, hide and wait.

Slipping the bag in between two large roots at the tree base, Abene straightened. Casting one final look around her, eyes squinting through the darkness, she departed.

On her way back to the fermette she passed Starling Farm. All seemed quiet and peaceful, the soft light of the kitchen glowed orange in the pre-dawn cold. Soon Jeans would appear in the doorway, his broad shoulders and long stride carrying him to the cow sheds to start the day. They would know to wait too, they'd discussed this possibility, so Abene didn't need to talk to them. But she was glad she'd checked by; it was good to see there were no soldiers swarming over her friend's home.

Sophie had simply been delayed, that was all.

Back home she tiptoed into the room she shared with Camille and Eduardo. They both slept peacefully, the boy snugged tightly deep within his blankets. The tension in her body sluiced away. Padding quietly to her own bed, Abene slipped beneath the covers hoping to catch an hour's rest before sunrise.

"Abene, wake up!"

Abene sat bolt upright in bed, eyes wide as they adjusted to the light. She'd overslept.

"Oh gosh, sorry," she stuttered, hurriedly rubbing sleep from her eyes as she swung her legs over the edge of the bed. "I can be ready, tell Eduardo I won't be a moment."

"Abene, stop." The mattress gave and Abene turned to face Camille.

Panic gripped her heart instantly as she took in Camille's strained blue eyes.

"What has happened? Where is Eduardo?"

Abene went to surge from the bed, to rush to find her child. But Camille stopped her with a firm hand.

"Eduardo is safe. He and Giselle are in his room playing. I told them to give us a moment."

Abene nodded slowly, panic calming as she took in the information. Brow creasing she eyed Camille. "Why aren't they at school? Why did no one wake me?"

Camille took a deep steadying breath and gripped Abene's hands. "You were out so late. I decided to let you rest. I planned to walk the children to school," she paused, subconsciously biting her lower lip before continuing. "Three army trucks sped past us on the road. Soldiers with guns. They were moving fast and didn't even glance at us. But I knew... I just knew..."

"Starling Farm?" Abene breathed.

"I hurried the children home, ordered them to stay and went to see... Abene, the soldiers were at Starling Farm."

Fear gripped Abene's throat in its fist. Coughing to loosen the tension, she looked at her friend. "Are they still there?"

Camille shook her head. "I do not know. I hurried back, to tell you. I know you had a handover last night."

Abene fought to control the rising dread that squeezed her lungs. "They didn't arrive," she said. "Sophie never made the handover."

Camille stared at her, eyes wide. "Who knows about us?"

"I have to think," Abene said, standing up.

"Abene, who knows?"

Abene turned to face her friend. "Marguerite knows. But Giselle is here, she won't give us away."

Camille stared at her, mouth working before. "People will reveal anything when they are desperate..."

Abene spun, heading for the door.

"Where are you going?"

"I have to see..."

"Abene!"

"Stay here, don't go out. I'll be back."

Grabbing her coat from the hook she raced from the farmhouse and onto the narrow dirt path that led to Starling Farm.

Despite Camille's warning, the sight of German trucks parked outside her friend's abode was still an awful shock. It was their worst fear come true. She crouched behind a tree by the roadside. As she watched, two soldiers appeared in the doorway, guns unslung, pointing back into the house. What happened next froze her heart. First Marguerite, then Jeans, appeared in the doorway, arms pressed to their backs by firm German hands. They were forced down the front stairs of the farmhouse and pushed to their knees on the icy dirt. One soldier, bearing the silver-trimmed coat of an officer slowly paced towards them. Abene couldn't hear his words, she was too far away. But it wasn't difficult to imagine.

The officer leaned close to Marguerite, before gripping a fistful of her hair and forcing her head back at a painful angle. Abene's hand went to her mouth in horror as Jeans surged forward to protect his wife. The butt of a rifle connected with his head and he fell to the ground, unconscious. Abene watched as the soldier stood above Jeans' felled body, rifle aimed at his head. The soldier looked up at the officer who paused, eyeing Jeans as he lay, helpless in the dirt. He flicked his hand.

The sound of rifle fire filled the crisp air and Abene flinched down behind the tree instinctively. The gun fell silent, its loud bangs replaced by a high-pitched scream. Marguerite had crawled to her husband's body, her hands running over his face, his neck and coming away bright red with blood. The officer looked up at two of his men. Slinging their guns on their backs they strode forward, hands gripping Marguerite and pulling her up. She fought, limbs flailing, mouth wide as she roared her pain and loss. But she was too small to fight the strength of two trained men. They hauled her up like a rag doll and half dragged, half carried her to the waiting truck. The officer was talking, pointing to the house. Three other soldiers turned sharply on their heels and headed for the house. They flowed like water, sounds of crashing furniture and smashing glassware echoing out into the frosted morning. Then, a plume of dark smoke began to rise up into the blue day, the bright orange of licking flames soon joining the black. The house had been set ablaze.

Abene gasped, eyes full of tears. The soldiers reappeared, climbing into the waiting trucks. The engines fired and they made their way out along the drive, the burning homestead in their wake. Abene sank down lower out of sight as they rattled past. Three trucks. Six men. For two farmers. As the trucks disappeared from view, Abene gave in to the sobs that had built within her chest. Her cries exploded from her mouth as she thought of Jeans' kind eyes and warm smile, now cold and dead in the dirt before his ruined home. And Marguerite was captured and at the mercy of the soldiers who had killed her husband and destroyed her life.

As her sobs calmed the heavy weight of understanding Abene forced herself to her feet. One foot and then the next, heading home.

Sophie had not arrived.

Starling Farm had been raided.

Jeans was dead and Marguerite a prisoner.

Had Sophie also been discovered? Was that why she'd not arrived at the oak tree the night before?

And what of the little girl she'd passed to the guides only weeks ago? Had they made it across the mountains to the safety of Spain?

How much of their network had been revealed?

Someone had talked. That much was clear.

What mattered now was how much they had told.

THIRTY-FIVE
ABENE

Time hung heavy, the sun slowly eking across the pale sky. Abene kept Eduardo and Giselle inside, not trusting them to stay near the farmhouse. She needed them in calling distance should an army truck arrive. What she would do to keep them safe, she did not know. Eduardo followed her instructions without bother. He was always happy to play indoors, especially as the seasons cooled. But Giselle was troubled, difficult. She complained about each lunch option Camille provided; where usually fish stew was her favourite, today it was too salty, the bread too hard. She fussed over the butter and argued Eduardo was, unfairly, given more cheese. Generally, she was out of sorts. Abene did not chide her. She knew Giselle well; she was a smart girl. This change in routine, not going to school on a weekday, especially now with the fear and pressures of the occupation, signalled danger. And Giselle knew it.

As the sun began to fade behind the pine trees that lined the farm, Giselle demanded answers. Hands planted on her hips, feet spread wide she announced, "It is time for me to go home."

Abene felt a shot of tension spark up her spine. She'd had

all day to consider an answer to this natural demand, yet with everything else that had occupied her mind, she'd not found a suitable response.

Turning to Camille, a plea on her lips, Abene sought her friend's calm counsel once again.

As she always seemed to do so naturally, Camille stepped into the fray. "Your mother thought you might enjoy staying a few nights longer," she began, moving to run a gentle hand through Giselle's fine hair. "The cows will soon need to shelter in the barns at night, and your father and mother have much work to do to prepare for the coming winter. It is the same here and across the region. We need the extra hours of work... and you and Eduardo will only be bored. Won't it be more fun to play here together?"

Giselle eyed Camille suspiciously. "It's never bothered them before—"

"Really?" Eduardo's piping voice cut Giselle off. "That's wonderful! Giselle, I can take you to see the wild mushrooms I found last Sunday. And we can help Camille with the evening milking..."

He prattled on, happy and excited, and took Giselle's hand, leading her from the room towards the door.

"Eduardo!" Abene caught herself and calmed her tone. She didn't want him outside, but realising that she needed a moment alone with Camille, relented. Forcing a smile to her lips she continued. "Stay close by, yes? And be back before dark."

"Of course, ma tante." Eduardo grinned at her, a smile of the purest, most innocent joy, before turning and drawing Giselle out into the dusk.

Abene sank into a chair at the kitchen table. Without a word Camille went to the sink, filling the kettle and setting it to boil on the hob. As the water gently warmed, she crossed to Abene, stopping beside her to rest a hand on her shoulder.

"What will you do?"

Abene didn't need to ask what she meant. Sophie had not arrived at the meeting point, their safe house was routed, and Marguerite was taken prisoner.

"Marguerite won't give us up. Giselle is safe here, that is all she has left."

Camille squeezed her shoulder, moving to make the tea. Placing the teapot on the kitchen table she took a seat beside her friend.

"Will you go back?"

Abene looked up, meeting Camille's eyes. She knew the answer was in her own stare. Camille turned away. For a moment she was still, a small muscle twitching one side of her tightly drawn lips. Then Camille exploded.

"They are gone! You know this. And the Germans are searching. There can be no other reason, no other way that they knew of Starling Farm. They caught Sophie and the airmen she seeks to save, and they gave Jeans and Marguerite up! They would have given you up too, if they knew where you lived."

"We don't know that—"

"I think we do."

"Camille," Abene reached for her friend's hand, but Camille pulled away, pacing from the table to the kitchen window. Abene watched as she rested her hands on the windowsill, eyes gazing out across the darkening farm. She waited. She understood. Camille cared for her and for Eduardo. Moreover, the discovery of Starling Farm and the passage of soldiers risked her family too.

After a long moment, Camille turned. Running her hands down the front of her dress she said, "The children are heading in. I'd best start supper."

"Camille—"

"And breakfast will be ready for you in the morning. Don't be late." She looked over her shoulder, fixing Abene with fierce eyes: a question and a demand. Abene blinked against the pain and fear she saw reflected in the twist of her friend's mouth, in the tears that threatened to flow down Camille's cheeks.

"I won't be."

Camille nodded once, hand rubbing roughly across her face, then disappeared into the grand pantry. Abene stayed at the table a moment, listening to the shuffle and bump of Camille sorting through the canned summer produce, gathering rice or potatoes from the cold store. The bang of the front door drew her attention. Eduardo and Giselle trotted into the room. Giselle's frowning concern was replaced now by a wide grin.

"Ah!" Abene chided playfully. "You two are covered in dirt. To the outhouse to clean for supper. And, Eduardo, change that shirt, it's filthy!"

"Si, ma tante!" he called as the two children disappeared into the depths of the house.

The mix of languages, so natural and unforced, drew a smile from her lips. As Abene watched him go, she felt her heart expand, as if it swelled, huge and bulbous, morphing out of her body to follow the boy as he loped away.

I will come back, she promised the silent room around her. I will always come back for my son.

Late that night, well after the house had drifted to sleep, Abene crept downstairs. As she padded to the front door a figure moved towards her from the darkness. Abene froze, sucking in a sharp breath. As her eyes adjusted to the faint light of the moon that dusted the room, Abene relaxed.

"Camille, what are you doing? You scared me half to death!"

Camille moved forward, orienting herself at Abene's side.

"I am coming with you."

"Camille? No, we talked about this. You stay here, watch over the house."

"No," her friend's voice was firm, determined. "I agreed to support you in this, but not to leave you as a lamb to the foxes. Tonight, I will be at your side."

Her whole being rebelled. This was her choice, her risk. She'd done all she could to keep her loved ones separate: Eduardo, Lourdes, Udane, Camille and Pierre... How could she allow this?

Camille eyed her in the dark. "I am coming," she hissed. "By your side or on your tail. I am coming with you."

Abene closed her eyes a moment, gathering her strength. She knew she could not sway her friend, and if she was honest, a part of her, deep and buried, was thankful. She was terrified of what she might find, or not find, by the oak tree. Having Camille by her side was something to hold on to in the dark of despair.

"Let's go," she said and stepped across the threshold into the bitter cold of night.

The field was dark and silent. A light breeze kissed the bare branches of the oak tree, filling the night with a soft rattle. Abene and Camille stepped quickly across the untended grasses of the field.

Several steps from the tree, Abene held up a hand. Gesturing in the dark she asked Camille to stay. To her relief, Camille obeyed. Abene moved forward, each step slow and purposeful. Her eyes were wide, pupils seeking every touch of starlight to guide her way. At the oak she crouched, shuffling around its base until she came to the two big roots and the gap in between. She plunged her hands into the darkness. Nothing.

She sat up, perplexed.

The supply bag was gone.

Slowly she stood, night dark eyes scanning around them. She detected no movement, no unexpected lights. Tilting her head she listened. Silence.

But... she leaned down, squinting in the pale moonlight. A

seam of moisture glistened on the bark. Reaching forward she pressed a finger into the shiny patch. Her fingers came away wet. And red.

Abene took a deep breath.

Someone had made it to the meeting point.

Someone was alive.

Quickly, she made her way back to Camille.

"So?" her friend whispered. "Nothing, right?"

Abene shook her head in the dark. "The bag is gone, and there is blood. Someone made it."

"Oh God!" She felt Camille move and imagined her friend covering her mouth in shock, as she always did.

"We have to find them," Abene said.

"But... how?"

Abene paused, mind whirling. "Stay by the tree. I'll be back."

Without giving Camille a chance to argue, Abene headed off into the dark. There was an old barn on the edge of the field, long abandoned, certainly not weatherproof. Its state of disrepair had been part of the reason for choosing this spot for the drop. No farmer was coming out here, not now. New development wasn't something you did under Nazi watch.

It was the only shelter for miles around, making it too obvious a target for patrols for Abene to use it as the meeting point, better to keep to the surrounding trees. But for an injured soldier, it was shelter and it was close.

Whoever had taken the bag was bleeding, badly. The mark on the tree was evidence enough of that. The survivor – dare she hope survivors – had not gone far.

She broke into a light jog, keeping her step as soft as possible while crossing the distance to the barn swiftly. As she approached she slowed her step, ears pricked, listening. The groan of pain was loud as it intruded on the silent night. Bracing herself she pushed open the barn door and stepped inside. The space was shrouded in darkness, the small light from the starry sky barely able to breach the space. She stood still, waiting, allowing her senses to adjust. The scrape on the floor, the panting breath of someone in trouble. Abene saw him. Laying prone in the centre of the dusty space was a man in slacks and a heavy coat. The sound of her arrival had shocked him, causing him to turn suddenly. Abene saw the flash of agony that creased his dirt-covered face. Lips parted, dry and split, as his hand came up in a gesture of placation.

"Désolé, sorry," he muttered, voice scraping from a parched throat.

Abene scanned the room, at his side lay the bag, open, the water bottle discarded, likely empty. She saw no one else.

"Where is Sophie?" she asked.

Surprise registered on the man's face and he forced himself up into a sitting position, hand now pressed to his gut. Abene could see a large red patch of blood staining the front of his coat. That was bad.

Abene stepped forward, voice harder. "Where is Sophie?"

The man's mouth opened and closed a few times, then his face fell into lines of sorrow as he shook his head.

"I am Gilles," he said.

Abene cocked her head. He was speaking French. Interesting. She moved forward slowly, not wanting to startle him. But as she drew closer, she realised she need not have worried. His skin was ashen, his face covered in a sheen of sweat, his eyes wide and glossy. Abene knelt before him.

"Can you move?"

He squeezed his eyes closed and pushed himself up onto his feet. A cry of pain escaped his lips. He stood before her on clearly unstable legs. Abene rushed to his side, gripping his arm.

"You can barely stand," she said, mind rapidly assessing his state of being and the distance they had to travel to the farm. "Are you sure you can walk?"

The man swayed in her arms, hunching over the wound to his front.

"There is no choice," he said.

He was right, Abene knew, but as she guided him to take his first step forward, and felt the weakness of his step, she worried that he could not make it.

"Wait," he said, stopping still. "Who are you? You know about Sophie but..." His words were cut off by a wheeze of pain from his lungs.

Abene braced him, allowing him time to regain his composure before answering. "My name is Abene, I work with Sophie. I left the bag..."

Gilles eyed her. Abene continued. "I was your contact, I will guide you to the safe house." She paused, realising that she could not in fact take Gilles to Starling Farm. Recovering, she continued. "Then I take you to Hendaye at the base of the Pyrenees, to cross. But..." she listened to his laboured breath. This man was going nowhere soon. "... Let's focus on getting you somewhere warm and cleaning up that wound."

"But the others... Randy, my friend. Have you seen my friend?" Abene saw the desperate hope in his eyes, hated the resignation that replaced it as she shook her head.

Gilles allowed her to help him out of the barn. About halfway to the oak, Camille joined them. "I saw you..." she said by way of explanation.

"Thank you. Here, take his other side. Gilles, this is Camille. She is my friend, you can trust her."

But Gilles was beyond fear, too drained from pain and blood loss, he clearly had no choice but to obey them.

The trek back to the farm took double the normal time as the two friends worked to manoeuvre Gilles down the road. As the farm came into view, Abene felt a swell of relief. Her muscles ached from the cold and bearing the soldier's weight for hours as they traversed the dirt track home, and her mind was exhausted from lack of sleep.

Coming to the front door, Camille paused. "Outhouse," she said.

Abene didn't argue. Carefully they moved Gilles around the circumference of the house, heading for the washroom. But just as they were about to slip inside, the dark night was flooded with light. Pierre stood at the back door eyes hard as he stared at his daughter and her friend.

Abene's heart lurched. This is not what she'd wanted, to put her dear friend in such an awful position. Pierre had taken her and her family in... She opened her mouth to explain, but Camille spoke first.

"The man is wounded. He will die if we do not help him."

Abene watched as Pierre paused, saw the fight between his instinct to protect his family and his sense of goodness as it filtered across his face. Then he sprang into action.

"Bring him into the kitchen, lay him on the table." Rolling up his sleeves he hurried back inside as Abene and Camille turned to guide Gilles into the main room of the house.

Pierre met them in the kitchen, helping them to lift Gilles onto the sturdy wooden table.

Pierre held his hands above Gilles' blood-soaked coat, and paused. "Is all right?" he said, looking directly into the bleeding soldier's eyes. Gilles nodded.

Pierre launched into action, unbuttoning the coat and pulling back the fabric to expose the wound.

Gilles' stomach was a mess of blood, dried black and fresh red.

Abene sucked in an involuntary breath of horror, her hand covering her mouth. Pierre barely paused. "Camille, boil water. Abene, fetch your mother and Udane. We will need more hands."

Abene stared at the old farmer a moment, then, driving herself into action, obeyed.

Lourdes and Udane came quickly, the questions she knew they longed to ask dying on their lips as they spied the prostrate man in the kitchen.

Pierre looked up from where he was gently mopping away the blood from Gilles' wounds. "Bullet fragments," he explained. "Not deep, but I have to clear the metal. Then he will need stitches. I have no pain medicine. You will need to hold him down. Take his legs and arms."

Without a word the women moved, Abene and Camille at Gilles' head, Lourdes and Udane at his feet. Pierre leaned down, pressing his forehead to Gilles' as he whispered something for the injured man alone. When he stood up, Gilles' eyes were wide, his mouth set in a line of grim determination. Pierre took up a pair of pliers and began.

It was bloody. Gilles' screams were horrific. The powerful thrashing of his limbs gave way to pitiful sobbing as he slowly lost his energy and finally consciousness.

Abene looked up at Pierre in fright, but Pierre's face remained smooth and focused. "It is always the way," he said, not looking up from his work. "They pass out from the pain."

Abene met Camille's eyes over Gilles' head. The horror of his time in the Great War dripped from those simple words.

After what seemed like hours, Pierre stepped back from Gilles' sleeping body, hands slick with blood. "Take him to my room, come." Between the five of them, they managed to carry Gilles' unconscious body up to Pierre's quarters. Once he was settled on the mattress, covers drawn up around him to keep him warm, Pierre spoke, "Now we wait."

"Lourdes, Udane, will you take the first watch? I need to speak with our daughters."

Lourdes nodded, stepping forward to perch on the edge of the bed. Udane took the chair in the corner.

Abene and Camille filed out of the room behind Pierre.

Back in the kitchen, the old farmer began the clean-up, wiping blood from the table and floor. Abene and Camille joined. They worked in silence until the kitchen was sparkling and fresh once again.

Pierre broke the silence. "He will need medicine, morphine." He looked at Camille, "But the Germans must not know."

"I can get some from the doctor's office, it won't be missed."

"You will be careful," Pierre said. It was not a question.

Then he turned to Abene. "This man, he is young and wounded. I know he is a soldier, that much is clear. The question is, why is he in my home?"

Abene swallowed, pausing to find the right words. Again, Camille cut in, "Abene is helping the resistance. They are sneaking soldiers out of occupied France, across the Pyrenees to safety. They are working to save France."

Pierre eyed his daughter, then turned back to Abene. "Were Jeans and Marguerite party to this?"

"Yes."

Pierre nodded.

"So this is why the Germans came for them? Something went wrong."

"It did. I don't know the details yet, but the man upstairs seems to be the only survivor."

Pierre paced away from the table, head lowered in thought. "I should have known Jeans would get involved in something like this. But I didn't expect it from you." He turned to face Camille.

Now it was Abene's turn to interrupt. "Camille is not involved. It is only me. I meet the soldiers at a set location and guide them to Starling Farm. Then, once they are recovered and the weather is suitable, I take them to Hendaye to cross. Camille only came today because—"

"—because it went wrong." Pierre's voice cracked like a whip, angry and cold.

Abene fell silent, shame punching her heart. His anger was right, it was justified. He had opened his home to Abene and her family, and she had repaid his kindness by risking his daughter's safety. This man, who'd seen war, then lost his wife... Camille was all he had left.

Unexpectedly, Pierre slumped. It was as if all the fight suddenly drained from his body. Moving on heavy, tired feet he sat down at the table. Camille and Abene sat too.

Eyeing them in turn, Pierre said, voice soft now, "We are at war, I know that. I fought once..."

Abene swallowed; Pierre's knowledge of how to stitch up a human had been on clear display.

"This war? I am too old. You are young, as I once was. I understand you must try. But the children must be kept safe, that is non-negotiable."

His eyes closed, his face drawn and weary. "The man can stay until he can walk, then he must go."

"But Starling Farm was raided, who knows if the other safe houses are intact!" Camille cried, looking at Abene.

But Abene knew Pierre was right. Resting a calming hand on her friend's arm she said, "I will take him, as soon as he can walk."

Pierre met her eyes across the table, and the promise was sealed. No matter what, Abene would get the soldier away from the farm, and keep Camille safe.

THIRTY-SIX

ABENE

Abene was in the kitchen feeding Eduardo and Giselle when Camille came down from her shift with Gilles. Neither of them had managed much sleep. Between the hours of finding Gilles and bringing him here, then the surgery and planning with Pierre, the sun had been peeking over the hills before either had found her bed.

But there was nothing for it. The day had started, the children were awake and they had a lot to discuss.

Camille took the chair next to Giselle and gently took the young girl's hand. "Giselle my darling, there is something you must know..."

The child didn't believe them of course. How could she? What ten-year-old could comprehend that her parents were gone, and may not be coming back? As Giselle screamed her tearful protest at Camille, Abene ushered Eduardo from the room. He knew what it was to be separated from his parents, and to become an orphan, he didn't need to relive that pain too closely. In the lounge, Abene took a seat and Eduardo came to sit beside her. Too large now to curl into her lap as he had when he was smaller, instead he snuggled into her side, seeking comfort. Abene wrapped her arm around his shoulders, pulling him close.

She watched his hands as they played with a button on his shirt, his gaze far away, processing. She waited. He would speak when he was ready.

"Does Giselle live with us now?"

"For a time, yes. But she has family in Bayonne. We will contact them. It is likely they will take her in."

"But not an orphanage?"

Abene felt her heart squeeze. She understood his concern. It was his experience after all. They were good to the children at the orphanage, kind and gentle. But nothing could substitute a mother's love.

"Not an orphanage."

She felt his body relax a little, then. "Why did the soldiers take her parents?"

Camille had been gentle in her description of the events at Starling Farm. Giselle didn't need to know her father was already dead.

"A misunderstanding, I am sure," Abene lied. It hurt to lie to Eduardo. Abene believed in honesty and trust. But this truth was too dangerous. Nothing mattered more than his safety.

"Will the soldiers take you?"

A fierce determination flooded her limbs. "No," she said and realised she truly meant it. Nothing and no one would ever take her from Eduardo's side. Eduardo snuggled closer, calming Abene's internal fire, and settling her nerves. Her hand soothed his hair subconsciously and she felt her eyelids drooping. Suddenly the boy sprang up. "I will check on Giselle, she will need a friend."

"That is very kind, Eduardo. But remember, if she needs to be alone, that is all right too."

"I will remember. But she won't want that. Giselle doesn't like being alone."

With that he trotted back to the kitchen in search of his friend, to offer what comfort he could. Once again a flood of love burst forth from her soul. Just eleven years old, what a beautiful young man he was growing to be.

Just then her mother appeared at the top of the stairs.

"He is awake," she said.

Gilles lay beneath the blankets, shivering.

"He burns with fever," Lourdes said.

"Likely an infection," Abene said. She perched herself on the bed beside Gilles and pressed her hand to his forehead.

"Go find Camille, see if she needs more help with the children. If you can relieve her, send her to town. We need the medications."

Lourdes nodded, leaving the room. Abene turned her attention back to Gilles.

"Water," he mouthed, lips too cracked and split to form proper sound. She reached over to the glass by the bed and held it to his lips, helping as he sipped.

When he was done his eyes began to close and Abene rose from the bed to sit in the little chair in the corner and keep watch in case he needed anything further.

"Abene?"

Abene jolted awake, blinking rapidly. She must have fallen asleep while watching over Gilles. Thankfully the young soldier seemed to be sleeping peacefully.

Camille was squatting before her, eyes sunken and rimmed in black smudges of fatigue.

"I gave him some morphine. It will help him sleep. I could not get much. The rations run short..."

"It will be enough," Abene said, sitting forward. "Sorry, I must have fallen asleep."

Camille smiled gently, cupping Abene's cheek. "You need rest too."

Shaking her head to clear the fog of sleep, Abene stood. "Where are the children?"

"Giselle and Eduardo are in the kitchen, helping Lourdes with supper preparations."

"How is the girl?"

"Dead on her feet. She won't be long from her bed either. It's been an awful day for her."

Abene placed a hand on Camille's shoulder, squeezing gently. "And how are you? I know the family have been close friends of yours since you were a girl."

Tears welled in Camille's eyes, shining silver in the afternoon light. "Marguerite was like a mother to me. She took me in when my own passed, and has always cared for me, and for Papá. My heart aches, it is true. But I must keep perspective. This is about Giselle, not me."

"We all have to grieve, Camille."

"And I will, but not yet. Now I have to be strong. Her family in Bayonne will welcome her. I will see her there myself, before the week is out. The sooner she is with them the better for her, and us."

Abene nodded her understanding of Camille's unspoken meaning. With the discovery of Starling Farm, everything had changed. And with this soldier hidden beneath their roof, no one at the fermette was safe. Abene rose from the chair to check on the sleeping Gilles.

"You have done enough today," she said, turning back to Camille. "Go, seek out your father. Take some time to be together. He will be hurting too."

"Merci," Camille whispered, dashing the tears from her cheeks.

Abene watched as she left the room, before perching herself on the edge of Gilles' bed.

"Who are you?" she whispered to herself.

Fresh faced, skin unlined, younger than her perhaps, and from a life more privileged than hers. An airman, she knew. Most of the men they snuck into Spain were Allied pilots, shot down over occupied France whilst on bombing raids across the country. But she'd never met one who spoke French. How many young airmen had she helped during her time working with Sophie and the Comet Line? Six? Seven? But she'd never really thought about them. Could barely picture any of their faces. Even the kind American Benjamin who had shown compassion to the small child Ana... Her heart squeezed thinking of the little girl. Before Ana, Abene had kept herself separate from her transports. They didn't offer stories of their lives, and she didn't ask. It was easier that way, keeping a distance between her and those she sought to help.

Just in case.

But Ana had changed that. The child had wedged herself into Abene's heart, opening her to those she helped. She sent a prayer that all that was befalling Starling Farm and the fermette had not followed the girl to the foot of the Pyrenees.

Now, as she watched the gentle rise and fall of Gilles' sleeping breath, it was as if the space within her that Ana had created sought to be filled more completely. And she found herself wondering of him and his life.

He was brave, or at least hopeful, to join up. What had driven him here to fight? What had brought any of the airmen?

She knew *her* reasons; everyone she loved was at risk. She would do anything for them. But why would someone travel across the seas and join a conflict that was not their own? What would inspire that choice?

He was kind too, she knew. In the fog of pain and fear, he'd still shown genuine concern for Sophie, and his friend Randy; that revealed a good heart. A man she would want to know, in a different life, free of the terrors of this one. Her lips parted in a heavy sigh. So much was lost in the wake of war, and so many lives were destroyed.

Moving a stray hair back from his sweat-beaded brow, Abene felt her resolve strengthen. This man had come here to a land that was not his own, to fight for freedom. Unlike Abene he had chosen that fight. He didn't deserve this fate. He would survive, this young victim of war. She would see to it. Somehow.

Gilles was wounded, badly, and needed time to heal. Abene kept watch at his side. For days he tossed and turned, crying out words at random, voice thick with delirium. Some words, Abene knew: *No! I'm sorry! Please!* Others were indecipherable. One broke her heart: *Maman!*

Did all men cry for their mothers, in the end?

Pierre checked in regularly, cleansing the wound with alcohol, his hands deft and trained. One night, he caught Abene watching his work. The smile he offered was sad and heavy. "I learned the hard way," he said, answering her question without it being asked. His time as a medic in the Great War had truly shaped Pierre. Right now, it was saving this man's life.

On the third morning, the soldier's eyes opened with the dawn. Abene stood from her chair and crossed swiftly to him, offering water to sip. He sipped from the cup, thin torso trembling from the effort of sitting up.

"Thank you," he croaked, falling back into his pillows, before remembering, "Oh sorry, merci."

Abene smiled and nodded, putting the glass back down.

The man scanned the room but made no attempt to rise. Abene waited in silence, watching his face. The roundness of youth still swelled his cheeks, even if the strain of injury had blackened the skin beneath his eyes.

"Where am I?" he asked at last.

"Safe," Abene said. "On a farm outside Saint-Jean-de-Luz."

"Saint-Jean..." the man trailed off, and then the light of recognition seized his eyes. "I am close then. In the French

Pyrenees. Who else is here? Did Randy make it? I have to find him..."

"Shhh, shhh, peace," Abene said, placing a hand on his sweat-soaked shirt to still him. "You are in no condition to do anything just now."

The man stilled, his breathing slowing as understanding settled over his face.

"It's just me, isn't it?"

Abene grimaced and nodded slowly.

He squeezed his eyes closed, a single tear escaping from between the lids. "We survived the crash, we made it to the rescuers. Thought we were home free..."

Abene waited patiently as the man spoke, processing his grief and loss. "Sophie told us we were nearly there, a contact would meet us then... bang! The Germans came out of nowhere. It was chaos. I was shot—"

He sat up suddenly, hands coming to his belly.

"Gentle!" Abene warned as he pulled up his shirt to expose the jagged wounds across his abdomen. He exhaled roughly. "Fieldwork," he said.

"The farmer here has experience in war. He saved your life."

The man looked at her again, face drawn and solemn. "You found me, brought me here."

Abene breathed out. "Yes. When Sophie didn't arrive, I went searching. You were the only one I found..."

He slumped back against the bed, face contorting in pain.

Abene licked her lips and thought of what she could offer this man, this stranger in his grief and pain. "You are safe here. We will get you healthy and then I will take you to Hendaye, to the next safe house."

"There is a safe house left?"

"I don't know," Abene answered truthfully. "But it is the only way..."

Her words trailed off as he turned his face to the brightening window. His mind, too full of the horrible truth, had switched off. Her plan to get him out of France would have to wait. Until then, keeping him safe from German discovery, keeping them all safe, was the priority.

"Rest, monsieur, regain your strength. Then we will see what comes next."

She rose, padding softly for the door.

"Wait," he cried, pausing her step.

"Thank you, Abene," he said, hand resting over his heart. Abene felt her throat tighten at the gesture, at his gratitude and his sorrow. They all bore so much in these fraught times. And there was still a long way to go. Bracing herself against the unknown before them, Abene nodded and left the room.

THIRTY-SEVEN

ABENE

They came a week later. One truck, two German soldiers and a polite knock on the door. "Officer Frederick Müller and Oskar Smitz, may we come in?" Pierre showed them through to the kitchen and offered tea. Camille, just returned from Bayonne, put on the kettle, and Lourdes snuck upstairs to warn Udane and Gilles to be absolutely silent.

"So, officers, how can we help you?" Pierre asked, taking a seat. Camille placed the teapot in the centre of the table and began pouring the hot liquid into cups. Abene hovered in the doorway, ready to grab Eduardo from where he played in the garden outside and run at the slightest sign of trouble.

The older officer, Müller, face clean-shaved, white showing at his temples, leaned forward, pressing his hands together in a gesture of contemplation. Fixing Pierre with a hard stare he paused, stretching the moment to the point of becoming unbearable, before leaning casually back in his chair, and opening his hands out as if in welcome.

"It is not you who can help us, but we who are here to help you," he said.

Pierre blinked, confusion furrowing his brow, his gaze

flicking up to Abene momentarily. Abene felt her heartbeat increase. What did these soldiers know? Had Marguerite broken?

Müller smiled into the tense silence, smoothing away an invisible blemish on his uniform before straightening his posture once again.

"We have been in the Pyrénées-Atlantiques for some time now, monsieur, we have come to know your communities. It seems to me that there is no conceivable way that you would not know of recent events at Starling Farm."

Abene tensed, her breathing halting. She watched as Pierre swallowed, his hands rubbing against his thighs in a nervous gesture. Probably drying away the sweat of fear from his palms.

"We saw the trucks, and the soldiers," he answered truthfully. "But we know nothing more."

The officer eyed him. "You were friends with the farmer, Jeans, and his wife Marguerite, were you not?"

Pierre gave a shrug, likely intended to be nonchalant, but it came off anxious, furtive. "We farm the same region, similar crops. We exchange small talk at market days. But I don't know if I would go as far as friends."

"Yet you harboured their daughter."

Abene's stomach dropped out of her body, horror gripping her heart.

Pierre did well. "Giselle is at school with my nephew, they are playmates. She was here the morning of the trucks..."

"... And you gave her shelter. Before sneaking her away to a family in Bayonne."

"I—"

"It is all right, monsieur," Müller said, holding up a hand to silence Pierre. "We found the girl. Fortunately, her story matches your own. She is of no interest to us. A child caught up in the betrayal of her family. No... it is not the girl who interests me, it is the timing."

Again he paused, allowing the tension to build. "Do you know why we arrested your neighbours? Monsieur?"

Pierre firmed his shoulders, before saying directly to the officer, "I do not."

The officer's mouth twitched into a small secret smile. "Yet on the night of their transgression, their child was here. That is interesting."

"I told you, Giselle and Eduardo are playmates at school—"

"So Marguerite has assured me."

The air went out of the room. Marguerite was alive. What had she told this officer?

"Eduardo..." Müller mused, "that is a Spanish name, yes?" He turned, eyeing Abene. "You are the boy's mother?"

She felt her stomach turn to water under his scrutiny. But she stood firm.

"I am."

"From San Sebastian, I am told."

Abene forced her features to calm, even as her every nerve felt poised and ready to flee. "Yes."

"How fortunate you are," the officer continued. "To be taken in by such a kind family. That is generosity that must be rewarded with honesty. And obedience."

"I am very grateful," Abene managed, mind racing, trying to assess how much this man knew. If she had to confess she would. She would do anything to save Eduardo.

"Abene has been a pleasure to have here," Pierre cut in unexpectedly. Abene shot him a look. No, no, she thought, don't defend me. Pierre ignored her pleading eyes and addressed the officer. "You can see I am ageing," he said, holding up his large, worn hands. "I am not the man I was in my youth. Abene is a great help with my farm work. I have given her shelter, yes, but she has repaid me tenfold."

He looked up at Abene, a soft smile on his face and she knew, despite the situation, he spoke the truth in his heart.

Gratitude flooded her, a tear springing unexpectedly to her eye.

The officer broke the moment. "How nice," he said, voice flat. "Well, Oskar and I have taken up enough of your time. We have more houses to visit, citizens to reassure." The two soldiers stood, straightening their jackets, something like regret swimming in the eyes of the younger man. But not in Müller's. "Rebellion, in any form, will not be tolerated," he asserted "Be careful, monsieur. Even your neighbours are not above suspicion. Can we count on your loyalty?"

Pierre stood slowly. "I know nothing of why you have taken Marguerite," he said, sticking to his story.

"Keep your ears and eyes open, monsieur. Even the most beautiful house can be built on a faulty foundation. Good day."

Müller turned for the front door, his boots ringing off the floorboards as he strode from the room. As he passed Abene he paused, face moving close to her own as he whispered, "As a survivor of the Civil War, you must understand the risk of subversion. And the folly. For the sake of your boy, I hope to never hear your name in my interrogation room."

Abene held his stare, heart pounding against her ribs so loud she was sure he could hear its rapid beat.

The officer gave a tight smile, then marched for the door, his colleague close at heel, and out into the late autumn day.

As the door closed behind the men, Abene's knees gave way and she sunk to the floor. Pierre was at her side in an instant.

"It's all right," she breathed, struggling to regain her composure. "I'm all right. I just need a moment."

Pierre remained crouched at her side. "Marguerite has held her tongue, for you, and her child," he said. "But the Nazis are no fools. There is a connection between us. They cannot prove our involvement, but they are watching."

Lourdes appeared on the stairs. "My daughter!" she exclaimed, seeing Abene on the floor.

"It is all right, Madre," Abene said, forcing herself to her feet. Pierre took her arm, helping her to steady her wobbling legs.

"I am sorry," she said, looking deeply into Pierre's eyes. "Please forgive the danger I have brought to your door."

"There is nothing to forgive. But we have a decision to make." His eyes flicked up, and Abene knew he was talking about the healing soldier hidden upstairs.

"Gilles has healed well. He is weak, he needs more time to recover."

"If the Germans find him here..."

"He can't make it, not yet."

"I can." They looked up. Gilles stood at the bottom of the stairs, Udane by his side.

"I heard the soldiers. You have all risked so much for me. I can never repay you for all you have done. But my presence here endangers you all. I will leave, tonight."

"Gilles," Abene said, turning to him. "We don't even know how to get you out yet. Starling Farm was discovered. The safe house in Hendaye may also be exposed—"

"I will find my way to Spain," Gilles interrupted. "I am a soldier, it will be all right."

Abene felt her chest tighten at his strength and determination. He was willing to push himself, to place his own life at risk for their safety.

She closed her eyes, mind racing. Even with a map and supplies, Gilles didn't know the region, and he was still healing. There was no way he could make it to San Sebastian alone. And even if he did, how could he find a friendly contact to transport him to Gibraltar?

If they let him go alone, hoping the safe house was intact, hoping he could make it, he would surely fail.

A realisation, undeniable and terrifying, settled over her shoulders.

"I will take you."

Gilles frowned at her. "There is no need. You said yourself that the safe house in Hendaye is likely routed. There is no reason for you to risk guiding me there. It is my chance to take."

"No," Abene said. "I mean I will take you to the safe house, and hope to find it occupied. But if need be, I will take you all the way, across the Pyrenees, to San Sebastian."

"Abene!" Lourdes gasped. "No."

"Madre," Abene turned to her mother, taking her hands, "I have crossed the mountains before, with you. I know the way."

"This is foolhardy," Gilles said, "I just need a map."

Abene rounded on him. "Just a map? Bah, you are the foolhardy one! Let's imagine that you do make it, alone, wounded, across the frozen ice of the mountains, across the top of Spain to my home town. Then what? Do you know San Sebastian? Or who or where to meet your transport to Gibraltar?"

"You don't know that information either," Gilles countered.

"But I know the fishermen," Abene said, mouth firming into a determined line. "I know the people. I will find you a boat to safety."

Beside her Lourdes released a tiny sob, drawing Abene's attention back to her mother. "You understand, don't you, Madre?"

"Si, ma cariña, si," Lourdes whispered, tears forming in her eyes. She reached forward, cupping her daughter's cheek. "You are so brave. I am so proud of you."

Abene leaned into her mother's palm, taking strength from her belief and pride. The truth was, she was terrified. Of the journey, of the risk, of the unknown. Yes, she knew San Sebastian and the men who worked the fish, eight years ago. Who knew who remained after so many years of Nationalist rule and terror? Who knew what kind of place her old home had become?

And leaving Eduardo... She pictured his trusting face, this

boy she loved. To walk away from him, the thought crashed through her, testing her resolve, pressing against her determination. She felt the sorrow swelling within her, felt her body pull away from the decision.

But there was no choice. It was her job to keep the boy safe and she had brought this danger to the farm. She would put it right. Gilles wouldn't make it on his own. And she wouldn't abandon him to such a fate. She would help him. Save the soldier, and protect Eduardo and Camille. Protect the ones she loved.

Lifting her head high, she stepped back from her mother's touch and addressed Pierre. "We will need supplies."

"Come," the old farmer said, "let's get you packed."

THIRTY-EIGHT

1981

The letter from Gilles had arrived months before.

It was a shock to me, and to all of us.

Juan wanted to ignore it... I knew we could not.

As he sits before me, I know I was right.

We are connected, this man and I. No matter what Juan might wish.

"I never knew," he is saying, eyes cast down, staring at his hands. "The war in France... it was horror and death and fear. But what you'd already seen, what you'd already endured. How did you keep going?"

Outside the sun is still shining brightly, but the shadows have started to lengthen. I stand, moving to the window; the cooling sea breeze will soon wash over my little house on the hillside, bringing with it the calm of evening. I stand at the window, allowing myself a moment to collect my thoughts. Outside the bright pink oleander flowers that grow wild in my garden dance on the breezes off the Bay of Biscay. I breathe deeply through my nose and smell their sweet scent through the open glass. It mixes with the salty brine of the waters off the coast. It is the scent of Donostia. It is the scent of home.

I return my focus to Gilles and smile softly. "You just do," I say.

He nods, accepting my answer in silence, but I can see he is not satisfied. In truth, nor am I. But it's all I can offer. I don't know how I made it through – the fear, the horror, the death and the loss.

My father...

So much was taken, all for the greed and power-driven desires of men. Franco in Spain, Hitler in France. They were the figureheads, but they did not act alone.

Silence is complicity.

But silence keeps you alive.

I made choices. And I survived. If I had my time again, would I do things differently? If war came knocking on the boundaries of my home today, would I strike back? Or cower and run?

I am older now, and my nation is settling into an uneasy peace. It is surprising how quickly complacency establishes itself. How fast people forget.

"My throat is dry," I say, seeking to shift my thoughts. "Can I offer you coffee? Only instant, I'm afraid. But it's good enough."

"Yes, thank you."

"Milk and sugar?"

Yes, one teaspoon, please."

I excuse myself to the kitchen, place the kettle on the hob, line up two cups and spoon out the grounds. So easy, so convenient.

Back in the dining room, I place a tray of biscuits before Gilles. "Help yourself."

He selects a chocolate-coated cookie, not one I baked. How we all have changed.

"Has it been difficult, returning here?" he asks.

I blink, surprised by the question. Yet I guess it is relevant in his mind. He had to find us after all.

"It has been good and hard," I pause, choosing my words. "I think it was really Juan who wished this return. His heart never found a place in France, nor his tongue!"

I give an indulgent laugh, thinking of my husband's appalling French. But I guess I am lucky; languages have always come easily to me.

Gilles is smiling, nodding. "I had trouble," he said. "Adjusting when I returned to Montreal. Civilian life was... slow."

"Juan experienced that too, after the war. But he found work on the fishing boats, purpose with our children. It got him through."

A light has come on in Gilles' eyes. "Yes, my children helped too."

"Tell me about them."

He eyes me cautiously, so I smile as open and wide as I can. I want to know, of his life, of his loves. I want him to have been happy.

"Two girls, Deidre and Amelia. And then my boy, James. They are all grown now. Beautiful, like their mother." He glances away, mouth twisting in regret. "I loved Jenny dearly, I tried to be a good husband, but..."

He looks down at his hands shaking his head distractedly. "I am not sure I knew how to be just a man again, after France."

I understand this. Saw it on the streets of Saint-Jean-de-Luz. In the eyes of the men who came back, heard it in their stories remembering fellow soldiers who never returned. "War changes us," I offer.

Gilles smiles briefly, a thank you for my words. But he has not felt them, not really.

"Where is your wife, now?"

"She lives in Maine, over the border. Our marriage was over for many years, but we made it work, for the kids. After James went to university in the States, Jenny moved out. We still talk regularly."

"There's still love there," I say, understanding.

"Yes, I think so." I see the gratitude in his eyes, it helps him to hear it.

And I wonder at my own marriage, at the connection between Juan and I. Borne of grief and loss, both broken and afraid. But at its core there is more, I think. It is why we are still together, despite all this world has thrown at us. We are united. I believe we always will be.

"The divorce was finalised last year."

"Is that why you are here? Why you decided to come now?"

Guilt clouds his eyes. "I should have come sooner, I know—"

"—Life is too short for regret," I interrupt. "You had your reasons. I understood. It was a lot, what happened, what we went through. We cope as best we can."

"Thank you."

I hear his thanks, but really, the words were for me. Gilles is not the only person weighed down by the pain of conflict, by the choices made and not made. By guilt, real or imagined.

My whole country carries this pain. And will for generations.

War does not end with an armistice.

It is when the guns go silent that the real fight begins.

PART 4

1943 – ACROSS THE PYRENEES

THIRTY-NINE

ABENE

The night air was biting. The porch wood rough against her knees. She wore trousers, borrowed from Pierre, and thick boots that belonged to Camille. At her side sat a bag of supplies: bread, cheese, dried beef, bottles filled with water from the well, thick blankets, cloth wraps for wounds, and a small jar of alcohol for swabbing. Wrapped in her arms Eduardo stood, his body shaking with the effort of holding in sobs as she said farewell. She clutched him to her fiercely, smoothing his soft hair, and breathing him in. The feel of his arms around her neck almost undid her resolve. How could she take this chance? How could she leave his side? What could possibly matter more than this child in her embrace?

And in those questions the answer rung, clear and true. It was for this boy that she must go. To remove the threat of discovery, to keep him safe as she had sworn to do. As her heart knew she must. If that meant she had to leave, then she had no other choice.

Taking a deep, steadying breath, she pulled back from Eduardo's arms. Holding him before her she focused, giving him her full and undivided attention. "Be a good boy. Listen to Camille and Pierre. Do your letters and numbers."

The boy nodded, lips quavering.

"And remember, you are my brave, brave boy. I won't be a moment longer than I must be. And then I will be back."

"You promise?"

Abene took his hand and pressed it to her heart. "I swear on the beat of my heart. I will come home."

Releasing a heavy breath Eduardo surged forward, back into her embrace, squeezing her with all his might. Gently she disentangled herself from his arms and, heart breaking within her chest, rose to her feet. The rest of the household were waiting by the door. She shook Pierre's hand, embraced her mother and Udane, then stood before Camille. Her dearest and truest friend.

"Camille, will you—"

"—I will love him as my own until you return. Eduardo will want for nothing. Ever."

The friends' eyes met, and an unspoken promise passed between them. If the worst happened, Abene knew Camille would always take care of Eduardo.

She turned from the assembled group. Gilles waited at the bottom of the porch steps, facing out into the dark forests that surrounded the farm. Slinging her bag of supplies over her shoulder she stepped down to him.

"Ready?" she asked.

His eyes shone in the warm light that seeped from the house. He nodded.

Waving to the gathered household, Abene said, "I will see you before you know it."

"Leave swiftly, and return faster," Camille called, gathering Eduardo to her side as the boy raised a hand in farewell.

Turning quickly as tears threatened to spill down her cheeks,

Abene and Gilles set off down the drive to the small gate that led to the dirt road. They would follow the backtracks between farms, avoid the main towns and roads, and travel only under the cover of dark. It would be hard going, a long and dangerous trek to freedom. Beside her, Gilles' tread was firm, his head held high. She hoped he would have the strength and health to make it.

At the gate Abene paused, glancing back a final time to the motley group that were assembled on the farmhouse porch. Bathed in the warm glow from the kitchen lights, enveloped, safe. Peace settled over her heart, they would be safe.

She was making sure of that.

Gilles could not remain at the fermette, the risk of discovery was too great. But he must not be captured by the Germans either, lest he reveal their involvement. Abene knew he would not give them away willingly, but soldiers knew how to make a man talk. The raid on Starling Farm was proof enough of that.

It was more than that too. Gilles was a good man and Abene couldn't stand by when it was in her power to help.

She knew the route to the Pyrenees, had guided many escapees to the safe house at the foot of the mountains. She would do so again and see Gilles safely from Nazi reach.

Secure in the belief that she had made the right decision, Abene opened the gate and stepped onto the dirt track.

They trekked through the night, the ground a mess of slippery mud beneath their feet, their breath a cloud of white mist before them, the pale moonlight casting the trees in silvered shadow. Though their pace was steady, Gilles' injury and the need for increased caution slowed them significantly. The Germans were looking for them. They had to keep well beneath the cover of the trees, avoiding the roads, It was a slower route, harder, and it wasn't long before Gilles began to lag. Abene adjusted her stride to suit him, staying close in the dark, support and comfort against the night. When he began to hunch in on himself, one hand bracing the still raw wound in his gut, Abene declared it was time to rest.

Gilles looked up from his focused march. "But there are hours left of darkness. I can keep going."

"This is the easy part," Abene said truthfully. "The mountain ranges will test us to the limit. It is better to conserve our energy now, so we are fresh when the ascent comes."

She read the conflict on his features, the war between relief at the promise of rest, and the fear-driven desire to keep moving, to get as far from Nazi reach as possible, and fast. But they were a long walk from safety, and Abene had made her decision.

They set up a small camp in a copse of pines that lined the boundary between two farms. Abene rationed out bread and cheese. They ate in silence, both alone in their thoughts, and their fatigue. Brushing crumbs from her coat, Abene pulled the blankets from her pack.

"Sleep close," she ordered, wrapping the rough wool around them. They snuggled together on the cold forest floor, a nest of pine needles and natural mulch their bed. Cocooned in the silent forest, Abene drifted to sleep.

The daylight hours came swiftly, the pale sunlight dappling across the forest floor. It did little to assuage the cold, but the light drew Abene from her sleep. Her arm was draped over Gilles, holding him tight to the curve of her own body. She tensed in surprise at the closeness of him, his musky scent filling her nose. Cold and asleep she must have sought his warmth. Now awake she should move away, allow some space between her and this man she barely knew. Yet as she lay beside him, listening to the rhythmic sigh of his breathing, still deep asleep, she found she didn't want to move. Closing her eyes again, she attempted to find her way back to sleep. The day was young, and she needed her rest for the night trek to come. But oblivion refused her request. Easing her arm from Gilles' body, Abene rolled onto her back and stared up at the canopy of trees, sparks of sunlight peeking through the leaves.

Her movement must have disturbed the sleeping airman, for he twitched, muttering under his breath before tensing, eyes snapping open.

"Peace," Abene soothed, laying a hand on his forehead. It was slick with sweat, despite the cold that enveloped them.

She watched as Gilles calmed his breathing, swallowing hard as he drew his mind from the darkness of his dreams back to the light.

His face turned to her, eyes meeting in the dawn light, so close she could feel his breath on her skin.

"You are all right," she whispered, hand smoothing along the light dusting of stubble that lined his jaw. "Bad dream?" Abene ventured.

A sheepish grin, a small shrug of his shoulders.

"They will ease, in time." She cupped his cheek. "Close your eyes," she whispered. "Rest. I am here. You will be safe."

His eyes blinked slowly as the fatigue of his healing body reached up to claim him back to sleep. As consciousness fled, his body eased into hers, his head coming to rest on her shoulder. Abene relaxed against his warmth, felt his slowing breath against her side. Soon her eyes became heavy and the morning drifted away.

Hours passed, the sun rose, birds singing to the day, breeze kissing through the pines above, and they slept.

They awoke around midday and shared more bread and cheese before Abene insisted on inspecting his wound. Gingerly Gilles unbuttoned his coat and lifted his shirt.

Abene suppressed a sharp intake of breath. One night of walking had already impacted the wound site. Dried blood lined the stitches where the wound had been stretched too far, fresh blood seeped at the corners. It was not healed enough for this journey, she knew, but what was the alternative?

Reaching into her pack she retrieved the small bottle of alcohol and a rag. Soaking the rag in the spirit, she carefully dabbed the fluid over the wound. Gilles tensed and hissed, but remained stoic, allowing her to clean the raw wound. When she was finished, he slumped back onto the dirt floor, breathing heavily.

"Sleep," Abene said. "We set off at dusk."

Gilles said nothing, simply closed his eyes, his breathing slowing and deepening quickly. He was exhausted.

Abene settled down beside him, determined to find her own slumber, but once again, rest would not come.

She woke Gilles as the gloaming light of sunset cast the trees in soft yellow, the sky a rich cobalt blue. They packed swiftly and set off once again, sticking to the forest edges, where they could easily duck back into the cover of trees should any unwanted attention arrive.

Their pace was slower than the night before, Gilles' steps tentative, movement clearly painful. Abene stopped him. Taking his pack of supplies from his back she slung it over her own shoulder. The weight was not so much extra for her to carry. "You have your own pack..." Gilles protested.

"You have a hole in your stomach," Abene retorted, striding on. Gilles didn't argue. That night she didn't allow them to stop early. She wanted to make it to the mountainside town of Hendaye before sunup. A part of her still hoped the safe house stood untouched, that she would find Mateo and Antonio, alive and ready to guide Gilles to Spain.

Moonlight gilded the frosted earth that lead to the small farmhouse she knew so well. It stood, still and silent, wrapped in night. No smoke rose from the chimney, no lamplight shone from the windows.

Abene held up a hand. "Wait here," she ordered. Dropping the two packs to the ground she crouched low and paced forward to investigate.

She was yards from the house when she knew. The front door was open, partially off its hinges, only darkness within. Cold and mute, the farmhouse was an empty shell. Abene took in a deep breath, sent a prayer to God that the occupants still lived, and then turned back to Gilles. And into the butt of a gun.

Her hands flew up instinctively, her breath puffing a thick white cloud of surprise before her eyes focused on the face beyond the end of the rifle.

"Mateo?"

Mateo held a finger to his lips for silence, before dropping the gun and stepping close.

"Sorry, I didn't realise it was you," he whispered. "What are you doing here?"

"I have a soldier, he needs to cross."

Mateo shook his head. "Not now, it is too dangerous. You can see we were raided. The patrols are tight and regular. We have been discovered."

"But you got away."

"The Germans came a week ago, we ran into the forest. But we dare not return."

Abene steeled her resolve. "Mateo, I have no choice. I can't keep this man safe on this side of the border. Please, we have to cross."

"I will not go, not now. Nor will Antonio."

"Then I will take him."

"It's too risky."

She stared at him in the pale moonlight, eyes desperate, and saw the moment he relented.

"Come," he turned, leading her away.

Deep in the forest, they met with Antonio, the other smuggler who helped lead men across the mountains. He squatted by a low fire, buried in blankets.

"Abene?" the surprise in his voice was obvious.

"She has a man to transport."

Already Antonio's head was shaking. Mateo held up a hand. "I have already told her, but she says there is no choice. You still have the espadrilles?"

Antonio shuffled to a bag, pulling out two pairs of canvas shoes and throwing them to Mateo.

"Wear these," Mateo said, handing the shoes to Abene. "They help with the damp on the mountains. Be sure to dump all your francs too. If you are captured the foreign currency will give you away. And here, he pulled a large square of folded paper from his own sack. "A map of our route. I always give one to the soldiers, in case..."

Abene unfolded the page, but the light was too dim for her to properly make out the markings.

"We have no food to spare," Mateo continued. "You will need to resupply in town. Bread and cheese are best. High energy, low weight."

"All right. Thank you, for all you have done for the people we have saved."

Mateo frowned, guilt cutting deep lines along his face. "I have a family too," he said.

Abene reached out, gripping his shoulder. "Be safe," she said.

"They are gone?" Gilles asked as Abene took up their packs once more, bracing herself against the flood of weariness that washed over her limbs.

"It is empty," she said simply, not wanting to explain the full truth. "I saw an old shed a mile or two back. We will make camp there. Rest. There is rain on the wind. We will see out the storm, and get some sleep ready for the next stage. Tomorrow I will head into town and resupply. So we are ready..."

A gentle hand squeezed her shoulder and Abene looked up, meeting Gilles eyes. "I am sorry," he said simply.

She didn't know why he was sorry. For her friends, now

prisoners of the Nazis, or dead? For the danger that lay ahead? For her separation from her family and loved ones? For the whole horrid mess that war created? All of it, or none of it, it didn't matter.

She was sorry too.

A sob swelled up in her chest, tears breaking free from her eyes. Gently Gilles pulled her to him, wrapping her in a comforting embrace. His arms were strong, and solid, despite the tremble of fatigue she could feel running through his body. She allowed him to hold her, allowed herself to give in to the comfort and support. She needed it, she realised. She needed him too. The only way through this next stage was together.

Collecting herself she stepped back. "Thank you," she whispered. He smiled at her in the soft darkness. "Let's get to that barn before sunup."

As the first patter of rain landed on the already water-laden soil, they stepped into the small barn. It was dusty, run-down, but dry. Collapsing in a corner they drew blankets around themselves, bodies tucked close for warmth. Abene was exhausted, too wrung out from walking, from loss and sorrow, from the strain of responsibility to even think of food. Instead, cradled in Gilles' arms, her eyes drifted closed as the soft patter of rain on wooden beams lulled her to sleep.

The rain shower passed by mid-morning and Abene, refreshed after a deep rest, made her way into the border town of Hendaye. Wrapped tightly in her coat she kept herself small and quiet, as she sought a market shop to resupply. Before her, the coastline of France gleamed in the winter light, along its cliffs the armaments of Hitler's Atlantic Wall defences. Holding her nerve, she pressed on. Around her the town went about its day, seemingly unaffected by the war that surrounded them. Until a patrol came into view. The warm banter, the unhurried pace, changed in an instant as shop owners and customers fell silent and shrunk in on themselves as if melting into the background, trying to blend into the terraced buildings of the stores. The soldiers continued their patrol, unfazed by the silent tension that followed in their wake. The silence remained long after the patrol had turned the corner to another street.

Moving swiftly Abene found a grocer and purchased more cheese and bread, some dried fish and beef. As she handed over the last of her francs, keen to relieve herself of the incriminating currency before they crossed into Spain the cashier eyed her, expression hard. But he asked no questions. It was better not to know.

Nodding her thanks, Abene left swiftly.

Back in the small barn she and Gilles shared a large meal, filling themselves to the brim, ready for the journey the dusk would bring.

As the sun sank low in the sky on their final day in France, Abene packed their bags and Gilles buttoned his coat. Standing at the door of the hut she turned to him. "Ready?"

"I am."

"Let's go."

FORTY

ABENE

The going was tough. Winter had already arrived on the mountain, bringing ice-coated pathways, the wind a frozen whip that bit at every inch of exposed skin. But they kept on. Juan had made it across in January; the knowledge of his crossing gave Abene hope that they too could succeed. She led the way, thigh muscles screaming as she pushed up, up, up the mountainous terrain of the Pyrenees. The trek was harder than she remembered, the cold and the dark rendering the path treacherous, and unpredictable.

Behind her Gilles laboured in silence, his breathing a heavy rasp.

Abene knew he must be in agony, the strain on his wound would be awful. But he didn't ask for rest and she didn't offer it. This part of the journey simply had to be endured. There was no alternative. Shelter was scarce and the fierce cold was a danger they could not avoid. There was no choice but to risk travel in the daylight hours, the terrain too treacherous to traverse in full night. The only option was to press forward, to cross the border and make it to Spain.

Sleet, cold and slippery, began to fall on the second day. It coated the rocks in a slick of wet, making them slippery and difficult. Their pace slowed, but Abene did not allow them to stop. As the sleet continued to flurry down, becoming firmer, thicker and heavier, it settled over their coats and hats, the wet seeping into the cloth, soaking through until it reached their flesh. Wet through, muscles burning, wicked winds whipping at their backs, they began to shiver as the cold took over. Abene knew they needed shelter, and soon. Remembering the old shepherd's hut Juan had found on their crossing eight years before, she adjusted their track, hoping her memory and God would guide her there.

The sun was rapidly descending casting them in the grey of gathering night as they came to a particularly steep incline, the jagged rocks sharp and unforgiving. Their pace slowed again, Gilles hunching down to use his hands to support his ascent. But Abene pushed on, the fading light and building sleet forcing her forward.

And then he slipped.

Abene barely heard it; the roar of the winter winds was so strong and forceful as it swirled about their heads. A small cry, the crunch of rock on rock. She looked back and watched in horror as Gilles tumbled down, sliding on his belly until his legs crashed into a larger rock that protruded from the mountainside.

Quickly Abene discarded her packs and, bracing herself with her hands, hurried down to where Gilles sprawled below.

"Gilles! Gilles! Are you all right?" She gripped his arm, rolling him over. A low groan sounded from his lips and his eyes fluttered.

"Gilles, get up. Come on, you have to get up." Around them the sleet thickened again, turning to snow. It coated the rocky outcrop, and the path ahead, dusting them in soft white. Fingers swift, Abene unbuttoned Gilles' coat. She didn't need to open his shirt. The white of the material was red with blood. She gasped, eyeing the soldier as fear lashed along her limbs. She had to get him to shelter and deal with his injury, and quickly. Moving behind him she wrapped her arms under his armpits. "I am going to push you up now, Gilles. You have to help me. You have to move."

He didn't answer, but she felt the muscles in his chest tense, ready for action. Bracing herself against the hard rock of the mountain Abene pushed. Gilles roared in agony as he worked to come to his feet. Standing, he hunched heavily over his middle, eyes wide, lips trembling.

"There is a hut," Abene explained. "It's not far, Gilles. We are almost there. We have to keep going, just a little further."

Gilles nodded, gasping for breath, and Abene urged him forward. They made their way back up the incline, Abene close behind Gilles, watching for him to slip again, ready to try and stop his fall. They passed the packs she'd dropped, and Abene made a mental note of their location. They pressed on, up and up and up until they broke over the crest of the hill. There, just a few yards down in the next valley stood the shepherd's hut. Abene released a sob of gratitude and sent her thanks to God for guiding her truly. Taking Gilles' arm she guided him down to the hut and settled him inside.

"Stay here," she ordered, though her words were unnecessary. As Gilles lay down on the dusty floor of the hut, she knew he was going nowhere without her.

As the last rays of sunlight dipped below the mountain peaks, Abene trudged back down the cliff face to collect their packs. Staggering and slipping, muscles spasming with pain and fatigue she made her way back to the hut and shut the door firmly behind her.

There was no light in the hut, and she had no dry wood for a fire. But they had blankets, and each other. Gilles' wound could wait. Feeling her way to him in the dark, she helped him to strip off his soaked coat and wrapped him in a fresh blanket, damp from the pack, but better than nothing. Pressing another blanket against his stomach she heard Gilles gasp in pain. "Hold this here, stop the blood."

His hand took the blanket. "Rest now," she crooned, soothing his rain and sweat-drenched hair from his forehead. "Rest now."

Wrapping herself around Gilles' shivering body Abene willed the meagre warmth of her body to flow into his. As the winds whipped around the walls of the hut, she sent a new prayer to God. She cared for this man in her arms, had committed to bring him safely into Spain. He deserved to make it to safety, to get out of France and live a life of freedom and hope. They all did.

"Please God," she prayed, "let Gilles survive the night."

Abene woke with a start. She sat up sharply, blinking rapidly as her eyes adjusted to the soft dawn light. Outside the wind whistled its harsh lullaby, but inside was still. Gilles sat steps away, rummaging in their packs. He must have awoken before her. Rubbing the sleep from her eyes, Abene crawled over to Gilles. He looked over at her, face pale and drawn, eyes tight with pain.

"Let me see," she said, pressing his shoulder gently to guide him to sit flat. He allowed her to unbutton his shirt, wincing as she pulled the material away from where blood had dried through it and stuck the shirt to his wound. Exposing his stomach Abene blew out a long, heavy breath.

Gently she ran her fingers along the jagged seam of his injury.

"How bad is it?"

"You've torn several stitches," she said, turning to the pack to collect the bottle of alcohol and fresh bandages. "There is a lot of blood. But you will live."

Gilles nodded.

"Lay back."

As gently as she could Abene washed the wound in alcohol. Once all the caked blood was gone she helped Gilles to a standing position and wrapped a bandage around his middle, hoping it would help reinforce the remaining stitches.

"I can go on," Gilles said.

"Not today you can't," she replied. "Besides, the weather is still harsh. Here we have shelter. We can rest a while until the storm subsides. Lie back down, I am going for firewood."

Gilles eased himself to the floor, pulling a blanket up under his chin, and Abene slipped out into the icy morning.

They passed several days in the hut, the sound of the wind and the crackle of the fire filling the space around them. The hut was small and dark, but that made it easy to keep warm. Gilles mostly slept, while Abene busied herself collecting wood and water from the valley outside.

At night they huddled close, the deep cold of the peaks of the Pyrenees encroaching even within the circle of firelight.

They shared stories to pass the dark hours. Gilles told her of his childhood in Canada. The son of a school teacher, his boyhood had been made up of harvest festivals and Christmas lights, of pumpkins and presents and hot chocolate and roasts.

"It sounds so beautiful, Canada."

"It is," Gilles sighed, falling into a wistful silence.

Abene rolled onto her side, resting her head on her hand she watched his face in the flickering flames. "Why did you come?"

"Sorry?" Gilles looked at her, frowning.

"Why did you join the Air Force? Why did you come here to fight?"

"Because it was the right thing to do."

Abene narrowed her eyes at him. Could his reason really be so simple? It was hard to believe.

"What?" Gilles asked.

"War is horror and death," Abene said. "No one chooses that."

"You are here," Gilles argued. "You are helping me. That was a choice."

"Because my home," a pause, "my *homes*, have been taken from me. My freedom, the safety of my son, was destroyed. I have no choice. You did."

She stared at Gilles. Watched as his features flushed in shame. "You are right," he admitted, voice soft. "It was more than honour. France and Canada, our countries are connected. My mother's family are French. When my best friend Randy signed up, talking of adventure, the feats of bravery, I wanted that too.

"We were assigned to a bomber squadron, in Yorkshire. Gunners, there to protect the plane, at least in theory. Our squadron raided deep into France," he paused, releasing a heavy breath. "War is not what we expected. I am no fool. I know that our raids did not only land on German heads."

Ana's terrified eyes appeared in Abene's mind. Her sanctuary exploded by Allied bombs, mother and father gone. She sent a fresh prayer to God for the little Jewish child and hoped she'd found safety.

"On the last raid, we were hit. Randy and I made it out of the plane, our parachutes worked. A farmer found us in a pine forest, took us to the network, and got us down to Sophie in Bayonne. She warned us we could surrender and Germany would let us live. Or we could attempt escape and if captured, we would die. We chose escape. But I didn't think about what it meant for those who helped us." He fell silent, eyes soft with regret.

"There were two others with us when we left Bayonne to meet you, Brits I think, though we really didn't talk. I didn't even see the Germans. Sophie pushed me aside. The others scattered. I was hit." His hand drifted over his wound. "I went down. Waited. When the Germans were gone so were the others. I couldn't find anyone... not even Sophie."

Abene closed her eyes, sorrow flooding her soul for her brave friend. Sophie had risked it all for what she believed. She deserved better than whatever fate she'd met in that barren field.

"I didn't know what to do. I was in such pain, losing blood. Somehow I found the checkpoint, and your bag, at the oak tree. I think... I think that kept me alive. Hope. I found the barn and waited..."

He broke off, wiping his eyes, swallowing hard. Abene stayed silent, still, listening to the sounds of the storm that whipped around their tiny hut.

Eventually, Gilles spoke. "I came to do the right thing and to be a hero. I believed that I could be part of a great victory. But I am not that man."

"War is not heroic," Abene said, voice thick with emotion and anger.

She felt his eyes on her and shifted uncomfortably. "What you are doing, here, helping me. That is heroic. I think."

Abene shook her head. "No," she said. "That is the right thing to do."

Gilles laughed and settled back into the blankets. An easy silence fell between them. Abene felt her eyelids grow heavy, and her breathing deepen. Just as she was about to drift into sleep Gilles whispered, "To me, you are the truest hero."

Their eyes met in the firelight, two souls broken by loss and war, two people at the edge of hope. As their lips met, nervous, tentative, Abene felt fire thrum through her skin, bolts of energy piercing her very core. Gilles cupped her chin, tipping her head back, deepening the kiss. Abene let her hands to run down his face, his neck, gently over his chest. She lay back, allowing him to move above her. He pulled her close, his body leaning into hers, then broke away with a grunt.

"Ah, sorry," he said, voice sheepish. "I forgot my limits."

"Your wound?" Abene sat up, reaching to check his stitches.

He caught her hand and pressed a kiss to her palm in the dark. "I am all right. Just got a little overexcited."

Abene grinned at him, placing a gentle hand on his cheek, before drawing him to her for another kiss, soft, loving.

"It is all right. We can lay together," she said.

"I'd like that," he replied.

FORTY-ONE

ABENE

When the sleet cleared and the clouds dried up, their journey continued. The going was slow, but mercifully uneventful. A clear, pale sky hung above them, the gentle sun guiding their steps. As they walked out onto the Spanish side of the plains that bordered the Pyrenees, Abene and Gilles sank to their knees. Breathing heavily, they swayed slightly as their aching muscles spasmed and cramped.

"We made it," Gilles managed through gasping breaths.

"We did," Abene agreed. There was still a long walk before them until they reached San Sebastian, but they had made it through the mountains to Spain. They were beyond Nazi reach. In theory at least.

But not yet safe from Spanish guards.

The first hurdle rushed past already in flood, the Bidasoa River, too full and flowing to attempt to swim, especially with Gilles' injury. The water ran along the border of France and Spain; the only crossing for miles in either direction was a shaky swing bridge, guarded by a patrol.

Abene led them downstream to wait. "Best to try our luck at

night." They made camp on the edge of a farmer's field. The cold still surrounded them, the clouds grey with the threat of rain, but it was not as biting and oppressive as it had been in the Pyrenees.

"The mountains are beautiful," Gilles said, eyes looking back at the snow-capped peaks they had just traversed.

"They are, better for a summer stroll though, I think."

Gilles huffed a laugh and settled down to rest.

When the depth of night shrouded their passage, they inched back to the dubious bridge. A single light shone from the guard house, the soft rumble of chatter and the laughter of relaxation echoing from the walls.

Abene held a finger to her lips, before pacing forward. One foot after the other, they traversed the rickety bridge, listening intently, waiting for the scream of a whistle, the shout of alarm that would signal they had been discovered. As Abene's feet squelched into the sodden mud of the far riverbank, relief flooded her senses. Turning back, she held out a hand to help Gilles stumble to her side.

Smiling at each other in the dark, they continued, one destination in mind: Abene's childhood home.

They arrived on the outskirts of San Sebastian two days later, having crossed ravines, more rivers, fields and rock.

Standing on the small road that led down into the town proper, Abene felt her eyes well with tears. This ground was her home. Eight years had passed since she'd walked on the land of her people. Eight long and heartbreaking years.

When San Sebastian had fallen to the Nationalists, she had lost everything. Her home, her culture, her beloved papá. She had thought there was nothing left, no joy or hope to keep her going. Then Eduardo had collided into her life, and Camille and Pierre, and she had found that life went on. Love had shown her the way back to hope and passion.

But she'd never believed she would walk the soil of her country again.

However changed, Spain was still the home of her heart.

"What can I do?" Gilles whispered at her side. Abene turned, smiling up at him. During their days on the mountain something had shifted between them, a new understanding and connection developing almost without notice.

"You are here with me, that is enough."

Gilles nodded, and stood in silence beside her, allowing her the time she needed for this moment.

"I can't risk taking you into the town," Abene said eventually. "Spain is neutral yes, but we have all heard the stories of Franco's double dealings. Who knows what we might find here. In the morning, I will go in alone."

"But what of your safety? You fled the Nationalists, just as I flee the Nazis."

Abene eyed the red roofs of her home town, the grey and turbulent waters of the bay beyond.

"I know Donostia. I know where to go and who to speak to. I will draw less notice alone."

"Fair enough."

"We will go to my old family home. It is on the edge of town, unlikely to have been occupied after we left. We can set up a base there until I find a way to get you to Gibraltar."

Gilles followed her across the outskirts of the city below and back up the hill to the small stone cottage that once rang with the love of family. It sat still and silent, the windows broken, the roof partially caved in. The land around it was brown and dead from winter, but clearly rough and unkempt.

"Still abandoned then," Gilles quipped. "We are in luck."

Inside the cottage was full of dirt and rotten leaves. Pigeons nested in the remaining beams of the roof, their poop covering the floor. Abene wrinkled her nose.

"We can clear a space for us," Gilles said, bending to gather up a clump of leaf material before grimacing and holding his belly.

"You rest," Abene said. "I will see what I can do."

An hour later she had managed to remove some of the dried poop from the floor, kicking it along the ground and out the door with her booted feet. There was nothing she could do for the smell.

"Come and rest." Gilles smiled. "It is not going to get any cleaner."

Lips twisting in a wry smile, Abene joined him on the mucky floor. "I am not sure how I will manage to be inconspicuous in the town," Abene said. "I think they will smell me coming."

Gilles wrapped an arm around her and released a laugh that brushed across her neck. Smiling at her own joke, Abene cuddled into his side, seeking and sharing warmth, and solace. She was home. The walls were cold and empty, the comforting scent of her mother's cooking absent from the air. This place that had once signalled safety and love, now desolate and cold. Beside her Gilles tightened his embrace, perhaps sensing her disquiet. Thankful for his companionship in this moment of internal conflict, she tucked in closer and closed her eyes.

They had made it past Nazi patrols, through snow-capped peaks and out of the storm of the Pyrenees. There was one final stage left on their journey.

Abene had to find a boat.

Abene stood stripped to her waist in the morning sunlight, canteen of water in her hands. Splashing the icy water over her body she rubbed her skin vigorously, trying to clear away some of the dirt and dried sweat. She hoped it would do some good. Pulling on a fresh blouse she'd kept for this day she turned back for the hut. Gilles' head quickly disappeared behind the doorway and Abene felt her lips quirk in a grin. Cheeky man, had he been watching her wash?

Smiling to herself she tried to smooth the wrinkles from the blouse, but the material was too soft and had been roughed up too much in her pack. She'd be wearing her coat anyway, it probably didn't matter.

She made her way back to the cottage.

"I will be back before sunset," she promised Giles. "Will you be all right alone?"

"Can you bring some more food? Something other than cheese and bread?"

Abene smiled. "I will try."

San Sebastian was exactly the same, and totally changed. As Abene walked towards the old town she felt her nostrils expand as they breathed in the familiar salty brine of the Bay of Biscay, the scent of frying mackerel on the breeze. But as she came to the sweeping beach she'd played on as a child, shock halted her step. Nazis. Two of them, standing on the curve of the bay, chatting companionably, with a slender woman. They were all rugged up in thick coats, the smoke of the soldiers' cigarettes blowing back into the city as the winds of the bay pushed past.

Abene stood frozen, unable to make her limbs respond.

It was silly, she told herself. They didn't know who she was, or why she was here. There was nothing to fear.

And yet dread flowed along her limbs, her breath quickening.

As she watched, another man appeared on the beachside path. Bulky and squat in a dark cloak, cigar puffing from his lips, he strolled along the waterside to join the group. The woman seemed to move away, but the new arrival wrapped a possessive arm around her waist. Abene was close enough to see her flinch. The man said something and the group laughed as one, the woman tittering nervously. She looked up.

Their eyes met and locked, recognition sparking between them.

The woman in yellow. Miren.

Abene had not thought of her in years. Not since that wet summer eve when she'd walked her home in the rain. Surprise lifted her eyebrows.

A curious smile parted the woman's lips and she seemed about to step forward.

Abene turned abruptly disappearing back into the narrow streets off the bay.

She would go the long way to her father's favourite inn.

The inn was warm and musty and full to overflowing. Abene's heartbeat stuttered as she scanned the patrons. Men she knew, older, greyer, thinner. And men she did not know. Even here, in the belly of her father's world, San Sebastian was changed.

Squaring her shoulders, she moved through the throng of eager drinkers; most ignored her, a few whistled, calling jeers. She spied old Luis, once her father's closest friend, and greatest rival. Luis looked up, and on seeing her did a double take before putting down his beer and pressing through the crowd to her side.

He took her elbow in a firm grip, steering her for the door. On the street he spun her, hands gripping her shoulders as he scanned her face.

"It really is you, ma cariña," he said, voice shaking, before pulling her into a crushing embrace. "Welcome home. Are you safe?"

"No," Abene managed against his barrel chest.

"Then you will come home with me."

. . .

Inside Luis's small home on the far side of town, Abene sat, rubbing her arms for warmth as he lit the fire and the stove. Soon a bowl of kokotxas, Basque-style fish-head stew, was placed before her.

It was over-salted, the cod chewy. It was delicious. It tasted of home.

Luis took a seat opposite her, sitting down heavily. He watched as she spooned mouthful after mouthful of stew into her ravenous mouth.

"More?" he asked when she had finished.

Abene nodded. He took her bowl and refilled it, right to the brim.

Abene ate more slowly now, savouring the familiar stew, enjoying the warmth that spread through her belly. After her nights crossing from France, it felt amazing.

Eventually, Luis spoke, "You have a place to stay?"

Abene shook her head. "Then you stay here," he said.

"I am not alone," Abene warned. Luis nodded slowly, eyes sparkling in the firelight. "Where is your companion?"

"The 'who' is more important. He is an Allied soldier. I have guided him across from France. He needs a boat to take him to Gibraltar. He is wounded—"

"Slow down," Luis held up a placating hand. "One step at a time. Where is this man?"

Abene lowered her eyes sadly. "My old home."

"First we must fetch him here. If he is in a similar state to you, he will need food and a wash..."

Abene blinked slowly, the warmth of the fire on her skin and her full stomach was making her sleepy. But she could not rest, not yet.

Luis came with her, a steadying hand at her back as they made their way to Gilles. He came willingly, with only a passing wary glance at Luis's gruff visage. Back at the house, they washed, and Luis heated up more kokotxas. Gilles ate hungrily, just as Abene had done. As the last rays of the sun had faded from the late November skies, they were both abed, fast asleep.

The final stage of their plan, passage for Gilles to Gibraltar, would have to wait.

FORTY-TWO

MIREN

Miren couldn't believe her eyes. The Basque girl whose father had been a fisherman. Abene. Older of course, thinner and tired. But it was her. Miren was sure of it.

She hadn't seen her late-night rescuer since the fall of San Sebastian back in 1936. Hadn't thought of her either. She still had her coat...

Hans laughed again and Hernandez squeezed her waist possessively. She gently broke free. "Gentlemen, I must take my leave. I have errands to run."

Even Hernandez waved her away affably and Miren strode after the woman as fast as she could. She made it into the narrow alleyways just in time to see the woman disappear around a corner. She hastened to follow. Keeping her distance, Miren followed the woman as she circled through the town, avoiding the bay, and the soldiers who likely still chatted on the shoreline. Eventually they came to an old tavern. Miren had never been to this establishment. Watching as a fisherman wobbled out of the front doors, passing Abene with a lecherous grin, Miren decided to wait outside.

The cold air gathered around her, seeping through her thick

coat. She tapped her feet, working to keep her toes from going numb. Why was she following the coat woman? It was an odd compulsion, yet it pulsed in her chest. Abene had helped her long ago. Perhaps she could again?

She pressed a hand to the tiny bulge of her belly, new and tight.

Life stirred within, she knew. At first, she'd ignored the symptoms, blamed the pause of her monthly bleeding on her poor appetite and the stress of Hernandez's dark presence. But now that almost three months had passed, reality had settled over her.

And filled her with dread.

She'd given up on herself long ago. Her abusive marriage, Anders' death. She saw no path, no future for the woman she had once been.

But this new life, this child of her body. How could she bring a baby into her world? How could she let Hernandez play the role of a father? She'd thought to throw herself at the mercy of her parents, to beg them to allow her to return beneath their roof. But she knew it was an impossible thought. Miren was married, and in Franco's Spain, marriage was "until death do us part". There was nothing her parents could do for her. But maybe there was something she could do for herself.

Breathing deeply, she snugged her coat tighter around herself. She had to act. There was no choice.

The door of the tavern opened, revealing the woman and a gruff old sailor. They walked together up towards the poorer part of town and into a small slum dwelling. Again, Miren waited and watched.

The sun was tracking down the sky when they appeared again, walking at pace back across town. Miren followed. They ended up at an old ruined farmhouse on the outskirts of the city, where the streets gave way to fields. Miren crouched behind a tree as three figures exited the abandoned hut. The new man was tall and fair, his eyes gleaming in the dusk. Her breath caught in her throat as a realisation dawned. He was a soldier. Her mind raced, joining the dots.

The safe houses in France had been routed. And Anders was gone. But that didn't mean there were no more airmen desperate to escape German-Occupied France. She stayed behind the tree watching as the trio disappeared back towards town. She didn't need to follow, she knew where they were going.

And she had something she could offer.

It was early morning when she knocked on the door to the small hut in the slums. Paint flaked off from the wood, sticking to her knuckles. She waited, listening intently. Heavy steps, a creaking door and the face of the old fisherman appeared before her.

His eyes widened in genuine surprise as he took her in. Few wealthy ladies frequented these parts, she guessed.

"Hello, señora?" he said. "Sorry, er... I think you have the wrong address."

He moved to shut the door but Miren jammed her foot into the gap, blocking his movement.

"I am exactly where I need to be. May I come in?"

"I... ah, look. I don't know you, señora. I am not in the habit of admitting strangers."

"Yet you took in two last night," Miren said, fixing him with a stare.

The man blinked in shock, his mouth opening and closing as he tried to work out how to respond.

"That can stay between us if you let me in. I have business with the woman." She held up her hand, and the old, worn coat hung from her arm. "A return, if you will. And a trade."

"I... all right." The man swung the door wide, stepping aside to allow her to cross the threshold.

The space inside was dank and smelt strongly of mould. She made her way down a short hallway.

"Kitchen, at the back," the man rumbled behind her.

Miren squared her shoulders. This was a risk, she knew. If her guess was right, then these people would be scared, and desperate. If she was wrong, they may turn her in. Her hand fluttered to her stomach once again and her resolve strengthened. She knew what she had to do.

The kitchen was tight and cramped, but warm. At the table sat Abene and the soldier. They looked up in surprise, Abene shooting to her feet, spoon held before her like a weapon.

Miren held up her hands in placation.

"Luis! What the hell?" Abene shouted as the old fisherman entered the room.

"She knew you were here. Says she has business with you..."

Abene rounded on Miren and Miren stepped forward, holding out the coat. "This is yours, I believe."

Abene blinked, stunned. Then looked back into Miren's face, recognition dawning.

"What do you want?"

It was Miren's turn to pause. Collecting her thoughts, she decided the only path was truth. "I believe you are here to smuggle this soldier out of Spain, to Gibraltar, or somewhere similar. But judging by the fact I saw you walking the streets in town, I believe you need help.

"I need help too, as it turns out. I think we may be useful to each other."

Abene eyed her sideways, then glanced across at the man who still sat at the table.

He shrugged in confusion, clearly not understanding her Spanish, giving away that her guess was correct.

"You have brought him a long way, but there is still far further to go. You need a boat or a car. Transport out of Spain. And I can help you with that."

"What do you want in return?"

"Rescue."

Abene moved around the table, never taking her eyes off Miren, then leant down to whisper in the man's ear. He nodded in thought, took Abene's hand and squeezed.

Then he rose from his seat, holding out a hand. "Gilles," he said. "Parlez-vous Français?"

The bread was rough and lumpy, but the lard was oddly satisfying. Miren leaned forward and cut herself another slice of Luis's morning bread. She'd not been so hungry in months.

"So, how do you think you can help us?" Abene was sitting opposite her, Luis and Gilles at her sides. It was rather like an interrogation. That thought made a giggle bubble up in Miren. After her years under Hernandez's reproachful scrutiny, this made for a very non-threatening interrogation.

"I know a man. Knew a man. He was working with the British to arrange passage out of Spain. I know who his contact was, the Attaché to the Consul in Bilbao. And, my husband is an important general in Franco's Spain, so I can feign a reason for contact."

"Franco!" Abene exclaimed, panic lighting up her eyes. "Luis, this is a trap."

"It is no trap, I assure you—"

"I know your father is wealthy, powerful," Abene interrupted. "This is a way to advance yourself—"

"No!" Miren came to her feet, furious. "My father was ambitious, true. But not for a long time now. And this has never been about that..." She looked at Abene, holding her gaze. "I watched you, when we were children. As you played on the sand with your friend, I longed to join you, to feel a part of something so... real." She paused, centered herself and continued. "I found that connection for myself, when I worked for the

Basque government before the civil war. The man I knew... he did all he could for a free Spain. He was important to me. Very important." Voice wavering with emotion, Miren fell silent. She wasn't ready to speak of Anders, not yet.

Something shifted behind Abene's eyes. "His name is Juan, my friend," she said, voice low. "I remember you too."

The tension of the moment evaporated. The two women faced each other, understanding flowing between them. Miren saw sadness in Abene's eyes, and knew her own reflected the same. Such different lives they'd lived, yet here in this moment they were exactly the same. Two women facing loss, two lives destroyed by war.

It seemed Miren had said enough.

Lowering herself back into her chair, she continued. "I have been lucky so far, but that luck is running low. I need to escape. Your plan is to get him out. What about you? Will you travel to a British Territory also?"

"No, my home is France. I will return there, to my family."

Miren nodded slowly. Perfect, she thought to herself, that is perfect. "Naturally I cannot go to Gibraltar, my association with Franco and his Nationalists is not amenable." And I will not risk a boat from Spain as Anders did, she thought, closing her eyes and squeezing out the memory. Opening them she continued. "But you have crossed from France... When you return, I will go with you."

She watched the information filter over Abene's face. The woman tapped a finger, thinking. "There is more," she said. "Gibraltar would welcome you, whatever your association. Why risk fleeing to France with me? You are wealthy, you have power. Why run?"

Miren shuffled in her seat, hands settling over her belly. "I have my reasons," she said evasively.

Abene's eyes widened. "You are with child..."

Miren closed her eyes and nodded once. "Wherever I go in

Spain, he will find me, and the baby. But if I can get out of the country..."

"Britain is out of the country."

"My baby will be raised Basque, as I was, and my father—"

"It is a tough passage," Abene said. "You don't look particularly strong."

Miren fixed her with eyes blazing with fire. "You do not know me."

Abene nodded slowly. "So, you arrange passage out for Gilles. And in exchange, I bring you to France. What then?"

"I stay with you, wherever it is you live. You keep me and my child safe until I can strike out on my own."

"You ask a lot. France is at war."

"I can pay. I have jewellery."

Abene and Luis exchanged a look. Abene returned her stare to Miren. "How long will it take you to arrange a way out of Spain for Gilles?"

"Give me a few days."

"And until then?"

"Until then, you stay here, keep out of sight. And I return to my husband. Everything must seem normal until the night we flee."

"All right," Abene turned to Gilles. "I don't see that we have a choice." Gilles smiled softly at Abene; Miren didn't miss the look of care that passed between them, perhaps even love. She didn't know if she really believed in love anymore...

Suddenly Abene stood up.

"Where are you going?"

"To get my map of the route through the Pyrenees," she replied. "I can take you back to France with me, but that's no good if something goes wrong, or if I am hurt. You need to be useful in the mountains. Pregnant or not."

Miren swallowed, resisting the urge to curl in on herself under Abene's direct stare. She was a tough woman, to be sure.

"Fetch the map then, I am a quick learner."

She watched Abene disappear into the house.

"Gracias," Gilles said softly, in heavily accented Spanish. "Thank you."

Miren offered him a smile.

Her plan was in motion; whether or not she would succeed was up to God.

FORTY-THREE

MIREN

The office of the British Consul in Bilbao was a beautiful building. Miren stood at the base of the grey stairs that led into the building proper. Around her, the winds of approaching December blew sea mist and the scent of seaweed through the streets. Icy, cold. The months of danger for her fishing port town, the months to stay safely indoors. She drew her cloak tighter around her as she glanced up and down the street. She didn't think she'd been noticed or followed when she boarded the bus to Bilbao. But with Hernandez's connections and power in the region, she could never be sure.

It was a risk she had to take.

Lifting her head high, she placed a heeled foot on the first step.

She would find Mr Chalmers and she would beg for his help.

There was an Allied airman in need. He would find a way to get Gilles out.

And then Miren would be free.

She mounted the stair, stepping quickly, pausing briefly at

the door to muster the very depths of her resolve, and knocked twice.

The bean stew was briny and overcooked, the vegetables more mush than pieces, and Miren could not get enough.

"You don't have to eat," Abene said from across the table, eyes on the rich bowl of stew that sat before Miren.

"She's welcome to my food," Luis said. "Everyone in this house is welcome."

Abene glanced up at the old fisherman. "I am not saying she shouldn't eat, Luis. I am saying she doesn't have to. You know she's used to different fare."

Miren slurped another mouthful of the stew into her mouth, savouring the warmth that spread through her body as it travelled down her throat. Since her wedding to Hernandez, food had lost its flavour and Miren struggled to eat. But here, in Luis's kitchen, she simply couldn't get enough.

"It's lovely," she said to Luis. "I am very grateful."

Luis nodded at her, a smile hovering at the corners of his lips. Then he looked at Abene and pulled a face. Abene shrugged, turning back to Miren.

"So, tonight's the night?"

Miren swallowed her latest mouthful, dabbing at the corners of her mouth with a serviette as she nodded.

It had been a week since she knocked on the door of the British Consul's office and asked for Michael Chalmers. The man had recognised her instantly, thank the Lord, and ushered her into his office swiftly. He expressed his condolences over Anders' death and Miren had nearly broken. But she'd held firm and explained what she needed.

"A Canadian Airman has made it across from France. He needs passage to safety."

Michael's eyebrows had practically hit his hairline. "I

wasn't expecting a transport. Not after... I will see what I can do."

He'd decided travel overland to Madrid and then Seville was too risky in the current political climate, so he arranged a fishing boat to take Gilles around the coast and down to Gibraltar. He needed the week to prepare. The night had arrived.

"Yes," Miren replied to Abene. "The boat will be at El Puerto for 11 pm, three lights shining from the rigging. But he won't wait..." she trailed off, thinking of Anders' ill-fated passage, eyes lowering as her heart constricted in her chest.

"We won't be late," Abene said firmly. "And we won't wait for you if you are."

Miren met the woman's focused gaze across the table. "You won't have to wait for me," she said.

Gilles, who was standing at the small kitchen window gazing out onto the laneway that bordered the slum house, turned to face Abene. They exchanged a few words in rapid French, and Miren could only vaguely follow. Then he smiled at Miren. "Merci beaucoup, from the bottom of my heart, thank you."

He placed a hand over his chest. Miren mirrored the gesture, a mix of apprehension and hope swirling in her stomach.

Luis and Gilles made their way from the kitchen, leaving the women alone. Abene stood, rounding the table to sit beside Miren. She took Miren's hand in hers.

"It will be all right," she said.

Miren glanced away. The fear of failure churned cold and solid within her, the imagined image of Anders shot dead, sprawled on the floor of a fishing boat, his blood mingling with fish guts and scales, haunted her dreams. What the mind could conjure could be worse than reality.

She prayed Gilles would escape the same fate.

But that would not be her path to freedom. No, her escape

would be on foot. The mountains of the Pyrenees lay in wait: tall, frozen, brutal. As Abene squeezed her hand, reassurance, warm and true flowed from the touch. And Miren believed this woman would see her to safety.

"How is the baby?"

Miren looked up at Abene, grateful for the concern. "Strong and well, I think." She rubbed her belly affectionately.

"Are you excited to be a mother?"

A heavy breath escaped Miren's lungs, the pent-up wash of worry borne alone. "I am. I love this little one more than I ever knew was possible. But..."

"But?" Abene prompted.

Overcoming her reservation, Miren continued. "It is a big thing, motherhood. I have not always been strong. If I am honest, I am afraid of what kind of mother I will be."

Silence fell between them and Miren wished she'd never confessed something so awful. Would it change how Abene looked at her? Would she no longer think Miren strong enough to risk their flight to France?

"Being a mother is the greatest privilege in the world," Abene said, voice soft and full of love. "When Eduardo came into my life, I swore I would do anything, *anything* to keep him safe. And I always will." She paused, turning to Miren with an intense stare. "You are here, risking it all for your child's freedom and future. I don't think you will be a good mother. I think you already are."

Miren regarded her, heart swelling. A single tear tracked down her cheek.

"Thank you."

Abene smiled, nodded. "So," she said, changing the subject. "Shall we go over the map again?"

"I feel sure you will guide me safely," Miren replied.

"Things can go wrong," Abene said. "Let's review, one more time."

"All right."

Miren pushed her flat of beef to the side of the plate. Her hunger at lunch had not returned and she could not face the juicy meat. At the end of the table, Hernandez chewed loudly. The sound grated on her already frayed nerves.

Not long now.

Pushing her plate away, she faced her husband. "Shall we retire to the smoking room? I can fix you a brandy?"

Hernandez looked up at her, eyes narrowing. He scanned her face, searching for any hint of non-compliance. Miren arranged her features in a mask of serenity, keeping her breathing steady.

At length, Hernandez nodded. "That would be delightful, my darling, thank you."

They walked to the smoking room together. As Hernandez settled himself by the fire, Miren moved to the drinks cabinet and poured a large measure of brandy and a slug extra.

Hernandez needed an early night.

Arranging her features into a warm smile, she turned, offering the glass to Hernandez. He took it, unaware of the larger than usual portion. Hernandez gulped down the liquid, leaning back into his chair as if all were in order.

"Another?" Miren offered.

"Please."

They sat in silence, the gentle crackle of the fire a soothing accompaniment.

As the hour drew to a close, Hernandez's eyes began to droop, lulled toward rest by the soothing warmth of the flames and the double doses of liquor. Miren watched as his head lolled, before flopping back to land against the back of his chair. The movement started him awake and his eyes flew open, a grunt sounding from his throat.

Blinking sleepily, Hernandez placed his now empty brandy glass on the side table.

"My darling, I fear I am more tired than I realised. I think it is time to retire."

Miren smiled, coming to her feet. She linked her arm with his and walked with him up to his room.

"Sweet dreams," she said.

"Get that beauty sleep."

"I will."

She closed the door behind him and shut her eyes, forehead resting on the wooden panel of the door as relief flooded her body. The plan had worked.

Now all she had to do was cross the top of Spain and she would be safe. She breathed out in a huff of anticipation. So much had to go right for this to work. And so much could go wrong. Placing her hands over her stomach she paused a moment, focusing on why she was here, why she must succeed. For her unborn child, Miren would make it to France.

She paced to her room. Moving quickly and efficiently, she drew on her overcoat and slung her pre-packed bag of travel clothes and jewellery over her shoulder, then slipped silently from her room. Step light and quick, she descended the stairs and crossed the hallway, heading for the door.

Her hand was on the doorknob when she heard the footstep.

Stomach plummeting, she turned, bracing herself for Hernandez's fury.

Juileta stood in the light of the open smoking-room door. The old lady shuffled forward, eyes taking in the scene before her.

Miren clenched her jaw. She offered no explanation, there was no lie that could save her now.

Juileta paused about halfway between them. Their eyes

met. Miren watched as the soft pity that always swam in her maid's gaze hardened into fierce determination.

"Go fast. Live well," Juileta said, voice low and firm.

Purest gratitude flooded through Miren. From her low position in this household of fear, Juileta had stood beside her, soothed her sorrows and worked to distract Hernandez's ire. She had done all she could for Miren.

"Come with me," the words were out before Miren had thought them through. Abene doubted Miren could cross the mountains. How could this old lady?

But Juileta shook her head. Then smiled.

"Raise your baby with love," she said.

Surprise shot through Miren. She had not realised the old woman knew of her pregnancy.

"I will," she promised. "Thank you."

She slipped through the door and into the bitter night and, hopefully, her escape.

FORTY-FOUR

ABENE

The soft knock on the door sounded at exactly 10:45 pm. Gilles and Abene tensed, looking at each other. Luis opened the door. A cold and shivering Miren stepped into the warmth of the house.

"Are you ready?" she asked.

Gilles took Abene's hand and gently squeezed, then nodded.

"All right. The boat is waiting at El Puerto. Code word: parsley. Follow me."

Abene embraced Luis. "Thank you for all you have done." The old fisherman nodded.

"Your father would be so proud of you."

Abene felt her chest tighten as his words settled over her soul. "Thank you."

"We have to go," Miren said behind her. "Come."

"Wait." Luis clasped Abene's hand, pressing something hard into her palm. She glanced down to find a small fishing knife resting there.

"In case," Luis explained. "Buena suerte. Good luck."

Smiling a final time at Luis, Abene turned, slipping the

knife into her coat as she took up her bag and followed Miren out into the dark of night. They walked single file across the centre of the city, heading swiftly for the bay. Around them San Sebastian was still and silent, the cold of coming winter keeping the residents inside the cosy warmth of their homes. The only sound was the clip of Miren's heels on the pebbled pathways.

"You brought boots too?" Abene asked.

Miren glanced up and nodded. "In my bag. If I am seen on the streets, I need to look like myself, coming home from a party. Boots would raise suspicion..." she trailed off and Abene didn't press. Miren was taking a great risk by helping them. But the risk was also her reward if it meant freedom over the border in France and safety for the baby inside her.

As they came to the bay's edge, a fishing boat came into view, three lights shining from the rigging. The signal. Miren pointed, and Abene nodded. They struck out from the cover of the streets and pathways that made up the town, and headed for the dockside...

... Just as a group of men appeared from within the old town. Their laughter and slurred speech rang across the moisture-thick air, white mists of breath and cigarette smoke puffing around them. The trio froze. At the centre of the group was a man in Nazi uniform. Clearly, the group had been warming themselves at a bar in the old town, enjoying the night and the company of each other.

Quickly, Abene gripped Gilles' arm, pulling him back into the shadows. Miren followed. They watched, wide-eyed with fear, as the group of revellers stopped on the path along the bay, leaning against the railing and watching the waters ebb and flow onto the sand.

"It is cold," Abene suggested. "They will move on soon."

But Miren shook her head. "There is no time. The boat won't wait. Not after..." She stopped before mentioning Anders' fate, the real risk Gilles was taking, and stepped forward into the street.

"Miren!" Abene hissed. "What are you doing?"

"I will distract them, move them on," she said. "Good thing I wore my heels." She turned back to Abene, pressing her bag into Abene's arms. "I will meet you at the rendezvous point. The old cottage. Wait for me?"

"I will not leave without you," Abene promised, slinging the extra bag on her back.

Miren addressed Gilles. "Bonne chance," she whispered and strode out into the dark.

Abene watched as she made her way to the group, her gait changing, hips swinging suggestively as she approached the men. They saw her, turning as one, their laughter taking on a deeper tone. Miren slipped between the men, face smiling. Abene fought for calm, her throat closing over in fear as the Nazi wrapped an arm around Miren's waist. Then, the group began to move. Back along the shoreline, towards the old town, away from the port and their waiting ship, disappearing into the streets beyond.

Abene and Gilles waited a moment, ears pricked. Only the gentle lap of the bay sounded before them. Taking a deep, steadying breath, Abene took Gilles' hand and led him down to the port.

The fishing boat was small and weathered, the man at its helm grey and hunched.

"Parsley," Abene said, eyes darting around them.

The old man paced forward. "You're late. I was about to leave."

"We are here now," Abene retorted.

The man snorted, turning from her to study Gilles. Suddenly, he lifted his hand in a salute. "For your service," he said.

Gilles blinked in surprise, then returned the gesture of respect. "Thank you for taking this risk."

"Ganiz," the man said, extending his hand to Gilles. The men shook.

"I will see you safely to Gibraltar. But we must depart, the further we can be from the port when the sun begins to rise, the better."

To emphasise his words Ganiz moved to the engine, turning a key. The boat's engine coughed and spluttered as it came to life, the hull vibrating against the dock's edge.

Gilles turned to Abene, eyes sad. "I guess this is goodbye," he said.

Abene smiled and drew him into a tight embrace. Pulling back, Gilles eyed her, his mouth twitching as if he wanted to say something. There was no time.

"Go," Abene said.

Gilles turned and stepped onto the deck of the boat. To the side, Ganiz had unhooked the ropes and returned to the wheel, ready to depart.

"Come with me," Gilles said suddenly, reaching across the space between vessel and dock, offering a hand to Abene. Her own reached up, taking his hand in hers. She stepped forward instinctively, then paused.

"It is not safe," Gilles pressed. "Come with me to where you cannot be hurt. We can return when the war is over. But come with me now."

Abene faltered, her heart beating faster. Her body swayed forward and she stepped onto the deck of the boat. "I will protect you," Gilles said.

She looked up into his eyes and saw the love and care swimming in those deep pools of blue.

Her heart cleaved. This offer, to travel on this boat, away from Spain and France, away from war and death and loss. To start again, fresh and new in another place. A place with Gilles.

It was a beautiful dream. One of escape and freedom. After nearly a decade of pain and loss, she longed to say yes. To step onto the boat beside him and sail to safety.

Ganiz fired the engine and the boat began to pull away from the dock.

And Abene stepped back.

It could only ever be a dream. For only in a dream was Eduardo there too, and her mother, Camille, Udane, Pierre, Juan. And only then could she leave with Gilles.

There had never been a choice. Waiting for her on the other side of the Pyrenees was her new home. Her family through blood and choice. Her Eduardo. He was the reason she had taken this risk, and travelled this far. She could never leave him.

"I cannot leave my family. I promised to help Miren to safety."

She watched Gilles' face fall and willed him to understand.

He held fast to her hand. She squeezed his fingers once more. "Be safe," she said and dropped his hand.

The boat pulled away from the dock, angling for the bay beyond.

"I will come back for you," Gilles called. "This is not goodbye."

"You know where to find me," Abene called back, eyes filling with tears. She stood alone, buffeted by the icy winds off the coast as the little boat chugged out across the bay. She watched its passage until the pilot light on the tall mast disappeared around the rocky outcrop. And she did not move, not until there was nothing before her but darkness and the sea.

The hut was still and quiet; only the soft light of a lamp glowed within the broken windows. Abene hastened to the door. She'd stayed longer at the water than she had intended. Miren would be worried, she knew. But she'd needed the time. Farewelling

Gilles had split her soul. She felt they'd bonded, truly and deeply, over their dangerous trek to Spain. He was strong and brave. And he had wanted her to go with him, had offered to protect her. And she'd wanted to say yes. To hang up her boots and let him take her in his arms and keep her safe. She'd been fighting for so long, conflict to conflict, unknown into unknown. She was tired, so tired.

But it was never a real choice. Abene would never abandon her family. Eduardo, Camille, Juan, Lourdes, no matter what horrors this world threw at her, she would always do what was right.

Words of apology already on her lips, she pushed open the door to the hut.

And stopped in her tracks.

There in the middle of the room stood Miren. And beside her, gun trained on her head, the Nazi soldier. A lamp sat at their feet, casting ghostly shadows on the back wall.

The soldier looked up, a sly smile spreading on his face.

"I knew someone would come," he said.

Abene's eyes flicked to Miren. The woman's face was pale with fear, her cheeks wet with tears.

Slowly Abene lowered her bags to the floor and raised her hands. Clearing her throat, she said, "Good evening, officer. I assure you, the gun is not required."

The man narrowed his eyes at Abene. "It is *Commanding Officer*, and I rather think the gun is perfectly required."

Abene's mind raced as she tried to work out what had led to this moment. What did this man know? What did he suspect?

She didn't have to wait long.

"It was surprising," he began, "to be approached by such a beautiful woman in the dark of night." The hand that gripped Miren's shoulder tightened and she flinched in pain as he spoke, just to her. "The others were happy to be led back to the bar, but my curiosity was piqued. Then I saw it, the flash of recognition in your eyes, before you turned away. So when you slipped away so soon after drinks were ordered, well, I had to follow..." He stopped, allowing himself a rueful laugh. Addressing Miren directly, he continued. "I recognised you too, you see. I've dined with you and your husband. I'm Pieter, Commanding Officer Pieter Weber."

Abene's glanced at Miren. Her was face cast down, watching the ground, her lips moving involuntarily.

"Commander," Abene said. "I am not sure what you think is happening here. We are just friends, meeting—"

"—In the dead of night, on the outskirts of town. Surely you don't expect me to believe this is innocent?"

Abene thought quickly; what possible reason could she offer up to this man to explain their presence? Her gaze fell on Miren's bag and a lightbulb lit in her head.

"We are simply getting a head start on tomorrow's journey."

Miren's face shot up, warning straining her features. Abene forged ahead. "My aunt lives the next village over. It is her birthday tomorrow. We wanted to surprise her."

The Commander eyed her. "So you would spend a night in a filthy hut?"

"It was a place we played as children," Abene tried. "It seemed... nostalgic."

He nodded slowly, face considering. And for one beautiful moment, Abene thought he might believe her.

Then he threw back his head and laughed. "You must think I am a fool!" he cried. "Besides, your friend here is not as clever as she thinks. I know she has been making enquiries at the office of the British Consul in Bilbao."

Miren gasped and Abene closed her eyes in defeat. "Who are you helping? Hmmm?" he crooned, leaning close to Miren's face. "What are you hiding?"

Miren gave a whimper.

"She knew nothing," Abene said, stepping forward. "She is innocent."

"Abene!" Miren cried.

"It was me, I snuck out of France. I wanted to come home, Miren was helping me return safely."

"A pretty lie," the man sniggered.

"It is the truth." Or at least partially. Abene raised her hands before her.

"You will not move!" The commander said, eyes fierce in the lamp light.

She froze. "Please, she whispered. "I just wanted to come home."

A cruel smile spread over his lips. "Then why are there two bags for travelling?"

Abene cursed under her breath and opened her mouth to speak.

"Enough lies. You are both coming with me." He pulled Miren against him roughly, locking her to his side. "The police will help us to uncover the truth. And God help you if it is as evil as I suspect. Crossing from France, that I believe. But you didn't come alone, did you? No. A visit to the British Consul in Bilbao can only mean one thing. I am no fool, I can see the pattern. You were helping traitors to escape from occupied France. You are working for the resistance."

"No!" Miren cried.

"Silence!" he shouted, before throwing her violently to the floor. She skidded on her knees, sprawling on the mucky wood. "Gather your bag, you are coming with me."

Miren was scrabbling on the floor, tears streaming from her eyes.

And with crushing certainty Abene knew what was before them. It would not take much for the officials to uncover their plan. The fishing boat that departed unexpectedly, the connection with the Consul. The commander's hunch would be proven correct. The boat would be found, Gilles turned over to the Germans. And she and Miren would be put on trial, or put to death.

She would disappear off the face of the earth, and her family would never know what had happened to her. She would simply never come back. Would Eduardo believe she'd abandoned him? Would Camille feel betrayed? And Miren, the child in her womb, would that stay their execution?

Or worse, would they torture Miren? And would she give away the location of the fermette? All Abene had struggled to save now hung in the balance. Would Nazi boots sound across the farmhouse floor, would Eduardo watch as Pierre was gunned down before him? Would he spend his final years of childhood in a concentration camp?

No.

It was too much.

It could not be.

She would not allow it.

Suddenly, with a clarity like a spark from God, Abene knew what she had to do.

Three people stood in the ruin of her childhood home, only one would make it out. Her hand slipped into her cloak, fingers wrapping around the butt of Luis' fishing knife.

Bracing herself she looked at Miren, a mother, like herself. It was good, this was right. Fixing the woman with her eyes she said, "Tell my family I love them. Tell Eduardo to always be brave. And tell Juan, I am sorry."

Miren looked up at her, confusion writ across her brow.

But Abene barely noticed. She turned to the commander. He stood, gun cocked, barrel pointing at her chest.

"Live well," she cried to Miren and then lunged forward.

"No!" Miren screamed, but all Abene heard was the rush of her own blood in her ears.

She struck out, aiming for the commander's belly. She got

close enough to see the shock on his face and smell the brandy on his breath. The knife pierced through his cloak, punching into the soft round of his stomach, right beneath his ribs.

Then she heard the bang. Loud and echoing, it ricocheted through her mind. Pain split her gut in two and she fell to the floor. Hands cupping the hole in her stomach she slumped down against the filthy floor. The commander was on his knees, bent over double, struggling to breathe.

The last thing she saw was Miren disappearing out the door, her eyes wide with terror and sorrow.

The last thought in her mind was Eduardo's smile.

Her brave, brave boy.

Now he would be safe.

FORTY-FIVE

1981

The tears are streaming from our eyes, the sorrow bleeding from our hearts. Our hands reach for each other, clutching together across the table, holding tight against the swell of grief and regret. Against the choice. Against the past.

"She was so brave," Gilles is saying, voice coarse from crying. "She saved your life. And mine."

I am seized by the sudden urgent need to explain, to justify myself, prove myself. This guilt and doubt, so long buried in the arms of my husband, floods forward once again, painful and vicious.

"I couldn't save her," I stammer, squeezing his hand as though life itself depends on it. "It was too late. The gun, the bullet. I had to run. I had no choice."

"Miren," Gilles goes still, his expression solid and clear. "I know."

Silence falls between us, both lost in our own memories, our own loss.

Gilles breaks that silence. "I asked her to come with me, to run away. I wish she'd chosen differently."

Acceptance of this fact settles over me, how much closer I truly came to death. But Abene chose her family, and then she chose me. In Juan's stories of his childhood friend, I have come to understand the woman who made that choice. And love her even more.

"In my dark moments, I wish she had chosen to live," I say. "But then I remember my daughter, my Adelina. And I can't feel guilt. My life meant hers. I would never choose something different."

Gilles nods.

"It broke me when I first learned she died," he says. "The war, it took so much from me. But taking Abene..."

I close my eyes and take a deep, steadying breath.

"I should have visited sooner. I promised her I would return. But when I knew she would not be there... Still, I should have come to thank you—"

"I understood," I interrupt. "There was nothing in France for you but terrible memories. Abene was the light."

"Yes, she was. But still."

"We have all made choices in grief. We did what we did. We cannot judge that with older eyes."

"Thank you," he says, and I see the weight of guilt lift from his shoulders.

And finally, I know the answer to my own question. Will I tell him the truth? My secret?

No.

The front door bangs open and Laia skips into the dining room. "Madre is coming. It is time to cook dinner."

I blink in surprise, then notice the deepening orange of the sky outside. It is later than I thought. Gilles stands, glancing at his watch, wiping tears from his cheeks. Clearing his throat he smiles at Laia. "Thank you, young lady, I quite forgot the time."

"Madre says we will walk you to the train."

"There is no need—"

"Madre said!" Laia insists, her little body going rigid.

I see the small smile on Gilles' lips as he accepts defeat. There is no arguing with Laia, or Adelina.

My daughter appears, arms laden with bags of shopping. She bustles past me into the kitchen. Soon the sound of rustling bags, banging cupboards and pots and pans rings out through the house.

"She's making Sukalki," Laia supplies.

Sukalki, a traditional Basque beef and vegetable stew, is Juan's favourite. He loves piquillo peppers. Very thoughtful of my daughter, something to comfort him after a challenging day.

"Come," I say to Gilles. "I will see you out."

On the front porch, we pause, embracing in the fading light. It is a real embrace this time. I feel the love and understanding flow between us. Our shared memories and pain are a little lighter now, after a day spent in common experience. Breaking apart, I pat Gilles' shoulder. "You are a good man," I say. "Thank you for it all."

Laia appears at Gilles' elbow, her hands planted on her little hips. "Well, come on, or you will be late!"

Gilles grins down at my granddaughter, eyes shining. He offers her his hand and she grips it firmly, leading him down the tiled street.

I watch as they begin the walk down the hillside, the Bay of Biscay shining before them. Adelina comes to my side and pauses before joining her daughter and Gilles on their evening trek to the train.

"So you didn't tell him?" she asks.

"No," I answer simply.

She accepts this in silence, but I can feel her question. I wait. Laia is skipping, her free hand waving in the cooling air. Gilles is laughing. It is a beautiful scene, this moment between my granddaughter and the Canadian pilot whose life I helped to save.

Adelina touches my elbow. "How can you keep it from him? When you know..."

I look at my daughter. Her bright eyes, her strong and determined face. All my love and pride in one place, my past and my future, everything I am or could ever be. I place a hand on her cheek, meeting her eyes.

"Because it's the truth," I say. Adelina waits, watching me. "Because the woman he loved never did come back."

She smiles, small and sad, eyes shining with understanding. She wraps an arm about my waist, hugging me gently before moving away. "I had better catch them up," she says, "Laia only has one speed: full!"

I huff a laugh to myself, tears now brimming in my eyes and watch my daughter striding down the road to join Laia and Gilles. The setting sun frames them in a golden light, a glowing image of what could have been if the world had turned differently. If Abene had chosen to run away with Gilles, if she had lived to return to San Sebastian.

But the world did not turn that way.

Abene saved me, and my child, and I will pray for her soul every day for that sacrifice.

That is my burden to bear, that and the secret I have chosen to keep. But I carry it willingly.

I stay on my porch long after my family has disappeared into the streets below. I should go in and start the stew, but the breeze off the bay is soft and salty. It smells of home. The same scent that greeted us when we returned here from France five years ago. A difficult choice, and the right one.

I still remember the shimmer of tears that lit my husband's eyes as he looked upon the bay below that first day, the relief that slacked his shoulders, a calm coming over his body that I'd never before known.

There was sorrow too. My parents were long gone, their graves untended. I take them flowers now, every Sunday. It is the least I can do. Few of Juan's old fishing mates still sailed, the fisherman's tavern long closed. I looked Carla up, and we met for coffee. The new lines of her weathered face matched my own, but no joy shone from her smile. In her furtive twitches and nervous hands, I saw the years of Franco's authoritarian rule. The oppression the Pyrenees had spared me. Our conversation was halting and strained. Too much life had passed for us both to find a way back to friendship. It was all right; I was no longer a lonely young woman desperate for a friend.

I had a family now.

As the sun disappears beyond the horizon, Juan appears. His gait is loping, and his limbs are loose. A smile lights his face as he sees me. He comes to me, wrapping his strong arms around me and pulling me close. A kiss on my forehead, a lock of hair smoothed from my face.

We stay like that for a moment, just the two of us, bodies pressed together in comfort and love, watching the waters in the distance as the day fades away behind us.

"What's for dinner?" he asks.

"Sukalki."

"Adelina and the family will be joining us?"

"Yes, she brought the groceries."

"Come then, let's get it cooking. I'll chop the piquillo."

He takes my hand and leads me inside. I close the door behind us.

And on the past.

The day is done. Now there is only my future.

PART 5

1943-1945 - AFTERMATH

FORTY-SIX

MIREN

1943 France

The fermette looked peaceful and still. Surrounded by frost-tipped grasses, a line of smoke from a wood fire curling into the pale blue sky. Miren trudged up the small hill towards the house, her feet crunching over the winter-hardened soil. Her breath puffed a white mist before her, irregular and jagged.

But she was here. Somehow, despite everything, she was here.

A boy, on the edge of adolescence, perhaps twelve or thirteen years old, rounded the corner of the house, logs of firewood in his arms. His eyes spied her and he paused.

"Camille! Pierre!" he shouted, before putting down the wood and racing toward her.

Coming to her side the boy took her arm. Miren felt her strength begin to fade, the last of her reserves fleeing.

"Madame!" he said. "Are you hurt?"

"Abene," Miren managed to pant. "Abene sent me." In her exhaustion, she had spoken Spanish, but the boy understood, answering her in her mother tongue.

"Abene?" the boy looked up over her head, eyes searching. "Where is my mother?"

"I... I am a friend."

An older man appeared, a yellow-haired woman at his elbow. The boy looked up at them, "She knows mother," he said.

"Abene," Miren breathed, vision dimming.

"Get her inside," the woman said.

Strong hands gripped her arms. Miren tried to step forward, to allow them to lead her inside. But the world was greying, her mind slipping. "I am sorry," she whispered, and the world went black.

She woke in a cocoon of blankets, the soft crackle of an open fire signalling safety and home. Turning her head slowly she took in a room of wooden boards and a small side table. Near the fire, a single chair, an old woman with grey hair sitting within it, hands occupied by knitting.

The lady must have heard the rustle of Miren's movement for she turned towards her. In her face, the shape of her nose and eyes, Miren saw Abene, and her heart cleaved. This must be her friend's mother. Sorrow swelled in her chest and she pushed herself into a sitting position.

The woman put down her knitting, rising slowly. She shuffled to the bed, perching herself alongside Miren's leg. Sad eyes, sunken and black-rimmed, regarded Miren.

She knew, Miren realised. Somehow, she already knew.

The woman smiled sadly. "Eduardo tells me you spoke in Spanish."

Miren managed a nod. Then the truth and the heartbreak rushed up from her heart. She opened her mouth to pour it out, to confess and absolve her guilt. "I am so sorry—"

The woman held up a shaking hand. "Not yet. You are weak, you need food. Not yet."

She rose and crossed to the door, calling out to someone named Udane, before returning to Miren's side.

"You have come from Spain? It is a long way. Here."

She took up a glass of water from the bedside table and held it to Miren's lips.

The door creaked and another old lady appeared bearing a tray of steaming soup.

Miren pulled her arms from the blanket's grip and accepted the tray. The soup smelt divine. Carefully, she scooped a spoonful into her mouth, the warm vegetable and beef melted on her tongue.

"I am Lourdes," the first woman said. "Abene's mother. And this is Udane, my lifelong friend. Eat, sleep. You are safe here. Recover. Then we will talk."

Miren eyed Lourdes, read the honesty in her face and took another scoop of soup.

"We will leave you. Call if you need anything."

The women left. Miren finished the soup and then slipped back into the black oblivion of unconsciousness; a deep and dreamless sleep.

She woke with a start, hands clutching for something in the distance that she could not see. As her eyes adjusted to the soft light of dawn she saw the younger woman, her blonde hair pulled into a long plait down her back. The woman stood and left the room without a word.

Lourdes reappeared with a tray of porridge in her hands. Miren ate dutifully as Lourdes sat by the fire, the clicking of her knitting needles ringing through the room. When she was finished, Miren put down her bowl.

Lourdes looked up and nodded.

"All right," she said. "Now you will tell me how my daughter died."

Tears spilled from Miren's eyes. "She saved my life," she whispered, voice hoarse from sleep and exhaustion.

"Of course she did," Lourdes said. "Now tell me why."

Miren spent a week in bed, resting and recovering from her journey across the Pyrenees. Periodically Lourdes or Udane would bring her food, taking turns to sit and keep her company through the long hours of her rest.

Nothing more was said about Abene and the circumstances of her passing, though the weight of deepest sorrow showed in the bodies of both women.

One day, shortly after lunch, the boy appeared at her door. He knocked softly, his bright eyes peering around the door. There was something familiar in his gaze, but Miren couldn't quite place it. Perhaps it was simply that he looked Spanish.

"Come," Miren said, offering a gentle smile.

He loped across the room, before taking a seat on the bed beside her.

Large brown eyes, full mouth, corners turned down in grief, he took Miren's hand. "She didn't suffer, did she?" he asked, hand clutching hers.

Miren took a steadying breath. The image of Abene as she'd last seen her, hands gripping her ruptured belly, the blood pooling around her collapsed body, filled her mind.

"No," she lied.

The boy's lips wobbled, his chest heaving with the effort of controlling his sadness. But he straightened his shoulders, holding his head high and firming his mouth. In that movement, Miren knew him. The small boy on the fishing boat who'd taken her hand and told her to be brave. Her lips parted in surprise and joy. He'd made it, Eduardo the orphan boy from San Sebastian had found a new home.

He turned to her. "I miss her," he said simply.

"She loved you so much," Miren said, truthfully. "You were the last words from her lips. You were everything to her."

He smiled at Miren, eyes glazed with tears. "We are having a funeral for her tomorrow. Will you be well enough to come down? Just to the field by the apple trees." He pointed out the window that opened to the farm beyond.

"I would never miss it."

The next afternoon, as the sun began to pale over the fermette, Eduardo appeared again at her door. He was dressed in a black suit; the sleeves of the jacket and trousers were too long and had been rolled up to fit, but he still looked charming.

Miren had washed herself in the basin provided and wore a dress borrowed from Lourdes. He crossed the room to her, offering his arm. She leant heavily on him as she made her way down the stairs, the pain in her blistered and torn feet still raw and abrasive.

Outside the others had already gathered. The old farmer Pierre stood beneath a bare apple tree, Bible clutched in his hands. To his left Lourdes and Udane stood, arms wrapped about each other in solidarity. To his right, a small group of women Miren did not know. The yellow-haired woman stood apart, alone. Eduardo dropped her arm, gifted her a smile then crossed to join the tangle of arms of Lourdes and Udane. The women welcomed him warmly, with smiles and kisses, cheeks glistening with tears in the fading sun.

"Abene was a rare and special woman..." Pierre began.

After, the family gathered inside around the kitchen table. Miren, unsure, moved to return to her room. "Eat with us?"

She turned to see Lourdes offering a hand of welcome. Miren smiled and joined them at the table. The blonde woman sniffed and stood up, crossing to lean against the sink, keeping a distance between them. Pierre eyed her. "You are all right, Camille?"

So that was her name. Camille simply nodded.

Udane served sponge cake, and Lourdes poured tea. They ate in silence, each alone with their thoughts and memories of Abene.

Soon Pierre cleared his throat and addressing Miren said, "We have talked it through, and there is a place for you here. If you wish it."

Miren looked up at him in surprise. "I... it was the plan, yes, but I do not expect you to keep to it, after Abene..." She stopped, swallowing.

Pierre nodded thoughtfully. "You helped her to save Gilles. And you are in need, that much is clear. We would not turn you out. Not if you need our sanctuary."

"There is more," Miren said, steeling herself. "I am going to have a baby."

Shock lit the faces of all in the room, and then a great smile broke out across Lourdes' face. "A baby!" she whispered. "Abene knew, didn't she?"

"Yes, she did," Miren said.

"Then you must stay, you and the new little one. This place needs new blood."

"I agree," Pierre said.

"Well, then, I would be so grateful to accept. I have money and jewellery. I can also pay."

"No, no, none of that," Pierre said. "That is for your child."

The back door banged shut and Miren looked up to see that Camille had left the kitchen.

Silence fell over the table. Miren chewed her cake. She understood it would take time for Camille to forgive her for the death of her friend. Perhaps she never would.

Over the next few months as winter numbed the land then thawed into spring, Miren came to learn the ways of the farm.

She helped in the kitchen mostly, cooking with Lourdes, while the men saw to the crops. Camille continued to keep her distance, only speaking to Miren if it were absolutely necessary.

Eduardo was a joy. His fascination with her growing belly and genuine excitement to meet the child within brought a light of hope to the farmhouse. A promise of a future to come.

No one spoke of the war that continued to rage outside their doors. They hunkered down, focusing on the boundary of the fermette and the people within.

With the hot winds of summer came the first cramps of her labour.

"To her room," Camille ordered. "Eduardo, boil water and bring it. Lourdes, Udane, with me. Father, keep out of sight."

Miren was ushered upstairs, and, surrounded by the women of the house, she laboured through the day. Camille never left her side, holding her hand and talking her through the ordeal. "I am a nurse," she said by way of explanation. Miren didn't really care, it was just good not to be alone.

As the sun rose on a steaming June morning, her daughter gave her first hearty cry. Camille sliced the umbilical cord with a knife and sponged the blood from the child's limbs.

"A girl," she said, placing the babe on Miren's chest, a softness in her eyes that Miren had never seen.

Her daughter was perfect. Dark fuzzy hair covered her crown, bright eyes watching her mother's face as her lips pursed, instinctively seeking her breast.

"What will you name her?"

"Adelina," Miren said. "For her father, Anders." The man she'd chosen to name as her daughter's sire, whatever the real truth might be. "And Abene, for my friend."

"Adelina Abene, it is a good name," Camille said, and their eyes met. In that moment Miren saw the anger in Camille's heart melt. Her daughter had unlocked the last door to surrender in Camille's soul, helping her to accept Abene's passing. Now Miren was truly home.

Soon after Adelina's birth, the tide of war changed.

From the beaches of Normandy, the Allies flooded across France, pushing back the Wehrmacht. By August Paris was liberated.

May 1945 brought the news: the war in Europe was over.

The Germans had been defeated.

The town celebrated, and Camille took Eduardo to join the festivities. Miren stayed on the farm, happy to keep her distance from it all.

One sunny day not long after Adelina's first birthday the man appeared at the gate. Miren was sitting on the small set of chairs at the front of the house, enjoying the sunshine as Adelina sat in the grass, fat baby fingers trying to pluck the daisies from the soil.

Tall and swarthy, his beard overgrown, the man lopped up the small hill, sack slung across his back. The front door banged and Eduardo appeared, flashing past Miren as he raced down to the man. Eduardo threw himself into his arms and the man lifted him bodily from the ground, a cry of joy sounding from his lips. The two made their way up the hill, coming to Miren, their cheeks wet with tears.

"This is Juan," Eduardo said.

Juan regarded Miren with dark eyes. A small smile of surprise on his lips.

"My son!" A cry sounded from the house as Udane burst from the doorway. Juan caught his mother up in his arms, holding her as she sobbed, her cries echoing through the trees.

"Where is Abene?" Juan asked.

"Come inside."

Miren stayed on her chair, face turned to the sun. This was

a time for the family. Juan had just returned from war to face a terrible truth. One she knew she was responsible for. She would give them space. Sadness and joy sat heavy within her. Juan, the boy with fire in his eyes, the man she knew Abene prayed for, Juan had made it. She smiled up at the sky and whispered to heaven, "He made it, my friend. He made it back."

The next day as Miren worked in the apple orchard, picking fruit for jam and cider, he approached.

Stopping a few steps away he looked down on Adelina where she played happily in the grass.

"She is beautiful," he said. "May I help her pick the flower?"

Miren nodded, watching as Juan crouched down beside her daughter and pulled a daisy from the soil before handing it to Adelina's clutching hands. A small laugh escaped his mouth as he smoothed the soft baby hair from Adelina's eyes.

Then he stood, stretching his back and stepping closer.

"I want you to know that I don't blame you," he said, face sincere.

Miren regarded him in the glow of the summer sun. "Thank you," she whispered, though her stomach tightened. These people had been so understanding. But she could not forgive herself. Not yet.

Juan cocked his head at her. "You do though, I see."

He came closer, placing a hand gently on her shoulder. "There are no good choices in war," he said simply. "Try to accept that. You are here, your baby is here. That is enough."

Their gaze met. The years of war, of loss and fear, had dulled the blaze in his eyes, but they were no less beautiful. He offered her a lopsided grin, then turned and walked back to the farmhouse.

He appeared again the next day, bending to scoop up her buckets of fruit, helping her to the barn. They stood together in the cool open space of the barn, sorting the apples into barrels: small for jam, large for cider.

"She didn't belong here," he began, voice soft. "I can barely smell the sea. Abene, she belonged on the water."

Miren plucked an apple from the bucket, pulled a leaf from its stem and placed it in the barrel, waiting for him to continue.

"But, somehow, she was happy here... I don't know if I can be."

He selected a new apple, eyes downcast. Miren took a moment, gathering her thoughts, then, "I am not sure either," she said truthfully. "Everyone has been so welcoming. Yet this is not San Sebastian. I miss my madre. I feel... disconnected. But..." she paused. Turning to Juan, Miren placed a hand over his, stilling his apple sorting. He faced her, expression open, hopeful.

"I think that's all right," she said. "We don't need to know. Not yet." She smiled at him then, small, but honest. "It is enough to just be. For a little while at least."

Juan nodded, tears misting his eyelashes, then returned to the apples. A comfortable silence settled between them as they worked.

They grew close over the next few months, Juan often appearing to help with Miren's chores or making time to play with little Adelina.

Miren observed his deep affection for Eduardo, saw how he gravitated to the children, and how they made him shine. And how his joy brought peace to her own restless soul. Slowly, but surely, she felt her heart opening to him as his easy companionship turned to friendship, shaping a place for her in this foreign land.

As the cooler breezes of autumn first began to stir the leaves from the trees, it seemed as natural as breathing when Juan took her in his arms and pressed his lips to hers.

His mouth was soft and warm, his touch gentle and unsure.

And Miren realised, she had found her future. She'd sacrificed so much, left her land, and her parents, knowing she might never return, might never embrace them again. But she'd done so for her daughter, and for herself. She'd done it for freedom. Once an impossible dream, far from reach and filled with pain. Now, there was something to savour. A glimmer of joy. A life to build with this man from San Sebastian and her child. Miren had finally been rescued.

FORTY-SEVEN

1981
Three months later

The bus station is bustling. Adelina is wrangling her three small children, her husband Alain balancing suitcases. Other families are milling about, babies on hips, mouths wide in cries for quiet, mothers chasing small children, fathers hurtling towards the bus carting suitcases for the hold. Juan and I stand separate. Arms hooked together, we move through the undulating mass of people trying to board. It is easier, we are only two.

On the bus, Alain has secured a cluster of seats.

"Laia, stand up for your grandmother. Samuel, stop poking the baby..."

I smile a secret smile to Laia as she vacates her seat for me. She is a good child. Comfortably in my seat, the driver announces our departure as the brakes hiss and the vehicle lurches forward. Samuel and Laia and the other children of families press their hands and noses to the large windows, breath puffing white against the glass.

Beside me, Juan takes my hand and squeezes gently. His eyes are sad.

I rest my head on his shoulder and give my body to the rocking of the coach.

We've made this journey every summer since we returned to Spain, and we will do so for as long as we are able. We have family to visit, after all.

The journey to the station at Saint-Jean-de-Luz is smooth today, the summer sun shining brightly down to sparkle off the green of the trees. As the mountains of the Pyrenees rise around us I am gripped by awe. How different this journey is now, how safe and easy. I look up at the sky; there is not a storm cloud in sight.

At the station, we disembark, a motley group of stressed adults and overexcited children. Juan moves ahead, hand tented over his eyes he scans the waiting crowd. I know he has seen the man he seeks when his body lifts, joy a physical, blooming thing that lightens his muscles. He glances back to me. "On the right, by the newspaper stand."

I nod, but he has already turned away, rushing forward.

I watch as he and Eduardo come together, grown men now, older, grey. Yet I still see the young boy and the weary soldier, the shine of tears on their cheeks. I always will.

The men embrace. Eduardo towers over Juan; he is now a man grown, with his own wife and children. His own family. Juan will always be part of that family. Adelina appears beside me, taking my elbow. I smile at my beautiful, strong daughter and we cross to the newspaper stand.

"Miren," Eduardo says, eyes bright with happiness as he embraces me, then Adelina.

"And Samuel! How you have grown!" he exclaims.

"I've grown too," Laia pipes.

"I see, I see." Eduardo ruffles her hair affectionately. "The truck is in the park, follow me. Here, let me help you with the suitcase, Alain."

We load onto Eduardo's truck, Laia on Juan's lap, Samuel squeezed between Eduardo and Alain along the front seat. Eduardo fires the engine and the truck starts forward towards the fermette.

As the farmhouse comes into view at the end of the drive, the world slips away. I am young again, exhausted to the point of collapse, my feet torn and throbbing, my Adelina in my belly. A lump forms in my throat. Laia turns to me. "It's okay, Abuela," she says, her small hand patting my face. I gift her a wobbly smile.

"It is," I agree.

As Eduardo brings the truck to a stop, his wife Amelie steps from the front door. Drying her hands on a tea towel she comes to greet us.

"Miren, Juan!" she says, face full of joy. "Come inside, I've just put on the kettle."

"Where is she?" Juan asks.

Amelie smiles knowingly. Of course, Juan will not rest and refresh. Not yet.

"Out the back, in the apple orchard."

He turns to me, question in his eyes. "Let's say hello," I agree.

She is why we have come.

He takes my hand and we round the farmhouse, continuing up the small incline towards the apple trees, leaving the family to settle in the house.

I see them beneath the trees, the glow of the summer sun shrouding them in an orange frame. Camille stands, still strong and straight. Her fine golden hair now streaked in grey, pulled into a bun at her nape. Beside her the wheelchair. From this angle I cannot see its occupant, only the back of her hair, vibrantly curled, still dark and full. Camille rests a hand on her shoulder.

I hear Juan's breath catch in his throat and he moves ahead. I am happy to let him go. This is why we are here, after all.

As he comes to the wheelchair he kneels and the memory, sharp and sudden, pierces my heart. I am back there, thirty-five years ago, on this farm, baby Adelina playing at my feet.

Back, watching the large, dark car advance up the drive, the curling autumn leaves swept aside in its wake. Back as Juan came to stand beside me at the front door. Eyes wary. The war in Europe over five months before, but still alive in his body.

Back as the man in black stepped from the car.

He'd walked up to us quickly, as two other people stepped from the vehicle. Another man in a suit and a woman, sturdy in nursing whites.

"Hello," the man had said. "My name is Doctor Beauchamp. Is this the property of Pierre Cambourd?"

"It is," Pierre said from behind us.

"And you are Juan Garcia?" he addressed Juan, whose eyes narrowed, face closing down in suspicion.

"I am very glad to have made it to the right place," Dr Beauchamp continued. "I am sorry it has taken so long to find you."

"I am sorry," Pierre interrupted, "but what is going on?"

"I work for the French Government, rehabilitating war survivors..."

Behind him the second man had lifted a wheelchair from the car, bending to check the spokes. Then the woman opened the back door of the car, leaning in. When she stood her arms were laden with the withered body of a woman, her hair patchy and worn.

A cry escaped Juan's lips and he was running, down the hill to the car. He fell to his knees beside the wheelchair and the withered woman now resting within it, his hands clutching her face.

"Fetch Lourdes!" he cried.

As he pushed the chair up towards them, realisation had dawned over me.

Abene.

Abene was alive.

Shock rattled my core as tears sprung into my eyes. "How?" the word breathed from parted lips as I remembered the bang of the commander's gun, the blood-strewn floor, Abene's glassy eyes. She was mortally wounded. Yet somehow, she'd survived. Had crawled from the hut into the San Sebastian night, miraculously alive. Was she found by enemy soldiers? Or betrayed by her fellow countrymen? I may never know. But somehow, beyond hope, Abene had survived.

"Please accept my sincere apologies," Dr Beauchamp was saying. "We had difficulty finding her records, and her family... Fortunately you recorded her employment here at your property. It was our only lead."

Lourdes came to the door. "Daughter!" her voice choked from her throat and Pierre grabbed her arm to stop her from collapsing to the floor.

"She is home," Juan said, voice braking. "Abene is home."

I looked down at the frail woman in the chair, hair patchy and ragged, skin sallow, cheeks sunken. But her eyes shone as bright as always. Eduardo arrived at the edge of the group. Abene looked over at him and a smile, perfect and true, spilt over her face.

"Home," she'd said.

We'd gathered at the kitchen table, cheeks wet with tears of joy and confusion as Dr Beauchamp explained.

"She was liberated at Ravensbrück camp in Germany. They'd had her working on a quarry. We took her straight to a hospital camp. She did well at first, but then her body crashed. She suffered a series of strokes."

"Why? What caused them?" Juan demanded, eyes wild, hand still gripping Abene's wheelchair. He was not letting her go, not ever again.

"Sometimes, when the body has been through so much trauma, it is too far gone. Organs, bodily systems, they have already begun to shut down. Restarting can be... unpredictable. We lost many..."

Silence fell across the table, each person lost in the horror of understanding. To survive the extremes of the labour camps, to be rescued, and to still die.

"Abene survived the strokes, but not without consequence. We have done all we can."

"Will she improve? Get better in time?" Lourdes asked, her mother's heart clearly breaking in two.

"The best thing is for her to be with family," Dr Beauchamp replied, eyes sad. "But there is hope. There is always hope."

As understanding settled across us all, realisation cut my soul. What horrors had Abene endured in that camp, at the hands of German officers intent on revenge? I would never know the extent. But what I did know was her strength. No patrol had ever come knocking on the door of the fermette, no policeman seeking a list of traitors. Despite her suffering and fear, Abene never gave us up. She kept us safe, until the end.

As the car disappeared down the drive, I'd felt my own resolve strengthen. Abene had suffered more than I could possibly imagine. But she had survived, she was here. And she was a fighter. The Nazis had done their worst, but my friend – my friend had not given up.

Despite it all, Abene had made it home, just as she'd promised. And here she would be cared for. Here, she would heal, and live.

The years passed. Juan and I declared ourselves married

before God. He knew that, technically, I was already married to Hernandez, in Spain. But Juan didn't care. He has seen me as his, and only his ever since. After the ceremony, we moved out. We invited Eduardo to come with us, to be a part of our family. But he chose to stay with Abene. I knew he would.

Adelina grew, fell in love with a fellow Basque man and married.

Pierre passed, then Lourdes and finally Udane.

Eduardo married a local girl and started his own family and his own farm.

But Camille stayed. Carer and friend to Abene. Now and always.

Before me Juan stands, gesturing me forward. I walk up to the group and hug Camille before bending down to press a kiss to Abene's cheek. Her skin is dry, and the lines around her mouth deep. But her eyes are shining. I look over at her easel, at the picture she has painted. My breath catches. It is a hut, surrounded by snow and ice, and the rocks of a mountain. I know this hut. It is where she and Gilles took shelter as they crossed the Pyrenees, revealed to me only by his recent visit. My heart clenches tight and I take her hand in mine.

She looks up at me, a peaceful smile on her face. "Home," she says. Her words never did return fully, but her spark, the light in her eyes, gradually strengthened. Nothing could ever dim that brightness forever.

"All right, ma cherie, let's get you inside," Camille says. She takes control of the wheelchair and begins the walk down to the farmhouse. Eduardo appears, striding up the hill, arms wide before he engulfs Abene, chair and all, in a tight squeeze. She never stopped being his mother, he never stopped being her son.

"Ready?" Juan is at my side, voice soft.

"You go down, I just need a moment."

He nods in silence, presses a kiss to my temple then ambles down to the farmhouse.

I stand alone, the apple orchard lush and green around me. The sun is low in the sky, casting all in a golden hue, picture-perfect French countryside. I breathe deeply the scent of fruit and earth, remembering the safety and love I found here on this farm on the edge of Saint-Jean-de-Luz.

I have lived a good life, I realise, despite it all. I overcame. In the end, I rescued myself.

A cool breeze drifts up the valley and I wrap my arms around myself as peace settles over the fields of the fermette.

The scuff of footfall draws me from my thoughts. Juan has come to fetch me from the gathering dusk. His eyes shine in the last rays of light from the setting sun, a mirror for the twinkling stars that are now scattered across the sky. I take his hand and allow him to lead me down the hill.

Inside they have gathered: Eduardo and Amelie, their children Pierre and Simone; Adelina and Alain, Laia and Samuel and baby Louise; Camille and Abene. Juan and I join them as Camille places bread and butter on the table. Eduardo pops a bottle of red, filling our glasses. Bowls of stew steam before us: rich and herby.

Abene is staring at me across the table, face calm and serene. Eduardo tucks a napkin into her jumper and settles to scoop stew into her mouth. Amelie is cutting bread. Juan takes up his glass of wine and raises it in a toast.

"To family," he announces, voice high and bright.

"To family," we chorus in return, sipping our wine.

"Home," Abene says suddenly.

"Yes," I say, as it all falls into place in my heart. The understanding Abene has known for so long washes over me, gentle and freeing.

This place is home to Abene, not because of the fields and trees, the house and its fireplaces. It is home because of Camille, Eduardo, Lourdes and Pierre. It is home because of Udane and Juan, and for a time, even me.

When I returned to San Sebastian, I thought I was going home. I found a nation changed and a city I barely recognised. My parents long passed, Hernandez too. Juan and I could have truly been married then, but it didn't matter. We were already one and we knew it. I returned seeking my history and traditions, and brought with me love and connection. I fought for that love, bled for it. I built it by choice.

In truth, I brought home with me. In my husband and daughter, in my grandchildren.

Home is not a place, it is the people that surround you, in the love that you share.

"To home," I say.

"To home," they all return.

I meet Abene's eyes across the table. The smile that often sits across her face is there, but for a moment, fleeting and unsure, I see more in her expression.

I see understanding, I see forgiveness. I see love.

Eduardo holds the spoon up to her lips and the moment is gone. She beams at Eduardo, her love for him open and clear.

And it is all right because now I understand. Despite it all, we have overcome. We have endured and suffered, lost and hurt. But we have also loved. We have lived.

Despite it all, we are home.

A LETTER FROM THE AUTHOR

Huge thanks for reading *The Girl Who Crossed Mountains*. I hope you were hooked on Abene and Miren's journey. If you want to join other readers in hearing all about my new releases with Storm, you can sign up for my newsletter.

www.stormpublishing.co/lelita-baldock

And for more information about all new releases and bonus content, you can sign up here:

www.lelitabaldock.com/writing-newsletter

If you enjoyed this book and could spare a few moments to leave a review that would be hugely appreciated. Even a short review can make all the difference in encouraging a reader to discover my books for the first time. Thank you so much!

I am drawn to the stories people forced from their homes and all they know. As the granddaughter of a refugee, I have seen first-hand the trauma and long-term impact displacement can have on an individual and their families, for generations. But I have also seen the strength of the human spirit that can be unleashed. It is this exploration of triumph over adversity that led me to the stories of the Basque people of Spain and their flight across the Pyrenees during the Spanish Civil War. In their survivor accounts I found terror and fear, but also love and spirit. I hope I have gone some way to sharing their strength with you in this narrative.

Thanks again for being part of this amazing journey with me and I hope you'll stay in touch – I have so many more stories and ideas to entertain you with!

Sincerely,

Lelita

ACKNOWLEDGEMENTS

What a journey it has been to research and write *The Girl Who Crossed Mountains*. The first novel I have written knowing it had a place with a publisher. And the first with a requested theme: women in World War Two.

The story of the Basque people is rich and deep, and I have only scratched the very surface in this narrative. I hope what I have shared resonates with readers.

A huge thank you must go to my incredible editor Kate Gilby-Smith from Storm Publishing. Your insights and emotional acuity have guided me to shape this novel into the story it is today.

Thank you to my friends and family for all your support in my author career and in life generally.

And to my beloved husband, Ryan, and my writing buddy Jazzy-pud – you are the foundation of everything. I love you.

Readers, for selecting my novel and coming on this journey with me, I am profoundly grateful. I hope you felt deeply and found escape in the pages of Abene and Miren's story.

Sincerely,

Lelita

Printed in Great Britain
by Amazon

45792518R00209